THE
PROTEUS
OPERATION

Books by James P. Hogan

The Code of the Lifemaker

Genesis Machine

Gentle Giants of Ganymede

Giants' Star

Inherit the Stars

The Proteus Operation

Thrice upon a Time

Two Faces of Tomorrow

Voyage from Yesteryear

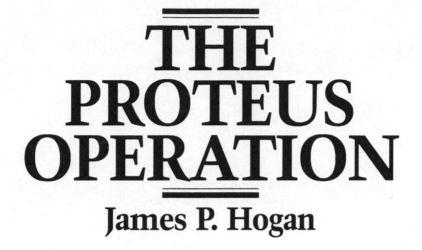

THE
PROTEUS
OPERATION

James P. Hogan

Bantam Books
Toronto • New York • London • Sydney • Auckland

THE PROTEUS OPERATION
A Bantam Book / October 1985

Library of Congress Cataloging in Publication Data

Hogan, James P.
 The proteus operation.

 I. Title.
PR6058.0348P7 1985 823'.914 85-47620
ISBN 0-553-05095-8

Published simultaneously in the United States and Canada

Bantam Books are published by Bantam Books, Inc. Its trade-
mark, consisting of the words "Bantam Books" and the por-
trayal of a rooster, is Registered in the United States Patent and
Trademark Office and in other countries. Marca Registrada.
Bantam Books, Inc., 666 Fifth Avenue, New York, New York 10103.

PRINTED IN THE UNITED STATES OF AMERICA
MV   0 9 8 7 6 5 4 3 2 1

TO

MICHAEL ROBERT

Who appeared on the scene somewhere around
the middle of the book . . .

into most distinguished company.

ACKNOWLEDGMENTS

The help and cooperation of the following is gratefully acknowledged:

Edward Teller, Eugene Wigner, and Isaac Asimov for their agreement to appear as "guest" characters.

The Franklin D. Roosevelt Library, Hyde Park, New York, for permission to reproduce the Einstein letter.

Robert Samuels of the Department of Chemistry, Georgia Institute of Technology

Mark Looper, Mike Sklar, and Bob Grossman of Princeton University

Brent Warner of the Department of Physics, Ohio State University

Steve Fairchild of Moaning Cavern, Murphys, California

Lynx Crowe of Berkeley, California

Charley, Gary, and Rick of Charley's Bookstore, Sonora, California

Ralph Newman and Jack Cassinetto of Sonora, California

Dorothy Alkire of Manteca, California

Dick Hastings and the staff of Tuolumne County Library, Sonora, California

U.S. Navy, Treasure Island, San Francisco

U.S. Air Force, Langley AFB, Virginia

And, of course, Jackie

Proteus

OLD MAN OF THE SEA in Greek mythology, to whom all of the past, present, and future was known, but who would assume various forms to avoid revealing it.

Only when he was captured and constrained to a particular manifestation could the future be determined with certainty . . . strangely reminiscent of the collapse of the quantum-mechanical wave function.

THE
PROTEUS
OPERATION

PROLOGUE

SUNDAY, NOVEMBER 24, 1974, dawned sullenly over the Virginia coast, with raindrops spitting from a wet, overcast sky, and ill-tempered squalls scuffing white the wavetops of a choppy, gunmetal sea. Looking like a flecked carpet unrolled upon the surface, a straight, foamy wake extended out of the eastern mists to mark the course of the nuclear-driven attack submarine USS *Narwhal*, now within sight of its home base at Norfolk and being escorted over the last few miles by a flock of lazily wheeling sea-gulls, filling the air with their raucous lament. From the sinister black of the submarine's hull to the dirty off-whites of the sea-gulls and the spray, the world was a composition of soggy grays.

The grayness seemed fitting, Commander Gerald Bowden thought as he stood with the first navigation officer and a sig-nalman, looking out from the bridge atop the *Narwhal*'s twenty-foot-high "sail." Color came with babies and flowers, sunny mornings and springtimes: new things beginning. But corpses were pale; the sick, "ashen-faced"; the ailing, "gray with exhaus-tion." Along with strength and life, color drained from things that were nearing their end. It seemed fitting that a world with-out a future should be a world without color also.

At least, barring some kind of miracle, the free world of the West that he was committed to defend—what was left of it—had no future. The latest Japanese provocations in the Pacific were clearly the long-expected prelude to a move against the Hawaiian Islands, aimed at the final strategic isolation of Australia. There was no possibility of the U.S.'s meekly acquiescing again to such an aggression, as had happened with the annexing of the Philippines to the Japanese Empire five years previously. War would automatically mean taking on the might of Nazi Europe plus its Asian and African colonies, too, with the Fascist South American states doubtless joining in at the last moment to pick up their share of the spoils. Against such odds there could be little doubt of the outcome. But the nation and its few remaining allies were grimly resigned to go down fighting if they had to. President John F. Kennedy had spoken for all when he pledged America to a policy of "No more surrenders."

Bowden shifted his gaze from the harbor entrance ahead to the fourth figure on the bridge, whose Russian-style, fur cap with backflap turned down against the wind, and paratrooper's jump-smock worn over Army fatigues contrasted with the Navy garb of the ship's officers. The dress was an assortment of oddments from the ship's stores that the soldier had changed into from the workman's clothes he'd been wearing when the *Narwhal* picked him and his party up. Captain Harry Ferracini, from one of the Army's Special Operations units, commanded the four-man squad and its accompanying group of civilians that had come aboard several days previously at a rendezvous with a fishing boat off the southwest English coast. What their mission had been, who the civilians were, and why they were being brought back to the U.S., Bowden had known better than to ask; but clearly, for some branches of the U.S. military, an undeclared, undercover war against the Third Reich and its dominions had already begun.

Ferracini had clear, still predominantly youthful features, with fine, handsomely proportioned lines, smooth skin, and a sensitive mouth. His complexion was dark, his eyes large, brown, and brooding, as befitted his name. If he felt any sentiments about the fate of the nation or the demise of democracy, his expression revealed no hint of them as he took in the indistinct Norfolk skyline, his eyes missing nothing, but shifting with the practiced laziness of somebody adapted to existing inconspicuously for long periods in hostile surroundings. Bowden guessed the soldier to be in his late twenties, although his disinclination to smile and the air of seriousness that he wore most of the time were the characteristics of an older man grown cynical with living.

True, Ferracini's kind of business bred inscrutability as a

safeguard and taciturnity as a habit; but in their few, brief conversations, Bowden had discerned a remoteness in the young soldier's manner that went beyond professional habit and revealed
an emotional chasm by which he, and others like Ferracini
whom Bowden had met on previous missions, seemed to distance themselves from the world of personal feelings and everyday human emotions. Or was it from the world of meaningful
things with beginnings, which now meant nothing and led nowhere? Bowden wondered. Was it a sign of a whole generation
reacting instinctively to protect itself from the knowledge that
it, too, had no future?

"Welcome home, *Narwhal*," Melvin Warner, the first navigation officer, read aloud as a light began flickering from the har-
bormaster's shack at the end of the outer breakwater. "Pilot
dispatched. Regret lousy weather."

"Somebody's awake early," Bowden said. "Either they're expecting VIPs today, or the war's started already." He turned his
head to address the seaman. "Make a signal back. 'Thanks. Com-
pliments on speed of service. Weather better three hundred feet
down.'"

"Launch approaching, starboard bow," Warner reported as the
signalman's lamp began chattering. He gestured toward the lines
of sleek, gray warships moored in the outer harbor. "There's one
of the big carriers in, Gerry. Looks like the *Constellation*."

"Reduce speed, open up for'ard, and prepare to take on harbor pilot," Bowden said. He turned toward Ferracini while Warner
translated the command into orders and relayed them below.
"We'll get you and your people ashore first, Captain. That'll free
you up as quickly as we can manage." Ferracini nodded.

A message had been received in mid-Atlantic, sent by a
Navy VLF transmitter in Connecticut on the long wavelengths
that submarines could pick up while submerged, advising that
Captain Ferracini and Sergeant Cassidy were urgently required
for other duties and would be met at the dock to receive further
orders. "They don't give you guys much of a break," Bowden
commented. "I'm sorry you'll be going so soon. At least it isn't
that way all the time, eh?"

"Not quite all the time, anyhow," Ferracini said.

"Just when we were starting to get to know one another."

"That's the way it is sometimes, I guess."

Bowden looked at the soldier for a moment longer, then
abandoned his attempt at conversation with a sigh and a barely
perceptible shrug. "Okay, well, we'll be docking in a few minutes.
You'll need to be getting back down to join the others in the
wardroom." He extended a hand. "A pleasure to have had you

aboard, Captain. Glad we were able to help. And good luck with whatever they've dreamed up for you next."

"Thank you, sir," Ferracini said, sounding formal. He shook hands first with Bowden, then with Warner. "The men asked me to express their appreciation for the hospitality. I'd like to add mine, too." Bowden smiled faintly and nodded. Ferracini climbed down into the bridge hatch and began descending the ladder below.

From the compartment below the bridge, Ferracini squeezed through another hatch and entered the pressure hull of the ship, beyond which yet another hatch and a third ladder brought him into the forward end of the control room, with its confusion of machinery, consoles, dialed panels, and equipment racks, the purpose of most of which he didn't understand. Crewmen were busy at stations extending away on both walls aft of the twin periscope stand and huge chart table. On the port side stood two padded leather chairs with cockpitlike control columns and arrays of hooded instruments, looking more like an aircraft flight-deck than the helmsman's and diving officer's positions on a ship. The seats were fitted with safety belts, which said enough about the *Narwhal*'s maneuvering capabilities; the dynamics of handling fast submarines came closer to flying through water than anything that resembled sailing in the traditional sense.

Bowden's executive officer and a detail of seamen accompanied Ferracini forward through the passageway leading between the captain's cabin and sickbay to the wardroom, where the passengers had been given bunking space for the voyage. He found Cassidy and the two privates, Vorkoff and Breugot, packing away final items of kit and helping the eight people they had brought out of England into top clothes suitable for going outside. Several of the civilians still looked drawn and emaciated, although traces of color were beginning to show on their faces after four days of rest, proper medical care, and the *Narwhal*'s generous rations.

"Pretty well done, Harry," Cassidy drawled, zipping up the last of the bags he had been packing. "How are things doing outside? Are we almost there?"

"Just coming into harbor. They're taking on the pilot," Ferracini replied.

"So how's home sweet home?"

"Wet, cold, and windy. Everyone ready down here?"

"All set."

Mike "Cowboy" Cassidy had a long, lanky frame, which he carried with an easygoing looseness that could be disarmingly deceptive, clear blue eyes, thick yellow hair, and a ragged mustache. Special Operations troopers were trained to work in pairs, and he had been Ferracini's regular partner for over three years. By all the measures of mood and temperament that the psychologists made so much of, they should have been incompatible, but each had refused obstinately to work with anyone else.

While the seamen carried the kit out, Ferracini looked around at the people in the wardroom. This would no doubt be their last time together as a group. Just as they had begun getting to know something about one another after four days in the cramped confines of the submarine, the voyage had ended, and they would all be whisked away in different directions. It was like life in general—nothing permanent; nothing lasting; nothing to attach roots to. Ferracini felt weary at the futility of it all.

The two scientists, Mitchell and Frazer, were still wearing oddments of the homemade uniforms of the Prison Guard Section, British Security Police—effectively a locally recruited branch of the SS—in which they had contrived their escape from the political concentration camp on Dartmoor. In earlier years, Mitchell, a specialist in high-temperature corrosion chemistry, had been forced to work in the program that was supposed to have led to the first German lunar landing in 1968. Frazer had been working on inertial guidance computers before Berlin ordered his arrest for alleged ideological failings.

Smithgreen—certainly not his real name—was a Jewish Hungarian mathematician of some kind who had managed, incredibly, to evade detection ever since England's surrender to Germany on the first day of 1941. Maliknin was an escaped Russian slave laborer who had worked on the German ICBM silos in northern Siberia. Pearce—again, undoubtedly a pseudonym— had bleached his hands and facial skin and straightened his hair in order to survive the African genocide of the sixties.

Then there was the woman who was called "Ada," slumped in a chair at one end of the wardroom table and staring vacantly at the bulkhead as she had for most of the voyage. England might have surrendered in 1941, but Ada never had. She had continued fighting a one-woman war against the Nazis for over thirty years, ever since the day when, as a young schoolteacher in Liverpool, she had watched her husband, father, and two brothers being marched away as labor conscripts for deportation to the Continent, never to be heard of again. Revenge had become her way of life. Using forged papers, disguises, and a score of aliases, she had reputedly killed one hundred sixty-three Nazis, including a Reich Governor, three district commissioners, the Gestapo chiefs of two British cities, and dozens of British collaborators in local government. She had been arrested repeatedly, had suffered interrogations, beatings, and torture; she had been sentenced to death six times, escaping on four occasions and twice being left for dead. Now, in her fifties, she was burned out, aged prematurely by a life of hatred, violence, and ordeals of the kind evidenced by the gnarled scar tissue at the ends of the fingers of her right hand, where nails used to be. Her fighting was done, but the information that she carried in her head would be priceless.

Ferracini's survey of the wardroom finally brought him to the young man with the mustache and the blonde girl who were known only by their code names "Polo" and "Candy." Both of them were U.S. agents returning home after an operational tour. Ferracini had no idea what they had been involved in, and it was better that things should remain that way.

Vibrations shook the structure, and the sounds of machinery came from nearby. There were no pointless dramatics among the company, or pretensions that their relationships would endure. After briefly muttered thanks and farewells, Ferracini and Vorkoff led the way out into the wardroom passage, down a level, and forward into the torpedo storage room, where one of the main loading hatches had been opened. They exchanged more good-bys with the ship's officers standing around the ladder below the hatch and then preceded their charges up and out through a hooped canvas shelter onto the narrow working space crowning the ship's precipitous sides. Ferracini went ahead up the gangway to join the sailors who had carried the kit ashore, while Vorkoff stayed at the hatch to help the civilians across the wet steel plates. Cassidy and Breugot brought up the rear.

The first thing that Ferracini saw as he came up to the level of the dock was a naval lieutenant standing in front of a bus that was waiting to take the civilians. The second thing he saw was the olive drab Ford sedan bearing government plates and parked fifty or so yards back, with a uniformed driver inside and an indistinct figure watching from the back seat. Although the window was misted, making details impossible to distinguish, the figure, with its rounded facial silhouette and the floppy hat jammed squarely on its head, could only be Winslade. That the car was flying a general's pennant and Winslade wasn't even in the Army meant absolutely nothing. In fact, it would have been typical. He should have expected as much, Ferracini told himself. He had never heard of personnel on active duty being intercepted for the next mission like this, before the current one was officially over; and whenever things started moving in the direction of the highly irregular, Winslade was usually involved somewhere.

The lieutenant, it turned out, wasn't authorized to accept the handover documents for the civilians. The bus was just to take them to the airfield on the far side of the base, he informed Ferracini, where planes were waiting to fly them to their respective destinations. The people who would be taking charge of them formally were at the airfield. "I'll see what's happening here," Ferracini told Cassidy. "You'll have to go with the bus to take care of the formalities. We'll pick you up later."

Cassidy nodded. "I'd hate to see 'em all sent back because we did the paperwork wrong."

"You guys can go with Cassidy, too," Ferracini told Vorkoff and Breugot. "You'll be able to find out over there about transportation back to base."

They exchanged farewells with Ferracini and boarded after the civilians. The naval lieutenant followed last, and the bus pulled away. Ferracini looked up and saw the white-capped figure of Commander Bowden watching from high on the *Narwhal*'s bridge. The figure raised a hand, and after a few seconds Ferracini raised his own in response. Then he shouldered his kitbag, turned away, and walked across the dock to where the Ford was waiting.

The driver, who had got out and was standing in front of the car, took Ferracini's bag and stowed it in the trunk. Inside, Winslade leaned across to open the door opposite him. Ferracini climbed in and shut the door. Succumbing to the texture and smell of the padded leather upholstery, he stretched back with a grateful sigh and closed his eyes to savor for a few precious moments the unaccustomed feeling of luxury and warmth enveloping him.

"I take it we have to collect Cassidy," Winslade's precisely articulated voice said while the driver was getting in. "Where to? The air base?"

Ferracini nodded without opening his eyes. "He's taking care of the papers."

"The air base," Winslade said, in a louder voice. The car moved smoothly away. "So, Harry, how did it go this time?" Winslade inquired genially after a few seconds.

"Okay, I guess. We got set up as planned. We got them out. We brought them home."

"All of them? I counted only eight."

"The three that were supposed to come through from London didn't show up. We never found out what happened. Pluto thinks there's a leak at that end."

"Hmm . . . that's unfortunate." Winslade paused and digested the information. "Does that mean Pluto's compromised?"

"Maybe. He's closing down the operation as a precaution—moving to Bristol and opening a new shop there, probably inside a month."

"I see. And our dear friend, *Obergruppenführer* Frichter? How is his health these days?"

"Lousy. He won't be hanging any more hostages."

"How tragic."

Ferracini opened his eyes at last and sat up with a sigh, at the same time pushing his cap back off his forehead. "Look, what is this, Claud?" he demanded. "There are proper places and procedures for mission debriefings. Why are you handling it, and why are we riding around in a car?"

Winslade's voice remained even. "Just my personal curiosity. The regular debriefing will be held later by the appropriate people. However, there's more pressing business to be attended to first. To answer your other question, we're not simply riding around, but going somewhere."

Ferracini waited, but Winslade left him hanging. He sighed again. "Okay, I'll buy it. Where?"

"We were going to the air base, anyway—flying to New Mexico."

"Where, specifically?"

"Classified."

Ferracini tried another approach. "Okay—why?"

"To meet some people whom I have no doubt you'll find interesting."

"Oh, really? Such as?"

"How about JFK for a start?"

Ferracini frowned. He knew that while Winslade had a way of playing with people sometimes, he never joked frivolously. Winslade smirked, his pale gray eyes twinkling behind rimless, semicircular spectacles, and his mouth stretched into a thin, upturned line.

In his late fifties at least, with a rounded face, ruddy complexion and nose to match, medium build, and white wisps of hair showing above his ears, Winslade would have cut a good figure as a jovial but slimmed-down Mr. Pickwick. In addition to his soft, floppy-brimmed black hat he was wearing a heavy gray overcoat with fur-trimmed lapels, a dark silk scarf, and brown leather gloves. He was clasping the carved top of an ornamental cane standing propped between his knees.

The most anybody seemed to know about Winslade was just as much as they needed to, which was never very much, usually no more than he chose to disclose. Ferracini, for sure, had never really figured out exactly who Winslade was or what he did; but he did know that Winslade walked in and out of every department of the Pentagon with impunity, dined regularly at the White House, and seemed to be on first-name terms with the directors of nearly every major scientific research institution in the country. Also, in talking with Winslade over the several years in which their paths had been crossing intermittently, Ferracini had formed the distinct impression of Winslade as a man who was far from new to the business of undercover operations—and not only theoretically, but in terms of hard, firsthand experience as well. He suspected that Winslade had been operationally active himself once, long ago, possibly; but he couldn't be sure because Winslade never talked much about himself.

The sedan slowed as it approached the gate leading out of the dockyard area. The barrier rose, and a Navy Police corporal waved them through while the two guards presented arms. Once through the gate, the car accelerated and turned in the direction of the air base.

Refusing to play further question-and-answer games, Ferracini clamped his jaw tight and thrust out his chin obstinately. Winslade shrugged, then smiled and reached into the briefcase beside him to draw out a neatly made, pocket-size portable radio, with a black front panel, silver knobs, and chrome trim. It was smaller than anything Ferracini had seen before, apart from secret military devices, and had a hinged cover on the front.

"Empire-built Japanese," Winslade commented as he flipped the cover open with a thumb. "You won't see anything like it here, but the children there carry them around in the streets. It even plays recordings on magnetic cassette tapes. Want to hear one?" He produced a tiny cartridge, inserted it into a space behind the cover, snapped the flap shut, and pressed a switch. Then he rested the radio on his knee and sat back in his seat, watching Ferracini's face.

Ferracini stared in disbelief as powerful, swinging music poured from the speaker, with a clarinet leading over several saxophones to a lively, thumping rhythm of accentuated bass. It was unlike anything that he had ever heard. The popular music of the seventies tended to be a mixture of militaristic and patriotic marches, Wagner and the dreary dirges of the people who thought America could save itself by going Fascist, and the wailing about doom and destruction of liberal-minded adolescents. But this? It was crazy. It didn't go with the times, either—or with Ferracini's present mood.

After a few bars of incomprehensible vocal harmonizing, a

male soloist came in with the lyric. Winslade tapped his fingers on the armrest beside him and nodded his head in time with the beat.

> *Pardon me, boy,*
> *Is that the Chattanooga choo-choo?*
> *Yeah, yeah, track twenty-nine,*
> *Boy, you can gimme a shine.*

Ferracini brought a hand up to cover his brow and shook his head, moaning tiredly. "Claud, gimme a break. I've just got off a sub that we've been cooped up in for days. We were over the other side for six weeks. . . . I don't need this right now."

> *You leave the Pennsylvania station 'bout a quarter to*
> *four,*
> *Read a magazine and then you're in Baltimore,*
> *Dinner in the diner,*
> *Nothing could be finer,*
> *Than to have your ham n' eggs in Carolina.*

Winslade turned the volume down. "Glenn Miller. Would you believe I used to dance to that?"

Ferracini stared at him incredulously, as if seriously wondering for the first time if Winslade really had gone insane. "You? Dance?"

"Certainly." A faraway look came into Winslade's eyes. "The Glen Island Casino was the best spot, off the Shore Road in New Rochelle, New York. That was the prize booking for all the big bands then. It had the glamour and the prestige. The main room was up on the second floor, and you could walk out through big French windows and look right across Long Island Sound. All the kids from Westchester County and Connecticut went there. Ozzie Nelson played there, the Dorsey Brothers, Charlie Barnet and Larry Clinton. . . . You really don't have any idea how the world was before the fall of Europe and the Nazi atomic attack on Russia, do you, Harry?"

Ferracini stared dubiously at the box in Winslade's hand and listened for a few seconds longer. "It doesn't make sense," he objected.

"It doesn't have to make sense," Winslade said. "But it's got a positive, confident sound to it. Doesn't it give you an uplift, Harry? It's happy, free, alive music—the music of people who had somewhere to go, and who believed they could get there . . . who could achieve anything they wanted to. What happened to that, I wonder."

Ferracini shook his head. "I don't know, and to be honest I can't say I care all that much, Claud. Look, if you want to take off on a nostalgia trip or something, that's okay, but leave me out of it. I thought we were supposed to be talking about the assignment that Cassidy and me were radioed about, that you said had something to do with the President. So, could we get back to the subject, please?"

Winslade cut off the music and turned to look directly into Ferracini's face. Suddenly his expression was serious. "But I never left the subject," he said. "This is your next mission . . . or I should say, *our* next mission. I'll be coming along, too, this time—heading up the team, in fact."

"Team?"

"Oh, yes. I told you we're on our way to meet some interesting people."

Ferracini struggled to make some kind of connection. Finally he shook his head. "So where are we going—Japan? Someplace in the Japanese Empire?"

Winslade's eyes gleamed. "Not *where*, Harry. We're not going any *where* at all. We're staying right here, in the States. Try asking *when*."

Ferracini could do nothing but look at him blankly. Winslade made a pretense of being disappointed and nodded toward the radio as if giving a hint. "Back then!" he exclaimed.

Nonplussed, Ferracini shook his head again. "It's no good. Claud, I still don't get it. What the hell are you talking about?"

"Nineteen thirty-nine, Harry! That's the next mission. We're going back to the world of 1939!"

CHAPTER
1

TWENTY-FIVE MILES SOUTH of London, near the town of Westerham in the Weald of Kent, Chartwell Manor and its estate stood amid a rolling landscape of woodlands, fields, and sleepy farming villages lying chilly and damp in the bleakness of an English February afternoon. Although cluttered now by such signs of modern times as clumps of roofs spreading among the tree-covered hillsides, buses and motor cars vanishing and reappearing along roads hidden by high hedgerows, and bridges and viaducts carrying railway lines south to the coast, the basic character of the scenery was as it had been for centuries.

Chartwell itself was a massive, two-storey, red-brick affair of indeterminate architecture, some parts going back to Elizabeth I, standing in spacious grounds and approached from the road by a curved gravel driveway. A lawn at the rear separated the main building and its outhouses from a cheerfully rambling layout of walled kitchen garden, rose gardens, greenhouses, stable, and summer pavilion, interspersed with flagstone terraces and copious shrubbery. Running water pumped from a reservoir at the bottom of the grounds returned via a system of fishponds, duckponds, cascades, and rockeries to enliven the gardens and provide a soothing background of rustling and chattering. Solid, immutable, and serene, the house and its setting epitomized the English ideal of secure, comfortable, leisurely contentment.

The Right Honorable Winston S. Churchill, parliamentary member for the electoral constituency of Epping, gazed out at the scene from behind his desk in the south-facing, upstairs study. Such serenity had not arisen of itself, as part of the natural order of things, he reflected. It had been fought for by a nation struggling for generations to win and hold a survival niche against forces of disruption, destruction, and violence that were not of its invention, but which had existed as part of human nature's darker side for as long as humanity had existed. Freedom had been won only at heavy cost, and to survive, it had to be protected jealously. As in the gardens below the window, the blooms and fruits of civilization, carefully cultivated over long periods of time, would soon be overrun by the weeds of barbarism if the gardeners relaxed their vigilance. Churchill made a brief note of the analogy for possible future use, then turned to relight his cigar from a candle kept burning on a side-table for the purpose. He blew a stream of smoke across the desk and resumed reading the speech that he had made to his constituents five months previously, late in August 1938.

It is difficult for us . . . here, in the heart of peaceful, law-abiding England, to realize the ferocious passions which are rife in Europe, he had said. During this anxious month you have no doubt seen reports in the newspapers, one week good, another week bad; one week better, another week worse. But I must tell you that the whole state of Europe and of the world is moving steadily towards a climax which cannot be long delayed.

That had been before the Anglo-French capitulation to Hitler at Munich and the throwing of Czechoslovakia to the Nazi wolves. The weeds were threatening to engulf the garden, and the gardeners were still asleep.

Churchill—he and a small group, predominantly of Conservatives—had tried to waken them. For years now, although persistently excluded from cabinet office and the inner ranks of government, he had been trying to waken them. Germany's withdrawal from the League of Nations and the Disarmament Conference in 1933, just nine months after Hitler came to power, should have given ample warning. But the nation hadn't heeded. The Nazi blood purge of the following year, clear evidence that a powerful, industrialized state was being taken over by criminals and subordinated to the gutter ethics of street gangs, had failed to provoke the indignation that could have extinguished Corporal Hitler's grotesque social and political experiment in its infancy.

And it had been the firm reaction of Mussolini, before he changed sides, not of the West, that had foiled a premature Nazi coup in Austria shortly afterward, in which the Austrian Chancellor, Dollfuss, had been murdered.

In 1935, when Germany openly defied the Versailles Treaty by introducing military conscription and announcing the existence of the Luftwaffe, the Allies had responded by sitting down at Stresa and solemnly registering an empty protest; then the British had rushed to make atonement by concluding a naval agreement that permitted unlimited German construction of warships, including U-boats—without so much as consulting their French partners.

"Peace at any price," the cry had been. And what was the result? That an extortionate price had been extracted, there was no doubt: Italy lost from the Allied cause, and Abyssinia surrendered to brazen, unprovoked aggression; Japan permitted to maraud across China with impunity; the Rhineland reoccupied by three German battalions flaunting themselves under the very guns of the French, who had done nothing; preachings of nonintervention in Spain while Franco was being installed with the help of German bombs and Italian bullets; Austria seized by brute force; Czechoslovakia abandoned to threats of force. Yes, the price had been high indeed.

And the gain? Not a penny's worth. There would be war yet before the reckoning was done, Churchill was certain.

In fact, the result had been a grave loss. If there was going to be a war anyway, it would have been better fought on the terms of the previous September than on those confronting the West now, in 1939. Czechoslovakia had been intact then, with one of the most capable and well-equipped armies in Europe. Churchill was convinced that the French should have fought. They should have fought in September 1938, when the Czechs rejected Hitler's ultimatum to Chamberlain at Godesberg and mobilized their army, and the British Cabinet was on the verge of rebellion against further appeasement. Then Russia would have come in through the treaty that pledged her to follow France's lead—and the Russians had been eager to act—after which Britain would surely have been drawn in, too, even without a treaty obligation. Public opinion would have seen to that, if nothing else. Then, the chances of crushing Hitlerism might have been good.

Instead, Chamberlain had rushed off, clutching his umbrella, to obey the summons from Munich, and while he was in the very act of handing the victim over to blackmail, he had publicly proclaimed his trust in the Führer's good will and honesty.

"We have sustained a total and unmitigated defeat," Churchill had told the House afterward, only to be greeted by jeers and a storm of protest. But delirious crowds had welcomed Chamberlain back from Munich, applauding rapturously when he waved his piece of paper and promised them "peace in our time."

In Paris, Frenchmen had wept for joy in the streets as the news spread that war had been averted. "The fools!" Daladier, the French Premier, muttered as he was being driven back from Le Bourget airport. "If only they knew what they were cheering."

Churchill sighed, shifted some papers, and took a sip from a glass of Scotch whisky and water. Reluctant as he was to admit it, he was forced to conclude that his own career, which at times had appeared quite promising, was leading him now, at age sixty-five, only toward an outcast's lonely failure. His political burial was already as good as arranged by the architects of national policy, still persevering in their belief that tolerance and appeasement would eventually satiate the dictators and win concessions in return. How many times now had the delusion been exposed for all who wished to see? Yet the blindness remained.

However, the end of a political life didn't mean the end of living, he reflected philosophically. He had tried his best to uphold what was right as he saw it, and he had never deviated from the guidance of the moral principles that he believed in. Not many men could say that, even at the end of lifetimes usually judged far more successful. That was adequate compensation in itself. He had a comfortable home and a devoted family. There were some stock-raising ventures that he wanted to experiment with. His *History of the English-Speaking Peoples,* begun ten years ago now, awaited completion. And there would always be plenty of painting. . . .

No. It was no good.

He thrust out his lower lip and shook his head. There could be no disguising the sadness and bitterness. It wasn't so much any sense of personal injustice that dismayed him—anyone choosing a politician's life should be prepared for the risks, after all—but the prospect of watching the institutions of freedom and democracy, which he had devoted his life's work to defending passionately, debasing and prostrating themselves before tyranny, brutality, and every other antithesis of decency and civilization. The consequence of giving the world such a precedent to learn from could only be a calamity.

But *why* was it happening? Nobody could be as blind as some people were pretending to be. The only explanation could be that they didn't want to see.

That was what was disturbing him more: his suspicions about the motives of some sectors of the influential social and political circles from which he had been ostracized. The West had been too eager to pour loans into bankrupt Germany. Too many occasions when firmness might have put an end to Hitler had been allowed to slip by on flimsy pretexts. Too much Nazi propaganda circulated too freely in too much of the English and French press. Too many apologists for Nazism were at work among the West's trend-setters and opinion-molders.

The rich and the privileged, he concluded, saw a resurrected and rearmed Germany, Nazified or not, as a shield against Russia. They would preserve themselves and their lineages by erecting a barrier that would prevent Communism from expanding farther westward.

That was something that Churchill would never be a party to. There could be no justification for protecting oneself from a thief by hiring a murderer. Heaven alone knew Churchill was no friend of Bolshevism, and he was not about to start unsaying any of the things now that he had been saying all his life; but the response to one odious ideology couldn't be to inflict a second upon the world. No end could be justified by setting loose the Gestapo, the SS, and the rest of the hideous apparatus of the to-talitarian Nazi state upon the hapless, helpless, long-suffering peoples of Europe.

The tinkling of the telephone on the desk interrupted his ruminations. He picked up the receiver, took his cigar from his mouth, and rasped, "Yes?"

"Mrs. Sandys is calling from London," the voice of his secretary informed him from the room downstairs that she used as an office. She was referring to Churchill's eldest daughter, Diana. "She insists on speaking to you, I'm afraid."

"Oh, no trouble, Mary. Do put her through."

"Very well." A buzzing sounded on the line, followed by clicks.

"Yes? Yes? . . . Is anyone there? Oh, confound this damn thing!"

"You're through, Mrs. Sandys." Click.

"Papa?"

"Oh, you're there, Diana. What's up? Is something wrong?"

"No, nothing's wrong. It's just that Duncan and I thought we'd do some shopping this afternoon while we're in town, and perhaps see a play later this evening. So we won't be back for dinner after all."

"I see. Well, thank you for letting me know. Have you told Elsie?"

"Mary said she'd take care of it. Is there anything you need that we can get while we're here?"

"Hmm . . . I don't think so, really. . . . Was that all? Mary made it sound like a matter of life and death."

Diana laughed. "No, that's not all. I wanted to say hello, too, and make sure you're feeling all right. You sounded as if you might be catching a cold this morning. I hope you weren't busy."

"Never too busy for you, my dear. No, I feel fine, thank you. It must have been just a passing sniffle. I'm sure you'll have a wonderful evening, and we'll no doubt see you later."

"I'm sure we will. Very well, I'll let you get on, then. We'll see you late tonight."

"Yes, yes. 'Bye for now, Diana. Give my regards to Duncan."

"I will. Good-by."

The line went dead, and Churchill replaced the receiver. As his mind returned to the grim specter of Europe rushing toward catastrophe, he remembered a rhyme about a railway accident. He got up from his chair and moved over to the window, at the same time muttering absently to himself.

> Who is in charge of the clattering train?
> The axles creak and the couplings strain,
> And the pace is hot, and the points are near,
> And Sleep has deadened the driver's ear;
> And the signals flash through the night in vain,
> For Death is in charge of the clattering train.

He had come across the lines in a volume of *Punch* cartoons when he was a boy back at school in Brighton.

"Ahem." Mary coughed discreetly behind him.

Churchill turned to find her standing in the doorway, a reserved, middle-aged woman with a pallid complexion and brown hair tied neatly back in a bun. She was wearing a plain black skirt and white blouse ruffled at the shoulders. She was looking mildly perplexed and holding some crumpled brown paper that looked like the outer wrappings of a parcel. There was a small package of some kind in her other hand. "Yes, Mary?" Churchill asked. "What is it?"

Mary came into the room. "This arrived a few minutes ago by registered mail," she replied, sounding puzzled. "It's most extraordinary, sir. I don't recall seeing anything quite like it before."

"What? Here, let me see. What's so odd about it?" Churchill went over to her and took the package, then moved back to his desk to examine it. It was about the size of an average book, wrapped tightly in thick, white paper, and sealed with strips of a shiny, transparent tape that seemed, from a corner that had lifted slightly, to be adhesive. A new type of packaging material, he presumed. There was a message written in bold, black letters on one side:

TO THE RIGHT HONORABLE WINSTON S. CHURCHILL, M.P.
STRICTLY FOR YOUR EYES ONLY

Churchill turned the package over. There were no other markings. "Hmm, this is rather extraordinary, isn't it," he mused. "Well, you can see what it says. I suppose we'd better play by the rules, eh? Thank you, Mary. You can leave it with me." He sat down, swiveled back to face the desk, and turned the package over again. Then he realized that Mary had stopped uncertainly after moving only a few paces toward the door. "Yes?" he said, turning again and beginning to sound irritable. "What is it now?"

Mary looked back at the package nervously. "It's just that I . . . well, that is . . . it couldn't be dangerous, could it—one of those anarchist bombs or something? I could call the police and ask them to look at it."

Churchill stared at the package, his face set in a scowl. Then he shook his head and waved a hand impatiently. "Oh, anarchist bomb, indeed. You really do read too many cheap thrillers, you know, Mary. It's probably nothing more than a futile attempt at humor from Bernard Shaw or somebody." Mary hesitated for a moment longer, then nodded and left, still not looking very happy. Churchill turned back to the desk once again, rummaged in a drawer for a large pair of scissors, and began opening the package. He handled it, he couldn't help noticing, just a little bit more gingerly than would have been normal.

Inside several layers of thick paper was a box with a lid, both formed from an unusual kind of milky white, translucent, moderately flexible plastic. He had seen a similar kind of plastic in some experimental electrical devices that he'd been shown, but he hadn't realized it was generally available to the public. Such was progress, he supposed.

The lid was secured by more transparent adhesive strip, and the inside filled to the top with pellets of a practically weightless packing material, again new to him. Inside the packing he found some photographs, in color and of a quality that Churchill had never seen before; a collection of artifacts that looked like tiny electrical components; a flat metal box, smaller than a cigarette pack, with rows of tiny buttons on the front, all carrying numerals and other symbols, arrayed in rows below a rectangular window; a second, similar box, but this time dismantled to reveal an astonishingly intricate interior; and finally a folded piece of note-paper.

Churchill picked up one of the photographs curiously. It showed an aircraft in flight, but an aircraft of a kind which to him was completely revolutionary. It had a long, needle-sharp nose, and angled-back wings; there was no propeller. A caption on the back read, *Supersonic jet-propelled interceptor/bomber. Speed: greater than 2.5 times sound. Range: 3,400 miles without in-flight refueling. Ceiling: 90,000 feet. Armament: 8 radio-directed heat-seeking air-to-air rocket missiles, range 20 miles.*

"What on earth?" Churchill breathed bemusedly. His face creased into an uncomprehending scowl.

The next picture showed a sleek, pointed cylinder that re-sembled an artillery shell, except that it stood several stories high, as could be seen from the figures standing next to it. Ac-cording to the caption on the back, it was an enormous rocket. More pictures showed unfamiliar machines, buildings, and un-identifiable objects. Another caption read, *Power reactor har-nessing the energy of the atomic nucleus on an industrial scale, using artificial transuranic element 239 as fuel. Output 800 Megawatts.*

Completely baffled by this time, Churchill set down the photographs and picked up the assembled model of the flat box with buttons. A cursory inspection revealed a small switch set between inscriptions ON and OFF, and pointing to OFF. He moved the switch to ON, and a row of numbers appeared in the rectangular window above the buttons. Pressing a button labeled CLEAR erased the numbers. The numeral buttons caused num-bers to reappear, and further experimenting revealed that the " + ," " − ," and other buttons performed simple calculations. Slowly it dawned on him that the device could be used for other calculations, too, relating to branches of mathematics that he had long forgotten, if indeed he had ever had any grasp of them at all—a conjecture which he would have been the first to admit as improbable.

Churchill was staggered as the meaning sank in. Even the newest of the desk calculators that he had seen demonstrated were hopelessly simple and clumsy by comparison to this—heavy, noisy, ungainly contraptions, packed with levers and wheels and resembling office typewriters. And yet he had been assured they were among the wonders of the age. If so, what kind of technology had produced the device that he was holding in his hand? Where could it have come from? He picked up the note-paper, unfolded it, and read:

Dear Mr. Churchill:

Please excuse this rather unorthodox method of announcement, but you will appreciate that the situation is an unusual one.

I presume that the significance of the enclosed articles will have impressed itself upon you. There is much to discuss concerning the security and future of the Western democracies and little time to be spared. Accordingly, I have taken the liberty of arranging luncheon in a private room at the Dorchester Hotel for 12:30 on Wednesday next, February 17, at which I would request the honor of introducing myself and my colleagues in person.

You are cordially invited to bring three companions, the choice of whom I entrust to your judgment. Needless to say, their discretion must be absolute, and their reliability beyond question.

If the date and time are convenient, please confirm to the hotel's assistant manager, Mr. Jeffries, contactable on MAYfair 2200.

I remain yours faithfully,

(Signed)
Winslade

"This is incredible!" Churchill whispered. He read over the letter carefully once more, and after that re-examined each of the articles. Then he sat thinking and frowning to himself for a long time. Finally he collected the items together again, locked them away in the desk, then picked up the telephone and jiggled the cradle.

"Yes, Mr. Churchill?" Mary's voice answered. She sounded relieved.

Churchill's tone was serious. "Put a call through to Oxford and see if you can find Professor Lindemann, would you, Mary," he said. "Tell him I'd like him to get down here as soon as is humanly possible. I've got some things here to show him that I think he'll find fascinating . . . quite fascinating."

CHAPTER
2

DUSK WAS FALLING AS the truck, a 1929 Dodge three-ton, rumbled into the outskirts of St. Louis. It was one of a mixed bag of used vehicles acquired at an auction in Albuquerque and paid for in cash that had been obtained via some illegal transactions in exchange for gold. With its valves reground, its timing reset, and its carburetor cleaned and adjusted, it sounded a lot healthier than it had a few weeks previously. New Mexico was days behind, and New York City was still days ahead. This was the third time that Harry Ferracini had driven across the central and eastern U.S.A. of early 1939, and already he had had enough of it.

"An era of romance and glamour, Harry—excitement and freedom," Winslade had promised during the months of intensive training that had preceded the dematerialization of the twelve members of "Operation Proteus," along with their equipment, from a top-secret military installation at Tularosa, New Mexico, and their reconstitution thirty-six years back in time via processes involving dimensions, waves, and fields that Ferracini didn't understand. "Gable and Garbo, Cagney and Bogart, the Walt Disney epics," Winslade had enthused. "The time when Babe Ruth coached the Brooklyn Dodgers. Orson Welles had just pulled his invaders-from-Mars stunt on the radio. Joe Louis was knocking out all comers. Sinatra had just gotten started with

21

Harry James. There was no war-industries conscription for civilians then, no government rationing of anything, and you didn't need a permit to travel out of state."

All true, Ferracini conceded. But he suspected that either Winslade had led something of a sheltered earlier existence or nostalgia had been playing tricks with his memory. For Ferracini had found nothing especially romantic in the spectacle of a nation dreaming and deluding itself down the road to oblivion while just an ocean away the pogroms had begun, families were being dragged from their homes to be stripped and beaten in the streets, and the orders of brown-shirted thugs were now law in cities where people had walked without fear for centuries.

A month had gone by since the Proteus team's arrival in 1939. In that time, Ferracini had seen the poor, still too traumatized after a decade of Depression despair to find energy for anything but surviving from one day to the next; he had seen the middle classes, holding the world at arm's length in their newspapers and protecting their newly regained respectability in isolationist cocoons of home comforts bought on time and movieland fantasy; and he had seen the children of the rich, escaping into a tinsel-and-glitter world of celebrities, moonlight over balustrades and roses, satin gowns, and white tuxedos—all acting as if ignoring reality would cause it to reciprocate and leave them alone.

All, that was, except for a few. There had been the Great War veteran that he and Cassidy had met in the cocktail lounge in New Jersey, for instance, who had denounced the Neutrality Act and applauded Roosevelt's moves to rebuild the Navy and expand the Army. A woman wearing an "America First" button had started yelling and calling him a warmonger, and when the man that she was with became threatening, the bartender had thrown him out—the vet, not the pacifist trying to start a fight. Typical, Ferracini thought, of a world that accused nations of being unreasonable for wanting to defend themselves. Here, all around him, were the roots and causes of the world that he had come from thirty-odd years in the future.

That was what the Proteus Operation was supposed to change. Personally, Harry Ferracini was beginning to think they didn't have a prayer.

A glow of light appeared ahead, where a couple of lamps strung on poles revealed a roadside diner and the outlines of parked trucks against the darkening shadows of the town. Cassidy, wearing a navy blue woolen watch-cap pulled down over his ears and a heavy overjacket on top of faded dungarees, hauled his long, lanky frame upright in the passenger seat and pointed.

"There. That's the place I meant—where we stopped on the last trip. And my stomach tells me it's getting near eating time, anyhow. What do you figure, Harry—time for a break?"

"Not good to use the same places," Ferracini said. "There'll be more when we come out the other side of town."

"What? Don't you remember them steaks and onions? And isn't this the place that had the cute little chick clearing the dishes—the one that was all made out of boobs and ass? Man, did she give you some looks!"

"That's the whole point—I don't want to be remembered."

Cassidy threw up his hands. "Harry, I swear you're turning paranoid . . . I mean, do you think you're gonna bump into the Gestapo or something here in the middle of Missouri? We're not across the pond. This is home turf we're on now."

"Come on, Cassidy. You know better than that."

"Okay, Harry, okay." Cassidy slumped back down in his seat with a sigh.

Ferracini was right, of course. All kinds of things could be happening two months from then, and there was no way of telling what might depend on somebody's just happening to remember the truck, a face, or something he'd overheard.

Although the training program had included a series of tutorials intended to give some idea of the physical theory behind the process, all that Ferracini had really been able to make of it was that the machine that had been constructed beneath the site at Tularosa was supposed to be capable of sending objects and people back into the past. That was what Winslade had been involved in, and why he had spent lots of time talking to scientists.

No actual transfers of people into the past had been effected previously. Only some preliminary trials had been conducted, which the scientists had described simply as "encouraging," without going into detail as to what form the trials had taken. Apparently the rapidly deteriorating world situation had made it imperative for the mission to proceed at once, without waiting for all the answers to be revealed.

Three months after the trials, in the large chamber deep below the Tularosa facility, an egg-shaped capsule the size of a blimp had vanished in a bluish glow from its supports amid tangles of machinery and windings, and reappeared thirty-six years earlier, shifted five thousand feet upward as a precaution against positional errors. A set of helium bags had inflated automatically to lower the capsule to the ground, and fifteen minutes later Ferracini had found himself standing in the New Mexico desert with the eleven other members of the Proteus mission, staring up at the night sky of January 1939. The time travelers,

after what had surely been one of the most awesome achieve-
ments in the entire history of the physical sciences, had arrived
by balloon.

The Tularosa machine was strictly a one-way device, a "projector," and January 1939 was the greatest "range," back in the
past, that it could reach. To complete a two-way connection, a
machine called a "return-gate" had to be constructed at the far
end, for which all the requisite parts and components had been
brought in the capsule. Based on actual timings of dummy-run
assemblies performed during training, the planners had estimated four to five months for the return-gate to be operational.

Since the first objective of the operation was simply to set up
a dialogue between the United States governments of the two
eras and not to create any sensations before this could be accomplished, the policymakers in 1975 had decreed that construction
of the return-gate should proceed covertly. Furthermore, for ease
of future logistics and communications, they had deemed an
East Coast, metropolitan location to be desirable. That was how
Ferracini and the rest of the mission's U.S. Group, officially
known as *Sugar*, came to be ferrying components from temporary storage in New Mexico to a leased warehouse on the
Brooklyn waterfront. They were transporting the more critical
parts themselves, by truck—things like computers and electronic devices whose futuristic origins could hardly be disguised.
The larger structural members and pieces of the dismantled capsule, which were deliberately made from materials available in
1939 and could have been anything, had been trucked into Albuquerque and sent on from there by rail.

The mission's second objective was to intervene in the political situation in England, where the year 1939–1940 had brought
disaster in the Proteus world. In this case, the mission could not
wait for the return-gate in Brooklyn to be completed. The pace of
impending events in Europe demanded immediate action by the
West's leaders if the collapse there wasn't to be repeated. Accordingly, Winslade and the other two members of the mission's U.K.
Group, *King*, had gone straight on to London, flying DC-3 to New
York and continuing by ship; Pan American's Clipper flying-boat
service to Lisbon wouldn't be operational until later in the year.

After crossing the Mississippi at the Eads Bridge, they
stopped at an all-night eating place on the Indianapolis road out
of town. The parking area at the rear was dark, but on entering
the diner they found a warm, cozy atmosphere with yellow
lights, good-food smells, and a coal stove throwing out heat from
one corner. Between one and two dozen people were sitting at
tables and booths around the room, most of them truckers. At

the far end, framed in the serving hatch of the steamy kitchen, a brawny cook was thumping down plates of ham and eggs and beef ribs behind a stout, Mexican-looking woman working at the counter. Posters, newspaper clippings, and photographs of baseball players were pinned to the walls, and an enormous wooden radio on a shelf by the coffee urn was playing something that Ferracini could recognize by now as Duke Ellington. In their leisure time during training, the team had been saturated with radio recordings and movies from the period.

No one paid much attention as Ferracini and Cassidy stamped snow and slush from their boots, undid their topcoats, and walked up to the counter to order two steak dinners. They picked up a cup of coffee apiece and carried them to an empty booth in the far corner, near a chattering group of respectably dressed younger people whose snatches of conversation sounded a little too intellectual for the surroundings.

"It's warm," Cassidy said, pulling off his cap and ruffling his flattened hair with his fingers. "Want me to take over for a spell when we get moving again?"

Ferracini nodded. "Sure, I could use a break. Maybe I'll try and get a few hours' sleep."

"Four days a trip, and that's going twenty-four hours. They could use a few interstates." Cassidy sprawled in his seat and looked around as he raised his cup to his mouth and took a sip. "I'm still getting over this whole scene, you know, Harry. No papers for anything, no permits . . . Claud was right about it—everyone here does pretty much what they want. And I thought he was just selling the mission."

"Mmm . . ." Ferracini replied.

Cassidy leaned forward and eyed Ferracini for a moment in the way he did when he was scheming something. "You know, Harry, sometimes I think, ah, well, a guy could do a lot worse than stick around in a place like this permanently, know what I mean? When Claud's got his machine and can do what he wants with it. . . ."

"You're crazy! Quit talking like an asshole."

"No, seriously. What's there for us where we came from? It's all over back there."

"That's why we're here—to change all that. It'll be different, okay?"

"You mean everything—we just go back through the machine sometime later and find a whole new world waiting?" Cassidy looked unconvinced. "Things don't happen that easily, Harry. And Claud and all those scientists back there—they tried to sound reassuring and make like it was all gonna work out okay, but if you really listened to them, they didn't really know, either. They didn't know for sure how this whole business works."

Ferracini frowned. "Come on, Cassidy, we've been here long enough now to see what it's like, what the people are like. You really want to live surrounded by jerks like these? They've got it made, and they're throwing it all away. They can't see past their noses to what's really happening. It's like a country of over-protected kids. I mean—"

Cassidy held up a hand. "Okay, Harry, okay—save it." He didn't want to go into all that again. Ferracini shrugged and lapsed into silence. Cassidy sat back and looked around, and after a short while leaned forward once more to rest his elbows on the table. "I figure we'll have earned ourselves a spell of R&R by the time we hit Big A—a day or two at least. I mean, I wouldn't want to risk going off the road through over-dedication to duty and fatigue or something, and bending any of Mortimer's parts. What do you think, Harry? Don't you figure we owe ourselves a forty-eight?"

Mortimer Greene, formerly director of the Air Force's Advanced Weapons Systems Development and Testing Center in Nevada, was head of the mission's three-man scientific and engineering group. As such, he was responsible for getting the return-gate assembled. Also, as overall second-in-command, he was in charge of *Sugar* while Winslade was in London.

Ferracini grinned faintly and pulled his coat off his shoulders to drape it on the back of his seat. "Oh, I guess probably we'll be able to justify something," he said. "But first we deliver the load. Then maybe I'll have a word with Mortimer about getting us a forty-eight."

Cassidy leaned closer across the table. "You remember those guys we were talking to in that place on West Thirty-fourth on the last trip?" He licked his lips and dropped his voice to a more confidential level. "Anyhow, it seems there's these high-class hookers over on the East Side. For a buck and a half you can get—" He broke off as the Mexican woman arrived and deposited two large plates of food on the table along with a basket of thickly cut bread.

Cassidy was about to resume speaking when a voice from the group at the nearby table rose above the general background talk and distracted him. It belonged to a pudgy-faced, youngish looking man with greased-down hair, wearing a maroon blazer. "Coughlin's right. Why should we get involved with any foreign wars? We bailed them out once before, didn't we, and what good did it do? They've never even repaid their debts. If you ask me, that was what caused the '29 Crash in the first place."

"That's what I meant," a girl in a blue coat said from across the table. "Their governments are all rotten, anyway. Wars are endemic over there. I hope Hitler does a good job and cleans the whole place up thoroughly. It could do with it."

"Hear, hear," a fair-haired man next to her agreed. "He's only taking back what's theirs, after all, and restoring some pride and discipline. As Fiona says, a bit more of that could do them all some good. I mean, what alternative do they have?"

"Well, there is Cha-amberlain . . ." the man in the maroon blazer said with emphasized sarcasm. Somebody sniggered.

A thin youth sitting on the other side of the fair-haired man ruffled his eyebrows, widened his eyes, stuck a finger across his upper lip, and waved a menu card over his head. "Yesterday, I had another talk with Herr Hitler," he declared, mimicking a prim English accent, and his companions erupted into laughter.

Ferracini glowered at his plate and chewed his food savagely. "Aw, why let it bug you, Harry?" Cassidy said. "They can't make any difference to anything."

"It's what they represent," Ferracini muttered. He shook his head. "This country doesn't have a chance, Cass. It's all over already."

At the next table the man in the maroon blazer went on, "Well, let's face it, Fascism does seem to work. Perhaps nothing else can in an industrialized age. I mean, democracy was fine in the days of landed gentries and that kind of thing, but look where it led in the end."

"You've got to have someone in authority," the girl in the blue coat said. "And the only other people who understand that are the Communists."

"Yes, and we all know what that means," the fair-haired man told them.

"Shirkers of the world, unite!" the thin youth exclaimed, going into his Russian impersonation routine.

Cassidy's patience snapped abruptly. Without warning, he whirled around in his seat, leveled his fork menacingly, and waved it up and down with a piece of steak still impaled on the end. "You people had better cut it right there if you know what's best for you," he warned, narrowing his eyes and speaking in an ominous growl. "You ain't been there—don't know nothin'." He jerked his head in Ferracini's direction without looking away. "See this guy here? Well, he knows. Two years in Spain, volunteerin' with th' Abe Lincoln Brigade. Got hi'self bombed by them

Fascists and ain't been right in the head ever since. Gets mean an' ornery real easy when he hears talk like that—see them big starin' eyes? So you just quit it right there if you don't want him gettin' mad, okay?"

Ferracini groaned beneath his breath. For a few moments of awkward silence, Cassidy continued to stare mean-eyed over his fork, his mouth grimacing crookedly beneath his shaggy mustache. Then, turning her head away with a sniff and making an effort to sound as if nothing had happened, one of the girls said haughtily, "Has anybody read *Of Mice and Men*? I find Steinbeck to be really so-o visual. . . ." The conversation picked up again, and Cassidy turned back with a satisfied grunt. Nobody else in the room showed any sign of having noticed, and the rest of dinner passed without further incident.

When they were ready to leave, Ferracini went to the rest room, leaving Cassidy waiting just inside the front door. But when Ferracini came out, he found that Cassidy had come back and was waiting in the dark, narrow corridor, stacked with potato sacks and vegetable crates, leading from the restaurant. Cassidy's normal easygoing air was gone, leaving him tense and alert. "What?" Ferracini asked.

"Guy hanging around by the truck," Cassidy said in a low voice. "I just caught a glimpse of him moving around to the far side."

"Figure it's a heist?"

"Maybe."

"See any others?"

"No, but it's black out there."

"How're we fixed?"

Cassidy nodded in the shadows toward a back door that opened to the outside from the corridor. "We could set up a sitting duck with cover going out that way. What d'you think?"

Ferracini moved forward to bring his face close to the glass pane in the door. He moved his head from side to side to scan what he could of the scene outside, then stepped back. He gave a brief nod. "Who's going to play duck?" There was an obstinate silence. He sighed resignedly. "Okay, I'll do it. On your way. I'll give you five minutes." Cassidy disappeared noiselessly out through the door, and Ferracini went back into the rest room to rinse his face.

Five minutes later, Ferracini emerged, sauntered back into the restaurant, and bought a couple of candy bars. He put on his coat, went outside, and walked into the shadows of the parking area and around to the far side of the truck, at the same time making a show of fumbling in his coat pocket for his keys.

The man came around the front of the truck to face him as Ferracini reached the cab. The light from a distant street lamp silhouetted his frame, tall and broad, with stooped shoulders. He was wearing a soft felt hat and shabby overcoat. Ferracini tensed expectantly, but the man stopped a few feet back. "Say, buddy, ya wouldn't happen ta be going as far as the coast, would ya?" he said in a wheezy voice. "Any chance I could get a ride? Got a woman and three kids back in Kansas. . . . Need work real bad."

"Can't do that, pal," Ferracini told him. "Rules. Boss checks up all the time." He took his hand from his pocket and held out a note, at the same time straining every nerve-fiber to catch any hint of movement behind him—a foot falling stealthily, or the almost inaudible intake of breath as an arm was raised to swing. This was the moment when he placed total trust in the timing and judgment of his invisible partner. "Here's a dollar—go get a meal."

Even in the darkness he could see the man's eyes widen. "A whole dollar! Say, are you sure you—"

"Take it and get something to eat. There's more guys inside."

The man took the bill, mumbled something in acknowledgment, and shuffled away toward the door of the diner. Cassidy materialized silently out of the blackness behind where Ferracini was standing. "No problem?" He sounded mildly disappointed.

"No—just a guy trying to find a job."

But taking precautions had long ago become second nature. Ferracini tossed Cassidy the keys, and five minutes later they were Indianapolis-bound once more.

CHAPTER 3

ANY PROCESS THAT INVOLVED tinkering with the past was bound to have implications which by normal standards would be judged peculiar. In fact, it wrought havoc with all the conventional notions of common sense, logic, and causality.

One peculiarity that followed from the ability of the machine constructed at Tularosa in 1975 to communicate with a return-gate assembled at some point in the past was that as long as the return-gate had, in fact, come into existence, it made no difference what particular sequence of events took place later in time to produce it. Thus, by setting the 1975 machine's range to the appropriate value, it could be connected through to the completed return-gate, up-and-running by mid-1939, as soon as the 1975 machine became operational. There was nothing which said that in the 1975 sequence of events, the mission scheduled to go back to build the return-gate had actually to have been dispatched.

Given that such a possibility was implicit in the bizarre logic of the situation, it was inevitable that the mission planners would exploit the fact to test the entire system's rationale before the final decision to send the mission was taken. And that was precisely what had been done: As soon as construction of the 1975 machine had progressed to the point of its being able to receive simple, static communications messages (handling objects would require additional hardware), a message had appeared from May 1939, confirming that the mission had arrived safely and was assembling the return-gate on schedule. This constituted the preliminary "test," which the troops were told had proved satisfactory.

President Kennedy had approved the final "go" order, and the mission had departed as soon as the minimum hardware needed to confer projection capability was installed. Further investigation of the physics, it was agreed, could be left for others to worry about later, along with such seemingly paradoxical issues as what would have happened if the mission were never sent, since it had evidently arrived, anyway. The main thing was to see the team on its way, safely removed from the uncertain world of 1975.

"Yes, yes, I can see your point, Anna, but it provided us with as much in the way of reassurance as anybody could have hoped for in the circumstances." Mortimer Greene, the mission's senior scientist and head of the U.S. *Sugar* group, straightened up and gestured with the crowbar that he had been using to open the crates around him. "The urgency of the situation ruled out any possibility of examining all the theoretical unknowns."

Greene was in his early fifties, of medium height and broadly built, with a solid, imposing face, heavy brows, a square jaw, and a white, clipped mustache. His bald, domed head, fringed by a half-moon of hair that petered out above his ears, was the kind that sculptors like to find when commissioned to produce statues of great personages. He was wearing a white shirt with maroon and black pinstripes, the sleeves rolled up above his elbows, and over it, red suspenders.

Anna Kharkiovitch, the congressional historian sent as the mission's current-affairs specialist, looked dubiously over the clipboard on which she was marking off items from a checklist. Of slight build, with graying hair, she was somewhere in her mid-forties, with gaunt features that retained traces of the striking lines that had graced her in earlier years. She had escaped from the Soviet Union prior to its final partitioning between Germany and Japan in 1950. "I know the information was all we had to go on at the time," she said. "And I'm not saying the decision wasn't taken in good faith. But all this talk about 'random statistical perturbations' doesn't explain what happened. The fact still remains that there was an error."

They were working in a large open space at the rear of the building code-named "Gatehouse," the warehouse off Van Brunt

Street in Brooklyn that had been leased from the New York Dock Company to house the return-gate. The front of the warehouse was screened off by a dummy wall of bales and packing cases that was more solid than it looked; the windows and entrances back of the screen had been sealed; and the whole building was protected by a system of detectors and surveillance devices that many electronics enthusiasts indigenous to the times would cheerfully have given a year's salary to study.

"An error, yes," Greene conceded. "But of what significance? What matters is that the gate was working. That's what we are here for, and it's all we need be concerned with for the time being."

"But that's my whole point," Anna persisted. "If one part of the message has been shown to be wrong, how can we trust any of it?"

Greene lifted the top off another crate and began lifting out cartons. "The fact that the message was received says that the gate was working," he said. "That much, at least, has to be true."

"But how could it have been mistaken about something as fundamental as the machine's location? Something very strange has happened. It worries me."

The problem was that they weren't supposed to have ended up in a warehouse in Brooklyn at all. Since there was nothing in the peculiar logic of the whole business that said it couldn't, the message from mid-1939 had sought to save the team the trouble of searching around for a suitable site for the return-gate by providing details of the one already acquired, from which the message was being sent. But the message had directed the team to a factory building in Jersey City, which it described as being empty and on offer for quick sale as a consequence of its two joint-owner brothers' getting into difficulty over gambling debts. When Greene and Anna flew to Jersey City expecting to conclude a quick deal, however, they had found the premises to be in use and not up for sale at all. They had managed to obtain the place in Brooklyn only after making a hasty tour of commercial real-estate brokers.

So what had gone wrong? Clearly, the members of the Proteus team could have no reason to mislead themselves. If the message had indeed come from the site in Jersey City as claimed, then why had the site turned out to be unavailable? If it hadn't come from Jersey City—a conclusion that now appeared inescapable—then why would the message have said that it had?

"Well, worrying won't do us any good at all now, Anna," Greene said. "The thing to do is keep going and not allow ourselves to get too concerned about bridges we don't have to cross yet." He looked down again at the crate he had been unpacking. "Now where were we? . . . These look like the JSK-23 resonators. Do you have the list there? It should be number thirty-seven."

"Ah . . . let me see, here we are—two pages."

"What about the actuator assemblies? Are they supposed to be here?"

Anna flipped over some pages to find another sheet. "Let me see. No, they're not scheduled yet. The primaries are in Load Five with Ferracini and Cassidy. They should be somewhere between Indianapolis and here by now."

"Then the secondaries must still be at Albuquerque, yes? When are they due—with Major Warren and Sergeant Ryan in Load Six?"

"Yes, that's correct."

"Fine. In that case we'd better—" A rasping sound from the ancient telephone hanging on a pillar nearby interrupted. "Excuse me." Greene picked his way between parts and boxes to answer it. "Yes, Gordon?" The call had to be from Gordon Selby, the only other person in the building at that moment, who was sorting out documents in the front office. Selby was one of Greene's scientific group. He was also the mission's engineering foreman and would be supervising the military personnel during assembly of the gate. As well as providing the security guard, the members of the military contingent had all undergone intensive technical training in order to assist.

"Oh? . . . Oh really?" Greene said into the phone. He was beginning to sound excited. "Does it sound like good news, Gordon? Very well, what does it say?"

While Greene listened, Anna returned her attention to laying out the contents of another crate. She had the feeling that Greene was more concerned about the discrepancy than he tried to sound. If he could explain what had gone wrong, why didn't he? If he couldn't, how could he be sure of anything?

She looked up inquiringly as Greene replaced the receiver with a jubilant flourish. "Gordon took a telegram up front a few minutes ago," he announced. "From Claud in London. It sounds as if everything's going as planned. They're meeting Churchill and three of his colleagues for lunch at the Dorchester on Wednesday!"

CHAPTER
4

THIS WAS NOT WINSLADE'S first visit to London. It was, in a somewhat strange manner of speaking, his second in less than a year. In the Proteus world, he had come to the British capital in August 1938, as a member of a U.S. intelligence-gathering tour of several European countries, sent to evaluate information being brought by fugitive scientists from the totalitarian dictatorships. Now, due to the extraordinary circumstances of the Proteus mission, he was back again, ten months later and thirty-seven years older.

He had also visited London in the years following Britain's ignominious surrender on the first day of 1941. Until 1960, he had been involved in espionage activities camouflaged by various U.S. diplomatic missions and embassy appointments. In that year, Germany's formal relations with the West were virtually ended when Heydrich, after engineering Borman's assassination and forcing Hitler to retire at seventy-one on the grounds of diminishing mental faculties, came to power as the new Führer. Winslade had thereafter made several covert trips in connection with the work that eventually culminated in Proteus.

Those later visits, he had come to realize since his arrival from America with the *King* group, had clouded his memories. He had remembered a London of drabness, disillusionment, and defeat, with a Reich Governor installed at Buckingham Palace, the swastika flying above its roof, and black-uniformed SS sentries at its gates. He had remembered jackboots crashing in mockery on old cobbled streets before the halls in which the Mother of Parliaments had been born. He had remembered curfews, midnight arrests, and streets of boarded-up shops. He had seen stooped, sunken-faced women, whose menfolk had been taken to provide forced labor in the conquered lands of Russia, hauling handcarts and mending roads, while their ragged children fought over spillings from garbage trucks. He had watched the nation's wealth being carried away to swell the Reichsbank coffers, and its art treasures being looted for the greater glorification of the Fatherland or for the embellishment of Goering's show palace at Karinhall, near Berlin. He had remembered the grayness of everything, the fear, the hopelessness, the sullenness. And over the years, his preoccupation with such memories had dimmed his vision of the London that he had seen as a young man, now so long ago, yet at the same time, little more than yesterday.

But now Winslade was seeing and feeling again the color and vivacity of the world that once had been as he strode with Kurt Scholder and Arthur Bannering across Hyde Park, jauntily sporting his adopted off-duty Guards officer's "uniform" of bowler hat, pinstripes, and tightly furled umbrella that was never opened, even when it rained. Cavalry troopers in khaki fatigues were exercising their mounts among the riders along Rotten Row; couples and lunchtime strollers ambled by the Serpentine Lake, where boys were sailing model yachts, and old ladies fed the ducks from wooden benches by the waterside. From the bandstand behind, with sunlight glinting off polished brass and tunics adding a dash of scarlet to the green, the band of one of the regiments of Foot Guards was playing a lively rendering of "The Man Who Robbed the Bank at Monte Carlo," complete with plenty of twiddly bits and oompahs, blotting out the distant rumble of traffic in Park Lane and Knightsbridge.

In the past few days it had all come back to him: the small, glass-paneled, Dickensian shopfronts of Bloomsbury and Mayfair, known by reputation for too many generations to have need of the opulent displays of New York's Fifth Avenue or Rome's Via Condotti; raucously jovial Billingsgate and Covent Garden markets contrasting with the staid dignity of Pall Mall and its gentlemen's clubs; exotic foreign odors wafting from the restaurants in Soho; the Bovril and Guinness neon signs in Piccadilly Circus; black, upright taxis and red, double-decker buses advertising Booth's gin and Gold Flake cigarettes; the underground with its

clattering tube trains; Holburn's swaying, round-ended trams;
the squat, redstone rotundity of the Albert Hall; Trafalgar
Square; The Monument; Westminster; beef at Simpson's in the
Strand; the pubs, with their ornamented doors of polished wood
and frosted glass, serving pints of Charrington's stout and
Watney's bitter with pork pies or bangers and mash. Like the toys
that come to life at night in children's fairytales, it was all mag-
ically real once again.

"Imagine how much of Europe is still like this!" Winslade
exclaimed to his companions. "Paris, Stockholm, Brussels,
Amsterdam, Copenhagen, all still free. Can't you smell the difference in the air? That's what this whole mission is all about.
Seeing all this reinforces one's determination to succeed."

Arthur Bannering, tall, upright, distinguished in appearance
and bearing, silver-haired and meticulously groomed, grunted
noncommittally as he walked beside Winslade with long, easy
strides. He was dressed in a black overcoat and homburg hat, and
he carried a leather briefcase. "Possibly, Claud. But determination and results aren't the same thing. I'll feel happier when
we've seen some reactions from Churchill and his people . . . or
unhappier, as the case may be."

Bannering was English and therefore sounded noncommittal
about most things. A former official at the British Foreign Office,
he was the Proteus team's diplomat. He had been deeply involved
in European politics up until 1940, when his department had relocated to Canada, after which he had gone on to work with the
U.S. State Department. The experience of returning seemed less
moving for him than it was for Winslade, perhaps because living
in England had ingrained his recollections more permanently;
and then again, perhaps he was just being British.

Since arriving in London, Bannering had developed the com-
pulsive habit of scrutinizing passers-by, especially in the vicinity
of Whitehall, where the British Foreign Office was located. He
found the thought irresistibly fascinating, he had confessed to an
amused Winslade, that at any moment he might encounter an
innocent, unknowing copy of his earlier self. That was just another of the peculiarities admitted by the strange situation in
which they now found themselves.

Kurt Scholder, second to Mortimer Greene in the team's scientific arm, said nothing as he walked on Winslade's other side.
Short and lean, wiry-limbed, with lined features and cropped,
steel-gray hair, he had lived in the United States for twenty years
after being smuggled out of Germany in 1955 in the course of
another Winslade-managed operation.

They left the park at Stanhope Gate and crossed Park Lane to the Dorchester, Winslade marching ahead and holding his umbrella high to keep the traffic at bay. Their private luncheon room was prepared with the table already set, and they were thirty minutes early as they had planned. Winslade ordered aperitifs from the small bar that he had asked to be installed in the room, and they settled back with their drinks to await the arrival of Churchill and his party.

The bar included a box of Churchill's favorite brand of cigars, purchased from Fribourg & Treyer in the Haymarket, and plenty of brandy and port. Scholder cast his eye curiously over the other bottles while he sipped a vermouth. He noted the selection of fruit and tomato juices. "So, you still think it will be Lindemann, eh?" he said, cocking an eyebrow at the other two.

Winslade smiled thinly through his Mr. Pickwick spectacles. "It won't do any harm to be prepared, anyway," he replied.

"Still in for a pound, then?" Bannering asked Scholder.

"Five pounds if you wish," Scholder told him. "Churchill will have recognized the importance of this. He will have taken it to the official government specialist committee, not to the academic all-rounder. Five pounds says it will be Tizard."

"Done." Bannering shook his head. "You're still thinking like a German, Kurt. Forget about official channels of reporting. Churchill values friendships more than procedures. Five pounds on Lindemann."

"Well, we shall soon see," Scholder grunted.

The reason why Winslade had refrained from specifying whom Churchill should bring with him had been to test the theories of rival Proteus-world historians by inviting them to predict Churchill's choices, and seeing who was right. The number of candidates put forward had been relatively few, indicating a measure of agreement that was reassuring.

As first choice everyone had agreed on Anthony Eden, the former Foreign Secretary, and thus Arthur Bannering's one-time chief, who had resigned early in 1938 over Chamberlain's snubbing of Roosevelt to avoid offending Mussolini. The majority had picked as second Alfred Duff Cooper, formerly First Lord of the Admiralty and the only government figure to have quit over Munich, with the dissenters opting for Bracken, Wigram, Morton, or Austen Chamberlain, the Prime Minister's brother.

For the technical expert that it was assumed Churchill would include in his party, opinions had been more divided. One group of the mission planners had opted for Professor F. A. Lindemann, head of the Clarendon Laboratory at Oxford and professor of experimental philosophy, which in those days had meant physics. He was a long-standing personal friend of Churchill's, and among other things had advised him on the fountains and hydraulics at Chartwell. He was also a confirmed nonsmoker, teetotaler, and vegetarian, which explained the variety of food and drink. The other group had favored Henry Tizard, chairman of a government committee formed to conduct a scientific survey of air defense. In 1935, Tizard's group had begun investigating reports of radio disturbances caused by passing aircraft, and from that beginning had followed the development of what would later be called radar.

The list of names had been a short one and had followed fairly automatically once Churchill was selected as the initial contact. Choosing him for this role in the first place, however, had been a far less straightforward business.

The political historians involved in planning Proteus had argued incessantly among themselves over whom the *King* group should approach first in England, but none of their nominations had commanded the unanimous vote of confidence that the importance of the mission warranted. Eventually, Winslade had settled the matter by asking surviving British statesmen and members of the Royal Family from that era who had escaped to Canada and the U.S. the question: If there had been a chance of preventing Britain's collapse in 1940, who, with hindsight, would have been the best person to do it? And the majority of those polled had replied, "Winston Churchill." The verdict came as a surprise, since the name had not figured prominently among the recommendations of the Proteus-world's experts. In their opinion, although Churchill's earlier career had seen its colorful moments and shown some potential for greatness, by the beginning of 1939 he was all but finished as a politician.

A descendant of the first Duke of Marlborough, Captain-General of the armies of Queen Anne and victor of the battles of Blenheim, Ramilles, Oudenarde, and Malplaquet, Churchill had first followed a military calling and served in India and the Sudan as an officer with the 4th Hussars. After that, sent to cover the South African war as a correspondent for the London *Morning Post*, he had earned a measure of fame for his part in rescuing an ambushed train and for his escape from a Boer prison camp. He took up politics on returning to England in 1900 and during the years leading up to 1914 had held a number of government offices, culminating in First Lord of the Admiralty by the time of the outbreak of the Great War. In 1915, however, he had been widely blamed, probably unfairly, for the failed attempt to force the Dardanelles and for the ensuing fiasco of the Gallipoli campaign. He had resigned from the government and returned to soldiering in the Flanders trenches.

His political prestige had shown some recovery to begin with in the postwar period, but acrimonious differences over Britain's India policy had kept him out of the MacDonald coalition of the early 1930s, and his exclusion from cabinet rank in Baldwin's later government had left him without influence until Britain's final fall. After the German landings at the end of 1940, he and a group of like-minded neighbors had refused to obey government orders against offering resistance, and all of them had been killed when they opened fire with rifles, submachine guns, and a mortar on the first column of the Wehrmacht to appear in front of the barricade erected at his gates. Churchill had long been one of the Nazis' marked men, and after his triumphal entry into London, Hitler had driven down to Kent especially to gloat over the burned-out remains of Chartwell Manor.

So, although Churchill had shown himself to be a man of some achievement, high principle, and considerable courage, little on the face of things singled him out as the savior that the Proteus planners were looking for. He was impetuous, inclined at times to be too easily seized by the romantic appeal of an idea to be practical about implementing it. Although considered a liberal rebel by many of the old-school Conservatives, he was nevertheless in many ways a backward-looking imperialist, and on top of that, well past his prime. And he had been virtually exiled to a political wilderness.

But further investigation and interminable discussions between Winslade, Bannering, and Anna Kharkiovitch had gradually put the issue in a different light. England, terrified by the still-fresh memories of 1914–1918 and mindful of the Red menace to the east, had been stupefying itself with delusions for years, acting as if solemn reaffirmations of faith in the good will of man could alter reality. Of course, *that* England had refused to listen to the truth; the truth destroyed the myths upon which its comforting delusions were based. Different people, appropriately, had spoken for *that* England.

But now it was blinking open its eyes and taking stock of its situation. After the short-lived euphoria of Munich, people across the nation had found themselves awakening to the sober realization that they did not feel reassured of having bought peace in their time, and that shame and guilt had not been appeased. Since then, although the papers gave no great exposure to the fact and most people continued to go about their business pretending that they weren't pretending not to have noticed, gas masks were being issued to every citizen; airraid shelters were appearing in all the cities; strange steel lattice constructions were springing up at intervals along the coast; and the Hurricane and Spitfire factories were working around-the-clock.

Now, at last, the nation was starting to heed the warnings that it had been ignoring. It would want facts now, not myths; it would look for direction, not empty reassurances. It made sense that the right people to speak for *this* new, awakening England would be the ones whom the old, sleeping England had rejected. And the person around whom these people were falling into orbit as they gravitated together was Churchill.

Furthermore, Winslade and his colleagues had begun to see, even Churchill's political ostracism could turn out to be more of an advantage than the hindrance it had seemed at first sight to be. Perhaps there was something to be said for picking as their contact a person whose public image and reputation had not been tarnished by association with the policies of recent years and who could in no way be held accountable for their consequences. Suddenly the verdict of the old-timers made sense, so much so that it seemed it should have been obvious all along, and in the end Churchill was chosen unanimously.

Bannering glanced at his watch after they had been talking for some time. "They should be here soon now," he said.

"Yes, Churchill was known for being punctual, wasn't he." Winslade drew on the cigar that he had helped himself to and exhaled luxuriously. Although he looked superficially relaxed, a glint of excitement showed in his eyes.

"You've been looking forward to meeting him," Bannering commented as he watched.

"He had none of the virtues I dislike, and all of the vices I admire," Winslade admitted. He puffed at his cigar again and thought to himself for a moment. "Not only that—the feeling of being back here is exhilarating, too. You know, the problem with America, Arthur, is that it went directly from barbarism to decadence, without the customary period of intervening civilization."

"Humph—you stole that from Churchill," Bannering accused. "I read it somewhere in one of his papers."

"Did I? Oh, maybe I did. Is it legally possible to plagiarize between one world and another? I wonder."

Kurt Scholder studied his drink and swirled it around in the glass first one way, then the other. "With Germany, the problem is a different one," he murmured. "There, you see, they went from civilization to barbarism without giving themselves a chance to enjoy any decadence at all."

A tap sounded on the door, and the maître d'hôtel appeared.

"The rest of your party is here, Mr. Winslade," he announced. "Mr. Winston Churchill and three other gentlemen."

"Ah, yes, splendid," Winslade acknowledged, rising to his feet. "Show them straight in if you would, please."

The maître d'hôtel held the door aside and ushered in a broad, stocky figure with thinning, red hair and a pugnacious jaw, dressed in a striped three-piece suit with polka dot bow tie; he was already familiar from the hours that the Proteus people had spent poring over photographs and documents. Behind him was Eden, tall, handsomely endowed with dark, wavy hair and a thick mustache, also wearing a three-piece suit. Beside Eden came Duff Cooper, shorter in stature and recognizable by his high hairline, straight mouth, and frank, open face with calm, thoughtful eyes. Finally, bringing up the rear, was another tall figure with a dark mustache, looking stiffer and more archaically attired than Eden, frowning suspiciously from side to side as the party entered. The corners of Bannering's mouth twitched upward, and he gave Scholder a quick, satisfied nod. The technical expert was Lindemann.

Bannering and Scholder set down their glasses, rose, and moved forward on either side of Winslade to greet their guests.

CHAPTER
5

THE WAITERS FINISHED CLEARING away the dishes and departed, leaving a hot plate with two fresh pots of coffee on a side-table. Winslade excused the bartender and accompanied him to the door, turning the key in the lock after the bartender had left. Then, instead of returning to his chair, Winslade clasped his hands behind his back and began pacing slowly by the windows along one side of the room.

The talk over lunch had been primarily social, to establish a conversational familiarity between the two groups. Despite their puzzlement and curiosity, the guests had refrained from pressing questions in the presence of the hotel staff; now, however, the time had arrived for more serious business. Churchill lit a cigar and sat back in his chair to follow Winslade curiously with his eyes. The room became very quiet.

"Mr. Churchill," Winslade began without looking around as he continued pacing, "I understand that among other things, you enjoy reading the works of H.G. Wells."

"That's true," Churchill agreed. He stared moodily at his brandy glass and snorted. "I have to admit that for the last few years I've had ample time for more leisurely pursuits. Yes, Mr. Winslade, I enjoy Wells's speculations and prophecies. The ability to foretell the future is an art much admired and, with mixed results, attempted by politicians also. The politician, however, must also be able to explain afterwards why his predictions didn't come true. But why, pray, do you raise the subject?"

Winslade replied obliquely. "How about his novel *The Time Machine*? Have you managed to include that in your readings? If so, what did you think of it? Was the premise plausible, do you imagine, or too farfetched to take seriously?"

Churchill sipped slowly from his glass and frowned. Lindemann stiffened visibly in his seat, his mouth clamped tight, while Eden and Duff Cooper exchanged wondering looks. It was clear in that brief instant that such a possibility had already occurred to them. That was as Winslade had intended. He had allowed several days for the notion to sink in and for its impact to dissipate before the meeting. Doing it that way minimized the risk of having to waste half the afternoon convincing an audience too overcome by incredulity to be receptive.

Winslade wheeled around to face the table and brought his hands up to rest on the back of an empty chair. "I trust we have already satisfied you that we are genuine, and that in any case we're not the kind of people who would attempt a foolish hoax," he said. His expression was earnest. The jovial manner that he had maintained through lunch had gone. "To avoid taxing your patience further, gentlemen—yes, we have come here from a future age. To be precise, we have traveled back from the United States of the year 1975."

Stupefied looks greeted his words. He went on, "By that year the world of the Western democracies has been reduced to North America, Australia, and New Zealand. The totalitarian systems that you see rising today have subjugated the whole of Europe, Asia, and Africa, in over thirty years of ferociousness and brutality aimed at world domination. The South American states are already committed to similar ideologies. What is left of the West faces a final conflict that will be waged by weapons of destructive power that few people in 1939 are capable of imagining. The odds against the West are overwhelming. It cannot hope to survive. All it can prepare for is a noble end." Winslade paused to run his eyes around the table. His voice fell to little more than a whisper. "But that is what we have come back to change, if we can."

There was a long silence. Bannering and Scholder waited impassively, while the guests at last faced squarely and grappled with the implications of the truth that they had been putting off in their minds to this moment.

Finally, Lindemann shook his head. "I don't know. I really

don't know." He glanced from side to side for support from his companions. "Look, I can't fault any of the evidence that you people have produced, and goodness knows I've spent time on little else since Winston showed it to me . . . but I don't have to tell you how preposterous the whole thing sounds." He tossed up his hands in exasperation. "What happens to causality and common sense if what you've said is true? How can you have come from a future that you now say you hope to change?"

Eden was recovering slowly from the trance that had gripped him. "It can't make sense, can it?" he said distantly. "Supposing that you did manage to change the whole situation in—when was it?—1975 . . . then the future that you came from wouldn't exist anymore, would it?"

"So where would you have come from at all?" Duff Cooper completed, taking the point and sounding equally mystified.

Winslade seemed to have been expecting the question and answered evenly, "We can't give you a complete explanation, I'm afraid. The machine employed was built in circumstances of extreme haste and urgency. There wasn't time for an exhaustive theoretical treatment of the subject."

Lindemann shifted uncomfortably in his chair. "This machine," he said. "What physical principles did its operation depend on? Was it a vehicle of some description, or what?"

The conversation over lunch had already identified Scholder as the scientist. Winslade nodded for him to take it from there, then turned away to stand staring out of one of the windows at the treetops of Hyde Park. Scholder cleared his throat, clasped his hands together on the table in front of him, and began, "The quantum-mechanical wave function is merely a spatio-temporal subset of a more complex entity that exists in a state of continuous transition between additional high-order modes. The collapse of the wave function represents merely the localization of an event in our particular subdomain of this super-realm."

Churchill caught Eden's eye and gave a baffled shrug, but continued puffing at his cigar without saying anything. Lindemann saw the movement and interjected, "You remember the talks we've had on the modern interpretation of atomic particles, Winston. The wave function is a mathematical description of where, with varying probability in space and time, a particle might be observed when an experiment is set up to detect it. When the experiment is actually performed and a definite result obtained, the wave function is said to 'collapse' to one of its possible solutions. Until that happens, the position and motion of the particle are indeterminate."

Churchill nodded, but his perplexed expression remained.

"So what's this 'more complex entity' that Kurt's talking about now?" he asked.

"Well, it sounds as if the wave function described by our laws of physics—what exists in the familiar universe of space and time that we perceive—is just a part of something bigger . . . a 'hyper-wave' function that exists in a state of continuous oscillation between our and other higher-order modes—'dimensions' I suppose you might call them. But this hyper-wave function can become localized in a form that manifests itself as a mass-energy quantum—a particle—in our subdomain, as it were, of the whole. Apparently, that's what we mean when we say that the wave function collapses."

Scholder nodded. "And it turns out that it's possible to induce relocalization into other subdomains—in other words, physical projection into them. Furthermore, some such projections involve coordinate shifts along the axes of what we perceive as space and time. Hence we have the basis not only for traveling through time, but for covering immense spatial distances as well."

"So . . . let me see. You're saying what?" Lindemann said. Only the sound of Winslade whistling tunelessly through his teeth while he stared out the window broke the silence. "But all that says," Lindemann objected at last, "is that basic particles are material condensations of vibrating patterns that extend into other 'places,' and that those condensations can be 'evaporated' and recondensed elsewhere. It doesn't say anything about sending a macroscopic object from one such place to another. How do you achieve that?"

"Sometimes many quantum events can be made to correlate in such a way that they add up to significant effects at the macroscopic level," Scholder replied. "The track of condensations in a cloud chamber, all caused by the passage of a single particle, is one example. The correlated relaxations of many excited atoms to produce coherent light from a laser is another."

"Laser?"

"Oh, I was forgetting. Something I'll explain another time. Let's just say for now that the pattern of bound wave functions that defines a macroscopic object can be relocalized simultaneously. In other words, the entire object can be transferred coherently to a different subdomain."

They continued for a while longer, and Scholder finished with an outline of the equipment involved. As Lindemann's questions became more specific, Scholder seemed to become evasive. Finally Lindemann said, "Without wishing to be offensive, Dr. Scholder, I must say that surprisingly little seems to have been known about the underlying physics. In fact, I'm tempted to express amazement that this machine ever came to be built at all. I do take it you were one of the designers?"

Scholder spread his hands and shook his head. "I'm sorry if I gave that impression. No, I was just one of the—how would you say?—the mechanics, as it were, who worked on the project. A little of the theory rubbed off."

"A quantum mechanic?" Churchill threw in, and guffawed to himself.

"Strange," Lindemann murmured. "I'd have thought that whoever was responsible for the enterprise would have sent along somebody who was conversant with the theory. And this other group setting up the return connection in New York—there isn't a theoretician among them, either?"

"There couldn't be," Scholder replied. "There was nobody like that available in 1975 who could have been sent. You see, the machine wasn't designed then. It wasn't even designed in our world. It was designed in another age entirely, following certain discoveries that didn't take place until the first quarter of the twenty-first century."

Lindemann was looking bewildered. "I don't understand," he said. "How could it have been built in 1975 if it wasn't designed until the 2000s? This is getting ridiculous."

"Because the machine that we built in 1975 wasn't the first one," Scholder answered. "The first one was built in 2025, and it connected back to a return-gate constructed in Germany in 1926. And that return-gate, gentlemen, is still operating there, over in Germany, at this very moment!"

Winslade wheeled around from the window. "That was how, in spite of the apparent paradoxes which you have so correctly drawn attention to, we have reason to believe that the past can indeed be reengineered," he said. "You see, it seems that it has been done before. That was how the world that exists outside these windows, with all its problems and dangers that you know of all too well, came to be that way. It was interfered with and changed from something else that existed previously."

A strained silence descended. Eden covered the upper half of his face with a hand, shook his head slowly from side to side, and moaned quietly, "Oh, God."

Churchill thrust his lower lip out pugnaciously and stared long and hard, first at Winslade, then at Scholder. Finally he said in a slow, measured voice, "If your intention has been to thoroughly confuse and bemuse all of us for the purpose of making sure that we stay here until we have listened to all you have to say, then I must congratulate you on what I have no doubt is already a resounding success. That being so, I trust that you will now attempt to dispel some of the confusion. Might I suggest that you begin at the beginning, wherever that may be in this bewildering chronological imbroglio, and proceed from there in whatever comes nearest to logical order? I think that would be appreciated by all of us."

Winslade nodded as if he had been expecting it. "Kurt here is actually from the twenty-first century," he said. "Let's begin with that." Lindemann slumped numbly back in his chair. Eden was still sitting with a hand half covering his face. Winslade smiled. "But first, a refill of our glasses, gentlemen. Allow me."

Winslade moved over to the bar and poured fresh drinks, which were passed around the table. Duff Cooper, whose wide brow had been contorting in knots as he tried to make sense of what had been said, leaned forward to rest his elbows on the table and interlaced his fingers. He composed a businesslike manner and said briskly, "Yes, let's start at the beginning. Now, Dr. Scholder, where and when were you born?"

"In the city of Dortmund, Germany, on July 15, 1990," Scholder replied promptly.

"And you are how old?"

"This year I shall have been alive for sixty-nine years."

"Having come back from the year 2025?"

"Yes."

Duff Cooper thought for a moment. "But 1990 to 2025 is only thirty-five years."

"I didn't go back directly to 1975. I went back to 1941, and then, thirty-four years later when it was 1975, went through the process again to arrive here. Thirty-five plus thirty-four is sixty-nine."

"Oh." Duff Cooper's composure evaporated. He sat back, shaking his head, and looked helplessly from one to another of his companions.

Scholder couldn't contain a thin smile. "Perhaps it would be best if I began by saying a few words about the world that I am originally from," he suggested. The others waited in silence. He went on, "Its history was identical to this world's up until the mid-1920s. The Great War ended with the Armistice of 1918 and the subsequent Treaty of Versailles. Germany was reconstituted as a liberal democratic state under the Weimar constitution. The Locarno Pact was concluded in 1925, by which Britain and Italy guaranteed the Franco-German frontier against aggression by either side, and in 1926, Germany joined the League of Nations."

Eden sat up again and listened while Scholder reeled off the events. "But after that it was different? You mean something happened to send everything off in a different direction somehow?"

"Let's not get our perspectives confused," Arthur Bannering cautioned. He had been talkative during lunch, especially with Eden on topics of foreign affairs, but the technical conversation since then had left him with nothing to contribute. "What Kurt is describing is the way things were 'originally.' If anything was sent off in a different direction, it was the world that we're in now—this one."

"Umm, yes . . ." Eden said. "Of course. I wasn't thinking about it that way."

Scholder resumed, "Europe continued to recover through the later twenties. Although the crash of the U.S. stocks and securities market in 1929 did trigger a worldwide economic recession, the situation was brought under control before the damage had gone too far."

"Interesting," Eden said. "You mean there wasn't the same world slump that we've just been through? How was it avoided?"

"It wasn't as bad, anyway," Bannering said. "The German Chancellor in 1930 was Heinrich Bruening, leader of the Catholic Center Party. He joined forces with the industrialist, Hugenberg, of the Nationalists, and—"

"No, I was there that year," Lindemann interjected. "You mean Hitler allied with Hugenberg, yes?"

Scholder shook his head and stared at Lindemann pointedly. "Oh, no, Professor. In the world that I am originally from, Hitler was never more than an obscure figure on the lunatic fringe of German politics. He wasn't involved in anything that mattered."

Lindemann started to say something more, but Churchill raised a hand. "Let them finish, Prof," he murmured.

Bannering went on, "The Bruening-Hugenberg coalition introduced a series of bold financial policies which led to a cooperative European program for economic recovery. Basically, their program involved extensive aid to the underprivileged, heavy reinvestment in new technologies, and a revitalizing of overseas trade, especially with Asia and the Far East. Japan later became a major partner, too, under the Inukai government."

"Inukai," Eden repeated. "But he was assassinated, wasn't he? Some right-wing militants were upset about the naval agreement that he signed."

"In *this* world," Scholder said softly. "It never happened in the one that I'm describing."

Bannering allowed a moment for Scholder's point to sink in. Then he continued, "The European-Japanese initiative impressed the Hoover administration sufficiently for the U.S. to revise its own policies, and the outcome was a worldwide commitment to cooperation and growth instead of protectionism and ruinous competition. By the middle of the thirties, prosperity had returned on an even wider basis than before."

"Hmm . . . concerning the actual details of the economic measures," Eden began, "what—" He caught a scowl from Churchill and raised a hand quickly. "But perhaps we can go into those some other time."

"Yes, make it some other time, Tony," Churchill grunted. He looked back at Scholder. "And?"

Scholder shrugged. "The effects quickly spread. An 'Eastern Locarno' was signed in Warsaw in 1935, guaranteeing the borders of the states between Germany and Russia. With the West visibly committed to settling its differences amicably, Russia's xenophobia began to relax, and with the easing of tensions, the right-wing reactionary movements that had begun appearing in the West declined—Mussolini, for example, was deposed in 1937. The Soviet Union grew into a superpower rivaling Europe and America, and the resulting competition compelled the gradual dismantling of the European colonial empires. Although local squabbles continued to break out in some places, by and large the never-again idealism of the 1920s was coming true at last. The world was turning away from war as a means of settling its differences."

"Sounds too idealistic," Duff Cooper murmured.

"Apart from anything else, the weapons that became possible in later decades made major wars obsolete, anyway," Winslade said. "The world had to turn to other ways."

Scholder continued, "As societies continued to modernize everywhere in the later years of the twentieth century, technological innovation became the primary source of wealth. Eventually, the successful harnessing of the enormous energy concentrations of the atomic nucleus, together with revolutionary electronic methods for processing information and automating work, advances in the biological sciences, and demonstrations of the feasibility of space travel, put a permanent end to fears of limits to growth and the finiteness of resources."

"So practical application of atomic power is possible, is it?" Lindemann said. "I often used to argue with Rutherford at the Cavendish Lab about that. And the weapons that you mentioned, were they atomic, too? I once estimated that a single device ought to be capable of generating the same explosive power as hundreds of tons of TNT."

"Actually, it works out at tens of thousands of tons, Professor," Scholder said. "And when you move on into thermonuclear fusion weapons, tens of millions."

"Oh, good heavens!"

Scholder resumed, "Through into the twenty-first century, the capitalist world became more socialist and the Communists more commercial as competitive pressures forced a retreat from the extremist doctrines of both sides. Global civilization was established. Living standards soared. Opportunity became available to all. Universal education bred freedom, independence of thought, individualism. The political, racist, and religious fanaticisms from earlier eras waned. The mass movements that they had engendered faded as popular support declined. Reason had triumphed over passion. The first true era of the Common Man had arrived." He finished by tossing his hands up in an animated sigh that seemed, strangely, to ask what had been the point of it all.

A short silence followed while the guests digested what they had heard. Then Churchill commented, "It sounds utopian. But you're saying that somebody interfered with the past in order to change it all? Why would anyone have wished that?"

"The overwhelming majority of people didn't," Scholder replied. "But there were a few who didn't see their situation as quite so utopian. The world's traditional oligarchies and ruling elites were finding that the people no longer needed them . . . or perhaps had awakened to the realization that they never had. Their power and their privileges were being eroded. They were becoming an endangered species."

Duff Cooper nodded as the probable sequence of events became clear. "Then the scientific discoveries that you mentioned earlier occurred," he guessed. "These oligarchs gained access to the new knowledge and used it to alter history in a way that would be more to their advantage. Is that what happened?"

Scholder nodded. "They saw an opportunity to preserve the world in which they had enjoyed the wealth and the status that they considered to be theirs by right," he said. "They saw a chance to learn from, and correct their mistakes. This time there would be no yielding to high-sounding principles of compassion or equality. They would seize total power and use it to resist social change, preserving themselves by ruthlessness, intimidation and the unrestricted use of force. That is what the Nazi system has been set up to accomplish."

Winslade straightened up from the chair that he had been leaning on and moved forward to stand at the end of the table. "They were a numerically small group, but still influential, even if their fortunes were on the wane," he said. "An international cabal formed mainly from wealthy hereditary ruling groups, drawn together by a common survival instinct. Their organization was called "Overlord," appropriately. Through confidential contacts that their positions enabled them to establish with the scientific community, they set up the project at a remote location in Brazil. Their machine was known as "Pipe Organ" for secrecy. It could project about a century back into the past—to be precise, to the year 1925."

"And that was where you worked," Lindemann checked, looking at Scholder.

"Yes."

Lindemann looked puzzled. "And nobody else knew what this place was? That seems unlikely. A scientific breakthrough of such a magnitude couldn't be kept secret, surely."

"The site that housed Pipe Organ was described officially as an experimental facility involved in a revolutionary method for transferring objects through space," Scholder replied. "The time-travel aspect of the physics was suppressed."

"But what about the people who worked there, the scientists? They must have known."

Scholder nodded. "Yes, we knew what the system was, but not what it was being used for. We were told that the far end of the link was a research station established purely to investigate the cause-and-effect mechanism of transfers through time. Only an inner group of the top scientists and officials knew what Pipe Organ was really for."

"So how did they justify the secrecy to the rest of you?" Lindemann asked.

"On the grounds that the possible impact of something as stupendous as time-travel needed to be assessed rigorously before any publicity could be risked," Scholder said. "It sounded like a reasonable precaution to take."

"I see." Lindemann nodded and seemed satisfied.

Churchill drew on his cigar and nodded slowly to himself as he thought over what had been said. "Their objective was to destroy the Soviet Union," he concluded. "They perceived its unchallenged emergence as the root cause of all their misfortunes, so they set out to destroy it. And their bludgeon to accomplish that end would be Germany."

"Exactly," Winslade said.

Eden was puzzled. "So did this, this Overlord organization actually create the Nazis? . . . No, wait a minute, it couldn't have, could it. The Nazis were around before 1925."

"They exploited them," Winslade said. "There had been the beginnings of the Nazi party back in the Overlord world's past, but it had never come to anything." He began pacing slowly by the windows again and explained, "Once Overlord had gained control of the technology that could give access to the past, they searched the historical record for a situation which, with the hindsight they now had, might have lent itself to being manipulated to their advantage. And they found one. They found an ideal opportunity in the circumstances that had existed in Bavaria in the early 1920s, after the Great War."

"Aha—enter Corporal Hitler," Churchill murmured.

Winslade nodded. "The region had become a hotbed of political extremism of every kind, and in particular of reactionary right-wing movements hostile to the Weimar government and all that it stood for. All the roving malcontents from disbanded army units were there, the free-corps bands fighting under officers from the Prussian old guard against the Communists, all committed to repudiating Versailles and restoring the old conservatism and authoritarianism."

Winslade tossed out a hand casually, as if acknowledging that the rest hardly needed to be spelled out. "In the course of their research, Overlord uncovered a party called the National Socialists, which since 1921 had been led by a former infantry corporal who had been temporarily blinded in a British gas attack at Ypres in 1918. As a party it was different from the rest—the only one that espoused the aims and ideals of the Right, while it applied the methods of the Left. Hitler had a sound grasp of mass psychology. He had launched himself on the popular tide of anti-republicanism, and he played on Germany's need to find scapegoats for its defeat and humiliation. At the same time, he understood the Germans' conditioned dependence on authority figures, and hence the potential appeal of firmness, determination, and violence. And he knew how emotive passions can be roused by the pseudoreligious trappings of ritual, color, pageantry, and most of all, a symbol. Perhaps one of the greatest inspirations of his misdirected genius was his design of a black swastika in a white circle on a blood-red flag as the emblem of the Nazi movement." Winslade stopped pacing and turned to spread his hands in a brief gesture of appeal. "A formidable combination, gentlemen. But not sufficient on its own to turn a tiny, unheard-of, political debating group into a militant force capable of taking over a nation.

"Hitler had the kinds of ideas that Overlord could harness to its own ends, and he had the drive to turn them into action . . . but he was impetuous and inexperienced. His attempt to seize control of Bavaria at gunpoint in 1923 failed dismally. He was arrested and locked up for a year in Landberg, and when he came out he found the party banned and its leaders feuding and falling away. He himself was prohibited from public speaking for two years. Chancellor Stresemann's policy of reconciliation with the Allies was succeeding, the French occupation troops were leaving the Ruhr, and Dr. Schacht had stabilized the currency. Prosperity was returning, and nobody wanted to hear about Nazism anymore. The Nazis had flourished in the bad times. Hitler was a fanatic and never ceased preaching his ideology of racism and hatred, but he didn't have the organizing ability to build and hold together a structure that would endure. And as the good times continued getting better through the late twenties, he faded away."

Winslade sighed and gazed at his audience with an expression of mock sadness. "It was such a tragic waste of talent. If only Hitler had know how to recruit, organize, and keep his party intact, he'd have been perfectly situated to take advantage of the bad times when they came back again after the Wall Street Crash in October 1929. Hitler didn't know that was coming, of course . . . but Overlord did. They'd blueprinted everything he needed to do to prepare for the situation, and their first agents from 2025 arrived in Germany in 1925 to begin his education. Their return-gate was operational by the following year, completing the two-way connection, and everything that's happened since has been the unfolding of the Overlord plan."

Winslade paused; his listeners were too astounded to respond. He continued, "By various stratagems, what had been merely an economic recession in Overlord's world was engineered into the worldwide slump that you've seen in this one. The Bruening-Hugenberg alliance that we mentioned earlier, for example, was prevented from happening by Hitler's joining forces with Hugenberg instead. The Inukai assassination was another part of the economic sabotage carried out by three agents sent back from 2025 for the purpose, who left Hamburg on a ship bound for Tokyo in February 1932.

Winslade nodded solemnly in response to the four incredulous stares greeting him from along the table. "Yes, gentlemen," he told them, "the whole Nazi operation as it exists today is being masterminded from almost a century in the future via a two-way transfer channel operating in Germany at this very moment. It has been going on since 1926. And the results require no elaboration. In the world that we have now, Hitler didn't just fade away at the end of the twenties. When Wall Street collapsed and the world reeled, he was ready and waiting with a thoroughly prepared campaign to capitalize on the people's disappointments and misfortunes, and on all of postwar Germany's fears, resentments, insecurities, and hopes.

"Yes, indeed, I think you'll agree that, with some help from his invisible friends, Corporal Hitler has managed admirably to bring events onto a course much more to his liking this second time around."

CHAPTER
6

A NIGHTCLUB IN THE cold light of morning was like last night's lover without her wig and makeup, or a movie theater when the show is over and the lights come on. The magic and the make-believe were gone, and only the reality that had been there all along remained.

Harry Ferracini yawned as he sipped a black coffee at one of the tables in front of the bar. He pictured in his mind the noisy, boisterous world of glitter, color, jitterbugging bodies, and laughing faces that had existed there a few hours previously. Now the place was transformed by bright yellow lights that revealed pipes and ducts below a ceiling previously lost in shadow, cables hanging between the spotlamps, and chipped paint at the bottoms of the walls. Chairs were upturned on top of most of the tables, the carpets in the aisles between them had been rolled back, and a white-haired janitor in a red flannel undershirt, a cleaning rag hanging from his back pocket, was mopping the floor. Cassidy and a few others were still at the bar talking to Lou, the bartender, while he restocked his shelves. Janet was standing by the edge of the dance floor crooning "Smoke Gets in Your Eyes" in a husky, off-key, blues voice, accompanied by a bored-looking, cigarette-smoking piano player. Somehow, she had changed into a sweater and slacks. Ferracini tried to remember . . . oh, yes, she'd gone home sometime between two and three in the morning to get some sleep because she had a mid-morning rehearsal tomorrow. That meant this was tomorrow, he decided.

The rest of what had ended up as a pretty wild night now existed only as a series of disconnected recollections. He and Cassidy had started out at the place on West Thirty-fourth Street; Cassidy upset the boyfriend of the redhead in the green dress. There had been the three Irish guys in the small bar with the accordion player, the ex-fighter with all the stories somewhere else, the two sailors with the chorus girls, and the pimp trying hard to sell them a "better place down the street." They'd met Janet and her friend, Amy, later, talked a lot, and come back with them to the place where Janet worked four nights a week as a singer—Ferracini couldn't remember the name of it. Things probably wouldn't have gotten so bad if it hadn't been Ed's birthday.

Ed, long since disappeared, was a buddy of Max, the owner, who was sitting at the next table, remonstrating with two men about city taxes and the costs of repairs. Short and stockily built, with a high, tanned forehead and crinkly hair, his tie and vest loosened and jacket thrown over the chair next to him, Max looked like someone who had been born to worry. He had taken a liking to Ferracini and Cassidy after Janet introduced them, and had invited them to stay on with his circle of after-hours friends, a half dozen or so of whom were asleep in a variety of postures around the room. Apparently, Max had been having trouble with a local smalltime gangster who was trying to put a protection squeeze on the business, and he was eager to beef up the ranks of his regular customers with men who seemed to know how to look after themselves.

New York City, 1939, was a far cry from the drabness of the austere, authoritarian America that Ferracini was used to. Just walking around Manhattan, watching the bustling crowds and looking at the goods on display in the store windows had been an experience. Being among people who were free to work as they chose, to buy anything they could pay for, to go anywhere they wished, and to become anything they were capable of becoming had been like breathing fresh air for the first time. Admittedly, the picture had a seedier underside, but maybe that seediness was the inevitable flip side of the coin. In a society where people were free to be whatever they wanted, some would turn out bad. Unconstrained, the spectrum would expand to extremes in both directions.

Yet at the same time, Ferracini felt anger and frustration. He had found post-Depression America—the real America that he had seen in the farmers, the ranch-hands, the miners, the loggers, the factory workers, the storekeepers, and the truckers that he had talked to all the way from Albuquerque to New York— barely dented in strength and spirit, lean, tough, and proud to have pulled itself through the worst without sacrificing its ideal of personal liberty, as so much of Europe had been forced to do. Here was what should have become the nucleus of a world alliance that could have taken Hitler apart.

But instead, America was squandering itself and partying all night, as it would while Europe fell to the Nazis, while Japan invaded Asia, and until Russia was destroyed. Then America would wake up, but by then, it would be too late. The colored lights and glitter of the make-believe would be gone, and only cold, gray, cheerless dawn would remain. Claud believed it could all be changed. Ferracini thought Claud was crazy.

"Ain't that right, Harry?" Max asked from the next table.

"What? I wasn't listening."

"We're gonna be seeing a lot more of you and Cowboy around here now. Guys who know Max get looked after okay. Get into the best places in town, no sweat. Meet lots of girls—nice girls, know what I mean? Max is a good friend."

"Yeah, why not? We'll see, Max."

"See, Harry's a smart guy. What'd I tell ya?"

"What line are you in, Harry?" one of the two men sitting with Max asked, tossing back the last of a drink. Max had introduced him earlier as Johnny.

Ferracini made an empty-handed gesture just as a blonde called Pearl came over from the bar and slid into a chair opposite. "Nothing in particular right now," he said. "Done a little bit of this, a little bit of that. . . . You know how it is."

"What'd you do last?"

"Trucking between here and New Mex."

"Ever work muscle? I can use help. It's good dough—fifty a week, and could get better."

"Sid says he's ex-Army," Max threw in. "Sid can tell. That right, Harry?" Ferracini shrugged.

"It wasn't the Army," Pearl said in a throaty voice. "They used to be with some secret spy operation that the State Department runs out of the embassy in Paris. Cowboy's been telling us about it over by the bar. They smuggled a real princess out of Austria or someplace. Say, Max, why can't we get interesting guys like these in here more often?"

Ferracini groaned beneath his breath and went back to drinking his coffee. Before Pearl could take the subject further, Janet, who had finished her number, came over to the table. "How do you think it went?" she asked, looking at Max.

"You're gonna work it into the routine tomorrow?"

"Sure, if you like it. Why not?"

"And you're gonna use the blue dress, okay? The one with the frills and stuff, that's got the cutaway top that shows plenty of . . . you know. . . ." Max cupped his hands in front of his chest.

Janet nodded with a sigh and a resigned smile. "I'll wear the blue dress," she agreed.

Max nodded his head rapidly and waved a hand. "Yeah, yeah, and sing the song. The song's fine."

"I guess I'm through for today, then," Janet said. She looked down at Ferracini. "If you and Cassidy can stand a subway ride uptown, I'll fix you both a late breakfast. You'll be able to clean up a little, too, and say hi to Jeff. Interested?" Jeff was Janet's younger brother. She had taken a singing job partly to help him through Columbia, where he was studying on a state scholarship grant to be a chemist. The two of them shared an apartment somewhere near Morningside Park.

"I'm interested," Ferracini said. He raised his head and called across to the bar, "Hey, Cassidy, Janet's inviting us to eat breakfast and meet her kid brother. Are we interested?"

"What's that—breakfast?"

"That's what I said. At Janet's place—say hi to Jeff, remember?"

"Oh, Jeff, sure—the chemist." Cassidy hauled himself carefully off the barstool. "Gotta say hi to Jeff . . . eat breakfast," he mumbled to the people he had been talking with.

"Get a load of this," Pearl muttered, lighting a cigarette. "It takes me all my time to find one guy I wanna take home. She walks out with two of them."

Ferracini stood up and helped Janet with her coat. "You've got a deal," he told her. "But no subway. With us you go by cab, okay?"

Pearl looked appealingly at the ceiling. "What, no Cadillac? Gee, I feel bad for you, Jan. Things must be getting really tough."

"Our chauffeur took it for his night off," Cassidy said as he joined them.

Max sat back in his chair and looked up. "So don't forget what I told ya, Harry. You guys come back and see us again, okay? And make it often."

"We'll see what we can do," Ferracini promised.

"Here, give me a call if you wanna talk some more about the job," Johnny said, giving Ferracini a calling card. It read, J. J. J. J. J. J. Harrington Enterprises, with a phone number.

Ferracini nodded. "Thanks, Johnny. I'll keep it in mind."

The three of them left the club through its double doors and walked along a short corridor to a flight of steps leading up to the street. "What's that?" Cassidy asked from Janet's other side as Ferracini was about to put the calling card in his pocket. Ferracini passed it to him.

"He's the New York agent for all the Austrian princesses who want smuggling out of Europe," Ferracini said. "The two of you ought to get to know each other."

Janet was somewhere in her latter twenties, with the petite, rounded kind of face that a button chin, high cheeks, and a girlishly turned-up nose made pretty rather than glamorous. She had large, green-blue eyes with long lashes, a puckish mouth that dimpled at the corners when she grinned—which was often, even after a night like the one before—and dark auburn hair that bounced around her face in loose wisps and waves in a way that seemed appropriate to the times—unlike the joyless, tight-bound styles typical of the seventies. She was refreshed after having enjoyed a little sleep the night before, and Ferracini and Cassidy were content to let her do most of the talking as the cab took them north along Broadway and onto Central Park West.

"Our pa was an engineer of some kind. When I was fifteen, we moved down to Pennsylvania so that he could take a job with one of the steel companies," she told them. "Well, when everything crashed they had to cut back, and he was laid off. He couldn't get any other work—nobody could—and we all ended up in a light-housekeeping room."

"Lighthouse?" Cassidy repeated. "You mean you were on the coast?"

Janet looked at him strangely, uncertain of whether he meant it as a joke or not. "No . . . you know, that's what you called it. Two-burner stove, icebox in the closet that the guy delivered a fifty-pound cake for every two days, bathroom in the hallway that you shared with the whole floor, all for seven dollars a week in a brownstone walkup on the edge of the slums."

"Sure, sure," Ferracini said, nodding knowingly. "So what happened to your folks? You said there was just you and Jeff now, right?"

"Ma overworked herself outdoors in the winter and got TB," Janet said. "There wasn't any money to buy proper treatment, and she died in '33." Her voice was matter-of-fact, without bitterness or self-pity. "Pa sent Jeff and me back to New York to stay with his cousin, Stan, who was a lawyer, and his wife, and he headed out West. There was supposed to be jobs in Oregon and

California. He said he'd send for us after he got himself fixed up, but all we ever got was a couple of letters with a few dollars inside." Janet shrugged and smiled. "Still, even that meant he didn't forget, I guess. Last we heard from him was over a year ago now, when he said he'd signed up on a freighter based out of San Francisco, going to Japan and places like that."

"So what happened with this guy Stan and his wife?" Ferracini asked.

"Oh, they're still around. They've got this huge house that they've lived in forever. When Stan's brother's business failed in Jersey and another cousin got laid off by Ford in Michigan, they all moved in with their families—twelve people to seven rooms and one bath. That lasted a couple of years. We ate lots of rabbit and relied mainly on somebody or other getting a WPA job, but usually that only lasted a few months. So when Jeff—he's a smart kid—won this scholarship to Columbia and I got the job at the Rainbow to help out—"

"Rainbow?" Ferracini queried.

"Max's place—the Rainbow's End. We've just come from there, remember?"

"Oh, yeah, sure . . ."

"Anyhow, Max got us the flat through someone he knows. It's only a couple of blocks from Columbia, so ideal for Jeff. And it's easier for me to get downtown to work, too. I work in a store in the day as well as sing, but today I'm off."

"Max got you the flat?" Cassidy sounded surprised.

"Oh, he can get a bit fussy at times, but underneath he's okay," Janet said.

The apartment was at the top of a tired-looking, stone-fronted, three-storey tenement situated in an alley somewhere between Seventh and St. Nicholas Avenues, south of 116th Street on the edge of Spanish Harlem. Laundry hung from lines strung to the buildings opposite, above small, walled-in yards. There were lots of children, dogs, and trash cans.

The final flight of stairs was dark and rickety, but the apartment itself, even though cramped by monumental furniture intended for the roomier houses of an age when servants had been plentiful, was warm, clean, and reasonably lit. It consisted of two rooms and a tiny kitchen, and was brightened by cheerful curtains and draperies, plenty of ornaments and knickknacks, some framed family photographs, and a selection of chocolate-box-top pictures of mountains, flowers, and lakes pinned on the walls, all, no doubt, a result of Janet's feminine touch.

The front room opened off the stairway landing. They found Jeff sitting at the table that took up the center of the room, contemplating a litter of tools around a partly dismantled toaster. The radio was on, and just as they entered, Molly at 79 Wistful Vista was shrieking, "Don't open that door, McGee!" to the accompaniment of thunderous crashings, clangings, and clankings.

Jeff looked like a student. He had a lean, almost skinny build, an unruly mop of hair hanging over his forehead, and a pale, owlish face adorned by thick-rimmed glasses. He was wearing a sleeveless pullover on top of a checkered shirt, worn-looking corduroy pants, and canvas shoes. The shelves behind him were packed with books and untidy stacks of papers, and the walls were covered with scientific charts and tables, clips holding more wads of paper, a street map of New York, some pictures of airplanes torn out of magazines, and a cutaway view of a battleship. The blankets half-pulled over the couch by the window indicated where he slept; the other room, behind the door at the rear, was Janet's.

"Jeff, this is Harry, and this is Cassidy," Janet said. "They're the two guys I told you about this morning—the ones I ran into with Amy last night. They were still at Max's when I got back, so I invited them home for something to eat. Guys, this is Jeff."

"Hi," Jeff said in a neutral tone. His face registered no particular reaction. Janet took off her coat and disappeared through the door into the back room. There were a few seconds of silence. Cassidy looked down at the table and pulled a face. "Know anything about toasters?" Jeff asked.

"Only that they work better in one piece," Cassidy replied. Jeff nodded distantly. "Anyhow, I thought you were supposed to be a chemist," Cassidy said.

"Well, I'm not really anything yet. Why? Know anything about chemistry?"

"Not really—except that you have to learn a foreign language to talk about sugar and salt."

"Oh, that reminds me—" Jeff turned his head and called in the direction of the open doorway through which Janet had gone. "We were out of sugar, milk, and bread, so I took a half-dollar and got some from the corner store. The change is in the tin."

Janet came back into the front room. "Thanks. That saves me a trip back downstairs. Now, how about clearing that stuff out of the way, Jeff, while I make some coffee and start breakfast."

During the meal, they talked about movies, song hits, and some of the people who frequented the Rainbow's End. Jeff had a low opinion of most of the ones he had met, dismissing them unapologetically as bums, which perhaps explained the coolness that he had shown Ferracini and Cassidy. Ferracini asked Jeff if he had plans for specializing in any particular kind of chemistry after he graduated. Jeff thought for a second, then asked, "Ever heard of atomic physics?"

Ferracini made a you-know-how-it-is gesture with one hand. "A little."

"There have been some pretty exciting developments in the last ten years," Jeff said. "Theoretically, anyhow, you ought to be able to get enough energy out of tiny amounts of some substances to supply the whole world easily—thousands of times more than from gasoline, for instance." He gave Ferracini a guarded look. "Does that sound crazy to you?"

Ferracini did a good job of looking just a little incredulous. "Well, I guess nothing's impossible until someone proves it is . . . and then that's only until someone else goes and does it, anyway," he said. "Didn't a lot of smartasses who should have known better tell everyone that steam engines wouldn't work and airplanes wouldn't fly—all kinds of things like that?"

Cassidy nodded from across the table. "Right. I guess if I had to, I'd put my money on guys like Jeff here making atomic gasoline work somehow in the end—or whatever you call it."

Jeff seemd encouraged by the response. "You seem to be more open-minded than a lot of people," he said.

Cassidy shrugged and made a gesture of magnanimity. "You don't only get bums and deadbeats hanging around the clubs, you know. You can bump into us intellectuals, too, kind of keeping up the standards, know what I mean?"

Jeff grinned at Janet and seemed to loosen up suddenly. "Maybe these two are okay," he told her. "You know, your judgment's improving all the time, Sis. There might be hope for you yet."

"Well, Jeff, I'm real glad to hear that," she said.

Jeff looked back at Ferracini and Cassidy. "Recently, we had one of the real big names in atomic chemistry join Columbia," he informed them. "He had to get out of Italy because his wife's Jewish. Enrico Fermi. Maybe you've heard of him?"

Ferracini frowned. He'd heard the name, he was sure. Hadn't Fermi been mixed up with the crash U.S. program to go all-out for an atomic bomb, back in the early forties before Ferracini was born? The American program had begun after the Germans astounded the world by suddenly producing the atomic bomb in 1942, the second year of their attack on Russia, and had succeeded just in time to give the U.S. twenty years of grace.

The Axis powers had taken until the late 1940s to complete the mopping up and partitioning of the Soviet empire and to set up the administration and resettlement of the new territories. Then came the wars of anti-Nazi Moslem insurgency in the Mid-

dle East and western Asia, which had given America its chance
to close the technological gap sufficiently to develop a workable
bomb. Thus, an immediate follow-up assault on North America
had been averted. Instead, the Axis powers had turned their attention southward in the late fifties and sixties to Africa, inflict-
ing the horrors of Nazi-style domination and genocide on its
black peoples to provide colonial empires for Fascist Italy and
Spain.

While Cassidy and Jeff continued talking with Janet about
scholarships and job prospects, Ferracini sat back and stared
through the window at the Manhattan rooftops. The voices
seemed to fade, and he found himself brooding about the mission
and their place in it.

The American A-bomb hadn't become a reality until late
1951; the Germans, on the other hand, had dropped their first
atomic weapons on Russia in July 1942. So how could Kennedy's
Task Force, standing by in 1975 for the return-gate connection to
be completed, hope to stop Hitler by keeping Britain and France
fighting if they could, and by bringing the U.S. into the war? If
America was still twelve years away from making an A-bomb,
and it tried taking on the Nazis now, the only possible outcome
could be its total destruction along with the Soviet Union's. The
only answer that Ferracini could see would be if Kennedy
planned to send bombs through to the West from 1975 to counterbalance Hitler's. But that, surely, would result only in all-
around devastation, with both sides being supplied from different
futures.

Unless, of course, something was done in the meantime to de-
prive the Nazis of their nuclear capability.

For normal security reasons, the precise role to be played in
the Proteus Operation by the military contingent under Major
Warren had never been disclosed. It had been said that they were
to provide security at Gatehouse, but none of the troops believed
that was all there was to it. During the training period at
Tularosa, they had discovered that all of the Special Operations
troopers had worked on clandestine assignments; that all of
them were experienced in undercover operations in Nazi-
dominated Europe; and that, perhaps most remarkably of all, at
one time or another, all of them had done tours of duty in the
Leipzig area of Germany, a hundred-odd miles southwest of
Berlin. All of that, surely, was too much to be coincidence.

And Ferracini knew well that nothing Winslade was mixed
up with ever happened purely by chance.

CHAPTER
7

THE TRAIL THAT HAD eventually led to the unraveling by U.S. intelligence of the real story behind Nazism began back in the scientific world of the 1930s with the birth of atomic physics.

In the early years of that decade, Enrico Fermi, then working at the University of Rome, had speculated on the possibility of producing artificial radioactive isotopes by bombarding substances with neutrons, which had been discovered recently by Chadwick at Cambridge. He went on to conduct a series of experiments along such lines and published various papers. But in late 1938, his work was interrupted when he visited Stockholm to collect his Nobel Prize and seized the opportunity to escape to the West from Mussolini's Fascism, accompanied by his wife, Laura, and their two children.

By that time, however, similar investigations were under way in other places, notably the Joliot-Curie Laboratory in Paris and the Kaiser Wilhelm Institute of Chemistry at Dahlem, in Berlin. Further experiments on the neutron bombardment of uranium had proved puzzling: analysis of the reaction products failed to reveal the heavy elements, such as radium, that should have resulted from the decay of artificially activated heavy nuclei. Finally, in December 1938, Otto Hahn and Fritz Strassmann in Berlin conducted an experiment which showed conclusively that while radium and other predicted elements were definitely not created by the neutron bombardment of uranium, certain much lighter substances, such as barium and krypton, were. For a while, the experts were unable to offer a satisfactory interpretation.

Hahn wrote a letter detailing these puzzling results to a former colleague of the two scientists, Lise Meitner, an Austrian Jewess forced to flee the country after Hitler's annexation of Austria, who was by then working at the Nobel Institute in Stockholm. It so happened that Meitner's nephew, Otto Frisch, who worked with Niels Bohr at Bohr's Institute of Theoretical Physics in Copenhagen, had come to Sweden to spend Christmas with her, and between them they worked out what had happened.

The uranium nuclei, instead of simply absorbing neutrons to become heavier, unstable isotopes as had been expected, were splitting into nuclei of lighter elements of approximately half the original weight. Unlike spontaneous radioactive decays, which undergo comparatively small changes in mass by ejecting single particles and therefore involve only minor releases of internal binding energy, the uranium nuclei had been induced to split, or "fission," resulting in enormous yields of energy.

At the end of his Christmas vacation, Frisch brought the news back to Denmark just as Bohr was about to leave for the U.S. to attend the Fifth Washington Conference of Theoretical Physics. Bohr announced the findings to the conference on January 26, 1939, and the proceedings degenerated into a flurry of frantic scientists, many still in black tie, rushing through the exits to set up repeat experiments in their own laboratories at Johns Hopkins University, the Carnegie Institute, Columbia, Chicago, Princeton, Berkeley, and elsewhere.

The experiments confirmed the practicability of fission—as isolated atomic events, that is. The list of unknowns that would have to be answered before the energy theoretically available from the nucleus could be tapped on a usable scale was daunting, however. Accordingly, after their initial excitement, the American scientists resigned themselves to many more years of patience and perseverance before a working device of any kind— bomb or power source—would be even in sight.

The news of the German weapons used against Russia in 1942, therefore, came as a shock. None of the experts could explain it. Hastily reversing his previous policies of tolerance and good will toward the dictatorships, President Burton K. Wheeler, who had been elected in 1940 on a strongly isolationist platform following Roosevelt's retirement from public life, gave top priority to a comparable U.S. program. At the same time, Wheeler commissioned a select group drawn from the various intelligence services to investigate and account for the astounding speed of the German research and development effort. Thus, a new team of specialists dedicated to scientific intelligence-gathering came into being, which in time grew larger and found itself a permanent place among the government's less publicized institutions. The group was designated "SI-7."

Remoteness from the scene of events, the difficulties of operating in Nazi Europe, and the rigorous secrecy maintained by the opposition all hampered progress, but the picture that emerged as the pieces fell into place indicated that there had been something very strange about the whole German nuclear program.

After Hahn and Strassmann published their results early in 1939, a number of speculative papers by German authors on bombs and power reactors had appeared in scientific journals, and further studies were initiated by the Ordnance Branch of the Army, the Reich Ministry of Education, a research laboratory of the Post Office, and several private concerns. But these activities were never effectively coordinated, and although the Germans were quick to ban the export of ores from the mines they had acquired in Czechoslovakia, their overall program suffered from competition among the different groups for uranium metal and oxide as well as other resources, from witholding of information, and from the jealousies that tend to arise in totalitarian bureaucracies.

With such constraints, the program shouldn't have had a hope of yielding an atomic bomb in anywhere near three years. And indeed, the records that SI-7 unearthed showed a hodgepodge of impractical attempts at reactor construction, a glaring theoretical error that had gone undiscovered for over half a year, and no evidence of the major industrial installations essential for weapons manufacture. Nevertheless, weapons had appeared, as if out of nowhere, in the summer of 1942. How, remained a mystery for many years.

By the early 1960s, further work by SI-7 had established that the puzzle of Nazi atomic research was not an isolated instance; similar anomalies existed in other areas of German technological development, too, such as the electronics being applied in the Nazi military and space programs, their advances in computer technology, and their development of high-performance aircraft. In all cases, innovations had appeared that couldn't be traced to identifiable origins, but which again seemed to have appeared ahead of their time, out of nowhere.

That this should be so was all the more baffling since it represented the opposite of what had been expected from the Nazi system. Serving no other purpose than to perpetuate the absolute power of its ruling clique, Nazism stifled free expression and dissent, repressing all forms of original thought and substituting instead its own barren slogans and mindless dogmas. Such a system could never support a truly creative process of free scientific enquiry. It was totally parasitic. As with the material wealth that it was unable to create but could only loot, so it was incapable of creating new knowledge; it could only consume what was ready-made and available for it to conscript by force.

Gradually, a common underlying pattern emerged: The real innovations, it turned out, had not been due to any ongoing process of general discovery; instead, they all stemmed from a sudden and astounding leap forward in concepts and theory that had taken place in virtually all of the sciences during a brief period of only a few years, beginning in the early forties. After that, the curve of new discovery ceased abruptly and reached a plateau. That was what had enabled the U.S. to catch up. It was as if an advance deposit of information had been credited to Hitler's account to be drawn on for the next twenty years. Where had it come from?

The answer came out of the work that Claud Winslade had been involved in ever since the time of Europe's fall, which overlapped but was separate from SI-7's operations. For over twenty years, Winslade and his group had been piecing together another story that went back to the twenties and thirties, and which had grown more bizarre and more incredible as each new fact fell into place. This story involved, among other things, documents spirited out of top-secret German archives, which contained references to names, places, and organizations that nobody had ever heard of. There were descriptions of scientific concepts and theories that were unfamiliar even to experts. Mysterious names kept recurring, of people whose records had been faked to make it appear they had lived normal lives in Germany, whereas, in fact, they seemed to have appeared out of nowhere, just like the German scientific discoveries that were preoccupying SI-7. And most extraordinary of all, there were repeated mentions of dates and events that appeared to have taken place not in any recorded period at all, but in the twenty-first century!

And that, Winslade's group finally deduced, was the thread that tied all of those mysteries together. Unbelievable as it was, the whole phenomenon—Nazism, the rise of Hitler, the spread of totalitarianism in the early part of the century—had been engineered and remote-directed from the twenty-first century. Winslade's group even produced drawings and design data for Pipe Organ, the machine that had initiated the connection, and for the secret Nazi installation called "Valhalla" that contained the return-gate back to it. Some individuals who had transferred back from the future for one reason or another were still in Germany, after being trapped in the twentieth century when the Nazi leaders had the Valhalla machine destroyed sometime around the mid-forties. A few of those people were contacted and smuggled out, despite their being held under conditions of maximum security, and brought to tell their story firsthand at the White House. Kurt Scholder was one of them.

A detailed study ordered by the President in the late sixties concluded that enough information had been collected for the United States to build a Pipe-Organ-type device of its own with a good chance of success, even if some of the theoretical issues remained obscure. So perhaps the West could prevent the doom that appeared to be inevitable by trying some meddling in history of its own.

One major limitation, however, presented itself. The range of such a device—the maximum time back in the past that it could reach—was related to the energy density attainable from the source used to power it. Pipe Organ had utilized an extremely high density fusion process, which was what had enabled it to project back a hundred years to 1925. Fusion technology was not available in the world of the early seventies. The next best thing would be a dedicated high-temperature fission process, for which calculations indicated that the greatest range attainable would be a little over a third of that for fusion, that is, to sometime around late 1938 or early 1939, assuming four years to build the machine and the components for its return-gate.

The period before that date would be "frozen"—inaccessible—and therefore immune to being altered. There could be no changing the things that had already happened in the world: Hitler established in Germany; Hitler's takeovers of the Rhineland, Austria, and Czechoslovakia; Munich; the Spanish Civil War; Mussolini in control of Italy; Abyssinia; the Sino-Japanese war in Manchuria. There was no way around being stuck with all of it.

Every day lost would freeze another twenty-four hours of events into the sequence of unalterable history. President Kennedy ordered a crash program to be launched immediately, and the Proteus mission departed on schedule four years later, in 1975.

CHAPTER
8

"AN AMAZING STORY!" ANTHONY Eden exclaimed when Bannering finished describing the intelligence activities that had led up to Proteus. Eden, immaculately attired, as usual, in a three-piece suit of dark charcoal herringbone and wearing the homburg hat that had become as much a public symbol as Chamberlain's umbrella, continued staring out of the taxicab window for a while. The traffic tangle at the corner of Trafalgar Square sorted itself out under the no-nonsense direction of a walrus-mustached bobby in pointed helmet and neck-high tunic, and the cab began moving again. "So what happened finally with Heydrich's prophecy of getting to the moon by 1968?" he asked. "Did they do it?"

Bannering shook his head. "The Nazi space program ran into difficulties, mainly through a poverty of innovation, as had been predicted. They'd spent their capital. America, on the other hand, had enjoyed an enormous influx of talented refugees from all over the place and was reinvesting the profits. Both sides put up permanently manned orbital platforms in the same year—1970. In fact, the U.S. was drawing ahead in a number of fields by then."

"But not enough to avert a clash eventually," Eden said.

"It could hold the dictators at bay for a while, but they had a preponderance of brute force and the lion's share of global resources. It was clear that when they realized time was only widening the gap against them . . ." Bannering made an empty-handed gesture and left the sentence unfinished.

Eden stroked a finger through his thick mustache. "I don't know, landing a man on the moon . . . It sounds like something out of one of Winston's H.G. Wells stories. Is it possible at all, do you think?"

"Oh, certainly," Bannering assured him. "In fact, in the world that Kurt came from originally, they did it. And I'm sure the America I knew would have been able to do the same in time, if it hadn't been forced to dedicate the national effort to defense and catching up with the Nazis."

"They did it? You mean they actually got there—a man on the moon?"

"Yes, in the late seventies."

"Amazing! And what did they find there?"

"A lot of rocks and dust. It's not really my department, Tony. You should ask Kurt about it when he gets back if you're interested. He's always happy to talk about things like that . . . at least, if Lindemann's questions haven't driven him to distraction by now."

Kurt Scholder had gone off under a suitable alias with Lindemann for a few days to see some of the defense work being done in the physics laboratories at Oxford, Cambridge, and Edinburgh, and also at some of the government establishments with which Lindemann had connections. Scholder was hoping to meet some of the better-known physicists of the day, such as Erwin Schrödinger and Max Born, whose escapes Lindemann had helped organize during his visits to Germany in earlier years.

Winslade had left the hotel with Bannering and Eden, but they had dropped him off at Westminster to collect Churchill, who had scheduled a private session with Prime Minister Chamberlain that morning to impress upon him the gravity of the European situation and to plead for more vigor in strengthening the armed forces and speeding up industry. Everyone who had been present at the initial meeting at the Dorchester had agreed, however, that they couldn't risk bringing Chamberlain into the Proteus secret at that time. Many members of the upper echelons of British society were sympathetic to the Nazi cause and blind to its menace, and Chamberlain's true loyalties and dispositions were uncertain. There was no telling who the information might have found its way to; the risk of a leak back to Berlin was the last thing the team could afford.

In July, the return-gate being built in New York would become fully operational, putting the present Roosevelt administration in direct contact with President Kennedy and the task group standing by in 1975. At that point, the Proteus team's primary objective would be accomplished, and what happened after that would be out of their hands. Their aim in the meantime was to advance Britain's state of preparedness to the greatest degree possible. To that end, Eden had been busy helping to mobilize the support of the leading public figures who had spoken out for firmness and stronger defense measures, such as Lord Cecil and Lord Lloyd, Sir Robert Horne, and Messrs. Grigg, Boothby, and Bracken, while Duff Cooper was meeting with publishers to call for a louder note of urgency in the popular press. Churchill himself had accepted the task of prevailing upon Chamberlain and other cabinet ministers directly. Winslade would be bringing him for lunch at the Athenaeum Club to compare notes on the morning's efforts.

There was time to spare before they were due at the Athenaeum, and Bannering suggested an appetizer in a small pub off Cockspur Street that he had been fond of using in his previous existence in London. Eden agreed, and the cabbie dropped them off with a chirpy "Ta, guv," as Bannering added a tip to the fare. They were not far from the Foreign Office, and as Bannering and Eden began walking, Bannering resumed his unconscious habit of scrutinizing the passing faces.

"You needn't bother looking this week, Arthur," Eden said, grinning as he noticed. "You're not here."

"What? What do you mean, not here?"

"Out of uncontainable curiosity I took something of a liberty, I'm afraid, and checked up on you with a friend of mine in the F.O. who works with Halifax," Eden said. Lord Halifax had been Foreign Secretary since Eden's resignation a year previously, in February 1938. "Yes, you are working there, in D14 under Saunders-Blenkinson, as you said."

"Well, I'm relieved to hear it," Bannering replied, with just a hint of indignation in his voice.

"But this week they've sent you to Paris to see Bonnet's people. Had you forgotten?"

Bannering frowned for a second, then nodded. "Yes, that's right—it was to do with that Franco-German friendship thing. Did I go this week?"

"Yes. You're not due back until Saturday."

There was a pause. "You know, Tony, I'm still not sure if I believe this whole business."

They entered the pub and climbed a short stairway to an upstairs lounge. Eden bought two gin and tonics at the bar, and they carried them over to a table in a far corner, secluded from inquisitive ears by carved partitioning and potted plants. "Haven't been here before," Eden said as they sat down. "Quite a cozy little place, isn't it."

The friendship agreement between Germany and France had been concluded in December. Through it, Germany hoped to loosen France's alliance with England; it had pried Poland away from its Western ties with a nonaggression pact in 1934. But Eden very much doubted if the signings of these sacred pieces of paper, solemnly ritualized before trusting peoples as if tablets were coming down from on high, really meant anything that mattered. "Nothing matters very much," Lord Balfour had said once. "And very few things matter at all."

"Penny?" Bannering said, watching his face.

Eden searched his mind for something else to talk about. "Last night at Winston's flat—you'd just started telling us about Hitler's early days," he said. "But then Randolph arrived and we all went on to something else. We'd been talking about Versailles. . . ."

Bannering nodded. He took a drink and set his glass down on the table. "We don't seem to have learned a lot in two thousand years, do we. The Romans would never have made the same mistakes, you know."

"Yes, I've read Machiavelli, too," Eden replied.

The Romans had a simple policy for dealing with vanquished enemies: they were either very generous, or else they were very harsh. Either they installed defeated kings in palaces with slaves, horses, guards, and more power than they had dreamed of before in their own realms, thus guaranteeing strong defenders who would always be loyal to Rome; or they would get rid of them permanently, along with most of their families and followers. The rationale was that anyone given reason for harboring a grudge shouldn't be left strong enough to do anything about settling it. At Versailles and after, the Allies had broken every rule by not only leaving strong enemies with a grudge, but in addition giving up their own power to defend themselves.

"Reparations was a misguided concept from the start," Bannering said. "You can't hope to cover the costs of a war by plunder these days. Modern industrialized economies are too interdependent. All it did was throw world cash flow into chaos. America was getting back about a fifth of what it was paying out to Germany in high-risk loans."

"A lot of people knew that at the time," Eden agreed. "But nobody had the courage to say so to electorates that had put up with four years of war and were demanding revenge."

Bannering nodded. "But the biggest mistake was leaving the

traditional German power structure intact, still controlled by conservatives and monarchists who would never accept the regime that the West was trying to impose. The ingredients for a revolution were there from the beginning. Hitler saw a road to power. Overlord saw a weapon to hurl against Russia."

Eden sat back in his chair and looked distantly up at the ceiling. "The impact must have been stunning," he mused. "Just imagine Hitler and Goering being confronted by people from years in the future who say they want to help promote the cause. How would somebody react to something like that?"

Bannering blinked in surprise. "Well, *you* should know, Tony," he said. Eden laughed, and they finished their drinks.

"Good for another?" Bannering asked.

Eden pulled his watch from a vest pocket and flipped open the lid. "Yes, there's time. Why not?"

"On me this time." Bannering went to the bar and a minute later returned with two refills.

"So Overlord took over Hitler's early operation," Eden said, prompting Bannering to continue.

"Yes. They spelled out the conditions that the Nazis would have to satisfy for their next power bid. Essentially they were one, an appearance of legality—the real revolution would take place only after power had already been secured by constitutional means. Two, the Army would be for the takeover this time, not against it. And three, they'd need the active backing of at least some of the respected institutions of finance and business. Overlord's agents practically ran the party's Brown House headquarters in Munich. They planned the organization and recruiting, and they dreamed up the Nazi state within a state, complete with all its offices and departments, that would be ready to emerge overnight to replace the existing structure of government when the time came."

"Yes . . . that is exactly how it happened," Eden said slowly. He thought over the things he had been told already. "So when Müller resigned the chancellorship and was succeeded by Bruening in 1930, Hitler joined Hugenberg to prevent the Bruening-Hugenberg coalition that had led to stability in the Europe that Kurt came from. After that, Bruening couldn't hold a workable majority, could he?"

"There were interminable elections," Bannering said. "The Nazis gained ground by selling the Army on visions of restored greatness and terrifying the business community with specters of what would happen if the Communists got in."

"They must have had inside help with the Army, though," Eden said.

"They did," Bannering confirmed. "Overlord had been busy in Berlin, too, looking for manipulable contacts on Hindenburg's staff. Their collaborator was Defense Minister Groener's right-hand man, Schleicher."

"Ah, so Schleicher was in it with them, was he?" Eden nodded slowly to himself, as if that had told him a lot. General von Schleicher had been in control of all press and publicity matters concerning the military. He was a born political intriguer, and in the early twenties had circumvented the Versailles restrictions by arranging for German tank and air officers to train secretly in Russia.

Bannering explained, "Overlord agents put Schleicher up to the idea of ditching Bruening and Groener, incorporating the Storm Troopers into the regular Army and using their combined force to subdue the Nazis, and then seizing control himself. Schleicher fixed things with Hindenburg, and after Bruening and Groener had gone, he had Papen wheeled in as a temporary stooge-Chancellor while the last vestiges of constitutional government were done away with. Then Papen was ditched, too."

"Making way for Schleicher, who in turn was just to clear the road for Hitler," Eden completed. "My word, what a tangle!" He exhaled a long breath and shook his head wonderingly.

"Oh, it gets worse," Bannering promised. "Schleicher assured Hindenburg that he'd be able to form a stable majority in conjunction with a section of the Nazis that Schleicher had been told would follow Strasser in a breakaway from Hitler. But that whole business with Strasser was a charade to set Schleicher up. The Nazis didn't split, and the situation that Overlord had been engineering all along came to fruition with double-crosses sprouting all over Berlin and enemies pouring out of the woodwork to pull Schleicher down from all sides. He resigned at the end of January '33, and Hindenburg gave Hitler the job after Blomberg confirmed the Army's support. But Blomberg had been duped, too. He thought the Nazis would only be used as a temporary expedient to achieve unity by exploiting popular nationalist feelings."

Eden sat back and sighed as he recalled what had happened after Hitler became Chancellor, and the machine that had been waiting in the wings was wheeled out and unveiled. All the apparatus of state—press, radio, police—was immediately commandeered and pressed into the service of the Party; all opposition to the Nazis was declared illegal, and those who refused to surrender docilely were subdued by terror. Reich Governors were put in charge of the states, centralizing German power for the first time in history and achieving in two weeks what neither

Bismarck, the Kaiser, nor the Weimar Republic had ever dared attempt. In the Reichstag, a guaranteed majority was created by the simple device of arresting potential opponents; then that majority was used to pass an act conferring exclusive powers on Hitler's cabinet. Thus, the dictatorship was established legally, by consent of Parliament. The first concentration camp opened at Dachau in the same month.

Eden nodded slowly to himself as a lot of things fell suddenly into place—Hitler's great blood purge in 1934, for example, which had supposedly been to reassure the generals by getting rid of the extremists who were turning the Storm Troopers into a rival private army. Obviously, its real purpose had been to eliminate Schleicher, Strasser, and no doubt many others whose usefulness had ended and who knew too much.

Thus, the domestic decks had been cleared for the opening shots of Nazi foreign policy. This had begun with a series of provocations to test the resolve of the Allies; and sure enough, the Allies had protested and blustered, but done nothing. Only Italy had stood by its word when Hitler risked his first foreign gamble. "What about Austria in 1934?" Eden asked. "I take it that was to find out who could be pushed around and who couldn't. People like Winston and I kept trying to tell everybody, but they wouldn't listen."

"That was when Overlord decided that Mussolini had to be induced to switch sides," Bannering said.

"Overlord was behind that, too?"

"Of course. They put Mussolini up to the idea of invading Abyssinia and becoming another Caesar. In reality they were sending him up as a trial balloon to see how Britain and the League would respond to unprovoked aggression. The results told them a lot."

"And then the Rhineland, eh?" Eden said.

Bannering snorted contemptuously. "Hitler was terrified. He issued secret orders for the troops to come scurrying back over the bridges at the first sign of trouble from the French. He only went through with it because Overlord threatened to get rid of him and start all over again with someone else if he didn't. All that talk afterward about his iron willpower and how he kept the generals in line was so much stuff and nonsense."

Then Austria had been seized, followed by the Sudetenland of Czechoslovakia after the deal at Munich. And now Ribbentrop had opened the by now familiar diplomatic offensive against Poland for the port of Danzig, and against Lithuania for Memel.

Suddenly, Eden felt daunted by the task ahead of them. For years now, this hideous juggernaut had been rumbling onward along its chosen course, guided by evil genius and perverted science from an age that Eden was unable even to imagine. How could they, a mere handful, hope to deflect it even for a moment, let alone stop it? Even with the New York machine operating in July, what would be the use of aid from 1975 when the Nazis had access to the technology of 2025?

In any case, there was so little time. Eden and his colleagues now knew that the conflagration which had led to the collapse of France and Britain and the end of civilized Europe had begun that very year, 1939, with a German assault on Poland in the last week of August. That was why Winslade's group had come straight on to England without waiting for the New York machine to be finished.

Bannering saw the bleak look creeping into Eden's eyes and guessed what he was thinking. He drained his glass and set it down. "Come on, Tony," he said quietly. "We'd better be on our way."

Churchill, too, seemed despondent when they met him and Winslade fifteen minutes later at the Athenaeum. Eden asked how the meeting with Chamberlain had gone. "I really don't know if the man is sincere, or if he's simply keeping up a loyal front for those who still think Hitler will protect them," Churchill said. "But in any case, I wasn't getting through. He still insists he has a personal rapport with the dictators that makes the notion of going to war unthinkable. He's certain of his ability to judge character, and he thinks Hitler is basically trustworthy."

"And when you reminded him of Hitler's record?" Winslade asked.

Churchill sighed and shook his head wearily as he began eating. "I was met by a wall of defensive myopia. He doesn't see things in the same terms."

There was a short, heavy silence. "And then?" Bannering prompted.

Churchill finished chewing and took a sip of wine. "I ventured a display of prognostication, which I hope will not show my trust in you gentlemen to have been misguided. I prophesied that Hitler will take the rest of Czechoslovakia within a month and expose all the pious words of Munich as worthless twaddle." That, of course, was what had happened in the Proteus world's history.

"Good," Winslade said, nodding. "And what was his reaction?"

"He said," Churchill replied, "that such a thing was out of the question because Hitler had given him his personal word on it. Danzig and Memel are Germany's final territorial claims in Europe."

It happened within the month as Churchill had predicted to Chamberlain.

The Nazis stepped up pressure on the tottering remains of Czechoslovakia, and in the early weeks of March coerced Slovakia into proclaiming independence. Its aging president, Dr. Hacha, was summoned to Berlin and bullied into issuing a public request for protection by the German Reich. German troops already massed on the borders promptly marched in to do the protecting. On March 15, after making the triumphal entry into Prague that he had always felt cheated out of by Munich, Hitler added Bohemia and Moravia to the Reich's Protectorate. Nothing was left but tiny Ruthenia, formerly Czechoslovakia's eastern tip, which proclaimed itself independent as the Republic of Carpatho-Ukraine. It lasted twenty-four hours before being seized and annexed by Hungary, to which Hitler had already "awarded" it.

In his address to the House, Chamberlain expressed his regrets, but maintained that the guarantee given to Czechoslovakia at Munich was no longer valid since it had been given against external aggression, whereas the state that it had been given to had ceased to exist through its own internal processes. The world sneered its derision.

The Churchill-Winslade group accepted gloomily that they weren't about to see any changes in Chamberlain's attitude. They braced themselves with anticipatory contempt for the speech that Chamberlain was due to give at Birmingham on March 17. But something unexpected happened. A very different man spoke at Birmingham, a man whose wishful thinking and delusions had exploded sometime in the forty-eight hours since his words to the House, and who didn't like what he was seeing plainly for the first time. Throwing aside the prepared speech on domestic issues that he had delivered in the Proteus world, Chamberlain roundly condemned the latest outrages, castigated Hitler personally for his violations of solemn promises, and concluded by accusing him openly of aiming at nothing short of world domination. Two days previously, in Parliament, Chamberlain had said, "Do not let us be deflected from our course." This was a right-about-face!

So the Proteus team could now point to one change at the level of international affairs that was due to their intervention. But viewed against the enormity of all the other things that

hadn't been changed and the events marching relentlessly onward toward August, the return on the effort expended seemed
pitiably small.

Later in March, German troops occupied Memel.

At the end of the month, Britain and France announced a
guarantee for Poland.

CHAPTER
9

ONE OF THE REASONS why Cassidy enjoyed being in 1939 was that he had a fiancée in his own future era. Her name was Gwendolen. She was ravishingly beautiful, slender in body, noble in bearing, virtuous in character and mind, cultured, sophisticated, sensitive, and charming—the perfect combination of lover, companion, confidante, and partner for life. Cassidy couldn't stand the sight of her: the "partner for life" bit worried him, and he found the thought of having to conform one day to the image of respectability that went with the package terrifying. But her family had made millions from chemical fertilizers, a sizable share of which would become hers with the maturing of a trust fund due on the first day of the following year. In the meantime, a pre-Nazi world seemed a good place for staying out of the way.

"You see, Harry, it's all a question of learning to think analytically and being objective," Cassidy said. Ferracini was positioning another section of former for the compensator windings. Cassidy stooped to inspect the fit, chewed infuriatingly at his ragged mustache while he squinted along an edge to check the alignment, then nodded and reached for the box of fixing pins. "You have to be scientific about things. So when we get through with the job here and go back home, FDR and JFK will have figured out a way to change history, Hitler won't have happened, and we'll all be let go because there won't even be any Army anymore. Then there'll be the wedding bells and stuff, and I'll send you guys some pictures of the yacht from the Bahamas." He chuckled gloatingly.

Ferracini tapped the fit tight with a soft-head hammer. "Oh, yeah? If you think so much is going to be changed when we get back, then what makes you so sure it'll all stop right there just to suit you? For all you know, she mightn't even have heard of you when we get back. So what does scientific objectivity say about that?"

"That's no problem," Cassidy said, shrugging nonchalantly. "I still know about her, don't I? I just track her down, give her my inimitable, irresistible routine, same as before, and it all works out. What is it with you, Harry? You know, sometimes I think you just go around looking for problems to invent."

"But at least I'm consistent," Ferracini retorted. "A month ago you were telling me it couldn't all just change that easily— maybe this would be a better place to stay. Now it's all the other way around. You see, that's another problem with you, Cassidy— you're inconsistent. How's anybody supposed to talk to someone who's always being inconsistent?"

"But you have to admit that I'm consistently inconsistent," Cassidy said. Ferracini sighed and turned to pick up the next section of former.

Paddy Ryan, the oldest of the three sergeants with the mission, looked down over his shoulder from the ladder on which he was standing. He was attaching piping to the growing framework overhead. He was short and broad, with a round, reddish, gnarled-looking face and straight, light brown hair, which he combed conventionally and parted on the left. "Ah, with Cassidy's luck, anything could happen. Even if we get back and find nothing's changed, and the big war breaks out, anyhow, he'd still make it through and find some way to use the assets. What about the other night—two full houses and a straight flush in three hands—who ever heard of luck like that?"

"Like I said, you gotta be scientific about things," Cassidy said.

"What's that supposed to mean?" Ryan asked.

"He cheats," Ferracini answered.

The sound of footsteps came from behind a capacitor bank to the rear, beyond which Floyd Lamson, the third sergeant, was welding more structural members amid showering sparks and intermittent flashes of light. A moment later the thin, gray-haired figure of Anna Kharkiovitch appeared, wearing a brown warehouse coat and carrying a box. She put the box down on a worktable standing by the wall and began taking out hydraulic valves, gauges, and other components. "Hey," Cassidy hissed. "That offer still stands. We could get out and hit the town tonight. Haven't you changed your mind yet?"

Anna smiled down at what she was doing and replied without looking up. "Tch, tch, such impetuosity—and in a grown man, too. You should learn to control yourself better, Sergeant Cassidy. Then, perhaps, I might see if I can fit you in. But it is difficult with so many admirers, you understand."

"I'll fight 'em all," Cassidy offered.

"Oh, my word—such flattery!"

"And then he'll run out on ya," Ryan said. "He's got another woman—lots of money, see? He cheats on everybody."

"Surely not the gallant Sergeant Cassidy!"

They worked on in silence for a while. Then Ryan said, "It's starting to look like maybe somebody else won't be getting away with so much cheating from now on. Claud and the guys in *King* are really lighting some fires under the tails of them English over there. First there was Chamberlain getting up on his hind legs at last and calling Hitler an out-and-out liar a couple of weeks back. Then them and the French face him up square and tell him they'll kick his ass if he messes with Poland. Now they're handing out guarantees left and right to anyone who'll take 'em. It ain't lookin' so bad."

In the first week of April, while Churchill was protesting at the scattered disposition of the British Mediterranean Fleet, Italian forces had landed in Albania and quickly took over the tiny country. Anglo-French guarantees of protection for Greece and Rumania followed soon afterward.

"You see, Harry, it's all changing already," Cassidy said. "There won't even be any war in August. Three months from now, we'll be shipping bombs through here from JFK to nuke the hell out of Hitler and all of them Fascists, and then we'll be on our way home." He tipped his cap to the back of his head and scratched the front of his shaggy, yellow hair while he surveyed his handiwork. "Leastways, that's how I'd do if it was up to me," he told anyone who was interested.

Ferracini shook his head as he began attaching the terminal lugs. "You can't pretend that everything you see in the papers is due to Claud and his guys," he said. "Most of it happened the same way in our history, anyway."

"Harry's right," Anna said. "The guarantees to Poland and so on were given in our world, also. They're not new—not something that we can claim to have instigated."

Cassidy snorted, but remained silent for once. Ryan came down the ladder to study a drawing and collect some more pieces. "That doesn't make sense," he said. "If the rich people over there were happy to let Hitler take on the Russians, why would they wanna go giving out guarantees? Why would they want the hassle of commitments that said they had to get involved?"

"Pressure of world opinion after Munich," Anna replied. "In our history, they were prepared to risk a sham war in order to be seen to have made a genuine attempt to stop Hitler. When it failed, they would be able to claim that they had tried. But, of course, it all backfired in their faces." She spoke the words bitterly, but at the same time with a hint of a grim satisfaction that she couldn't quite suppress. The country being set up, after all, had been her own.

"You make it sound like they knew it was gonna fail," Ryan commented.

"Of course they knew," Anna said. "It had all been agreed to secretly by some of the more powerful names among the Western aristocracies. What else do you think Ribbentrop's little jaunts to London and Paris were for—to be the darling of the Mayfair set?" She made a face as if she were experiencing a bad taste. "That was why Hitler could afford to be so cocksure about clearing the way between him and Russia. He knew he'd be up against token opposition only—a charade put on for appearance's sake."

Anna had never talked about her experiences in Russia during the German and Japanese onslaught. As Ferracini watched her, he got the feeling that the visage of hardness and determination that he saw was a mask acquired in later years, with the contours beneath still carrying a memory of a face that had once been young and soft. She reminded him of another woman that he had seen somewhere . . . the former schoolteacher from Liverpool that they had brought back to Norfolk on a sub. It had been on his last European mission before Proteus. He couldn't remember her name.

"So it's still happening, right now," he said in a strangely flat voice. "Across the ocean out there—there are still people on our side who don't want to see Hitler stopped. We really are right back where it all started." The realization had never registered quite so strongly before.

"That's why Claud and the rest of *King* are over there," Anna said. "So let's hope that we'll soon start seeing changes to more than just speeches."

Behind them, Cassidy placed the last stiffening bar over its slot in the completed former. "I still say we oughta nuke the hell out of all of 'em" he muttered, and hammered it home with relish.

The phone from the front office rang, and Ferracini went to answer it. The voice of Major Warren greeted him, speaking quietly but urgently. "Get up here with Cassidy right away, but make it slow and casual. We've got uninvited guests. Have the others standing by on condition Fox in case there's trouble."

Ferracini acknowledged, and the line went dead. "Major Warren," he announced as he replaced the receiver. "There might be trouble up front. It's a Fox alert. Cassidy, he wants us out there— but go easy."

As Cassidy and Ryan put down their tools, Ferracini produced a Colt .45 automatic from a toolbox beside him and slipped it inside his coveralls. He went around the capacitor bank at the rear to where Floyd Lamson was working. Lamson lowered his torch and looked up inquiringly. "Fox alert," Ferracini told him, and went on past, heading for the front of the building. Meanwhile the others had picked up their own weapons and were following behind to take up their assigned positions. Ryan and Anna covered one of the two doors leading through the steel-reinforced façade of bales and crates screening the machine area; Lamson went to the other door to await the arrival of Gordon Selby, who had been resting in the back section with Captain Payne. Ferracini and Cassidy went on into the front area of the warehouse.

Mortimer Greene, in vest and shirtsleeves as usual, was confronting four men out on the loading platform above the dock where two of the trucks were parked. The tall, blue-chinned figure of Major Harvey Warren, erect and unmistakably military despite his brown corduroy pants, baggy green sweater, and leather cap, was standing a few feet back, outside the open door of the front office from where he had telephoned. Across the parking area below the dock, the small portal set into one of the main doors was open, and the front of what looked like a black Buick was partly visible outside.

One man was doing the talking and seemed to be in charge among the four. He had flaccid, clammy-looking features with fleshy lips, a wide nose, and dark, sardonic, somehow fishlike eyes. He was dressed ostentatiously in a light gray hat with a glittery band, raccoon-skin overcoat, silk scarf, and crocodile-hide shoes. The other three, standing a few paces back, were all big, broad-shouldered, and more or less uniformly attired in variations of double-breasted suits and felt hats. One of them, who was chewing gum, moved his head a fraction to run his eyes over Ferracini and Cassidy as they appeared from the rear, then looked away again, still working his jaw indifferently. Greene was tight-lipped and angry. Warren was eyeing the visitors up and down with parade-ground scrutiny, weighing the potential opposition.

"It's just a risky area around here—all the way along the waterfront," Fat-lips was saying, keeping one hand thrust in his overcoat pocket and gesturing with the cigar that he was holding in the other. He spoke in a bored, lazy voice, while his gaze wandered up and about, all over the visible interior of the premises. "Accidents happen all the time, especially fire accidents—bad ones. There's all kinds of stuff stashed away around these docks, know what I mean? Nasty, dangerous stuff—like oil, paint, gasoline . . ." He shook his head sadly and flicked an inch of ash onto the floor. "See what I mean, Pop? It can happen anywhere, any time at all. A place like this could be wiped out. And that'd be a real shame now, wouldn't it . . . all that nice stuff . . . them trucks down there . . . lotta money to lose."

Greene's face, and even the bald crown of his head, had paled. His white mustache seemed to bristle of its own accord. "How much?" he demanded curtly. Ferracini caught Cassidy's eye for a moment. Cassidy, it was clear, was still all for nuking them. But military discipline prevailed.

"Aw, for this place . . ." Fat-lips looked around again and gestured carelessly. "Say, two hundred a month—fire insurance, with the special protection plan against arson included. You're gonna need that, Pop—like I said, all kinds of nuts loose around this area."

Greene drew a long, deep breath, held it for a few seconds, then exhaled sharply and nodded. "Very well. Now get out. You're wasting our time."

Fat-lips turned his head momentarily to his three clockwork goons-in-attendance and indicated Greene with a nod of approval. "That's what I like to see—someone being smart. Being smart and cooperating like that can even get a discount later, maybe."

"Get out," Greene repeated. His face was beginning to color.

Fat-lips's expression hardened and his pretentious air evaporated. "First of every month," he snapped. "One of the boys here will collect. And no funny stuff, Pop—accidents happen to people around here, not only to places." With that, he nodded to his entourage and led them across the loading platform and down the short flight of iron steps to the bay where the trucks were parked. They left through the small door and closed it behind them. Seconds later, the sounds of car doors being slammed came from outside, followed by an engine starting.

Still breathing heavily, Greene turned back toward the others and stamped straight past them into the office, slamming the door behind him. They heard the car reverse outside the main doors, then stop, change into forward gear, and move away. Ferracini's tension relaxed. Cassidy was set to blow a gasket. "Are we supposed to just stand here and let bums come in and talk to the boss like that?" he seethed, throwing up his arms in protest at Warren. "We coulda blown 'em away. What are we, a kid's picnic outing or something?"

"The professor was right," Warren told him. "It's only for a couple of months, and what does a few hundred dollars matter, anyhow? Trouble would only attract attention. We don't need that." Cassidy knew all that already. The outburst had been just his way of letting off steam. He nodded resignedly and turned away, punching a fist into the opposite palm.

"Tell the others they can stand down," Warren told Ferracini. Then he went into the office to join Greene.

"Come on, Cowboy," Ferracini said. "Time to stop being an asshole and get back to work." They walked back around a stack of bales toward one of the concealed doors. "Mort said earlier that if we get the Quadcomp finished we can take some time off tonight. Maybe we could introduce a couple of the guys to Max and his friends."

"We've taken worse than those jerks apart with our bare hands," Cassidy grumbled.

"Save it for the real war, if it happens," Ferracini advised.

That evening, Greene would agree to only three leaves of absence among the military contingent, and Floyd Lamson went with Ferracini and Cassidy to the Rainbow's End. They took Gordon Selby along, too.

For Ferracini this wasn't far from home. He had been born just a few miles to the north, in Queens, and grown up across the river in Hoboken. As they crossed the Brooklyn Bridge in a cab on their way into the city, he was struck again by how little the view that he remembered of the Manhattan skyline differed from the one he was seeing now. Most of New York's architectural character had come with the building boom of the thirties, and nobody had found the time or the motivation to change it very much in the years afterward as the conflagration across the seas grew into a world catastrophe.

A branch of his family had established itself in America in successive waves of migration from Italy through the early decades of the century. His own father, taking his boyhood sweetheart with him, had crossed the Atlantic in the thirties, over ten years before Harry was born. He had chosen to emigrate rather than to be conscripted and sent away to places no one had heard of, in order to slaughter defenseless natives for the greater glory of a strutting oaf like Mussolini. They married, and the family had already acquired two sons and a daughter when Harry arrived in 1947. By that time, his father had worked hard, set up as a partner in a successful hardware business in Queens, and become a proud, patriotic, naturalized American. He celebrated his new citizenship by giving his new son a good, solid, American name; he'd have none of the "Antonios" and "Romanos" that inhabited his relatives' families in legions.

But Harry never knew his parents. His mother died when giving birth to him, and his father was killed in an electrical accident less than a year later. The children were found homes among the various relatives, and Harry was raised by an uncle and an aunt who lived in Hoboken.

His Uncle Frank worked as a spiderman on construction sites. In the evenings, he boxed in the local gymnasium; from time to time, he won trophies and some extra cash at clubs in the area. He taught Harry that people had to be prepared to defend themselves and the things they valued "because there's always people out there ready to take what they can't earn, if you let 'em." The same went for countries too, Frank used to say. If America, England, and even Russia, maybe, had only had the guts to stick together and fight Hitler while there was still time, then things mightn't have gone the way they did. Harry's father had always felt the same way, too. "He'd have been real proud of you, Harry," Frank had said when Harry announced, upon leaving school, that he was volunteering for the Army.

As a boy, Harry remembered looking at the photographs of his parents in Frank's house, wishing he could have known them. He tried to picture the kind of life they had led in a free Europe, and then the coming of the tyranny that had driven them to flee. He was saddened to think that after such effort and sacrifice to find freedom to live without interference and raise their children the way they wanted, they should have lived to enjoy so little of what they deserved. He had blamed the Fascists, the Nazis, and everything connected with them. Perhaps that was why he had joined the Army.

The incident that he had witnessed earlier in the day bothered him. It bothered him because, enraging though the spectacle had been, there was nothing else, realistically, that Mortimer Greene could have done. Did that mean, then, that there was nothing the democracies could do against Hitler's blackmail, either? If so, the mission was already doomed to failure.

Ferracini had never known Winslade's boundless confidence to be misplaced. He hoped more than ever that it would turn out to be solidly based this time. But he still couldn't see it.

CHAPTER
10

MAX'S PLACE WAS busy, and Janet was due to sing that night. Jeff had decided to take some time off from his books and his university friends and had come into town, too. He had even put on a jacket and necktie for the occasion, and despite his owlish face, his heavy glasses, and his mop of rebellious hair, he managed to look not too much out of place. In fact, to his freely admitted surprise, he was having a good time. A friend of his from the same department at Columbia—somebody named Isaac Asimov, who entertained hopeful notions of becoming a famous science-fiction writer one day—had declined an invitation to come along, claiming that he wanted to work on a new story idea. So Jeff had expected to spend a bored evening watching exhibitions of noisy mindlessness with nobody stimulating to talk to. Instead, he had met Gordon Selby.

"Walter Zinn has been running a lot of the experiments, and somebody called Szilard—Leo Szilard, I think—is involved, too," Jeff told Selby. They were sitting at a corner table near the bar with Ferracini and Pearl. Cassidy and Floyd Lamson had learned to jive and were bobbing and yelling with a couple of other girls somewhere out on the crowded floor. "Szilard's another Hungarian who got out and went to England, but he moved here sometime last year. Anyhow, they use a mixture of radium and beryllium as a neutron source, and bombard uranium oxide with the neutrons."

"And they've found fission neutrons?" Selby queried again.

Jeff nodded. "I'm pretty sure they have. I heard something about Szilard making phone calls to Teller and Merle Tuve down in Washington that sounded as if they had. Apparently, they have to use paraffin to slow down what they call 'photoneutrons' into 'thermal' neutrons."

Selby pursed his lips. He was lean and swarthy, in his late thirties. The dense, black hair that normally adorned his head in rich waves was now cut shorter, thirties-style, and he had a heavy but neatly trimmed beard. He tended to keep his business to himself and spent a lot of his free time roaming around the New York bookstores and art shows. Ferracini guessed that Selby had thoughts of investing early in the works of new names that were destined to command better prices in years to come. Such smuggling from the past was against the rules, but Ferracini couldn't see any reason to worry unduly about it.

"I'm kind of surprised that you know so much about it," Selby said to Jeff. "I wouldn't have expected students to be involved."

Jeff grinned. "Well, it's not exactly official—I'm just interested in the subject, I guess. And in a big university . . . well, there's always somebody who'll talk to you if you approach them the right way. Academics aren't big on censorship."

"Have you talked much about this to anyone else?" Selby asked uneasily.

"Not really. I can see why some people might consider it a sensitive subject right now, but Joliot's paper in *Nature* last month pretty much said the same things, anyway. And I've heard that Zinn and Szilard are working with Fermi and a couple of other guys to put out their own paper any time now."

Selby was wondering how much of Overlord's decision to equip Hitler with atomic weapons for the 1942 Russian campaign might have been due to mistaken impressions of an intensive official program being launched in the U.S. He knew from the subsequent record, and Jeff didn't, that a lot of arguing was going on right at that time in the office of George Pegram, professor of physics and Dean of the Graduate Schools at Columbia, over suggestions for voluntarily withholding details of the uranium research being conducted there. Also, Szilard had convinced Pegram, Fermi, Teller, and Tuve that the implications were serious enough to justify government involvement. Accordingly, Pegram had written to the Chief of Naval Operations in March to advise of the possible imminence of a new explosive of revolutionary destructive potential. In a follow-up visit to Washington to elaborate further, however, Fermi and Tuve had been virtually thrown out as a pair of cranks. So much for an intensive official U.S. program.

"The last thing I heard was that Fermi wants to build a pile big enough to support a chain reaction," Jeff said. "But he's not sure yet whether to go for carbon or heavy water as the moderator. He looked at Selby curiously for a few seconds. "You seem to know a lot more about this kind of thing than most people," he commented. "Where did you learn it?"

"Oh, I worked out west in Berkeley," Selby lied. That seemed far enough away. "Cyclotrons."

"With Lawrence?" Jeff sounded interested. "A pal of mine moved out there. He still writes—tells me all about what's going on there. It sounds like terrific stuff."

"That was a couple of years back," Selby said hastily. "I came into an inheritance. Now I'm just living up in the hills on my own for a spell, reading, thinking, and figuring out what I'm going to do with the rest of my life. I don't know anything about what's going on anywhere."

Pearl stopped talking to Ferracini while she lit a cigarette and looked across the table. "Hey, you two, we're still here, you know," she said raising her husky but not unattractive voice. "How about trying English for a change? Do you know what they're talking about, Harry?"

"Beats the hell out of me. I just leave 'em to it."

"She's right, Jeff," Selby said, relieved. "We ought to quit."

"Try getting to know some of the girls, Jeff," Pearl suggested. "There's some good-looking ones in here tonight. Go ask one of them to dance, why not?"

Jeff wrinkled his nose and shook his head. "Not really—I'll pass."

"Why, for chrissakes?"

"Aw . . . it's too much like a sex-substitute. I'll take the real thing or nothing."

"Gee, get a load of this! Is that a new line, Jeff?"

"I dunno—maybe. Think it's got chances?"

Pearl threw her head back and laughed delightedly. "It might have, but don't hold your breath." She looked at Ferracini. "Know something, Harry? This kid's gonna be okay. Hear that, Jeff? You're okay."

"Well, that's nice to know," Jeff acknowledged.

"I thought your sister was due out before now," Pearl said, looking around. "Where is she?"

The band slowed to a smoochy rendition of "When the Blue

of the Night," and the crowd on the floor began thinning out. A few seconds later, Cassidy and Lamson appeared, heading toward the table with their women. Cassidy was steering a small, bright-eyed, bouncy-looking girl, his hand draped loosely on her waist. He introduced her as Molly, and her companion as Nell. Molly evidently knew Pearl already. "I didn't realize he was with you!" she squeaked excitedly. "You never told me you knew a real, live, bomber pilot, Pearl. Who else have you been hiding?"

"Fancy that—I must have forgot." Pearl glanced at Ferracini and shrugged resignedly.

Floyd Lamson was almost as tall as Cassidy, with the same kind of lean, loose-limbed build; but he was clean-shaven and darker, and had high cheekbones, thin lips, a tapering face, and narrow eyes, suggestive of a trace of American Indian. Lamson specialized in knives, handguns, ungentlemanly hand-to-hand things, stealth, burglary, lockpicking, safecracking, and other such noble branches of the martial arts. "So, where's this singing lady you said we were going to meet?" he asked, looking back at the dance floor. "I thought she was due on by now."

"Don't get excited, Floyd," Cassidy said, dropping into his chair and ignoring Molly's squeal of protest as he scooped her onto his knee. "Harry's got plans in that direction. He'll deny it if you ask him, but I can tell. Pilots have this uncanny instinct, see. It's the night flying that does it."

"I was asking the same thing," Pearl said. "I haven't seen her anywhere for a while."

As the conversation around the table drifted onto something else, Ferracini took his glass and eased himself back in his chair to stretch a little, at the same time allowing his gaze to drift casually over the people nearby. George, the pianist who played for Janet, had appeared on one of the stools at the bar and was sitting hunched over a drink. He seemed tense and nervous about something, and his hand shook visibly as he raised his glass. Lou, the bartender, came over to say something to him, and then moved away with a deadpan expression, seemingly picking up strong don't-bother-me signals on his bartender's radar. Something was wrong.

Ferracini sipped his drink for a few seconds. Then he put down the glass, murmured an excuse, and went to the bar. He stopped by George, without looking at him directly. "What's happening?" he asked in a voice low enough not to carry.

George took another quick gulp of his drink but didn't look up. "Nothing that concerns you, Harry. It's just . . . problems with the place. Don't worry about it." George was scared.

"What kind of problems?" Ferracini asked. Then suddenly he

was alarmed. "How come you're not down there playing yet? Where's Janet?"

George waved a hand vaguely at the passageway leading into the club from the front stairs. "There's some kind of trouble back there, I'm not sure what. . . . Max's office . . ."

Ferracini turned and looked in the direction George had indicated. One of the inner double-doors to the club was open. In the passage beyond, a group of people were collecting coats at the hatcheck desk, and more were coming down from the street. "What kind of troub——" Ferracini began, and then broke off as three men came out of the door to Max's office. Two of them were visible just fleetingly before they mingled with the other figures and disappeared up the stairs to the street, but that was all Ferracini needed to recognize Fat-lips and Gum-chewing Goon. "Okay, George, I think I know," he muttered softly, and drew away.

"There's nothing you can do about it," George called after him as Ferracini started walking toward the doors.

"We'll see," Ferracini threw back darkly.

Max's office was a mess when Ferracini let himself in seconds later. The ornamental wall clock, the flower vases, a typewriter, and a couple of pictures were lying smashed on the floor. Some of the furniture had been broken. Drawers had been pulled out and emptied, and papers were scattered everywhere. Max was leaning against the desk, sniffing and dabbing a blood-soaked handkerchief to his nose and mouth. An eye was swelling already, and his clothes were disarrayed. Before Ferracini could say anything, Martha, the plump, middle-aged woman who did the bookkeeping, peered out from the bathroom at the rear of the office, where water was running. She looked white and shaken.

Then Janet's voice said, "Thanks, Martha, I'll be okay. Who's that out there?"

Ferracini strode grimly across the room and moved Martha aside to find Janet stooped over the washbasin. Her hair was ruffled, and she was holding a wet facecloth to a bruise on her cheek. She saw Ferracini in the mirror and tried to grin. "Hi. Now you've seen me at my worst." White with rage and unable to speak, Ferracini could only reach out and put a hand on her shoulder.

"Some guys were here—" Martha began.

"I saw 'em."

"They messed up the place and started slapping Janet about a bit to put the pressure on Max," Martha said. "Max tried to go for the ape in the fancy clothes, and . . ."

Ferracini squeezed Janet's shoulder and went back into the office. "You okay?" he asked Max.

Max nodded painfully. "I will be. Get me a drink, willya, Martha—a stiff one."

The door opened and George came in; he stopped and gaped around him in dismay. "Oh, my God, I never realized . . . I thought they were just talking. I wouldn't have just sat there if I'd known, Harry, honest. . . . I thought—"

"It's okay," Ferracini said tightly.

Then Cassidy slipped in, closing the door noiselessly behind, and took in the scene with a glance. "Watched the way you left—figured you might need a backup," he told Ferracini.

"Do you know who these bums are?" Ferracini asked Max. "Where they hang out, things like that?"

"Johnny does, but he ain't here yet," Max answered. "That was why they came early. They're the ones we've been getting a hard time from for a while now."

Cassidy looked at Ferracini. Suddenly he became apprehensive. He'd seen that expression on Ferracini's face before. "Hey, now, just wait a minute, Harry," he cautioned, holding up a hand. "Don't get carried away by any wild ideas, now. . . ."

An hour later they were back in Max's office, which was looking a bit tidier. Johnny "Six Jays" had arrived, talked for a while, and gone back out to the bar to collect a pal of his, who he said would be better able to answer some of Ferracini's questions. Max was in the bathroom at the back, leaving Ferracini and Cassidy on their own for the moment.

"This is crazy, Harry," Cassidy hissed, keeping his voice down to an urgent whisper. "Isn't it you who's always telling me this is an A-plus priority mission that we're on, that nothing, but nothing, is allowed to jeopardize? I know it's bugging you and all that, but we can't go after those bums. You're outta your cotton-pickin' mind, man!"

"Are you in or out?" Ferracini asked him stonily. His face was determined. Cassidy sighed hopelessly; Harry was serious all right.

Before either of them could say more, Max, patched and bandaged, came out of the bathroom, and a moment later Johnny Six Jays and another man entered from the passageway. Floyd Lamson was with them, too, looking curious. Johnny sat down on a corner of the desk near Ferracini and looked at him dubiously. "I don't think you understand what you're talking about taking on, Harry," he said. "Iceman Bruno stays holed up most of the time at this place he's got out at Pelham—big place, with at least a couple of his gorillas there all the time. It's practically a fortress. You wouldn't even be able to get inside."

"Oh, really?" Ferracini sounded unconvinced. "Tell me about it, Johnny," he invited.

* * *

Back at Gatehouse on the Brooklyn waterfront, the lights were burning through the night, as usual. Major Warren, Captain Payne, and Sergeant Paddy Ryan were in the back area, installing cable runs on the machine. In the front office, Anna Kharkiovitch was showing Mortimer Greene a summary of the study she had been conducting for the past few weeks, comparing everyday events as reported in the news with the corresponding items contained in the records from their own times. She had uncovered a whole list of further discrepancies.

"I can't find any differences before the date of our arrival here in January," she said. "But from then on, these things keep appearing—small things, admittedly, but how can they be explained?" She paused to invite comment, but Greene just continued staring with a distant expression at the papers she had spread open on the desk. Anna gestured again at the sheet that she was holding. "Here's another. Item: The Joe Louis versus John Henry fight at the beginning of February. According to our microfilms, Henry was knocked out in the second round for a full count. But at Madison Square Garden a couple of months ago, the fight was stopped at the count of five in the first. Item: Pope Pius XI died in February—except it happened a day earlier in our records than was reported here. Here are samples of the same day's issues of the same newspaper—they're not the same." Anna tossed the paper down on top of the others. "I could go on, but you can see the kind of thing. This sounds insane, I know, but it's almost as if we're, well . . . somehow in a different world. . . . But how could that be?"

Greene stared down at the desk for a long time without saying anything. "It's strange, I agree. . . ." he said at last. Then he sat up suddenly and became more brisk. "Nevertheless, we mustn't allow worrying about it to hinder our work. I'd like some time to go through what you've done here. In the meantime, why don't you go back and carry on with the others. I'll join you shortly."

After Anna had gone, Greene sat for a while turning over the pages of her notes. Then he picked up the phone and gave the number of the Hyde Park Hotel in London, where the time would be early morning. The operator advised that there would be an hour's delay on transatlantic calls. Greene placed the call and then went back to help with the work at hand.

And hour and a half later, he was back in the office, talking to a sleepy-sounding Winslade. "I'm keeping up morale here and not letting anyone become alarmed," he said, "but the truth of it is, I think we might be in trouble, Claud—real trouble."

CHAPTER
11

AT THE TIME OF the Munich crisis, Churchill had said there could be no European security without an Eastern front, and there could be no Eastern front without Russia. But the Russian approaches to the West for a united stand against Nazism had been rejected; furthermore, despite the treaty that obliged them to aid Czechoslovakia in the event that France did so first, the Russians had not been included in the Munich conference at which the Czechs' fate was settled. But then, who would invite a potential victim into the room where the alibis were being hatched?

As the summer of 1939 approached, two opposing currents were influencing Anglo-French policy-making. Pulling one way were the traditionalist forces who held the view that a Nazi-Communist collision might not be such a bad thing; that if the two systems ended up destroying each other, then probably so much the better. This school was prepared to accept a token Polish commitment, but on no account to be drawn into any pact with the Soviets that would mean continued entanglement in the conflict after Poland collapsed. Pushing the other way was the increasing pressure of Churchill and his followers, motivated from behind the scenes by Winslade's group, who knew where Hitler was leading the world, and who were happier at the thought of leaving the West's differences with the Soviets to be resolved some other time.

The resulting British actions were ambiguous. Thus, only a day after his defiant words of March 17, Prime Minister Chamberlain had rejected as "premature" an approach by the Soviet Foreign Minister, Litvinov, for a conference to discuss an anti-Nazi front, just as had happened "before" in the Proteus world. In April, Litvinov renewed his attempt with a formal proposal to the British ambassador in Moscow, just as before; the British government turned it down, just as before; and in May, Stalin replaced Litvinov with Molotov, just as before. Litvinov had been Russia's strongest advocate of collective security with the West, and the Proteus people had hoped to bring about changes in British policy sufficient to prevent his departure. On this issue, therefore, Winslade and Churchill were compelled to concede failure.

On the other hand, Britain suddenly announced that it was calling up its reserves to bring the Army, Navy, and Air Force up to war strength. That was something which had not happened "before."

"The problem, you see, is that Chamberlain is trying to pursue two irreconcilable goals," Kurt Scholder told Professor Lindemann across the compartment of the coach. Their train was just entering the outskirts of Chelmsford, in Essex. They were returning to London from the Air Ministry Research Establishment at Bawdsey Manor near Felixstowe, where Scholder, under a suitably contrived alias, had met Watson-Watt, Henry Tizard, and other government scientists to offer some thoughts on radar, aircraft interception, fighter ground-control systems, and related topics. "He's woken up to the immediate menace, yes, but he still can't bring himself to accept Russia as a major force in European affairs. He wants to curb Hitler with all these guarantees, but at the same time keep Russia out. It can't be done."

"Well, at least the country is starting to show some teeth," Lindemann said. "Some of that influence might get as far as Moscow and affect the talks there for the better." He didn't sound very hopeful.

"Maybe." Neither did Scholder.

One of the first things Molotov had done upon taking up his new appointment was make overtures for improving relationships with Germany. To avoid being left out in the cold, Chamberlain had responded belatedly by instructing his own representative in Moscow to open talks with the Russians, too. But in the Proteus team's world, these talks had been half-hearted and had served only to reinforce Stalin's suspicions that he was being maneuvered toward a war that the West planned to wriggle out of. So Stalin had stood back later, in August, when Hitler stormed into Poland and the Allies declared war in the expectation of being free of it within a month or two; he had looked on impassively when the tiger they had ridden about-faced and ate them. His own turn had come later.

"What a strange existence you've led, Kurt," Lindemann said. He had a reputation among his contemporaries for being somewhat abrupt and showing limited patience for ideas that differed from his own; however, understandably, he tended to be more accommodating where visitors from the future were concerned. "Twice now, you've been through this extraordinary process, and each time you've ended up further back in time than when you started. You must be beginning to feel like a—oh, I don't know—some kind of chronological Wandering Jew."

Scholder smiled. "But at least this time I have a feeling of having changed for the better. I saw enough of the nihilism of Hitler's Reich in the last world I was in—and then Heydrich's, which was even worse."

"That sounds hardly possible."

"Oh, yes. The state came to extend its power and presence totally into every facet of the individual's life. Everything you did, everywhere you went, everyone you met or talked to—all was supervised, scrutinized, regulated. Every activity had to be reported—even a stamp-collecting club or a children's sports team." Scholder tossed up his hands. "The children! They were practically taken away, brutalized and indoctrinated, even in pre-school years. Because Nazi superstitions concerning race and heredity were law, the weak and the mentally feeble were sterilized and taught simple tasks, if they were of any potential use at all."

"And if not?"

"They were eliminated from the race by a program of compulsory euthanasia."

Lindemann stared, horrified. "Surely not," he protested. "How could something like that be enforced? I mean, what if the parents refused?"

Scholder smiled humorlessly. "They didn't refuse. You can't imagine what it was like. The family had ceased to exist. Individuals had no rights or liberties. They existed simply to serve the state. The state owned everybody." He gestured at the picturesque townscape outside the window, which vanished suddenly as the train drew into Chelmsford station. "This is a different world, Professor—civilized and free. It has hope yet for a future.

Quaint and old-fashioned, certainly, but in the ways that matter, it's more like the place that I came from originally."

"That world must seem an eternity away by now," Lindemann remarked. "You were how old when you left there in 2025—thirty-five, you said?"

"Yes."

"Did you have any, any . . ."

"Family there? Yes. I no longer think about them. There's no point."

"Oh . . . I'm sorry."

"I was a physicist working on the development of fusion propulsion systems for interplanetary spacecraft," Scholder said, seeing Lindemann's awkwardness and moving the conversation along. "The new breakthroughs in physics were relevant to my work as well as fascinating in their own right, and I began specializing in them." He shrugged. "Overlord's agents introduced themselves and made a proposition that it was impossible to refuse, financially, and the next thing I knew I was working in Brazil."

"And from there you went back to the Nazi Germany that had been created in 1941."

"Yes."

"Working on the bomb program for Hitler's assault on Russia the following year."

"That is so."

"Were the bombs manufactured there in Germany?"

"Not manufactured. They were assembled from prefabricated parts shipped through from the future. Overlord didn't want to equip Hitler with a full-fledged industry of his own. I suppose they didn't want him to forget who was in charge."

Lindemann wrinkled his nose and rubbed it hesitantly with a knuckle. "Weren't there any, ah . . . any moral problems—with conscience or anything—I mean, working on something like that?"

"While we were in Brazil, we didn't know what the nuclear explosives were being sent through for," Scholder said. "We were told they were for routine engineering work—demolitions, excavations, that kind of thing. That wouldn't have been unusual."

"But when you actually went back there?"

"Well, then the working conditions were suddenly very different. We had no choice. They preferred using people with relatives back in 2025 because of the pressure it was possible to exert."

"Oh, how dreadful!"

"Most of the Nazis' methods were originated by Overlord.

They really weren't very inventive themselves. The attempted putsch in 1923 was about their limit—hardly memorable for its brilliance or originality."

The train had stopped, and, for a few seconds, Lindemann watched the activity on the platform. "So how did you come to get stuck there?" he asked at last. "Was that something else that you had no choice about?"

"I'm not really sure what happened," Scholder replied. "You see, several years later, the Nazi return-gate back to 2025 was destroyed. A number of us who had come from that time were trapped in Germany as a consequence. We never did find out what happened. Our best guess was that after the Soviet Union was disposed of, the Nazis decided they no longer needed further help from Overlord. They had become an unstoppable force in their own world and saw a clear road to complete domination. Afterward, I was drafted into other things."

"And Overlord never projected another one-way team back to find out what happened?" Lindemann mused. "I assume there was no reason why they couldn't have."

"Apparently they didn't. . . . At least, if they did, I never heard of it."

"Mmm . . . that seems strange." There was a pause. "And the stage was set for Nazism to engulf the world without hindrance—as it proceeded to do. So what happened to the future that you came from in the first place? How could it ever have come to pass at all?"

"I don't know," Scholder said. "Perhaps it no longer exists, somehow."

"If that's true, how can there be a return-gate in Germany right now that's connected through to it?" Lindemann objected. "A connection, moreover, that you say won't be broken for several years?"

"I don't know," Scholder replied again. "It mystifies me, too."

"Well, let's hope that we get some good news today or tomorrow from New York."

"Let's hope so."

For it was nearing the end of May, and according to the information received in 1975 before the mission's departure, the first exchange of simple static messages ought to have been taking place just about then. Only the uncertainties of cross-ocean communications made it impossible to say for certain when confirmation would reach them in London.

The compartment door opened, and a woman in a flowery, wide-brimmed, floppy hat came in, struggling with seemingly innumerable bags, packages, purses, and parcels. "Are these seats taken?" she panted. "No? Oh, thank goodness!"

"Allow me, madam," Lindemann said, rising dutifully to assist.

"Thank you. You're so kind. Oh—do be careful with that one. It has china in it."

An elderly clergyman entered behind the woman, followed by a man in a business suit, a burly, red-faced man in a checked tweed jacket and cloth cap, who could have been a farmer, and a younger couple. They jostled around and found seats, while Lindemann wrestled the woman's encumbrances up onto the overhead luggage rack; then Lindemann regained his place in the corner and picked up his copy of the *Times* from the seat to make room for the woman to squeeze between him and the farmer.

"Presents," the woman explained as she sat down.

"Really?" Lindemann replied mechanically.

"Toys, mainly."

"I see."

"I'm going to visit my daughter in Kensington."

"How interesting." A note of hollow dread crept into Lindemann's voice with the sudden realization that he might be trapped in such conversation all the way to Liverpool Street station.

"She has three children—my grandchildren."

"I'm sure you find them delightful."

The clergyman opened a magazine, the farmer and the businessman found places to stare at adjacent to each other's heads, and the couple began talking in whispers. Lindemann had just folded his paper to prepare for the crossword, when the woman stood up again to take off her coat. "I'm terribly sorry—I didn't realize it was so hot in here," she said.

"That's quite all right, madam," Lindemann assured her.

The woman folded the coat, stuffed it up among her other belongings, and sat back down. Lindemann returned his attention to his crossword, at the same time feeling inside his jacket for a pen. Then the woman began rummaging inside the purse that she had kept on her knee, and Lindemann had to draw back his shoulder to make room for her elbow. "Oh dear, I thought I'd put my ticket in here," the woman said. "It must be in the other one." She stood up again and began searching through the bags on the rack. Lindemann moved his knee and leaned away to make room once more, baring his clenched teeth as he nodded politely in response to her smiled apology.

Smirking behind his hand, Scholder looked away to the scenery outside as the train began moving again. But at the same time there was a worried look in his eyes.

This was the nation that was talking seriously about taking on the Nazi military colossus. In rural Essex and other places, Scholder had seen determined-looking spinsters on bicycles, pedaling through villages to pin airraid precaution bulletins on Post Office notice boards; he had watched retired Great War colonels drilling yokels with broomsticks on cricket greens and cramming their astonished heads into gas masks; he had observed Sunday-fete demonstrations of extinguishing fireworks with sand and a stirrup pump to show how to deal with incendiary bombs. It all typified the nearest that the English seemed able to get to working themselves into a war frenzy. They really believed they could stop Hitler by playing games like that.

But then, they hadn't seen what Scholder had seen. They hadn't seen the desert of rubble that was Moscow after the atomic attack; or the mountains of corpses in the Polish extermination camps; or the films of Africans being herded into pits by the thousands to be incinerated by napalm. They hadn't been where Scholder had been. They just didn't understand.

Winslade and Bannering were waiting at the end of the platform at Liverpool Street, which meant that something unexpected had happened. Scholder and Lindemann stepped up their pace as they walked by the locomotive, still venting steam and smoke after its exertions, and read from the expressions on their faces that the news was not good.

Winslade, wearing a trilby hat and tan trenchcoat, drew them aside from the throng streaming by from the train. "Trouble," he said without preamble, keeping his voice low. "They should have opened the connection from Gatehouse this morning. It didn't work. Nothing came through from the other end."

Scholder stared disbelievingly. "Nothing at all? You're sure the channel was operating correctly?"

"The channel was operative," Winslade said. "But nothing activated it from the other end." In other words, the apparently infallible test performed before the team's departure from 1975 had been worthless.

Lindemann looked aghast. "What do you propose doing?" he asked Winslade.

"Getting over to New York right away. I'd like you to come too, Kurt. Arthur will be staying here to carry on with Churchill and the others—turning the Russians around might suddenly have become more crucial than we thought."

"Another week at sea?" Scholder sighed miserably. "Oh, how I hate ships!"

"That won't be necessary," Winslade said. "Eden has managed to fix us a couple of seats on one of the Clipper mail flights that Pan Am has just started. We'll be there by tomorrow night. Mortimer has suspended further work on the gate in the meantime."

A sickening feeling of fear clawed at Scholder's stomach as he looked around and took in the scene of reunited couples meeting and embracing in the station, parents leading children by the hand, a porter loading suitcases onto a cart—just ordinary people leading their lives, bothering no one, and wanting only to be left alone. And he thought of the broken, gray-faced, emaciated people that he had seen in his visits to England in the years after its capitulation in 1941. Was it all now destined to happen again as he remembered? Perhaps it had been unalterable all along.

And what made the thought even more agonizing was the realization of what it would mean for him personally. He had spent thirty-four years in the previous world, and had seen the meaning of Nazi conquest firsthand. Was he now trapped with no escape from yet another past, destined to live through those same years of horror and despair all over again?

CHAPTER
12

REGARDLESS OF HOW IT was always done in the movies, the guard dogs used by the German police and military couldn't be dealt with by anything as simple as tossing them a piece of doped meat; they were trained to eat only the food fed to them by their handler. It was unlikely that the Dobermans loose in the grounds surrounding Iceman Bruno's residence at Pelham would have been trained anywhere near as rigorously, but one of the things that made Sergeant Floyd Lamson better at his job than most was that he made minimum assumptions and took maximum precautions. He dropped a sack filled with old clothes and scented with aniseed over the wall from a perch in an oak tree standing just outside a corner remote from the house, and used an air rifle equipped with a night-sniper's sight to pick the dogs off with fast-acting tranquilizer darts when they came to investigate. He had watched the place long enough, both night and day, to know there were four of them and that no guards would be roaming the grounds.

On receiving two green signal-torch flashes from Lamson, Ferracini and Cassidy relayed them to Paddy Ryan, who was concealed in the foliage outside the main gate. Then they scaled the wall easily using ropes and grappling hooks. They found the electrical wires strung through the coils of barbed wire on top, and before starting to cut a way through, made bypass connections to avoid setting off alarms. Meanwhile, Ryan moved up to the gate and affixed a small, shaped charge that would cut through the locking bar to afford a quick way out if one was needed later. He attached a detonator, threw one end of a pull-line trigger in through the gate to be retrievable on the inside, and then connected the trigger to the detonator. Then he retreated back into the shadows and followed the foot of the wall to where Ferracini and Cassidy had gone over. He found the rope they had left hanging and joined them on the far side. They waited a minute or so for Lamson, who had dropped directly into the grounds from the tree to administer shots to the dogs that would keep them out for the rest of the night; then the four of them began threading their way silently in loose single-file through the shrubbery toward the looming silhouette of the house.

For reasons that he hadn't disclosed, Mortimer Greene had ordered a halt to further work on the machine after tests of some kind that he and Gordon Selby had conducted all through the previous night and into the morning. Also, apparently, Winslade and Scholder were on their way back from England in a hurry. So presumably the tests hadn't worked. What it all added up to, Ferracini wasn't sure; but it did mean extra leave for the troops, and Ferracini had persuaded the others that it was time to pay Iceman the visit they'd been planning for some time.

Counting the ins and outs through the afternoon and evening had yielded the tentative result that there were nine other men inside the house besides Bruno, and also three women. All of the ground-floor and second-floor windows were formidably barred and probably wired, and the pattern of lights suggested that the occupants were moving mostly among the rooms at the lower front of the building. That was convenient, for the easiest way in that Lamson had identified was a small, circular window tucked high up on a rear wall, just below the eaves in the angle of a large gable. That window hadn't been barred; "obviously" there was no way for anyone to get even close to it.

At the house, Ferracini and Cassidy moved off around a corner into the shadows on the north side and ascended a vertical recess between a wall and a projecting pillar of fluted stonework, which they climbed by bridging across with legs and arms. From the top of the pillar, using rubber-soled boots to provide friction grips for most of the way, and a spike forced into a crack in the mortar to get them over one awkward spot, they traversed horizontally along a line of ornamental brickwork to a corner and followed the corner up to the roof. High against the night sky, they pulled themselves around the overhang and vanished; a few

minutes later, the end of a line tied in a series of overhand loops
sailed out from somewhere above the round window and dropped
into the flowerbeds where Lamson and Ryan were waiting.

Lamson climbed the ladder of loops while Ryan steadied the
bottom end; then, when Lamson was up to the height of the window, Ryan pulled the rope outward and inward again to swing
Lamson in underneath the overhang of the eaves. On the third
swing Lamson hooked the wooden window ledge with a fine-
barbed grapnel attached to a rock-climber's étrier, and then he
stepped into the étrier to give himself a stance where he could
work on the window. The window yielded quickly, and Lamson
climbed through. He secured the rope for Ferracini and Cassidy
to lower themselves down hand-over-hand from above, while at
the same time Ryan began climbing the other section of the rope
from below.

"Yeah, yeah, I gotcha." Bruno Verucin, known as the Iceman
because of his opulent tastes and predilection for diamonds,
tilted himself back in the chair behind his wide mahogany desk
and nodded into the telephone. He puffed out a cloud of smoke
and hooked the thumb of the hand holding his cigar in his suspenders. "Like I said, Pete, the whole idea is to get us set up off
Atlantic City the same way they're doing out West. That ship
that Tony Stralla's rigged out as a floating casino outside the
three-mile limit at Santa Monica is making three hundred grand
a month—did you know that? Yeah, that's what I said, Pete—
grand—a month. Well, that's what we're out to beat, okay?"

From an armchair in one corner where he was lounging with
one leg propped up on a stool by the bar, Bruno's lieutenant, Fred-
die Numbers, raised his eyebrows and looked across at One-
Round Connahan, who was leaning by the door, chewing gum,
looking bored. Connahan remained expressionless and carried on
chewing.

"That's right," Bruno went on. "It all depends on the Kraut
signing over the boat, the crew, and his whole operation with no
strings . . . Wally Fritsch, his name is. He's in trouble over the
money he owes, and I can put the screws on him there. . . . Yeah,
yeah, I hear ya, Pete. Wally's here now, and we're negotiating the
deal. . . . Not yet, but we're working on it. . . . Okay, I'll call you
back as soon as it's final. . . . Sure thing. Trust me, baby, okay?
When did I ever fail to deliver?"

Bruno put the phone down and looked at the other two.
"Pete's getting anxious. Maybe it's about time we went back
down to see how the negotiations are doing, huh?" He laughed at
his joke and got up from the desk. Numbers rose to his feet, One-

Round straightened up from the wall, and they followed Bruno out of the den.

They went down some stairs with thick carpeting, across an ornately furnished hallway with many doors opening off it, and along a corridor that led past an open room in which some hoods were playing pool. Finally, they descended more stairs and stopped outside a closed door. Bruno gave two sharp raps, and the door was opened from the inside.

The room was sparsely furnished, with just a bare table, a closet, and some upright wooden chairs. Two more of Bruno's strong-arm men were there, their ties loosened and shirts wet with patches of perspiration. A third man, in his mid-fifties, looking bruised and haggard, was slumped in a chair at the table. Blood showed at a corner of his mouth, and he was breathing in labored gasps.

Bruno crossed the floor and came to a halt, his knuckles resting on the tabletop. He looked down and shook his head reproachfully. "Too bad you're not as smart as I thought, Wally," he said. "Looks like you been giving yourself a tough time. So, I said I was a reasonable guy. You had enough time to reconsider yet?"

"You go to hell, pig's fart," Fritsch wheezed through lips that were starting to stiffen. He had a strong German accent.

Bruno's expression darkened. He slapped Fritsch hard across the face. "Talk to me like that again, boy, and you get your feet toasted, understand? Now, my patience is just about run out. You got one more chance to sign the paper before I get really mean."

Fritsch shook his head. "I vill not do ziss. You go unt fry in your own fat first."

"It's gonna be tough," one of the hoods murmured. He was known as Fairytoes on account of his two-hundred-eighty-pound bulk. The other, who was called Charlie, lit a cigarette and looked on expressionlessly.

Bruno glowered for a second or two longer. "Then bring the dame down and see how he likes that," he snapped. One-Round turned and went back out the door.

Fritsch's eyes widened. "Her you leef out of ziss!" he protested, rising to his feet. "It doesn't—"

Fairytoes cuffed him back down again. "Listen when da boss is talkin'."

"Waddya think I brought her here for—a bridge party?" Bruno sneered. "I told ya I'm a busy man. I don't have time for fooling around."

Fritsch looked genuinely scared for the first time. "But everyzing I make . . . years of vork, it all goes into ziss business. Vat you talk about now vould be giving it away." He shook his head.

"You talk about offers, so make der offer. . . . But ziss . . ." he shook his head again, "iss robbery."

"Ah! Do I hear a new voice of cooperation?" Bruno said, nodding approvingly. "Does that mean you're willing to talk now, Wally, boy?"

"Always I haff said I vill talk. But you haff never given even ze chance to talk. You talk only of take, take, take."

Bruno reversed a chair and sat down on it with his elbows spread along the top of the backrest. "Okay," he sighed. "I'll give it to ya one more time. Now hear me good, Wally, because this is the way it is. . . ."

His jaw moving mechanically, One-Round clumped up a short flight of stairs at the back of the house and came to the landing outside the room where they had left the girl, with Chins keeping an eye on her. He tapped and called, "Chins, it's me—Connahan," then turned the handle and pushed the door inward. There was no response from the other side, and he had just begun registering that the room was strangely still, when a finger tapped him lightly on the shoulder. He started to turn automatically.

An arm streaking upward like a piston, fingers of the hand curled back to expose the heel, smashed into the nerve plexus at the base of his nose and straightened him up for the knee already jackknifing into his crotch. He doubled over without a sound and was already out before an edge-handed blow to the base of his skull made sure he'd stay that way for some time to come.

The hooded figure in black caught him before he could fall, and a second, similarly clad figure came out of the room to take the feet and carry the limp form back in. The woman standing by the vanity, plain in looks and modestly dressed, in her late twenties or early thirties, watched, terrified, as they laid their burden on the floor away from the door and behind the bed, alongside Chins. One of them stooped to take One-Round's gun from its shoulder holster, frisked him quickly for other weapons, and straightened up, satisfied.

"Look, whoever you are, I don't have anything to do with this," the woman whispered tensely. "I don't belong here. I'm—"

"Shh!" The nearest of the hooded figures cut her off with a curt warning gesture. The other stood listening for a few seconds by the door, then nodded.

They ushered her out and over to a bathroom across the landing. One of them took the key from the lock as he pushed her not too roughly but firmly inside. "Stay in there," he murmured. "We'll be back." The door closed, and she heard the key turn. Then there was silence.

Fritsch shook his head and looked dazed. "I don't know. . . . Maybe. But leave her out of ziss business."

Bruno looked at him contemptuously. "You don't seem to have gotten it into your head yet that you ain't in no position to give me terms," he said. "You owe money, and the debt's overdue."

"Ze money I can raise," Fritsch protested. "Luck has not been good zese months. . . . But I vill need a little time."

"You don't have any time, and I need that ship. I'll be the one who says when." Bruno broke off and looked around the room, suddenly puzzled. "What the hell's happened to One-Round? I thought I told him to bring the dame here."

Numbers shrugged. "Probably he stopped off at the bathroom."

"What for—to decorate it? Go find him willya, Toes. Get them here."

Fairytoes nodded and started to leave, but as he reached the door, one of the hoods from the poolroom opened it from the other side. Toes shouldered his way past him and disappeared. Bruno looked irritated. "What now, Arch?" he asked the newcomer.

Arch gestured vaguely in the direction he had come from. "The phones are out, Boss. I figured y'oughta know."

Bruno scowled first at Numbers, then at Charlie. "They can't be—I just talked to Pete on the phone. I need to call him back, too. Check it out, willya?"

Arch shrugged. "I already did. They're out."

"What about the private line in the den?" Bruno asked.

"Ain't sure." Arch stuck his head back out the door and called up the stairway, "Hey, Mack, is the private line in the den out, too?" There was no reply. He tried again, louder. "Mack, wassamadda widdya? Ya gone deaf up there or sump'n?" Arch frowned. "Are you there, Toes?" he shouted. Nothing. He looked back inside the room. "I don't get it. Toes walked up there just a second ago."

Bruno and Numbers looked at each other. Bruno got up uncertainly from the chair, his face suddenly suspicious. "Something funny's going on," he muttered. He elbowed his way past Arch and stood looking along the passage and up the stairs outside. A foreboding silence greeted him from the rest of the house. "Arch, Numbers . . ." He inclined his head at each in turn. "We'll take a look. Charlie, you stay here with Wally. I wouldn't want him to get ideas about taking any walks."

They went upstairs in the direction that Fairytoes had taken. Jackets were hanging on the wall in the poolroom, a couple of half-finished drinks were standing on the edge of the pool table, and a cigarette was still burning in an ashtray. Nobody was in sight, and nobody answered when Bruno called.

"You got a rod?" Bruno asked Numbers in a low voice.

Numbers felt below his arm. "I left it hanging on the chair in the den," he said. Arch produced his own gun and peered warily back out into the corridor. It was empty.

"Let's get up there. We need to collect more equipment," Bruno told the other two. "Something spooky's going on around here." He motioned for Arch to go first and positioned himself close behind, allowing Numbers to bring up the rear. Nothing stirred as they made their way cautiously back to the hall and up the carpeted stairway to the floor above.

Arch went through the door into the den. He was already flat on his face and out cold when Bruno entered just a few paces behind. Facing him over Arch's prostrate form was a tall, menacing figure dressed in a black, hooded, tight-fitting tunic, and over it a belt and harness holding gun, knife, coiled line, and assorted tools and pouches. Bruno yelped with fear and ran back out onto the landing. Numbers had disappeared, and a second hooded figure was turning back from the banisters as the crash of something limp and heavy splintering a piece of furniture came from below. They grabbed Bruno by his shirt, bundled him back into the den, and slammed him down into the large chair at the desk. One of them jerked his head back by the hair and knocked it alternately left and right with a rapid series of open-hand slaps, then delivered a straight-fingered jab to the V below his rib cage, knocking all the wind out of him and paralyzing his breathing.

Bruno recovered painfully, gasping and heaving for breath. He focused his eyes to find one of the intruders lounging in the armchair by the bar, drinking beer from a bottle and eating caviar off the end of a wicked-looking, double-edged dagger. He had thrown back his hood to reveal a lean, lazy-eyed face with shaggy yellow hair and a droopy mustache, and was leering at Bruno with evident enjoyment. The other, who was standing between the desk and where Arch was lying unconscious, had also uncovered his head; he had alert, narrow eyes and high cheeks, and he looked mean.

"And then there was one," Cassidy said. He scooped some more caviar out of the can resting on the edge of the desk and smacked his lips approvingly. "You know, you really shouldn't go getting yourself mixed up in things you're not big enough to handle, Pop."

Bruno's jaw shook for a few seconds, but no sound came out. His face was pale, and beads of perspiration were appearing on his forehead. "Who are you? What's this all about?" he managed finally. He gulped, licked his lips, and shifted his eyes fearfully from one to another. "Look, if I did something that crossed somebody big in town or anything, it wasn't intentional, know what I mean? We can straighten things out. There's no need for misunderstandings."

Cassidy grimaced distastefully. He threw the empty bottle into the wastebasket and took his .45 from his belt, squinting along the barrel as he leveled it at Bruno's head. Bruno whimpered incoherently with terror. Cassidy turned the gun away and nonchalantly shot the face out of a photograph hanging on the opposite wall. "We can split the action," Bruno offered when the glass had stopped flying. "Fifty-fifty . . . Whatever . . . Anything's negotiable. I'm a reasonable man." Cassidy shot the inkwells off the desk in front of him. Evidently Bruno had said the wrong thing again. Bruno swallowed hard and looked at Cassidy strangely all of a sudden. "I know you from someplace. . . ."

"We're from the Federal Department of Insurance Company Licensing," Cassidy told him. "Especially fire insurance. We've been getting complaints from your customers." He fired once into the bottles behind the bar, once at the mirror above, and a third time through the clock by the window while Bruno flinched at the reports and the crash of more shattering glass. "That's official notice that your license has been revoked. Uncle Sam's got a reputation to think about, and you haven't been doing a good job to help him keep it clean. Get the message—Pop?"

Then Bruno remembered. "Those new guys by the water down in Brooklyn . . . the ones who moved into Maloney's old warehouse—you were with them!"

"Now you're getting the message," Cassidy said.

Headlamps from a car turning into the driveway outside lit up the window for a few seconds, which meant that Ryan had opened the gates. Then a frightened squeal sounded from just outside the door, and Ferracini came in behind Fritsch and the woman who had been locked in the bathroom. Two other girls were with them—a bubble-headed blonde clad in a negligee, and a heavily made-up redhead in a bathrobe. The blonde's eyes were bulging with fright; she looked like the one who had been doing the squealing.

"Trust Harry to find 'em," Cassidy murmured.

Bruno's eyes widened further when he saw Ferracini. "He was there, too! Look, whatever it was we walked into down there, we'll stay out of from now on, honest. I didn't—"

"Looks like we messed up somebody's plans for a romantic evening," Ferracini said, nodding to indicate the blonde and the redhead. "I guess these come with the decor."

"Who are the other two?" Cassidy asked. The woman was still distraught at the man's bruises.

"Reluctant guests," Ferracini said. "We just got here before it was her turn. You don't change your style, do you, Bruno? Maybe it's time someone taught you a lesson about politeness to ladies."

Cassidy's eyes hardened. "Bruno's starting to get wrinkles around the face," he commented. "We could smooth some of them out for him. There should be a laundry room with an iron in it around here somewhere." He emitted a laugh of gloating anticipation, unfolded from the chair and stood up. Lamson began moving forward menacingly. The blonde screamed.

"No!" Bruno shrieked. He fell out of the chair and onto his knees, clasping his hands imploringly. "I'll back off . . . anything you say, okay? I won't be any more trouble. Just name what you want . . . anything."

"I never thought I'd see the day," a new voice said. "Don't bother to get up, Bruno—it suits you." Johnny Six Jays came into the room, accompanied by two of his pals. Paddy Ryan was behind them. Johnny looked around and whistled. "Boy, these guys don't fool around! They've taken out your whole army, Bruno. You'd better be in a listening mood because we've got a lot of talking to do."

"Who are these guys?" Bruno asked in a bewildered voice. "How are they mixed up with you?"

"You're not asking the questions," Johnny reminded him. "Let's just say for now that you moved in on an operation down in Brooklyn that's a lot bigger than you'll ever understand. The people who are running it aren't pleased, okay?" That was all he'd been told; it was enough. More headlights came from the driveway. Johnny turned to Ferracini. "That'll be the rest of the boys arriving. I guess we can handle things now. If you guys wanna get along, that's okay. It'll be mainly family business from here on, anyhow."

"Probably best," Ferracini said.

Johnny ran an eye over the people who had arrived with Ferracini. "I know these two tramps," he said, inclining his head toward Bruno's girls. "Any idea who the other two are?"

"They're okay—just two people that Bruno's been pushing around. Want us to take them, too?"

"Sure, why not? . . . And thanks again."

"Any time—our pleasure," Ferracini said. He looked at the man and the woman with him. "Do you need a ride?"

"Yes—ve ver brought here," the man told him.

"Come on," Ferracini said. "We'll take you home."

CHAPTER
13

THE REARMOST PART OF the Gatehouse building consisted of several levels of partitioned areas that the team had adapted for living quarters, recreation, and additional work space. In the room that she used as a reference library and office, Anna Kharkiovitch sat at a large wooden table covered with neatly arranged and labeled piles of newspapers, magazines, and files, conducting her ritualized daily search of the news for discrepancies from the events recorded in her own future. By her chair stood a steel cart with a bank of microfilm file drawers below and a viewer on top.

Her face was somber as she worked. Clearly, the past they were in differed subtly from the past that had been recorded in the future they were from. It was true, as Mortimer Greene had pointed out, that the whole purpose of the mission was to alter that future, and that goal could hardly be accomplished without changing the events that had led up to it; but she was finding changes in events which could not, by any stretch of the imagination, be causally connected to anything the team had done. Surely that didn't make sense. How could anything be affected by their mere presence? Greene had been trying to appear unperturbed, but Anna interpreted this as a brave public face to avoid demoralizing the team. She had confided her misgivings to Gor-

don Selby, and he, too, had admitted to being far from happy
about the situation.

The papers from a few days previously carried stories of the
official visit by King George VI of England and Queen Elizabeth
to Canada, where they had met the five-year-old Dionne Quin-
tuplets. Now preparations were being made for the impending
arrival of the royal couple in the U.S. as guests of President Roosevelt. As had been recorded in the Proteus world, the same
Choctaw-Chickasaw princess had been engaged to tell Indian
tales at the planned hot-dog party at Hyde Park, and Kate Smith
and Alan Lomax would be singing to entertain after the state
dinner.

Anna wondered if the visit was meant as a demonstration of
Anglo-American solidarity to make Hitler think twice. If so,
then whoever had dreamed up the idea still didn't understand
Hitler. Even the majority of Germans still didn't understand
Hitler. She had talked to Kurt Scholder since his arrival in the
U.S. with Winslade, and he had admitted the failure to bring
about any real changes in Britain's defense preparations so far. "It's
like the Little Pigs—they're building a straw house to keep out
the wolf over there," Scholder had said to her. It would have been
hilarious if it weren't so frightening.

Winston Churchill, a firm monarchist who had stood
staunchly by the King's brother, Edward, in the abdication crisis
of 1936, had wanted to tell the King about the existence of the
Proteus mission, and to use the opportunity of the royal visit for
the British sovereign personally to bring President Roosevelt into
the secret. Winslade, however, had vetoed the proposal. His orders, he had claimed, were expressly to leave matters of Anglo-
American relations to be handled by the appropriate people after
the link to 1975 was established.

But in reality Winslade was concerned about security, Scholder had told Anna. Although interviews in Canada in the early
seventies with the King's daughters, Elizabeth and Margaret, had
failed to reveal any reason for doubting the King, Winslade had
remained reluctant to involve any members of European aristoc-
racy or royalty. The network of family trees and social connections was simply too uncertain to be trusted; but he hadn't
wanted to risk offending Churchill by saying so.

It was all such a complicated business. Anna sighed and
turned her attention back to the paper that she was studying. A
dispute between union leader John L. Lewis and Madam Labor
Secretary Frances Perkins over a new contract was reported just
as had been recorded in the Proteus world; Clark Gable and Car-

ole Lombard had announced their surprise wedding in Arizona, just as recorded; and Franco's victory parade in Madrid was reported just as recorded. But then Anna found another item that was different: In her records, General Malin Craig, the Chief of Staff of the U.S. Army, had completed his tour in August, after forty-one years of service; now, however, he had retired early, in May, and been replaced by somebody called George C. Marshall. Anna shook her head hopelessly. Proteus couldn't be responsible for something like that. There was no rhyme or reason to any of it, no pattern that she could discern. She entered the details and references into her notes and turned to another page.

Immediately, an item in the "Crime" section caught her eye under the headline TOO HOT FOR ICEMAN. The article hadn't even existed in the same newspaper from the 1939 that Anna had known. She spread the page out and read:

> The New York Police Commissioner told reporters yesterday that gangland feuding may have rid the city of one of its noted undesirables, Bruno "Iceman" Verucin, long suspected of major involvement in gambling frauds and protection racketeering. According to underworld informants, Verucin has been run out of town by rivals, and his entire operation reduced to a shambles.
>
> The news came after an amazing assault in true-to-form "Batman" style on Verucin's heavily guarded Pelham mansion by mysterious intruders in black, who defied supposedly impenetrable defenses, walked up walls, and stormed the premises to take Verucin captive and hospitalize four of his gun-toting henchmen.
>
> Fifty-two-year-old Verucin, notorious for his alleged part in . . .

The report went on to give details of Verucin's previous criminal career and suspected recent dealings before returning to the happenings at Pelham.

Something about the accompanying photograph drew Anna's eye back again. The face seemed vaguely familiar, but she couldn't place it. She shook her head and continued reading.

> Miss Sally Jackson, another of the guests present at the time of the incident, described them as "terrifying, like out of a comic book—you know, the guys who are always decked out in masks and capes and that kind of stuff. They were all big—seven feet, at least—and dressed in black with all kinds of things hanging every-

where like airplane pilots in movies. I guess they must have had goggles and helmets. . . . Yes, that's right— they definitely had goggles and helmets. They must have parachuted onto the roof."

It brought to mind some of the training films that Anna had seen of the Army Special Operations units. She sat back in the chair; her eyes narrowed thoughtfully all of a sudden, and she looked at the photograph again. Then she set the paper down, got up, and left the office.

Downstairs, at the large table in the middle of the partitioned space that served as the mess area and off-duty recreation room, Cassidy picked up the cards that Ferracini had dealt and fanned them. "The trouble with Germans, Harry, is that they're all robots," he said as he inspected his hand. "They're only happy when they've got someone to tell 'em what to do. Otherwise they don't know their asses from holes in the ground and they start worrying, know what I mean?"

"I still say it's more an abdication of responsibility," Ferracini said. "Let the leader make the decisions. And if it all screws up, well, you're just the same as everyone else, so it's not your fault."

Cassidy frowned at the cards he was holding. "Say, what is this, Harry—you been taking lessons somewhere? . . . Anyhow, they'd have been a lot better off if they'd shot the whole bunch of leaders as soon as they started getting outta line. That's what the Russians did with theirs. It wasn't their fault if the bunch they ended up with turned out to be worse than the bunch they got rid of. At least they tried to do something. You know, Harry, I kinda like Russians."

Captain Edward Payne, the mission's doctor, industrial chemist, and officer in charge of Gatehouse security, was sitting in an easy chair in one corner. Propped on his knee was a catalogue of the New York World's Fair, which had opened a month previously at Flushing, on the north shore of Long Island, in celebration of the 150th anniversary of George Washington's inauguration. He and Gordon Selby planned to go to see it when they could find time.

The exhibition covered a 1,216-acre site and had cost $125 million, Payne read as he thumbed the pages. The area was divided into zones, each of which was dedicated to a specialized depiction of the progress of man and civilization. There was a Hall of Transportation, a Hall of Communication . . . halls of Production, Health and Public Welfare, Government, Education, Recreation and Amusement . . . all of it adding up to and reinforcing the central theme underlying the whole event: "Building the World of Tomorrow." The intention of it all, the introduction read, was to show the significance of today's scientific and material achievements and how they would enable the world to live and work in harmony—to provide an interpretation of the modern world and where it is leading. There was a Central Theme Building, through which visitors would be carried on a moving platform to view the World of Tomorrow.

Payne snorted quietly. The visitors wouldn't see a firestorm raid on Calcutta by Japanese heavy bombers, a slave labor camp in Siberia or the Middle East oilfields, or some of the grotesque medical experiments performed without anesthetics by the Nazis' so-called doctors.

Despite Cassidy and Ferracini's bantering over cards, the mood at Gatehouse was tense. Anna was upstairs, no doubt immersed in her work; Selby was barricaded behind *The New York Times*, next to the coffeepot; Ryan was listening blank-faced to *Amos and Andy* playing from the radio on its shelf; and Lamson was dismantling, cleaning, and reassembling his gun for the third time that morning. Nobody wanted to admit the nervousness they all were feeling while they waited to hear the outcome of the conference going on in the front office between Winslade, Greene, Scholder, and Major Warren. But at the same time, none of them could take the pretense to the point of feigning indifference. They all knew that they all knew.

Something had gone very wrong with the project. The mission should have made contact with its own times, and it hadn't. It was now clear that the communications connection from 1975 hadn't been a link back to them, because at their end nothing had happened.

Payne was a doctor, not a physicist or a philosopher, but it seemed to him that the answer had to lie in the existence of not just one, but many worlds, all differing from one another in ranges of variation that stretched from the barely perceptible to the totally distinct. If so, then could the 1975 machine have somehow connected through to the wrong one? He rubbed his chin and stared at his book while he thought about it. But if that were true, then how could some other world's past have a Proteus team in it? Only one team had been sent, and that team was right here, in this world. No, the explanation didn't make sense. Nothing made any sense.

The sound of footsteps descending wooden stairs came from outside the room, and a few seconds later Anna came in.

"And here's one of my favorite Russians," Cassidy said, looking up. "You working overtime again, Annie? Come on, sit down. We'll teach you to play the game."

"Thank you, but another time. I have to take another rain check, I'm afraid."

Cassidy sighed. "I'm losing my touch, Harry. Look, you're my best buddy. You'd tell me—do I use the wrong soap?"

Anna smiled and walked over to where Payne was sitting. "Are you busy, Ed?" she asked.

Payne looked up. "No, just killing time like everyone else. Why?"

"I'd like another look at some of the surveillance pictures from a few weeks back."

Payne hesitated for a second, then nodded, set down the catalogue that he was reading, and got up. He followed Anna out of the mess area and along the passage outside. They came to a door, which Payne unlocked and opened to reveal another office. "Movie or stills?" he asked as they entered.

"Stills will be fine," Anna answered. "I'm interested in those gangsters who were here—the ones Mortimer talked to. I'd especially like another look at their leader."

Payne walked over to some metal filing drawers and opened the top one to pull out an index. "We should have some sets of facial shots of those guys already enlarged," he murmured as he scanned one of the sheets. "Yes, here we are." He opened another drawer and flipped quickly past several tabs, stopping at the next to pull out one of the brown envelopes containing blowups of shots from the security cameras hidden around the building. "Out of curiosity, what do you want them for?" he asked as he handed the envelope to Anna. His voice sounded more than just idly curious, but she pretended not to notice.

"I just want to check something," Anna replied vaguely. "Thanks, Ed. I'll return them as soon as I'm through with them."

She took the envelope back upstairs to her own office. Inside, she sat down at the table, took out the photographs, and compared a couple showing Fat-lips with the picture accompanying the article that she had been reading earlier. There was no doubt about it: Fat-lips was Bruno "Iceman" Verucin.

Anna sat back in her chair and pondered what it might mean. Despite his fastidiousness at times, the troops had a genuine liking for Mortimer Greene—which was only to be expected, since an inability to command their respect would have disqualified him from the mission in the first place. And there was no dout that they had been angered by Fat-lips's effrontery, especially Cassidy; but that wouldn't have constituted a sufficient reason. Anna couldn't see soldiers who had been trained to Special Operations standards of discipline making a personal issue out of something like that. There had to be something else. And she was beginning to suspect that she wasn't the first to have spotted the connection. She had seen Payne's expression when she told him which pictures she wanted.

The buzzer on the intercom unit to one side of the table interrupted her thoughts. She stretched out a hand and pressed a button. "Yes?"

"Anna, it's Ed again," Payne's voice crackled from the box. "Claud and the others have come out. They want everyone assembled in the mess area. Could you come back down, please?"

"Yes, of course. I'll bring the pictures, too. They've told me what I wanted. I'll see you in a moment." She switched the intercom off.

And then, as she rose from the chair, Anna recalled overhearing Ferracini and Cassidy talking about the same Fat-lips and his cronies beating up some friends of theirs at the club they frequented in New York. One of them was a girl that Ferracini in particular had sounded uncharacteristically incensed about— much more than a Special Operations trooper ought to have allowed himself to be.

"Ah, so that was it," Anna said softly to herself, smiling as she slipped the photographs back into the envelope. "She must be quite a lady."

Since all seemed to have gone well, she could see no purpose in starting a fuss now. But not everybody, of course, might feel the same way. She picked up the envelope and left the office to go back downstairs.

CHAPTER
14

ANNA CAME BACK INTO the mess area to find that the others from the front office had arrived and were waiting for her. Kurt Scholder had found a seat near Selby; Mortimer Greene was standing by the door; and Major Warren had pulled a chair up to the table at which Ferracini and Cassidy had been playing cards. Winslade paced in the open space in the center of the room while Anna found herself a chair. He was wearing a polka-dot bow tie—a favorite style of Churchill's that Winslade liked and had adopted—but for once his manner failed to match the mildly eccentric joviality of his dress. The others watched and waited silently. At last he stopped and drew himself up to face them directly. His expression was serious.

"Last month," he began, "Hitler and Mussolini announced the full military alliance that we have been expecting, which they call the 'Pact of Steel.' It commits them to armed assistance in the event of either's becoming engaged in hostilities and affirms a common foreign policy of conquest and domination. A day later, on May 23—assuming events have continued to follow the course familiar to us—Hitler should have called a conference of his military chiefs in Berlin and told them bluntly that war is inevitable if further successes are to be achieved. In fact, their 'Case White'—the operational plans for the attack on Poland—

will already have been submitted by the Army General Staff. Danzig is just a pretext. The decisions that will plunge Europe into catastrophe in August have already been taken."

Winslade made a brief, empty-handed gesture and swept his eyes quickly around the room. "The purpose of this mission was twofold. First, to set up a return-gate here in the United States in order to counterbalance the forces operating behind Hitler. Second, and of more pressing urgency, to bring about some improvement in the condition of England and France." He took a long breath, held it for a second or two, and then exhaled abruptly. "It's my duty to tell you all now, officially, that so far we appear to have failed in both objectives. We cannot pretend that the results of our efforts in Europe have been anything but disappointing. And the situation here, you all know. The communications connection back to 1975 has not been established as was anticipated, and we are forced to acknowledge the possibility that it may never be."

Winslade clamped his mouth shut and looked back at his listeners poker-faced, waiting for the full meaning of his words to register. Silence fell for a few moments, then was broken suddenly by a sharp snapping sound as Floyd Lamson bit right through the pencil that he was chewing. Gordon Selby and Anna stared at the floor; it was as they had been suspecting for some time. Ryan was looking dazed.

Captain Payne brought his fingertips up to his brow and shook his head. "Then how . . . If the pilot channel isn't opened, that means we won't be able to get the main transfer port operating, either."

Winslade nodded curtly. "Quite."

Ferracini's first reaction was a numb inability to comprehend. It would soak in slowly, in its own time. He knew at a rational level what the words meant, but emotionally he was detached, groping unconsciously for any distraction. And suddenly the look on Cassidy's face, jaw hanging open and eyes wide with shock, seemed uproariously funny. "Hey, Cowboy, maybe you won't be sending us those pictures of the yacht from the Bahamas, after all," he heard himself say. Cassidy gaped at him, but was too stupefied for the moment to answer.

Mortimer Greene nodded. "Harry's got it. What Claud's saying is, there mightn't be any way back."

Winslade stared unblinkingly through his spectacles. "Yes. And just to be sure there are no misconceptions, let me spell out for you what that means. Three thousand miles away across the ocean, the Nazi machine is daily gathering momentum on a course that is already set for war. The plans are laid. The generals who opposed them have been replaced. The German Army has grown to fifty-one divisions, nine of them armored, after only four years—it took the old Imperial Army sixteen years before 1914 to build up from forty-three divisions to fifty. In the same period, the Luftwaffe has gone from nothing to twenty-one squadrons and two hundred sixty thousand men. And to back it all up, Hitler has the guarantee of support from an age that is fifty years ahead of even our own.

"And what do we have to stop it? Let's plan for the worst, as we must, and assume that the return-gate situation won't change." Winslade spread his arms and swung his body left and right, appealing personally to every individual in the room. "Just ourselves—the eleven of us here, and Arthur Bannering back in England—to do what we can with a France that is surely lost to defeatism already, a tired and apathetic England, a cynical and suspicious Russia, and an American ostrich that doesn't yet understand the threat to be global." He shrugged and showed his empty palms again. "There will be nothing from 1975. No Kennedy with a prepared group waiting to take control, no military reinforcements, no advanced weapons as insurance against Hitler's atom bombs. We're on our own."

Ferracini's mind reeled. At least nobody could accuse Claud of not telling things the way they were. That was Winslade's way, he had learned. Winslade would flatten people with the blackest of possible pictures, and then stand them back on their feet again, a piece at a time, in such a way that the only hope available was the one he was offering. That was how he had talked most of them into joining the mission in the first place.

Gordon Selby ran a hand through his wavy, black hair and looked across at Scholder. "It's definite, Kurt?" he said. "We really don't have any idea what's gone wrong?"

"Well, we're not sure, anyway," Scholder replied, a curious note to his voice. "But we think there might be a way to shed more light on the mystery."

Ferracini realized that a glint was creeping into Winslade's eyes. Suddenly, he recognized the familiar conjuring trick being worked again—all hope made to vanish in a puff of smoke by one hand, and then tantalizing hints given that something else was being concealed in the other. Anna Kharkiovitch had seen it, too. "What are you telling us, Claud," she demanded. "That there might still be something we can do after all—seriously? But where would we start? . . . There's so little time. . . ."

Gordon Selby asked, "What did Kurt mean when he said

there might be a way to shed more light on it? How? I thought Mortimer said yesterday that it looked as if we might need an Einstein or somebody to figure out what's happened."

Winslade beamed suddenly. "Right on the nose, Gordon! So, we'll do that. Let's get Einstein in on it!"

"What?" Selby blinked uncertainly.

Winslade produced his rabbit. "He's just across the bay from here, at Princeton, isn't he? And the whole purpose of the mission was to make contact with Roosevelt and the present U.S. government, yes? Well, even if we can't put JFK on the line, we can still go ahead and talk to Roosevelt ourselves, anyway. And through him, we'd be in a position to get the entire U.S. scientific community working for us if we needed to."

As if on cue, Greene came forward from the door and stood beside Winslade. "Construction work on the gate will be carried through to completion, which means you've all got plenty to do," he announced. "Major Warren will post new schedules and rosters later this afternoon. Are there any more questions in the meantime?"

It was like a last-minute reprieve from a death sentence. All of a sudden, life seemed to have returned to normal as they had known it for the past five months. Everyone became talkative as a mood of relief and enthusiasm to get back to work took over.

"How are we going to contact Einstein?" Payne asked.

"We're not sure yet," Greene replied. "It's not simple. You can't get anywhere on the phone—the operators at Princeton have strict instructions about protecting his privacy. They get crank calls all the time."

"Why not send him a letter like you did to Churchill?" Ryan suggested.

"We're not sure if it would be reliable, Paddy," Winslade said. "Einstein really is the original absent-minded professor. He gets mountains of mail. Who knows who opens it, how much of it gets through to him personally, and what happens to half of what does? When he came to the States in '33, he missed having dinner at the White House because he never read the President's invitation."

"You're kidding!"

"No, really. Another time, he used a $1,500 prize-money check as a bookmark and lost both—the book and the check."

"It might be better to approach Roosevelt first," Anna said.

"We may have to," Winslade agreed. "But getting to the President isn't the easiest thing in the world, either. Churchill was accessible because he was a private citizen. But we are looking at various possibilities."

Winslade's manner became more brisk. "Our other objective was to bring about an improvement in Europe's state of readiness. Since it now appears that, for the time being, anyway, we'll have to do without some of the resources we were counting on, a military alliance between the West and Russia is more important than ever. That was one of the reasons why Arthur stayed in England. Since politics with the Russians has suddenly become so important, we might end up sending you over there, too, Anna, to work with Arthur and Churchill. They're trying to get Anthony Eden sent to Moscow instead of Strang."

In the Proteus world, the talks with Russia had deadlocked over the refusal of Poland, Rumania, and the Baltic states to allow passage of Russian troops through their borders, which made it difficult to talk seriously about Russia's aiding them against a Nazi attack. In an effort to move things, Molotov had requested Lord Halifax, the British Foreign Minister, to involve himself personally. Halifax had declined, however, and sent instead a relatively junior Foreign Office official called Strang, who had limited negotiating powers and needed constantly to refer back to London for instructions.

"That was why you left Arthur over there?" Anna asked, frowning.

"Yes," Winslade replied.

Anna's frown deepened. She knew that Winslade's directive from President Kennedy in the Proteus world hadn't said anything about trying to get Eden sent to Moscow in place of Strang. Therefore, the idea had to be something that Winslade had improvised on his own initiative. But if that was why he had left Bannering in London, then Winslade must have known that the gate wasn't going to work—or at least, he must have had a pretty good idea—even before he returned to the States. Suddenly, Anna found herself wondering just how much more Winslade might know that he had been less than forthcoming about.

When the meeting was over, Scholder and Major Warren stayed behind talking in the mess area, while Winslade and Mortimer Greene returned to the front office. Winslade closed the door, and Greene poured himself some coffee from the pot on the warmer in one corner. He stirred in a spoonful of sugar and sat down heavily at the desk. "I didn't expect it to go so well, Claud," he confessed. "It's nice to see you're not slipping." Winslade produced a cigar and looked absently at a large map of the world pinned to the wall. Greene sipped his coffee. "Do you think Einstein will be able to do anything?" He sounded dubious.

"Who knows?" Winslade replied. One thing I know for certain is that if you don't buy a ticket, you don't get a prize."

The answer wasn't exactly comforting. "And if he can't help?" Greene asked.

Winslade turned from the wall and peered down at Greene through his flat-topped spectacles. "Well, let's suppose for the sake of argument that he can't," he suggested. "How would you feel about it?"

"Personally, you mean?"

"Yes."

Greene sipped his coffee again. "I gave that a lot of thought while I was waiting for you and Kurt to get back from England," he said. "And you know, Claud, the more I thought about it, the more I found myself wondering if it would really be so bad. I don't have any real ties back in '75. My wife died eight years before we left, as you know. We had no children, and I was never very close to the rest of my relatives, if you know what I mean . . . hadn't even seen most of them for years. I guess I'd turned into a kind of academic recluse, burying myself in mathematical physics and coaching students." He snorted to himself. "Maybe they were my substitute family."

"None of the team has any strong ties back there," Winslade commented. "This fiancée thing that Cassidy tells everyone about isn't as serious as he makes out, you know. In fact, he'd be far better off out of it."

Greene was only half-listening. "But what was the point of trying to do anything for students in that world?" he went on distantly. "What worthwhile purpose was left for science? What future was there? At least here there might be a chance."

"Is that all?" Winslade asked. His tone said that it shouldn't have been.

Greene stared at his cup. When he looked up again, a harder glint had appeared in his eyes and his mouth was set in a determined line. "No, Claud, it isn't," he said. "Everything was finished back there. Oh, sure, America was going to fight in the best traditions of honor and so on, but it was a hopeless gesture. Our way of life was finished.

"But here it's different. Yes, there are problems, but everything isn't lost. I don't know how, but there might be some way yet of stopping the Nazis." Greene brought his palm down hard on the desk. "Goddam it, Claud, after the things we've seen, I'd fight them with my teeth and nails if that's what it takes. At least in this world we've got something worthwhile to fight for, for a change—a chance for things to turn out differently. And even if it doesn't work out, then at least we'll go down with our self-respect intact. How could we say that in a world that had surrendered itself like sheep?"

Winslade seemed satisfied. "Eventually, the others will come to see things the same way," he said. "In fact, subconsciously, most of them do already. And if Dr. Einstein provides them with an acceptable rationalization while they are adjusting to that perspective, then he will have served us more than adequately."

Greene looked apprehensive suddenly. "But we are going to try approaching him?" he said. "I mean, that's what you've just promised the troops. Besides, we can't let the opportunity just slip by."

"Yes, don't worry, Mortimer," Winslade said reassuringly. "After all, who knows—we may find we have a winning ticket."

There was a short silence while Winslade at last lit his cigar. Greene leaned back in the chair and stared at the door. "Okay, so, changing the subject, what are we going to do about this Bruno Verucin business?" he asked.

Winslade exhaled a stream of blue smoke. "I suppose it is quite definite that our people did it," he said.

"No question about it." Greene waved toward a newspaper lying on top of one of the desk trays. "We double-checked with the surveillance pictures, but I was never in any doubt, anyway— that's him in there all right. Nobody came for any money on the first of the month. It happened when work on the machine was stopped and I'd given them extra leave. The ammunition inventory shows five rounds of .45 caliber unaccounted for."

"And you still want a full inquiry and disciplinary proceedings," Winslade said.

"You can't be serious about just letting the whole thing ride," Greene protested. "I mean, it constitutes a major violation of just about every regulation you can name, and on a mission like this . . . And then there's Harvey Warren to think about. He's the senior military officer. How's he supposed to retain any authority if we do nothing? What about his professional image?"

"Not to mention yours, of course," Winslade remarked mildly.

Greene started to object, but checked himself when he saw the futility of pretensions. "Yes," he said, thrusting out his jaw, "mine, too."

Winslade turned his back on the map that he had been looking at and puffed at his cigar. "There's no reason to suppose that they think we know," he pointed out.

Greene scowled and shifted uncomfortably in his chair. That was true, but the answer had clearly left him far from satisfied. "Look," he said, "running *Sugar* group smoothly is my job. How am I supposed to do it if we're going to let anyone who wants to go off and fight private wars whenever he feels like it?"

"Would it make any difference if I tell you that Special Operations soldiers are not just more clockwork products from the military machine?" Winslade said. "I've worked with them for years. They're selected and trained for independence and initiative. Traditional discipline doesn't work with them. Trying to assert authority heavy-handedly only earns contempt."

"So how do you command any respect from people like that?" Greene asked.

"By showing them some."

"For behaving like thugs and jeopardizing the whole mission?"

"No. For being thinking, feeling human beings and not mindless zombies like the creations of the SS."

Greene stared moodily. "I'm not sure I see your point," he said grudgingly. His voice hinted that he did, but wasn't about to admit it so readily.

Winslade helped him out by accepting the remark at face value. "Try and understand the frustration that the men have been feeling," he said. "They've seen with their own eyes what Nazi conquest means, and to them the message of what's happening in Europe is obvious. But they have to watch the spectacle of the West's leaders lining up to bow and scrape before the dictators, and there's nothing they can do about it.

"But there was something they could do about the other Hitler—Bruno. You talked about self-respect a few minutes ago, Mortimer. The troops have theirs, too. How could they condemn the failure of the world's leaders to resist intimidation, and at the same time do nothing themselves when their friends were intimidated? You see, they had to do it. If they weren't made that way, they wouldn't have been picked for this mission to begin with."

Greene eyed Winslade dubiously for a few seconds. At length, he gave a resigned nod. "Okay, Claud. I'm not sure yet if you've totally convinced me, but I'll go along with it and pretend we don't know. How about Harvey Warren, though? He's my second-in-command here. Will he be able to accept it without feeling undermined?"

"I'll talk to him this afternoon," Winslade promised.

The atmosphere in the room had lightened considerably. "I must say, I'd like to have seen it," Winslade said, chuckling suddenly. "Do we know who was involved?"

Greene wiped his mustache with a knuckle. "Harvey thinks Ferracini must have been in on it because of the way he reacted to the girl being beaten up at the nightclub," he said. "Very likely, he was the instigator. Also, he's been pretty close to the boiling point for months."

"Mmm, that sounds like Harry," Winslade agreed. "So that would automatically implicate Cassidy, too. Besides being virtually Harry's Siamese twin, he has high principles, too, strange as it may sound. He takes individualism to the point of being socially obnoxious at times, but that's just his safety valve. Harry doesn't have one. So who else? Floyd, I imagine—the operation had 'Lamson' stamped all over it."

Greene nodded. "Probably Ryan . . ."

"And the other captain—Ed Payne?"

"Unlikely—Payne's too much of an intellectual. Also, he reported the deficit in the drugs, which would be hard to explain if he'd been involved. I doubt if he even knew the others were planning it."

Winslade nodded as if the assessment was pretty much as he had expected. He was about to say more when a tap sounded on the door, and Major Warren's head appeared. "Am I interrupting?" he inquired.

"No, no, come on in, Harvey," Winslade said. "What is it?"

Warren looked slightly mystified, as if not quite sure how to put what he wanted to say. "Er, it's about the problem you referred to earlier—about getting in touch with Einstein. We may have found an answer."

Winslade and Greene exchanged surprised looks. "What kind of answer?" Greene asked guardedly.

"Well . . ." Warren motioned back over his shoulder with his eyes. "Cassidy says that he and Ferracini know some of Einstein's acquaintances. He says they can put us in touch."

"Cassidy!" Greene exploded. "How can he possibly know anyone remotely connected with Einstein? It's just another of his cock-and-bull stories, for God's sake. He—" Greene stopped in response to a motion from Winslade.

"Go on, Harvey," Winslade said.

"I know it sounds crazy, but he really does seem serious," Warren said. "He claims they know some of the physicists at Columbia, such as Fermi. . . . And he also mentioned Leo Szilard, who filed a joint patent with Einstein for a heat pump when they worked together back in the twenties in Europe."

Greene slumped back in his chair, totally bemused. "Fermi? Szilard? How would somebody like Cassidy even have heard of names like those?"

"That's what I mean," Warren said. "He does seem to know what he's talking about. And what's more, Gordon Selby was with them a couple of times in town. He's also met some of the people they know, and he says there just might be something to it."

CHAPTER
15

JEFF FROWNED THROUGH HIS owlish glasses at the turntable and innards of the disembowled wind-up phonograph standing on the table in the front room of the apartment, and probed with a screwdriver to adjust something inside. He mounted one of his 78 r.p.m. records in place, slid the control switch to "play," and lowered the needle. After a few seconds of hissing, a jolly but scratchy voice singing to a tinny-sounding accompaniment filled the room.

> *I press the middle valve down,*
> *The music goes round and round.*
> *Oh-ho, Oh-ho, Ho-ho!*
> *And it comes out here . . .*

It was too fast and squeaky. Jeff stopped the record and turned a screw further. An ominous *boingggg* came from inside. He sighed and looked up.

"I'm not sure, but I'll try," he said. "Things have changed since the Szilard and Fermi papers appeared in *Physical Review* in April. The people involved seem to be applying a kind of—I don't know what you'd call it—voluntary self-censorship.

They're not publishing any more information on their research, and they've clammed up."

"Any guesses why?" Gordon Selby asked from where he was sitting on the couch next to Cassidy. He had a pretty good idea already, but was curious to hear what Jeff made of it.

Jeff shrugged. "If a chain reaction's possible, it might give you a way of making much bigger bangs than you can get with ordinary explosives," he said. "There are people in Germany who are just as capable of figuring out what the Hahn-Strassmann experiment means as anyone here—Heisenberg, for example. Why risk giving them extra clues?"

"How about the guy who's doing the experiments—Fermi?" Cassidy asked. "He sounds pretty approachable. What are the chances of talking to him?"

"None, right now," Jeff said. "He's lecturing at Ann Arbor in Michigan for the summer. There's somebody called John Dunning who's been working with him that I could try, though. But it is getting difficult. Asimov—he always wants to know everything—tried to find out from Professor Urey a little while back what's going on with all the uranium experiments we keep hearing about, and he nearly got his head bitten off. Everybody's clamming up about it."

Opposite Jeff, Ferracini stared moodily at the table as he listened. Why the hell couldn't Cassidy simply have told Claud that they knew a student from Columbia who might be able to suggest some names to approach, instead of leaping in with both feet and saying they knew Fermi? Claud and Mortimer had seemed interested and asked for an introduction. But instead of backing down when he had the chance, Cassidy had plunged on. "Sure, no problem, Claud. Just give Harry and me a day or two to fix it, okay?"

Later, Winslade, knowing Cassidy of old, had asked Ferracini for the real story. To Ferracini's consternation, Winslade, instead of quietly calling the idea off and trying another approach, had been happy to let them go ahead, even though Ferracini had given little for their chances. And now, sure enough, Fermi wasn't even in town, and the people who were weren't talking to anybody. Even Selby seemed to be realizing to his discomfort that the academic freedom taken for granted in 1939 didn't extend to quite the extremes that his first conversations with Jeff had led him to imagine.

Ferracini didn't understand what game Winslade was playing. If he had wanted to give Cassidy a mild rap on the knuckles for talking through his ass, he would have found some other way to do it than by exposing him to ridicule in front of the team. That kind of thing wasn't Claud's style.

Janet, who was sitting by the door leading into the back room, studied the toe of her shoe. "Who are these people you work for?" she asked suspiciously. "Why should they need to involve Jeff? It doesn't make sense. If they're politicians or something like that, why can't they go through the faculty dean? If they're scientists, how come the scientists at the university don't already know them?"

The question was not entirely unexpected. "They represent a consortium of private interests that are concerned about the possibility of Hitler getting his hands on a super explosive first," Selby told her. "They're willing to put up funds for comparable research over here, but before getting mixed up in a lot of red tape and bureaucracy, they want to talk informally to the scientists involved—to be sure that the implications are what they seem to be."

"I see." Janet could have tried harder to sound convinced.

"What about Leo Szilard?" Selby asked, looking at Jeff. "He's involved in the experimental work, too, isn't he? And he's Hungarian—another European. He might know something about the German work as well as about what's happening here." What really interested Selby was that Szilard was an old personal friend of Einstein; he didn't want to complicate the conversation even further by mentioning Einstein's name to Jeff just now, however.

"I don't know," Jeff replied. "I'll talk to Dunning and a couple of others tomorrow. We'll have to wait and see what happens."

Nothing more could be done about the matter that evening. The talk drifted on to the university and its buildings, the Morningside Heights area in general, and from there, to the subject of travel in and out of Manhattan. Jeff thought it ought to be possible to live a fairly full life in the subway system without ever coming out on the street at all. "There's practically a second city down there," he said. "You've got lunch counters, barbers, shoeshine stands, shops, and most of the big buildings connect to the subway, too. For instance, you could live at the Commodore, work in the Chrysler Building, eat at Savarin's, shop at Bloomingdales, swim at the St. George in Brooklyn, see a movie at the Rialto, and even get married in the Municipal Building, if you wanted."

Selby became engrossed in one of Jeff's textbooks, and Jeff and Cassidy started fiddling with the phonograph again. Ferracini said he was getting hungry, and Janet offered to go for some take-out food from a Mexican restaurant on the next block. Ferracini said he'd go with her.

It was evening when they came out, but still warm from the sweltering day. Lights were coming on in the street and over the fronts of the bars, restaurants, and dime movie houses standing intermingled with dry goods stores, butchers, groceries, and vegetable stores, many of the latter displaying mangoes, tamarinds, cassavas, pimentos, and other foods typical of so-called Spanish Harlem a few blocks farther east. There were plenty of people about, especially Puerto Ricans and Latin Americans. Children were still out on the streets, swinging on ropes around streetlights and playing hopscotch on the sidewalks; one group was jumping on a discarded bedspring. Teen-agers lounged on corners or around the cavernous tenement entranceways, and older people in flower-patterned cotton dresses and colored shirts sat talking and watching the world go by from the steps leading up to their apartment houses.

Europe had fallen to the Nazis years before Ferracini was born, and Asia and Africa were devoured while he was still growing up. By the time he became aware of the world and its situation, America was on a war economy and preparing itself for the final conflict that everyone accepted as inevitable. That was the only America he had known. But he had heard and read of the times before that, when life had been different, and places with names like London, Paris, and Vienna, each with its own allure of mystery and excitement, had been parts of a free world that people hoped to visit one day. For a few brief years after the Great War, the world had begun turning away from centuries of imperialism and oppression; its peoples had at last started learning to live together. And America, surely, with its throngs of every race, language, color, and creed daily rubbing shoulders in the streets of New York and San Francisco; with the ocean liners docked beneath scores of flags in its harbors; and its Clipper flying-boats bringing Tokyo hours closer, had pointed the way forward to the world as it might one day have been.

He felt strange walking through the streets of that America of long ago. This was how it should have stayed, he told himself. He could feel freedom all around him, a sense of vitality that had been absent from the times he remembered. There were still signs of the Depression, to be sure, and the nation still had its share of problems, but underneath, it was confident and optimistic, its conviction unshaken that its problems could be solved. It was the America that the father and mother he had never known had come halfway around the world to find: an America that still had faith in itself.

"You said once that you were from this area, didn't you, Harry?" Janet asked as they walked.

Ferracini returned abruptly from his reverie. "Oh, yes. That's right."

"Whereabouts? Farther east, maybe—the Italian quarter?"

"We've got some family there, but my folks moved out, to Queens. They both died when I was a baby. I grew up with an aunt and uncle over in Hoboken."

"Getting too crowded—when your parents moved out of the city, I mean?"

"Too Italian."

"That sounds strange."

Ferracini shrugged. "Italians, Sicilians—they like being surrounded by things they know. They like the ways and customs they're familiar with. So, when all the immigrants started coming over, people from the same villages started clustering together. Pretty soon, you could see Italy coming together again like pieces of a jigsaw puzzle. Well, my father said he didn't come all that way to find he was back in Italy again—he'd come here to be an American. So, they moved across the river."

"When did they come over to the States?"

She was fishing. They stopped to cross Seventh Avenue. He didn't want to have to lie or be led into contradicting himself. "Look," he said, "I thought we were going to get dinner, not start a cross-examination. Questions bother me. That was all a long time ago. It doesn't matter any more."

"I didn't mean to be nosy," Janet said. "Just curious." She was silent as they crossed the avenue through a gap in the traffic. When they reached the other side, she seemd agitated by whatever was going through her mind, turning her head every few seconds to glance at Ferracini uncertainly. As they reached the restaurant—a small, but well-kept place with a large, colorfully lettered menu and list of take-out items in the window—she could contain herself no longer. "Who are you?" she asked, drawing Ferracini aside from the door just as they were about to enter. She kept her voice low to avoid attracting the attention of a couple talking nearby, but it was insistent. "All of you—Cassidy, Gordon, Floyd, Paddy—the whole bunch. Jeff told me he's astounded by some of the things Gordon knows about—and in that area, Jeff's nobody's fool. But how could Gordon know all those things and not be a household name among the people at the university? Jeff's asked around, and nobody's even heard of him.

"And then there's the way you guys took care of Iceman and his apes—Johnny Six Jays told me all about it. There was a lot more to it than got in the papers. Max says you're ex-Army, but I talked to Sid, and Sid doesn't think there's any unit in the Army that could operate like that." Janet shook her head. "Now, don't get me wrong, Harry—it's great to see the heat's off Max now, and I'm as delighted as anybody about the account with Bruno getting squared up at last. But you didn't do it just for us. You did it because Bruno tried muscling his way into whatever you're doing in that place in Brooklyn." Ferracini swallowed hard and hoped he didn't look as alarmed as he felt.

"Bruno told Johnny about it after you and the others left," Janet explained, catching something in Ferracini's expression. "You see—there is something very strange going on. And when people that I don't know all that much about, but who are mixed up with something very strange, start trying to involve my kid brother in things that professors won't talk about and the Nazis seem very interested in, I start to worry. Jeff might be smart in a lot of ways, but sometimes he trusts people too much. So don't tell me it's none of my business, because I think it is my business. You're not just a trucker, Harry. Who are you and those other people, and what do you want?"

Ferracini eyed her circumspectly while she waited for a response. He had long seen that she was an intelligent girl, and now she expected the fact to be recognized. "You don't buy what Gordon said?" he asked her.

Janet gave him a pained look. "Businessmen might want to talk to scientists, but they don't hire private armies to go after the likes of Bruno," she said. Ferracini nodded with a sigh. He'd expected that. Selby hadn't known about the Bruno escapade; if he had, he'd have come up with a better story. Janet shook her head. "No, Harry, I don't buy that."

Ferracini closed his eyes and massaged his eyelids with his fingers. "Do you trust people too much as well, sometimes?" he asked her.

She shook her head again. "I don't think so. I've been around a bit more than Jeff."

"Do you trust me?"

Janet scanned his face. His expression was intense; his eyes, unblinking. "What's that supposed to mean?" she asked.

"It means I can't tell you."

In the long silence that followed, their eyes did all the talking that was necessary. She had wanted him to credit her as a person capable of thinking; he had done so, and now was asking for his own frankness and integrity to be respected in turn. Then Ferracini said, "We're not working for any foreign government or other interests, so if that's what's worrying you, forget it. We're strictly for Uncle Sam. That good enough?"

Janet studied his face for a while longer, then nodded, satisfied. "Let's go get the dinner," she said.

* * *

Winslade knew about the security-consciousness that had spread through the U.S. nuclear community during the first half of 1939, and he was under no illusions about the likely response to strangers trying to gain access to sensitive information through a graduate student. But he hadn't wanted to react negatively to an offer of help from one of the team, even if it was based on exaggerated claims, certainly not at a time when the team had just suffered such a tremendous shock. In fact, he had seen the situation as an opportunity to boost morale, especially that of the military contingent, from whose ranks the offer had come.

To succeed, however, the approach would need some quiet string-pulling from behind the scenes; Winslade was an old hand at that.

It so happened that Leo Szilard had spent some years in England between leaving Hungary and arriving in the U.S. During that time, he had worked with Professor Lindemann at the Clarendon Laboratory in Oxford. While Ferracini and the others were sitting down to their meal of chili, tacos, enchiladas, and hot sauces in upper Manhattan, Winslade raised Arthur Bannering on the phone in London and told him to locate Lindemann and have him call back as quickly as possible. The return call came through at Gatehouse just under an hour later.

"No, there's nothing new on the gate," Winslade told Lindemann. "The situation's still the same. Look, I might be needing both Mortimer Greene and Kurt over on this side for a while, so I'm going to send Gordon Selby over with Anna to update you. He's very knowledgeable, and I think you'll get on well with him."

"Very well," Lindemann agreed. "But that can't be what Arthur asked me to call you about. It sounded far more urgent."

"Correct," Winslade said. "I've been thinking some more about this idea we talked about before I left."

"Getting Einstein involved, you mean?"

"Yes. It seems worth a try. I agree with you—our best approach would probably be through Szilard. Now, for reasons that I'd rather not go into right now, some of our people are going to try contacting Szilard through Columbia. The trouble is, nobody at Columbia knows them, and everybody there is getting paranoid about secrecy. So, what I'd like is for Szilard to talk to the Columbia group first and make sure they know that when our people try to introduce themselves, it's genuine and it's important."

"Hmm, I must say it sounds a rather roundabout way of

doing things," Lindemann commented. "However, as you wish. What, specifically, do you want me to do?"

"What I'd like you to do, Professor, is call Leo Szilard from England, if you would, and brief him as follows . . ."

As Winslade had anticipated, Jeff's first attempts the following day to approach members of the uranium research group at Columbia met with frosty responses. Nobody would talk about the subject, nobody knew anything, and one doctor of chemistry threatened to call the FBI.

And then, suddenly and for no apparent reason, everything changed. That afternoon, by which time Jeff had reached the depths of despondency, John Dunning sought him out in the Chemistry Department and amazed him with an attitude that had undergone a complete about-face in a few hours. "I'm sorry I was a bit abrupt earlier, but we can't let just anyone come poking around in this kind of work," Dunning said. "Anyway, I'm not sure how, but apparently Szilard has been expecting you to show up, and he's very anxious to meet those people you talked about. He'd like them to call him direct."

Gordon Selby called Winslade from the Columbia campus with the news. "Let's try calling Szilard right away," Winslade said to Greene, dialing another number as soon as Selby had hung up. "We might just catch him before he goes home."

"Let's hope so," Greene said anxiously. "There isn't any time to lose."

There wasn't. They had also heard from Arthur Bannering that afternoon of another failure on the English side of the operation: Eden's offer to meet Molotov in Moscow had been declined. Strang was still being sent, as had happened in the Proteus world.

CHAPTER
16

DR. EDWARD TELLER WAS a broad, heavily built man with dark hair and thick, bushy eyebrows, a prominent nose, and craggy features. He had been born in 1908 in the Hungarian capital, Budapest. Gravitating naturally toward a career in mathematics and physics, he had studied at some of Europe's most prestigious institutions through the mid and late twenties, a time that had seen the rise of quantum mechanics and which represented, perhaps, one of the most exciting periods in the history of the physical sciences. He had been taught by such giants as Arnold Sommerfeld in Munich and Werner Heisenberg at the University of Leipzig, worked at the University of Göttingen and Niels Bohr's Institute for Theoretical Physics at Copenhagen, and attended scientific gatherings organized by Fermi at the University of Rome. Hitler's rise to power had driven him to England, after which, in 1935, he had accepted an offer of a professorship at George Washington University, Washington, D.C. There, he joined a former colleague from Europe, Russian-born George Gamow, in conducting theoretical studies of nuclear processes.

Teller had been present at the momentous Fifth Washington Conference on Theoretical Physics in January when Bohr announced the Hahn-Strassmann results, and by the summer of 1939 was being urged by Fermi and Szilard to join the uranium fission research group coming into existence at Columbia. Accordingly, Teller obtained leave of absence from George Washington University and moved with his wife, Mici, to take up temporary residence in an apartment in Morningside Heights. Fermi was methodical and even-tempered, whereas Szilard could be explosive and bombastic at times. The two of them disagreed often and didn't get along well, and Teller suspected that one of the reasons why he had been invited to Columbia, apart from his specialized knowledge, was to act as a peacemaker and help them work together.

Having seen for himself how attempts to placate the aggression emerging in Europe were merely taken as signs of weakness, he had reluctantly reached the conclusion that only firmness stood a chance of producing a deterrent effect, and that war would probably be inevitable eventually if Hitlerism was to be eradicated. Like his compatriot Leo Szilard, Teller already believed firmly that a uranium bomb was possible, and he entertained no illusions about what the consequences would be if Hitler got his hands on one first. Hence, he viewed the project with a seriousness that went beyond the purely intellectual involvement which, for the time being at least, seemed to be about as much as many of the Americans were capable of showing.

Around lunchtime on a sunny day in early July, Teller walked stiffly—he had lost a foot at the age of twenty in an accident inolving a Munich streetcar—down the broad steps below Columbia's Low Memorial Library on West 116th Street and checked his watch as he stopped to wait on the sidewalk. Szilard had refused to say over the phone what justified his insistence that Teller drop whatever he was doing in order to go with Eugene Wigner from Princeton—yet another refugee Hungarian physicist—to join Szilard at a strange address in Brooklyn, and he had refused to listen to any of Teller's excuses. He had sounded excited, even for Szilard.

Perhaps Szilard had met with better success from the Navy this time, Teller thought to himself. Despite Fermi and Tuve's abortive attempt last March to enlist official support for fission research, Szilard had used the occasion of the American Physical Society's meeting at Princeton in June to press another appeal on Ross Gunn, an adviser to the Naval Research Laboratory. The Navy's more sophisticated scientists had shown some interest in uranium, though more on account of its potential as a submarine fuel than through any insight to its explosive possibilities, but in desperation Szilard was following any lead.

No, that couldn't be it, Teller decided. All Szilard was looking for was a grant from naval research funds of something in the order of $1,500; even if the Navy had agreed, it would hardly have warranted the kind of reaction that Teller had heard over the telephone.

Teller turned and looked up at the building's rounded outline, formed of incongruously blended Roman dome and classical Greek façade, its massive stonework imposing among the surrounding structures of red brick. It had long been abandoned as a library and now served as the campus administration center. Perhaps there had been a breakthrough in the theoretical work on moderators going on over at Princeton, he reflected; or maybe somebody had come up with a new suggestion for concentrating uranium 235.

The big problem confronting fission researchers by the summer of 1939 was how to initiate and sustain a chain reaction. No useful release of the energy locked up inside the atomic nucleus would ever be realized if every nuclear fission inside the uranium fuel required a neutron fired in from the outside to trigger it; the energy released by the fissions would represent no useful gain over that expended on injecting the neutrons. If, on the other hand, the neutrons that were now known to be released in the fission event itself could be directed to cause fissions of more uranium nuclei, and so on, then a self-sustaining chain reaction would rapidly be set up and continue without further outside help, releasing more and more energy at an exponentially increasing rate. Clearly nothing of this kind had happened in Otto Hahn's laboratory in Berlin; if it had, nobody would have been left in a suitable condition to report the results that had so electrified the scientific world.

To cause a further fission, a released "fission neutron" would have to be captured by another uranium nucleus. Fermi had established that the probability of this happening depended critically on the energy that the neutron carried; furthermore, the energy that fission neutrons were released with was too high. For a chain reaction to be feasible, therefore, a "moderator" substance—to slow the neutrons down—would be required in addition to the fuel. Szilard had been investigating various candidate substances. Heavy water was a possibility, he had reported, but all things considered, graphite would be a better one to go for; and for once, Fermi had agreed with him. But how much uranium and how much graphite? Nobody knew.

It was clear too—and fortunate—that not all of the uranium atoms present in the experimental samples were being split. Only a small proportion were, which presumably represented a particularly susceptible isotope. Niels Bohr and Princeton's John Wheeler had concluded from theoretical considerations that fission didn't take place in the common uranium 238 isotope, but was restricted to the comparatively rare uranium 235. After some initial skepticism, the community of U.S. nuclear physicists had generally accepted this pronouncement and begun talking about the possibility of an explosive, fast-neutron chain reaction inside metal consisting of the pure 235 isotope only. To achieve it—assuming it was possible—the U-235 would somehow have to be separated out of the naturally occurring U-235 and U-238 mixture, and concentrated. Now only one atom in every 140 was of the required kind. The two kinds were chemically identical, and they differed in mass by only three parts in over two hundred. How to go about separating them was far from obvious.

That was not the only problem. Even if the rare 235 isotope could be extracted, how could enough of it be concentrated to make a bomb? Only an ounce or so of metallic uranium existed in the whole of the U.S., and nobody knew how much would be needed to make a bomb, anyway.

The toot of a horn sounded from behind, and moments later Eugene Wigner's car came to a halt by the sidewalk. Wigner, lean-framed and bespectacled, with a high forehead, thinning hair, and a rounded, open face that split readily into an easy, toothy smile, leaned across to open the passenger door. He was six years older than Teller and unfailingly gentle-mannered and polite. They shared the same political views and had first met at a seminar that Teller and some fellow-students had attended with Heisenberg at the Kaiser Wilhelm Institute in 1929. Einstein had been present, too, on that occasion.

Teller climbed in, and the car pulled away. "I hope you weren't waiting long," Wigner said in his high-pitched voice. "I got caught up in a snarl getting onto the George Washington Bridge."

"Don't worry about it. I had to cancel a lecture, so I'd only just arrived." Teller, by contrast, had a thick, guttural voice.

"I take it you've no more idea of what this is all about than I have," Wigner said. "Poor Leo sounded as if he were on the verge of cardiac arrest."

"None," Teller replied. "I've been trying to think of possibilities . . . but we'll soon find out, I suppose. Do you know where this place is?"

"Only that we go south and get over to the other side of the city." Wigner felt inside the glove compartment and thrust a folded street map and an envelope with directions scrawled on the back into Teller's hand. "You're navigating, Edward."

"Oh, God—but I don't know this city! I've only just arrived here."

"Neither do I. I'm not sure anyone does."

"Oh, well, let's see . . . Brooklyn . . . I think it's down by the bay somewhere, isn't it? Yes, here—we have to cross the river. Okay, Eugene, take the next left, which ought to be Cathedral Parkway. We'll get across town while we're still north of Central Park."

They reached Second Avenue, followed it down the East Side to Chinatown, and crossed the East River to Brooklyn via the Manhattan Bridge. Then they took a wrong turn and found themselves on the grimy, cobblestone streets of the Navy Yard area, with its flophouses, crumbling tenements, and greasy restaurants. After extricating themselves, they entered the central Fulton Street district, only to get lost once more among bustling downtown streets clogged with automobiles, pedestrians, and clattering streetcars, where neon signs blinked throughout the day in the false twilight below the elevated railroads.

At last, they came to the sprawling waterfront area between the Atlantic and Erie shipping basins, and slowed to a crawl through the maze of massive, gray loft buildings, warehouses, docks, and railroad sheds, trying to follow the hasty directions that Szilard had gabbled over the phone. Finally, at the back of a jumble of run-down older buildings separated by narrow lanes and alleyways, Teller motioned for Wigner to stop. He pointed at a gloomy, brick warehouse with blackened windows and closed doors standing at the end of a dock and overshadowed by a larger warehouse on one side, with a railroad siding and an iron bridge spanning a canal on the other. "That must be it," he said.

Wigner stared dubiously. "Are you sure?"

"Here are the notes you made. It's as they describe."

"This becomes more and more peculiar."

Wigner eased the car forward again, and they parked before the large doors at the front of the warehouse. Teller looked around warily as they got out; nobody was in sight. Then the small door set into one of the larger ones opened, and a figure in a crumpled jacket, loosely knotted tie, and gray flannel pants stepped out. He was broad and stockily built, and had a heavily jowled face with a solid chin, high browline, and wide mouth. It was Szilard.

Two men were with him. The first was tall, dark-chinned, and unsmiling, and wore baggy corduroy pants with a plaid shirt and brown leather cap. Szilard introduced him as Major Harvey Warren, U.S. Army. Wigner glanced at Teller apprehensively. Although Szilard was a first-rate scientist capable of some dazzling insights, he was known among his peers for leaps of imagination which at times could border on the reckless. Teller wondered if maybe Szilard had really let the strain get to him this time. The other man had a pinkish complexion and thin white hair, and his eyes twinkled mirthfully behind quaint half-round spectacles. He was soberly, but meticulously dressed in a plain, dark gray suit with striped shirt, silver tie with a red lion motif, and jeweled clip. His name, Szilard said, was Claud Winslade. He was "with the government."

They entered the warehouse and crossed a bay in which several trucks and other vehicles were parked, then ascended a short stairway to the loading dock. Here they met Mortimer Greene, a man in his fifties, with a bald head fringed by graying hair at the back and sides, and clipped mustache. Winslade described him as "also a scientist"; with him was another man, frail, with a deeply lined face and close-cropped gray hair. His name was Kurt Scholder; he, too, was a scientist, apparently. He spoke with a discernible German accent. "Where are you from?" Teller asked curiously.

"Dortmund, originally."

"I know it vaguely. When did you come to America?"

Scholder smiled mysteriously. "I think we should leave that question until a little later," he said. They moved on.

In the dim light farther back from the loading dock, Wigner and Teller could see nothing but bales and crates stacked high into the darkness below the roof. Major Warren led the way around a protruding wall of boxes into a narrow passage between the stacks, and then around another bend; it was like being in a military trench system, Teller thought to himself. And then a section of what had looked like a dead-end wall of crates swung aside to reveal itself as a camouflaged door—and a sturdily built door at that, they could see as they passed through.

Suddenly, they were in a completely different world of clean, painted, partition walls, false ceilings, and bright lights. Teller and Wigner turned instinctively as the door swung shut behind them, and saw to their astonishment that not only the door, but all of the rearmost stacks of crates formed a façade screening a false wall that reached up to the roof. Nearby, a partly enclosed room opened out to where they were standing. Winslade walked over to it and beckoned for them to follow.

Inside stood a desk and a couple of chairs; some charts and tables were pinned to one wall, and a rack containing automatic weapons was affixed to the wall opposite. But what attracted the attention of the two newcomers was the bank of instrumentation cabinets and electronic equipment standing on a table at the back. They walked up to it and gazed in amazement.

The front panels were compact and elegantly styled, unlike

the ugly and cluttered fronts of the black boxes they were familiar with. In addition to recognizable devices like switches and buttons, the panels contained other things that were new: luminous screens displaying lines of text; windows containing glowing numbers; two spools wound with some kind of ribbon behind a small glass door; a telephone handset of strange, streamlined design. Some of the rectangular screens were showing pictures: the loading dock they had just come from, other interior views that meant nothing, and a series of scenes from outside the building. Teller had seen some examples of experiments with "television" while he was in England, but never anything as clear as this.

Winslade operated a control on one of the consoles and indicated a screen that was showing a portion of the roadway outside. The view began changing, sweeping slowly by to cover all approaches as the camera moved. He keyed something into one of the arrays of buttons, and a screen that had been blank came to life to show Wigner's car stopping a short distance away, then turning and coming forward to park, and finally Wigner and Teller getting out and walking up to the door. "Terrible manners, I know, but sometimes these things are necessary," Winslade commented cheerfully.

In one corner was some shelving carrying an assortment of boxes, tools, reels of cable, and what looked like strange kinds of electrical components and subassemblies. Szilard picked something up and thrust it into Wigner's hand. It was a thin board of some greenish, translucent substance, covered on one side by a pattern of metallic lines and shapes, and on the other by several rows of small, black, rectangular capsules and an arrangement of colored disklike and rodlike objects. Szilard pointed at one of the black capsules. "That's the equivalent of a whole electrical cabinet, Eugene!" he exclaimed. "It contains microscopic configurations of silicon crystal—equivalent to thousands of vacuum tubes—more than you could get in the room!" Wigner turned the board over in his hands and stared at it, nonplussed. Teller shook his head incredulously.

"What does it do?" Winslade asked for them. "Oh, things like this, for example." He moved forward and tapped at a typewriter-like keyboard. The screen in front of him activated to read, COMMAND MODE. Winslade entered the word BASIC, which appeared letter by letter as he typed. Evidently he was writing direct to the screen. The questions MEM ALLOC? and FILES? whatever they meant, followed, and to each he tapped in a response. It was uncanny. Winslade was actually interacting—conducting a dialogue—with the machine.

Finally the word READY appeared, and Winslade typed RUN "TICK TACK." A moment later, the heading WELCOME TO COMPUTER TICK TACK TOE appeared at the top of the screen, and below it the familiar grid. At the bottom, a caption advised I'LL PLAY "O." YOU PLAY "X," and asked WHOSE MOVE FIRST? (Y/M). Winslade typed Y, and at once an O filled one of the corner boxes.

"Care to try your game?" Winslade asked, turning to face his two speechless guests. "Or would you prefer chess?"

"And this is just trivial!" Szilard interjected, waving his hands at the other two excitedly. "It can calculate—algebraic and trig functions, hyperbolics, matrices, whatever you want—in seconds! It remembers information—anything. You can recall things and change things in an instant. It can draw pictures—graphs, functions, shapes. It practically understands English!"

Neither Teller nor Wigner could form a coherent question just at that moment. Winslade looked from one to another for a few seconds, not without some amusement and then said, "Leo is right. This is a triviality. You will be wondering, of course, who we are, what we are doing here, and how it comes to concern yourselves. Excuse my taking something of a liberty like this, but I'm sure that when you know the answers you'll agree this was the quickest way to avoid a lot of tedious questions and possible misunderstandings. Follow me, if you will, gentlemen."

He led them to a door that led through a high partition extending almost from one side of the building to the other. On the far side they stopped dead, their mouths hanging open and eyes wide with disbelief.

In front of them was an enormous machine unlike anything either of them had ever seen. Its general form was a cylinder eight to ten feet in diameter, lying horizontally in a heavy steel framework with its underside about six feet up from the floor and the near end almost over their heads. The other end disappeared into a tangle of pipes and cables, immense electrical windings, contoured yoke-pieces, and ancillary latticework, making it impossible to judge its length. More machinery and electrical equipment filled the spaces in the framework beneath. An overhead railed platform, reached by several steel ladders leading up from the floor at various places, projected from the side of the cylinder and ran completely around it at its midheight level. Teller had seen some strange experimental apparatus in laboratories on both sides of the Atlantic, and machinery employed by all kinds of industries, but never anything like this. Its purpose was unimaginable.

They followed a narrow walkway along the floor below the

machine, between workbenches, boxes, metal housings, and cubicles, stepping over tubes and cable runs, and ducking their heads to avoid supporting struts and girders. As they picked their way through toward the rear of the building, Winslade remarked casually on some of the things around them. "Superconducting magnets generating fifty thousand gauss. The windings are kept at four degrees Kelvin by liquid helium, and carry up to forty thousand amperes per square centimeter. Not bad, eh?

"Waveguides transmitting electromagnetic energy at microwave frequencies—gigacycles per second. Just what you'd need for an echo-principle aircraft detection system."

They reached the end forty feet farther on, where the cylinder terminated in a steel, boxlike construction facing out over a wide end-section of the railed platform. An opening the size of a garage doorway led into the box, and blocks, chains, and lifting tackle hung from the roof above.

At the rear of the building, they left the space housing the machine and went through a door in another partition to find themselves in a suddenly more domestic and homey setting of closets and easy chairs, a table with cards scattered on top, the smell of cooking wafting from not far away, books, magazines, a coffeepot in one corner, and a radio turned low. Two more men were waiting here, and Winslade introduced them as Captain Payne and Sergeant Lamson, both, like Major Warren, from the Army. The group comprised a dozen persons, all told, Winslade said, but the others were elsewhere at that moment.

"So who are we, and what do we want?" Winslade swung around to face Teller and Wigner squarely. "We can help with many of the problems that you are involved with currently. For example, you, Eugene, are working with Leo, trying to answer a lot of questions concerning neutron moderators. Graphite seems suitable, but you need to know the path-length for slowing fission neutrons down to the right energy for capture." He looked at Teller. "But for an explosive device, will concentrated U-235 chain-react with fast neutrons? If so, what critical mass would be required, and how rapidly would it have to be assembled? I could go on."

Teller looked thunderstruck. "Now, just a minute," he whispered in a horrified voice. "How do you know what problems we are working on? This is a—a highly sensitive area. I . . ." He shook his head and looked at Wigner. "I don't understand. What's going on?"

"I don't know, Edward." Wigner was looking just as lost. He turned back toward Winslade. "Who are you? What department of the government are you from?" he demanded.

Szilard had been bottling up his emotions for as long as he was able. "That's a time machine out there!" he shouted, hopping from one foot to another and jabbing his finger in the direction they had come from. "They're not from anywhere in this world at all. They've come back from the future—back from 1975!"

Teller looked at Wigner. Wigner looked at Teller. They both looked at Szilard, then at Winslade, and finally back at each other. "He's gone mad," Teller said in a flat voice. But at the same time there was a curious undertone hinting that he already half believed it. The look in Wigner's eyes said the same thing.

Winslade nodded. "Yes, we are from the future," he said. "Therefore, naturally, we know something of your work. But we have our problems, too. The machine out there is called a return-gate. Its function is to establish a return connection to our own times, via which information and objects may be transmitted. It has been constructed to specification and operates correctly according to all our test procedures, but we are unable to make contact with the 1975 end. The situation is especially strange because we appeared to have made contact successfully with this end before we left." Winslade spread his hands and shrugged. "We want to know what's gone wrong."

CHAPTER
17

THE VAST MILITARY BUREAUCRACY that directed and administered the German war machine was centralized in a group of massive, imposing buildings lying along Bendlerstrasse, in Berlin. On a corner of Bendlerstrasse and a stone quay fronting the Landwehr Canal, the Ministry of Defense stood behind a classically columned façade approached by broad stone steps. Farther along the street lay the Headquarters of the Army General Staff, its gray fieldstone complex stretching back almost as far as the landscaped meadows and lakes of the Tiergarten. Numbers 72–76 of what was called Tirpitz Ufer, a roadway by one of the side canals, belonged to the austere, five-storey granite edifice that was headquarters of the Abwehr, the German military intelligence service.

In an office situated at a corner of the building on the third floor, two floors below the office of Admiral Wilhelm Canaris, the department's chief, Lieutenant Colonel Joachim Boeckel read a routine copy of a report that had come through from the Bremen branch, which handled most of the espionage and general intelligence information from the United States. The report was from a former Baltic ferry master of the Stettin, Malmö, and Copenhagen runs, who, although he had been living in the New York area for five years now, was still a loyal Nazi and eager to further the cause. He was still in the sailing business and had acquired a sizable boat, and Berlin had stayed in touch because of his knowledge of local waters and potential usefulness in getting other agents ashore in times to come if the need arose. His name was Walther Fritsch. Lately, it seemed, he had run into problems with some criminals who wanted to use his boat.

Boeckel smiled and looked up to call across to his trim and shapely, raven-haired secretary, tapping at a battered typewriter behind a paper-strewn desk in the opposite corner. "Hey, Hildegarde, listen to this. Do you remember grand-admiral Walther, who sends us snippets from America?"

Hildegarde stopped typing. "Oh, yes, the one with the boat. What's he done now?"

"Roosevelt and the Jews must be onto him," Boeckel said. "They've sent in their underworld to rub him out."

"Are you being serious?"

Boeckel grinned. "Apparently, some gangster was trying to pressure him into handing over his boat for some reason or other. Poor Walther got a bit roughed up. That niece who moved over with him was involved, too."

"Was it bad?"

"Oh, no, he's all right. But he talks here about a mysterious band of black-clad desperadoes who materialized from nowhere, stormed the house in which he and the girl were being held, vanquished the villains, and got them out. It even made the New York papers—here's a clipping. Ever hear a story like that before?"

Hildegarde regarded him dubiously from beneath long, black eyelashes. "Lots of times," she said. "Do you think he's very . . . stable?"

"Oh, it's wildly exaggerated, no doubt of that," Boeckel said. "Probably he got himself mixed up in a feud between rival gangs or something. But you're right—the strain might be getting to him. . . ." He frowned and added absently, "We might need him for some quite important operations one day. I do hope we can trust his reliability."

Hildegarde came around her desk to open one of the filing cabinets near Boeckel. "American decadence is getting to him," she said as she stooped to consult a document inside one of the folders.

Boeckel looked approvingly at the curves of her body through her crisp white blouse and black skirt. He patted her behind and allowed his fingers to linger lasciviously for a moment. Hildegarde tutted reproachfully, but didn't move.

"Can I take you to dinner tonight?" Boeckel asked. "Hoeffner's again, maybe? You liked the band there."

"But not the people."

Boeckel shrugged. "Okay. Then somewhere else."

"Hmm . . . something tells me that you've more than just dinner in mind."

"What could possibly give you such an idea?"

"Oh, young, handsome lieutenant-colonels are all the same."

"Really? And how might you know?"

"Never mind."

"Very well, I admit it." Boeckel tossed up his hands. "So, what's wrong with good, old-fashioned, German decadence?"

Hildegarde smiled as she went back to her chair and sat down. "I can meet you after seven," she said. "But don't act so presumptuously. It's not nice to be taken for granted." Boeckel initialed the report on his desk and tossed it across to her. "What do you want me to do with it?" Hildegarde asked.

"Well, let's not dismiss it too offhandedly. Put it in the carry-forward file to come out for review, oh, say two months from now. We'll see what else has happened then. But if you ask me, Hildegarde, I think you're right—it's the American culture. Our friend the grand admiral has been reading too many *Superman* comics and allowing his imagination to be carried away by them."

CHAPTER
18

NEWS CAME FROM ARTHUR Bannering in England of what at last seemed like a significant alteration of events: Chamberlain had agreed to the demands the Russians had been pressing for high-level military talks on concrete defense measures.

In the Proteus team's previous world, the British and French governments had persistently declined this proposal because of their reluctance to divulge military secrets without a political treaty; on the other hand, as evidenced by their choice of Strang to go to Moscow, they had been in no great hurry to conclude any treaty. This had confirmed Stalin's suspicions and strengthened his resolve not to be drawn into a Polish commitment, which would have been purely academic in any case, since the Poles had remained just as determined not to allow Russian troops through their territory. This had given the British Cabinet its excuse not to pursue the defense treaty with the Russians: they had shown themselves before the eyes of the world to have been willing, and it would be Poland's own fault now if she were invaded.

Sure enough, she was—four days later, on August 26. To satisfy world opinion the British and French went ahead soon afterward with their declaration of the sham war against Germany which Hitler had been expecting. The Polish campaign was over by the month's end. Through it, Stalin sat tight and presented an impenetrable face, while behind the scenes his own preparations went ahead frantically. For now that the Germans and Russians were facing each other across a common border, there could no longer be any doubt what the Germans were preparing for, just as soon as Hitler extricated himself from his Western entanglement.

But now, in this world, it was still July. The sudden show of solidarity with the Russians might be enough to deter Hitler from launching the attack, Anna Kharkiovitch thought as she gazed at the gray, foam-flecked waters of the Bay of Biscay. But this would be the last opportunity to save the situation in Europe. Everything depended on its being seized and exploited vigorously.

Beside her, Gordon Selby closed the magazine that he had been thumbing idly. They had flown from Miami to Lisbon on Pan Am's newly inaugurated transatlantic Clipper passenger service, and stayed overnight at the Hotel Duas Nocas to await a connection to Poole, in Dorsetshire, on an Imperial Airways flying-boat from South Africa.

"You know, I think I've come to terms with it," Selby said, turning his head and leaning across to speak closer to her ear. After twelve hours in the air the day before, they had learned to be almost oblivious to the constant roar of four sixteen-cylinder aero-engines. "If we do end up being stranded back here, we might be better off in the long run."

Anna nodded as if she had been expecting something like that. "And you're wondering if Claud knew it would happen."

Selby looked surprised. "How did you know?"

"I've been wondering, too."

"Well, what do you think?"

Anna studied his face. "Out of curiosity, what difference would it make to you?" she asked. "Do you have any ties that would make you want to go back?"

Selby shook his head. "None, really."

"No family or anything?"

"My parents were in the Congo when it was overrun and didn't get out fast enough—my father was a mining engineer there. Nobody ever found out what happened to them."

"How old were you then?"

"About twelve. I was back in the States when it happened, on school vacation. I finished growing up in an orphans' home and never got close to anybody. I wanted to be an engineer, though. It seemed . . . well, like a way of respecting my dad, I guess. Maybe a psychiatrist would tell me that I ended up in nuclear engineering because of a subconscious desire to make bombs to throw back at them before it was all over."

Anna smiled. "You think so?"

"I don't know, but I cheered as loud as anybody when Kennedy stood up and said we were through with being pushed around."

"You see, it's the same with all of us," Anna said. "Nobody on the team has any compelling reason for wanting to go back, and everyone has a score to settle with Hitlerism. It's as if Claud picked us with that in mind."

Selby pursed his lips behind his black, pointed beard. "So, are you saying that Claud knew the gate wasn't going to work?" he asked.

"I don't know. Let's just say that I don't think he was taken completely by surprise. I believe he was hoping for the best, but he was prepared for the worst when it happened."

Selby nodded. "I know what you mean. Why did he pick the particular mix of people we've got, for example? Some good technicians and a couple of engineers would have been enough to assemble the gate. Were a historian and a diplomat necessary?"

"Exactly. And were all the military people necessary for security?" Anna asked. "Even if they were, why do they all just happen to be experienced in overseas undercover work, especially in Germany?"

The Sunderland droned on, and parts of the French coast came into view in the haze on the horizon ahead. After a minute or two of silence, Anna asked, "Does Claud want the gate to work, do you think? Or is this business about Einstein just a ploy to keep up morale until we've all adjusted to the idea of not going back?"

"You mean did he knowingly abandon a lost cause in our world for the chance of a different outcome here?"

"Yes—just that."

Selby thought for a while, then shook his head. "I don't think so. Sure, he was prepared for what's happened, but he'll do everything possible to get the connection working if he can. Claud can be objective and calculating when the job demands it, but he's human underneath. He wouldn't just leave our world to its fate, with complete disregard for the people in it who were relying on us."

"What makes you think that?"

"The fact that I'm here, on this plane."

"So?"

"My field is nuclear weapons, which is no doubt the reason I'm on the mission. If Claud's only interest were defeating Hitler in order to build a nice, comfortable world to live in, the most important thing would be to get an American A-bomb program moving, okay? Well, if that was what he wanted, I'd be back there helping to start it." Selby spread his hands briefly. "But Claud didn't do that. Instead he sent me over to Europe. Why? To get me out of the way for a while and make sure that the scientists back there aren't distracted from the thing he wants them to concentrate on, which can only be the gate. That says to me that he's serious about Einstein. I'm just the insurance in case it doesn't work and we end up having to make our own bomb."

Anna nodded and seemed relieved. "Yes," she agreed. "That was how I saw it, too. I was hoping so much that you'd say that."

They lapsed into silence for a while. Then Selby looked up from his magazine again and said, "What about Cassidy, though? He's got a reason for wanting to go back."

Anna turned her head. "Because of that girl he talks about? Oh, you can't take that too seriously. You know what Cassidy's like."

"You don't think he is engaged, then?"

"Quite possibly he is, or maybe was, once. . . . But do you really think it would be so much of a tragedy if they didn't go through with it?"

Selby rubbed his nose with a knuckle and grinned faintly. "I guess not. But then the whole thing was bizarre from the beginning. I mean, Cassidy's okay in his own way, but he can be a bum. How did he ever get mixed up with a family like hers anyway?"

"Bum?"

Selby tossed his hands up in a candid gesture. "Well he is, isn't he? Let's be honest."

Anna looked at him curiously for a few seconds. "You don't really know Cassidy, do you, Gordon?"

"Why, what's there to know?"

"He comes from one of the wealthiest families in the southwest—the direct heir to an oil and minerals fortune. But he despised the people around him for living lives of luxurious banality at a time when the country had its back to the wall, so he walked out and became a plain trooper in the Army. As you said, Claud would never have picked the kind of jerk that Cassidy sometimes pretends to be."

Selby stared at her in astonishment. "How do you know about it?" he asked.

"Harry told me the story after we arrived in New Mexico— we were driving into Albuquerque in one of the trucks for something or other. I'd been a bit hard on Cassidy over something, and Harry wanted to straighten the situation out. Those two work well together."

That would have been typical, Selby thought. Harry wasn't the team's greatest talker, but for some reason it seemed natural for him to have confided something like this to Anna. "Hmm, strange," he remarked. "You seem to have a knack for getting along with the troops."

"It's not really strange," Anna told him. "When I was younger, I fought with the Siberian partisans for five years before I got out. I'd killed ten Nazis by the time I was seventeen. When I was eighteen, an SS colonel ordered all the men in my family's village to be shot. I went to bed with him so that I could cut his throat while he was asleep. You see, Gordon, Special Operations soldiers and I speak the same language."

Back at Gatehouse, Professor George Pegram, head of the Physics Department and Dean of the Graduate Schools at Columbia, had collapsed weakly into one of the chairs in the mess area, stunned from the things he had learned in the last sixty minutes. Winslade, Greene, Scholder, and others from the Proteus team, along with the three Hungarian physicists, were standing and sitting in various positions nearby. Pegram had been out of town, and over a week had gone by since Szilard's first frantic phone calls from Gatehouse to Teller and Wigner.

"Before you recover your wits, George, yes, we know there are seemingly impossible logical contradictions," Szilard said. "But trying to grapple with them at this stage would be futile. Take it from me—I've tried. We all have. So has Lindemann over in England. It needs a different kind of approach, a mind with a knack for questioning the obvious and for seeing the problem from the angle that everyone else misses. That's why we want Einstein."

"More than just Einstein," Winslade said from where he was standing in the middle of the floor. "According to our original plan, the President and certain members of the government should already have become involved. I don't see any reason why a technical hitch should justify delaying that any further, especially since we may find we need access to all kinds of resources that a word from the White House could unlock."

"In short, we approach the President through Einstein," Teller said to Pegram.

Pegram blinked dazedly, shook his head, and at last found his voice. "Yes, I can see what you're saying. But why not go to Roosevelt direct in the first place?"

"Think about it, George," Wigner suggested. "Fermi and Tuve were thrown out as cranks when they tried a direct approach to the government, just to get backing for fission research. Do you really want to be the one to go back and tell them we're into time machines now?"

Pegram nodded glumly. Wigner was right. Szilard had received a letter only a few days earlier, politely but firmly turning down their second attempt at interesting the Navy. "Einstein's prestige would carry the right weight," Pegram agreed. "But how is he going to get the message to Roosevelt? I mean, with all due respect to him, could we rely on him to carry out a job like that? You've heard the stories. . . ."

"I have negotiated suitable arrangements already," Szilard said, sounding just a little officious. "Gustav Stolper, the Austrian economist, recently introduced me to somebody called Alexander Sachs, who's an economics consultant to the Lehman Corporation and also a personal friend of the President's. I've talked to Sachs, and he has agreed to deliver a letter to Roosevelt personally, signed by Einstein."

Pegram looked aghast. "You've talked to him already? For God's sake, Leo, we can't allow information of this kind to—"

"Oh, of course, I didn't tell him anything about Proteus or the machine here," Szilard said impatiently. "We're using uranium research and the possibility of a fission bomb as a cover story. The real subject will be divulged later, only to Roosevelt in person."

Pegram looked at Winslade. "You're happy about this, Claud?"

"Oh, yes. Leo was kind enough to clear it with us before he said anything to Sachs," Winslade replied.

There was nothing more to be said. Pegram looked around one more time and then nodded. "Very well, let's go and talk to Einstein. Can you arrange a meeting in Princeton, Leo?"

"He's not there," Szilard replied. "The last I heard was that he's rented a cabin or something somewhere and gone off to sail his boat. So, first we'll have to find him."

And so it came about that on Sunday, July 30, 1939, while Teller and Pegram were at Gatehouse with Greene studying the construction of the machine, Leo Szilard and Eugene Wigner found themselves driving with Winslade and Scholder in Wigner's car, looking for a summer house belonging to a Dr. Moore, somewhere in the vicinity of Peconic, Long Island.

CHAPTER
19

IT WAS PAST 3:00 A.M., and Stan Shaw, "your very good friend, the Milkman," was babbling a cheerful news bulletin between commercials on WNEW's all-night radio program. Ferracini was dozing, chin on his chest and chair tilted back to rest his feet on the large table in the center of the mess area. Cassidy was sprawled in an armchair behind a newspaper, and Floyd Lamson was sitting on the floor with his back to the wall by the coffeepot, whittling an owl from a piece of wood to add to the collection of animal forms that was beginning to adorn the room. The rest of the team at Gatehouse were either asleep or with Einstein and the other visitors, who were still examining the machine.

Ferracini was picturing again the house that he had lived in as a boy, a yellow-painted wooden house with a brown shingled roof, near the gas station that one of his Uncle Frank's brothers owned. He remembered Frank, lean and muscular, coming home from the construction jobs he worked on across the river in Manhattan and talking over dinner about ball games and plans for fishing trips. When the news in the papers was bad, he talked about the things the Nazis were doing in Asia and Africa. Aunt Teresa would become very quiet when Frank talked about things like that.

In the evening, Frank and Harry would sometimes listen to a

fight on the radio, with Frank blocking and jabbing to the commentary as he followed the action blow by blow. Some nights he would shower, change, and pack his kit to go to one of the clubs where he boxed himself, or watched a match. On those nights, sometimes, Aunt Teresa used to sit down with Harry by the fireside and tell stories about the old days in Italy before Mussolini and the Fascists.

Life then sounded so simple and carefree, with lots of singing, dancing, and weddings in the village church. The world had seemed to be just a small community of relatives, friends, and familiar faces such as Father Buivento, Luigi the Mayor, Dino the wagonmaker, Rodolfo the dairyman, and more whom Ferracini could still picture from his childhood imaginings. His fantasies had mirrored the security and contentment of the age at which he had created them; sometimes, in harsher moments of later years—waiting inside a troop carrier to parachute out into the Greenland night during arctic training, maybe, or lying motionless for hours on an Alpine ridge while search parties with dogs combed the slopes below—he had thought back wistfully to that make-believe world of warmth and caring, where everybody knew everybody and all had a place to belong.

Now, strangely, he felt he had found something very close to that in the New York of 1939. The remoteness from their own times was forging a bond among the members of the team that made them seem like a family in many ways; and the circle of regulars at Max's, the Indian restaurant upstairs, Mooney's bar along the block, the pool parlor across the street, and other places that Ferracini was getting to know had a friendly familiarity that was a new experience to him.

Back in January, he remembered, he had felt contempt for the America that he had found existing before the holocaust years of the forties; but something in his perceptions had changed since then. Although Roosevelt's New Deal had included its share of failures and miscalculations, it had nevertheless succeeded in inspiring the nation with the determination it needed to help itself. And the nation, responding with rugged optimism, had pulled itself through the economic blizzard of the thirties, its basic human values of compassion and respect for individual freedom still intact. It had avoided succumbing to the forces of tyranny, hatred, mob-rule, and violence, which the same problems had unleashed across Europe. Ferracini was beginning to think that there was something to be proud of and a lot that was worth preserving in a people who could do that.

"Says here that with good behavior, and providing he pays the twenty grand he owes, Alphonse Capone'll be eligible for release from jail in November," Cassidy announced over the paper that he was reading.

"Where's he at?" Lamson asked from his position on the floor.

"Some place called Terminal Island off San Pedro, California."

"Well, I hope he behaves himself and stays in line this time," Lamson drawled. "Otherwise, we might have to teach him some manners, too, like Bruno." He set down his knife and turned the wooden owl in his hands to inspect it. "What kind of rap did they get him on in the end?" he asked.

"Forgot to mail his taxes," Cassidy said.

Lamson shook his head reprovingly. "Didn't make his protection payments, huh? Well, I guess that's what happens."

At that moment, the door leading to the machine area opened softly, and Einstein appeared. Cassidy put down his paper. Ferracini took his feet off the table and sat up. Lamson set aside his owl and rose awkwardly to his feet. Einstein held up a hand and seemed apologetic for the intrusion.

"Please, any need to disturb yourselves, there is not," he said in his quaint, heavily accented English as he came in and shuffled across to the table. "I am looking to get the cup of tea, if possible. Back there, politics they are all talking—such a dreary subject, even for one who understands, which I do not pretend to. So I ask where the bathroom is, and I sneak away." He winked conspiratorially at Ferracini and whispered behind a raised hand, "I can always tell them I get lost trying to find the way back. It's amazing what you can get away with when you're supposed to be absent-minded."

Although he had, by this time, acquired a snowy halo of wispy hair, Einstein was noticeably younger than the image depicted in the better known photographs of later years. He had a high forehead, dimpled cheeks, and a stubborn chin. His eyelids drooped downward at the sides, and in combination with his ragged mustache, would have given his face something of the look of a sad walrus, were it not for his bright eyes and the mischievous half-smile playing around his mouth. He was wearing a frayed brown sweater and shapeless pants, and had arrived with Szilard and Wigner early in the evening.

The others eyed each other uncertainly for a few awkward seconds. "Tea," Lamson mumbled. "We got some hot water here. Don't know about any tea, though. . . ."

"In the cupboard underneath," Cassidy prompted.

"Where the sugar and cream are," Ferracini said needlessly.

"Oh, yeah . . . lemme take a look."

Einstein pulled up a chair and sat down at the table, at the same time stretching the neck of his sweater to take his pipe from a shirt pocket. "You know, this year I have my sixtieth birthday. In all this time, never do I learn to drive the automobile, and only just have I mastered the intricacies of a camera—too much fiddling and twiddling and fussing, you understand." He gestured over his shoulder with the stem of his pipe. "And now this machine of yours you spring on me—an old man, set in his ways and his thoughts, who was foolish enough to believe he had caught a glimpse of how God was thinking when He designed the universe. Always I am telling myself that when we see complications in Nature, then what we are looking at is not yet the truth. Underneath, truth is always the simplest. But now this! How am I to reconcile the things I am hearing now with the faith I refuse to abandon that Nature reasonable and orderly is, and unreasonably malicious is not?"

Lamson squatted down and buried his face in the cupboard, while Cassidy made an extended performance of folding his paper. Loyalty in combat situations and so forth was all very fine, but this was something else: Harry was on his own.

Ferracini swallowed and made a conscious effort to look smarter than he felt just at that moment. "That sounds kind of strange, sir—Professor," he stammered.

"'Dr. Einstein' is good," Einstein said. "So what is so strange, Captain, yes? Or is it the first name that you prefer, being American?"

"Harry's fine—everyone else uses it here, anyhow. . . . Oh, you being confused by something complicated, I guess. Most people think of you as being about as complicated as a guy can get."

"Is not true, Harry." Einstein looked around him invitingly. "And? . . ."

"Er . . . oh, I'm Cassidy."

"Floyd."

"Harry, Cassidy, and Floyd. You know, always I have used just one soap for the shaving and for the face-washing. Most people, they use two soaps. But, I ask, why there is need to use two soaps? Those are the things that make life too fiddling and twiddling, like cameras—more things to do that aren't important, and more things to remember that don't matter. So always I use just one soap."

Ferracini was perplexed. Here was probably the greatest physicist of the century, he'd been told—supposedly, one of the greatest minds of all time, who had just been confronted by people from the future and the reality of time-travel—looking like a benign, Chaplinesque grandfather and rambling on genially about cameras and shaving soap. Ferracini didn't know what he was supposed to say. Army training hadn't covered situations like this. The other two seemed to be having the same problem.

"So you are with the Army," Einstein said, pulling tobacco from a worn pouch that he had produced from somewhere and packing the tobacco into his pipe. "Cassidy and Floyd, you are sergeants, I was told earlier—yes?"

"That's right," Cassidy said.

Einstein nodded. "In Switzerland, when I was a young man, they turn me down for military service, because I have flat feet and varicose veins, they say. But then, perhaps, it was more serious in the world that you are from. The whole country has become a military camp, to me it sounds."

That was a tricky subject. Einstein had refused vehemently to have anything to do with German militarism at the time of the Great War, and the soldiers were unsure how to respond without risking offense. Cassidy said cautiously, "It had gone past politics or economics. The only choice we had left was to surrender what we believed in, or else to defend it with everything we had. If you'd seen the things that were happening all over the rest of the world. . ."

"But I have seen the things which for years now are already happening in Germany," Einstein said. Just for a moment there was a hint of sharpness in his voice. He nodded in acknowledgment as Lamson placed an enamel mug of steaming tea in front of him, then relaxed with a smile and a sigh. "Your worrying is not necessary, Cassidy. People, they do not understand. . . ."

"*Wir können uns auch auf Deutsch unterhalten, wenn es Ihnen lieber ist,*" Lamson interjected as he sat down. (We can continue the conversation in German, if you prefer.)

Einstein's eyebrows shot upward in surprise. "*Das habe ich wirklich nicht erwartet, dass ihr alle Deutsch sprecht!*" (I really didn't expect this—that you all speak German!)

"We've all worked overseas in Nazi Europe," Ferracini said, switching to German also. "You had to speak German to get picked for those kinds of operations."

"So where did you learn it?" Einstein asked, looking around the table.

"Army school, most of us," Cassidy told him. "The training was intensive in everything. It had to be—your life was at stake, usually for months at a time."

Einstein nodded. "Yes, I suppose so. . . . But, anyway, where were we? Ah, yes—people don't understand. Because I refused to contribute to the war effort in 1914, they think I'm one of these pacifists who want us to pay any price for peace, as if 'peace' could be anything but an illusion under those terms."

"You're not?" Lamson, who had decided that Einstein was human after all, sounded mildly surprised.

"Not if it leads to the kind of world that you three are from." Einstein held a match to his pipe and puffed several times. "Certainly, I deplore aggression and violence as a way of solving problems. They can only lead to worse grievances and problems in the long run. But being prepared to defend yourself if you have to is not the same thing. This monstrosity consuming Europe is a cancer of the tissues of civilization. When the body is infected, it mobilizes its antibodies and destroys that which is alien to it. So, too, must the planetary organism. In other words, I accept, regretfully, that there are some evils that can only be stopped by force. Appealing to their better nature is as futile as attempting to reason with a virus."

Einstein shrugged. "So, when, in Belgium, they asked me if young men should go to do military service, I answered that they should not only go, but go cheerfully, because they would be helping to save European civilization. But the pacifists, who had misunderstood my position all along and tried to adopt me as a patron saint, howled in fury and denounced me as a traitor."

"Maybe they were accusing you more of being inconsistent," Lamson suggested. Ferracini was surprised. For Lamson to express an opinion about anything in more than a grunt or a monosyllable was unusual. Einstein seemed to be having the same effect on all of them.

Einstein shook his head. "Really, there is no inconsistency. I am opposed to the cult of militarism and the suppression of freedom by force of any kind. Twenty-five years ago, resisting war served that goal. With the situation that exists today, however, the only hope that the free nations have for survival is the strength of their armed forces. So, the means that are different superficially, at a deeper level serve the same end." He thought for a moment, and his eyes twinkled. "Or, as I suppose you might say, 'Everything is relative.'"

Ferracini grinned faintly and caught Cassidy's eye. Cassidy nodded back in a way that said, this guy is okay.

Lamson shifted his weight in his chair and frowned, then looked up at Einstein. "So, do you think it's possible to avoid it— the kind of future we're from?" he asked. "Even if we do avoid the mistakes that led to that mess, who's to say we won't walk straight head-on into another one? There are plenty of mistakes around, just waiting to be made."

Einstein shrugged. "Maybe, maybe not . . . I'm no longer young enough to know everything. I suppose I still have faith in people, despite it all," he said.

"The older you get, the less you know?" Cassidy queried, raising an eyebrow.

"Oh, but it's very true," Einstein assured him. "Except for scientists, of course. They never know anything at all." The other three exchanged puzzled looks. "It's true," Einstein told them. He sipped his tea and puffed a cloud of smoke from his pipe. "Most of the world still doesn't have the faintest notion of what science is. They think it is all madmen in white coats who want to take over the world with giant cabbages that eat people . . . But science isn't a *thing* at all—like electricity or gravity or atoms. Those are *subjects* that might be studied in a scientific manner, but science is the *process* itself—the process of studying them, or anything else, for that matter. It is a process for arriving at conclusions about what is probably true, and what is probably not. That's all. Its end product is simply reliable information. And the problem of knowing what to believe—what is true and what is not—is surely the most important problem that the human race has been grappling with for as long as it has existed. How many isms and ologies have been invented, all purporting to have the answer? And what were their answers worth?" He looked around. The others waited without interrupting.

"Most systems set out to prove or rationalize something that they have made their minds up about already. But that's a hopeless way to proceed if what you really want to know is the truth. Science doesn't do that. Its goal is to understand what's really out there—what the world is really like—and it accepts that whatever the reality is, it will be totally uninfluenced by what you or I might choose to think, or by how many others we might persuade to agree with us. The truth isn't impressed and doesn't care. That's why scientists don't pay much attention to debating skills. We leave those to lawyers and theologians. The eloquence and emotional appeal of the way ideas are presented has nothing to do with whether they're right or not."

"Pretty obvious when you think about it," Cassidy commented. "Just plain common sense."

"But that's all science is, Cassidy," Einstein said. "Formalized common sense. And since the purpose is to understand the world as it really is, and not to persuade anybody of anything in particular, there is no place for deception, especially unconscious self-deception. You can't get away with fooling yourself. Because all that will happen at the end of the process if you fail to detect your errors is that your aeroplane won't fly. The laws of

Nature, you see, can't be deceived. So there is a strong underlying ethical principle woven into the very fabric of the scientific process—something which is all too often overlooked. Wouldn't it be nice if the same were true in certain other fields of human activity?"

Einstein put down the mug and sat back to spread his hands on the table. "So instead of trying to prop up the things that it would like to be true, science does the opposite—it tries everything it can think of to bring its ideas down. That's what experiments are designed to do—to prove theories false. And if the theory survives, it comes out so much the stronger. Hence, like an evolutionary process, which indeed it is, science is all the time testing itself and correcting itself. It thrives on questions, challenges, dissent, and criticism. The most ruthless scrutiny that it is subjected to is its own. And so it stays healthy and grows sturdier.

"But how pathetic and fragile are the systems of thought that daren't expose their followers to any dissenting view or alternative explanation. Such systems are forced to ban what they have no answers for, and to suppress everything they can't compete with. Eventually, they wither, and they die. Eventually, the oppressors always end up being buried by their intended victims."

Einstein took his pipe from his mouth and nodded solemnly. "So it will be with Hitler and his 'Reich that will last a thousand years,'" he assured his listeners. "And that, gentlemen, is why I continue to have faith in people."

CHAPTER
20

THE CLASSICAL NEWTONIAN UNIVERSE was an orderly affair of billiard-ball particles hurtling around on gravitational and electromagnetic trajectories and bouncing off one another according to straightforward rules which in principle operated down to arbitrarily small scales of magnitude. Thus, it was a vast machine, and only the limits of observational accuracy and the sheer number of observations that would have been required prevented the motions of all its parts from being specified precisely at any instant that might be chosen. Every past and future state of the machine, everything that had happened in it, was happening, or would happen, could then be computed by applying Newtonian laws to this all-embracing snapshot and extrapolating it forward or backward in time. Whether such a stupendous computation was possible in practice was beside the point; the conclusion still followed that the universe was determinate, its future states unfolding as inevitably from past conditions as the cycles of the planets or the alignments of parts in a clockwork toy. This might have been good news for hedonists or conscience-plagued criminals, but it bothered those who believed in free will and liked to believe that free will had some part to play in the shaping of humanity's future.

By the close of the nineteenth century, however, the straws

of irrefutable experimental data were accumulating on the back of accepted theory, and the revolution in physics that followed had, by the 1920s, permanently demolished any notion of the subatomic realm as simply a Newtonian world in miniature. It was made up not of intuitively familiar, billiard-ball-like objects that occupied definite positions in space, moved along exact paths, and behaved generally as ordinary things do; rather, it was made up of perplexing new conceptual entities without parallel at the everyday level, which could be described accurately only in the abstract mathematical formulations that emerged as quantum mechanics.

Of particular consequence, events in the quantum-mechanical world were not determinate: A given present situation did not lead inexorably to an automatically defined future one. What was usually described as a particle, for example, ceased being a solid, immutable "thing" located in a pointlike "place", and became something that physicists called a "wave function"—a vibrating haze that moved and spread through space, its shape and density pattern changing continually.

A haze made up of what?

Nothing that had any physical attributes. But when it encountered another such entity, for example, by interacting with a measuring instrument designed to find out something about it, the act of interaction caused it to take on the properties more commonly thought of as "particle," which would instantly localize somewhere within the volume where the haze had been. Where it would localize exactly, nobody could say for sure. All anyone could say was where, probably. The density of the haze at any point as it vibrated and changed gave, from instant to instant, the probability that the particle would be found at that point.

Quantum-mechanical billiards, therefore, was played with the balls zipping around inside separate smokescreens, and it was never possible to predict in advance precisely what the outcome of a given collision would be. But it was possible to predict what it would probably be, and such predictions could be tested by experiments based on repeating an event many times and observing how frequently its various possible outcomes, in fact, occurred. Judged on the basis of its predictions in this way, quantum mechanics turned out to be, perhaps, science's most successful theory ever.

The universe was no longer clockwork; but neither had it reverted to being clay capable of being molded to freely expressed human will, either. For the laws of chance had replaced those of determinism. The idea of dice running the universe bothered some people even more than that of rigid causality. One of the most notable among them was Albert Einstein.

"Niels Bohr and I went over this again and again," he said in German to Winslade, Scholder, Teller, and Szilard. They were standing in one of the cluttered instrumentation bays below the raised walkway running alongside the return-gate cylinder. They had been studying a section of the system, and on the far side of a partition wall formed by electrical panels and a vacuum pump, Wigner, Greene, and others from the Proteus team, were repeating some of the tests. "The thought of being a lemon in a fruit machine has always struck me as even more repugnant than being a tooth on a cogwheel," Einstein said. "So, I view the theory as still incomplete. The reason it yields uncertainties is that experiments aren't sensitive enough yet to uncover the variables that operate at even finer levels."

Szilard shook his head. "I've never accepted that. If there's no experimental evidence of such variables, then there's no justification for assuming they exist."

"I feel the same way," Teller agreed. "Only the mathematical formalism has been verified, nothing else. The idea of invisible variables serves no other purpose than to satisfy your ideological conviction, Albert. It's imposed metaphysics, not physics."

"So, you don't subscribe to any interpretation," Scholder said.

Teller spread his hands. "Give me a guideline to construct one, and I'll consider anything. But if it's based on intuition, it will probably be misleading and hinder more than help. We've seen that time and time again."

"What other approach is there?" Szilard asked.

"Allow the mathematical formalism to yield its own interpretation," Scholder replied. "Don't try to impose anything on it."

A faraway look came over Einstein's face. He stood up from the box that he had been sitting on and paced slowly toward the far wall, where he halted before a tool locker, his hands clasped behind his back. "Yes, philosophically that's an interesting proposition. . . ." he said.

The others watched him for a second, then looked away as Scholder went on, "Couldn't the big mistake all along have been in viewing the quantum realm as some kind of ghost world whose symbols represent only possibilities? Couldn't the symbols of quantum mechanics represent reality faithfully, just as much as those of classical theory?"

"Faithfully?" Teller glanced uncertainly at Szilard, then looked back at Scholder. "Well, anything's possible, I suppose. But what does that mean?"

Szilard frowned as he thought about it. "How could it even be possible?" he objected. "There are two ways in which the wave function of an object can change. It can evolve continuously and predictably in time in the manner described by its differential wave equation; or alternatively, it can interact with the wave function of another object, such as when an electron interacts with a measuring instrument, in which case the change is discontinuous and the result will be one of a number of discrete possible outcomes, each with a given probability. But the two are fundamentally different. The first implies an isolated system, and the second doesn't. That must give contradictions if we attempt to interpret it literally. How can an inherently self-contradicting model represent reality?"

"Perhaps it's our assumptions about reality that we should be questioning," Einstein suggested to the tool locker. He turned to face the others. "Very well, let us allow the mathematical formalism to yield its own interpretation. So, what kind of interpretation had it yielded by the twenty-first century, Dr. Scholder?"

"Contemporary physics regards the process of interaction—observation, if you will—as the collapsing of the wave function into one of its possible outcomes," Scholder replied. "Which particular one it will collapse into is indeterminate, and the various possibilities can only be assigned a probability distribution." The three twentieth-century scientists waited expectantly. Scholder went on, "But this collapsing process and the assignment of probabilities to the outcome do not follow from any of the dynamic equations of the system. They are consequences of an *a priori* convention imposed upon the formalism—an assumption every bit as metaphysical as what Edward accused Albert of a few minutes ago."

There was a short silence. "But what alternative is there to collapsing the wave function?" Szilard asked at last, looking puzzled.

"Not collapsing it," Scholder said. Nobody could dispute the logic of that.

Szilard brought a hand up to massage his eyebrows. "But if we don't collapse the function to one of its outcomes, we'll be left with all of them," he said slowly. "Wouldn't that force us to postulate the reality of all of them?"

A distant gleam had come into Einstein's eyes. He paused as if to recheck his thoughts before voicing them, and then began nodding slowly. "Yes, that is being honest, is it not?" he murmured half to himself. "Simply to take the mathematics as meaning what it says and not try to constrain it with preconceptions of what it ought to mean or how we think anything ought to be."

"That's right," Scholder said. "Now follow that through and face up to the implications squarely."

Szilard and Teller stared at each other as they grappled with the meaning of it. Then Einstein began nodding his head more vigorously. "Yes, why not?" he whispered. "The real universe could be far vaster than we have ever imagined—a gigantic superposition of staggering complexity, in which every interaction generates its own set of branching outcomes. And since there is nothing in the formalism to designate any branch as being any more real than any other, why can't they all be equally real?"

"Let's make sure I'm getting this right," Szilard said to Scholder. "You're saying that if there are n number of possible outcomes of an event, it isn't true that Nature somehow picks one of them arbitrarily, by chance."

Scholder shook his head. "Why one rather than another?"

"No rules. No reason." Einstein said. "Those are the dice that I have always said God doesn't play with."

"Then what instead?" Teller asked.

"All of them," Scholder replied simply. "When a die is rolled, why can't the decomposition of the state vector represent a branching function that leads to six different worlds, all equally real, where each one contains a different result?"

Teller slumped back in his chair by the electrical panels. Szilard got up and began pacing restlessly, rubbing his chin with a knuckle while he struggled to come to terms with the proposition.

Einstein looked at Scholder. "So, the unpredictability would follow not from one outcome's being selected randomly from a possible six, but from uncertainty about which of the six branches an individual would experience," he said. "In other words, which outcome would come to correlate with his sense of identity. His memories would be a correlated set of outcomes of previous interactions, a kind of path traced through a tree of constantly branching possibilities."

"Yes," Scholder said.

There was a short silence, interrupted only by the sound of Szilard's pacing and Payne's voice from the far side of the partition, muttering numbers to somebody. "But there would have to be a different copy of him in each of the six worlds," Szilard said at last. He stopped, and his eyes widened as the full implication registered. "Copies of everything, in fact—the world, everything—not just six times over, but for everything happening, everywhere. . . ."

"Now I think I am beginning to see a little more clearly where this is leading," Einstein said. He took out his pipe and began filling it.

Szilard went on, "Any cause, however microscopic, could ultimately propagate its effects throughout the universe. If what Kurt's saying is true, then every quantum transition in every star, every galaxy, every remote corner of the cosmos, is splitting the universe into copies. . . . Every one of countless billions of variations multiplying at the rate of countless billions every second . . . an infinitely branching tree in which everything that might happen, does happen . . . somewhere."

"You see what I meant by the universe being bigger than we thought," Einstein said. "What we perceive turns out to be an infinitesimally tiny part of the whole, a path traced through the totality by a correlated set of memories and impressions." He puffed his pipe and gave a satisfied nod. "I must say that it appeals to me. The entire ensemble is deterministic, for all possible outcomes of any cause are firmly embedded in it; and yet the path traced through it by an individual's experiences can be influenced by what we call free will, in ways we have yet to understand. Yes, gentlemen, this makes me feel much happier."

The other two nodded slowly as they took it all in. It was becoming clear now how multiple futures could exist that couldn't have evolved from present circumstances: how Hitler, for example, could be in communication with a 2025 in whose history a Nazified Germany had never existed. The line of events that had led to the future where Nazism was unknown and which Kurt Scholder had come from still existed somewhere in the ever-branching tree of possibilities and outcomes. It existed, in fact, as just one of countless lines leading to a whole sub-tree made up of countless Nazi-free futures, a countless number of which had sent countless Kurt Scholders back into the past, and, no doubt, a countless number of which hadn't.

And it was clear what had gone wrong with the communications connection from 1975: somehow, a crossed line had occurred, giving them contact not with their own selves as they had assumed, but with some other version of themselves who were from some other 1975 and had arrived in some other 1939.

This still didn't help with the immediate problem of getting the return-gate operational. The gate was a slave device, operating passively in response to the main projector that was supposed to activate it from 1975, at the same time conveying from 1975 the required operating power—to prevent Gatehouse from sucking Brooklyn's generating grid dry. The gate wasn't designed to make calls out. But on the basis of what Scholder had said, there ought to have been lots of versions of the 1975 projector attempting to call in. But nothing was happening. Something was fundamentally wrong, somewhere.

Szilard was looking curiously at Scholder. "What I don't understand is why, if you knew about all this, you didn't explain more of it to Lindemann when you were in England," he said. "He didn't seem to have any inkling of these concepts when I talked to him by telephone."

Winslade moved across from where he had been listening. "I asked Kurt to be vague over there because of their uncertain situation and the risk of leaks," he said. "We couldn't afford to let the Germans pick up even a whisper of things like this being discussed on our side. But you can see now why we need help. The situation makes no sense. What, I wonder, did the team who got through from that factory in New Jersey know that we haven't figured out yet?"

Einstein nodded. "We need a better understanding of the physics of this strange new domain," he said. "Then you people will be in a better position to tackle the practical issues. Here, we have one end of a communications link that is in working order. The other end, we know, is talking, but nothing comes through. What could account for that? An interesting problem, I think."

Over on the far side of Manhattan, Jeff and his fellow student Asimov were walking down the steps of Schermerhorn Hall at Columbia after a lecture. "You ought to take some time off and get into town sometime to meet them," Jeff said. "That guy Gordon that I mentioned knows all kinds of things about atomic physics. It beats me where he got it from."

"Maybe . . . if I can find some free time," Asimov said. "But right now I'm working on another idea for a story."

"Oh, what this time?"

Immediately Asimov became more enthusiastic and began gesticulating as they walked. "Well, there's a spaceship trapped on a planet that's deep in the gravity-well of a giant star. The crew are trying to send a distress message out. But because of the time dilation caused by the gravity field, their time runs slower and they don't realize that all their radio frequencies are shifted. . . ."

"Would they be able to survive if the field was that strong?" Jeff asked dubiously.

"Yes, well, that's the part I'm trying to figure out," Asimov admitted. "But what do you think?"

Jeff reflected for a while, then shook his head. "I don't think you'll be able to make it work," he replied dubiously.

CHAPTER
21

THE EVENING WAS STILL young, and the Rainbow's End was fairly quiet. A couple of people were at the bar and some more groups and couples at the tables, mostly city workers and businessmen easing up for an hour with a drink and some talk before going home. Few of the regulars had arrived yet, and nobody took any notice of Walther Fritsch as he checked his coat at the door and stood looking around while his eyes adjusted to the lighting—he had left on his dark glasses. Then he walked across the floor and took one of the empty stools at the bar.

"Hi," Lou, the bartender, greeted gruffly as Fritsch sat down. "What can I getcha?"

"Good evening. Er, perhaps der Stin-ger, please?"

"One Stinger" Lou turned away and reached for a glass.

Fritsch scanned the place again, just to be sure. Neither of the two men who had given Fritsch and his niece a ride back into Manhattan—the big fair-haired one with the mustache, or the darker, olive-skinned companion—was present; nor was there any sign of the man they had called Johnny, who had arrived at the house later with the gangsters. Feeling more secure, Fritsch turned back to the bar and picked up his drink.

It hadn't proved difficult to trace the girl named in the newspaper article. She had given him the lead to the Rainbow's End, which, she'd told him, was where Johnny Six Jays usually hung out. She'd never seen or heard of the ones called Cassidy and Harry before, though.

Berlin's failure to mention his report in their last message had been disappointing. He felt they weren't taking him seriously. He wanted to produce something that would convince them of his worth. Events were sweeping toward a climax in Europe, and at such a momentous hour it behooved loyal Party members everywhere to contribute their maximum effort. And besides, Fritsch was curious, personally.

"A cozy place," Fritsch remarked. "I take it ziss is not its busiest."

"It'll liven up later," Lou grunted.

"My first visit here. My name is Johann, incidentally."

"Glad ta meetcha."

Fritsch took a slow sip and set the glass down. "I, ah, I vonder if you might possibly be able to help me. I'm trying to locate an old friend, who I understand comes here occasionally."

"Okay."

"His name is Cassidy—tall, yellow hair, vit der mustache. He has a friend called Harry."

"Harry and Cass? Sure, they come in here sometimes. Haven't seen 'em for a day or two now."

"Vill they be here tonight, do you happen to know?"

"Sorry, no idea."

"I see. Zank you." Fritsch raised his glass again while Lou moved away a short distance to fill an ice bucket. "I haffn't seen him for a vile now," Fritsch went on absently. "Vat he is doing these days? Do you happen to know?"

"You've got me."

George, the piano player, turned from where he had been half-listening on the next stool. "I can help you, mister," he said. "He's trucking these days out of someplace over in Brooklyn, didn't someone say?" He glanced at Lou, but Lou frowned, shook his head, and moved to the far end of the bar. George didn't catch the warning. "One of the warehouses around the basins south of the bridge," he told Fritsch. "I think someone said it was Maloney's old place—yes, that was it—Maloney's."

"Tell me again vere ziss is," Fritsch said, leaning closer.

Lou, standing with his back to them at the far end, shook his head again as he set out dishes of olives, pickle slices, and pretzels. If Johnny Six Jays was happy to mind his own business about what people like Harry and Cassidy did, then that should have been good enough for everyone else. George blabbed too much. One day it would get him into trouble.

* * *

In Brooklyn, meanwhile, the group at Gatehouse had spent the first day of August polishing the last details of their plan for approaching President Roosevelt, which remained unchanged in its essentials: The seriousness of fission research and the possibility of an atomic bomb would be used as a pretext to attract official attention, and the full story would be revealed when top-level contact was made. Nothing could be risked that might lead Hitler and Overlord to suspect they might not have a monopoly on Pipe Organ technology; nothing could be committed to paper, therefore, that remotely hinted at the existence of the Proteus mission or its purpose.

On August 2, Teller and Szilard made a second trip to Einstein's rented summer house, this time in Teller's 1935 Plymouth, and took with them the final draft of the letter they had composed for him to sign. It read:

```
                              Albert Einstein
                              Old Grove Rd.
                              Nassau Point
                              Peconic, Long Island

                              August 2nd, 1939

F.D. Roosevelt,
President of the United States,
White House
Washington, D.C.


Sir:

    Some recent work by E.Fermi and L. Szilard, which has been com-

municated to me in manuscript, leads me to expect that the element uran-

ium may be turned into a new and important source of energy in the im-

mediate future. Certain aspects of the situation which has arisen seem

to call for watchfulness and, if necessary, quick action on the part

of the Administration. I believe therefore that it is my duty to bring

to your attention the following facts and recommendations:

    In the course of the last four months it has been made probable -

through the work of Joliot in France as well as Fermi and Szilard in

America - that it may become possible to set up a nuclear chain reaction

in a large mass of uranium,by which vast amounts of power and large quant-

ities of new radium-like elements would be generated. Now it appears

almost certain that this could be achieved in the immediate future.

    This new phenomenon would also lead to the construction of bombs,

and it is conceivable - though much less certain - that extremely power-
```

ful bombs of a new type may thus be constructed. A single bomb of this
type, carried by boat and exploded in a port, might very well destroy
the whole port together with some of the surrounding territory. However,
such bombs might very well prove to be too heavy for transportation by
air.

-2-

The United States has only very poor ores of uranium in moderate
quantities. There is some good ore in Canada and the former Czechoslovakia,
while the most important source of uranium is Belgian Congo.

In view of this situation you may think it desirable to have some
permanent contact maintained between the Administration and the group
of physicists working on chain reactions in America. One possible way
of achieving this might be for you to entrust with this task a person
who has your confidence and who could perhaps serve in an inofficial
capacity. His task might comprise the following:

a) to approach Government Departments, keep them informed of the
further development, and put forward recommendations for Government action,
giving particular attention to the problem of securing a supply of uranium ore for the United States;

b) to speed up the experimental work,which is at present being carried on within the limits of the budgets of University laboratories, by
providing funds, if such funds be required, through his contacts with
private persons who are willing to make contributions for this cause,
and perhaps also by obtaining the co-operation of industrial laboratories
which have the necessary equipment.

I understand that Germany has actually stopped the sale of uranium
from the Czechoslovakian mines which she has taken over. That she should
have taken such early action might perhaps be understood on the ground
that the son of the German Under-Secretary of State, von Weizsäcker, is
attached to the Kaiser-Wilhelm-Institut in Berlin where some of the
American work on uranium is now being repeated.

Yours very truly,

A. Einstein

(Albert Einstein)

Szilard took the signed letter to Alexander Sachs, and at Sachs's suggestion added a memorandum of his own, making the point that a chain reaction with slow neutrons was a virtual certainty, and one with fast neutrons, though less certain, would make a bomb highly probable. Then Sachs wrote a covering letter of his own to complete the dossier and departed to arrange a suitable appointment with Roosevelt.

And so, for once, everything appeared to be going smoothly. . . .

Until a highly agitated Anna Kharkiovitch called from London.

"Claud, you won't believe what they've done over here," she almost screamed in the ear of a startled Winslade. "Chamberlain's sending a fossil admiral to head up the military talks in Moscow—he's pratically on the retired list! And the staff he's taking with him are only tacticians. They don't have any strategic experience. And even if they had, they don't have any negotiating authority. It's straight out of Gilbert and Sullivan. And that's not all. Claud, do you believe this—they're going there by boat!"

"Damn!"

"Russians won't stand for it, Claud, certainly not after the way they were snubbed at Munich. Stalin has set up people like Voroshilov, Shaposhnikov—some of the highest Soviet officers. They're serious. They want to talk business. This will only drive them straight into the arms of Hitler."

Sure enough, Hitler, sensing an unexpected opportunity, instructed his ambassador in Moscow to drop the word that Germany wanted to improve relationships. The Russian response was positive, and by the second week of August, while Admiral Drax and his party were still chugging sedately up the Baltic, Hitler was pushing for the German Foreign Minister, Ribbentrop, to meet directly with the Soviet premier. Stalin agreed, after extracting as a prerequisite handsome concessions in a trade and credit agreement. On August 22, it was announced publicly that Ribbentrop would be arriving in Moscow the very next day.

The implications were catastrophic as far as any hopes of averting the attack on Poland were concerned. By the time Ribbentrop left Berlin, Winslade was already on his way back across the Atlantic. Major Warren accompanied him this time in order to observe the military situation firsthand and meet some of the British commanders. He wanted to explore the possibility of getting replacements from the British Army for the military reinforcements that should have materialized in July from the Proteus world.

Winslade and Warren arrived in London in the early hours of August 25. By that time, the Russo-German Nonaggression Pact had already been signed. Hitler's road into Poland was wide open.

CHAPTER
22

WINSLADE HAD NEEDED TO be away for a short while to really notice, but something was different in the atmosphere pervading England. It manifested itself not as anything obvious or dramatic, but as a subtle alteration in the mind and mood of the people, and the tenor of the press that mirrored them. He wondered if perhaps he had been looking for the wrong things too soon. The untiring efforts of Churchill and the others had perhaps been achieving results, after all—results, possibly, that would prove more important in the long run, and from which all else would flow in time.

"Abaht time, too, if there is a punch-up, that's wot I say," the porter carrying the bags remarked in the elevator when Winslade checked back into the Hyde Park Hotel with Major Warren. "Mister 'itler's been arstin' for trouble long enough, and it's time someone give it 'im. Russians? They don't make no difference to me. A lot o' bloody good they were last time!"

A new resolution and firmness seemed to be taking hold in the higher levels of government, too, Bannering said, when he and Anthony Eden arrived at the hotel for breakfast the next morning. The day before the Nazi-Soviet pact was announced, the British Cabinet had reaffirmed categorically that the obligation to Poland would in no way be affected. By August 25, two days after the pact, negotiations were being rushed through with the Polish ambassador in London to get signatures on a formal treaty before the day was through. This was in sharp contrast to the attitude taken in the previous world, where the Allies had used the Polish refusal to accept Russian aid as an excuse to declare their guarantee invalidated. Now the guarantee was firm, even though this time Russia and Germany—for the moment, anyway—were solidly in cahoots.

The political scene throughout Europe was confused, and few doubted that war could be more than days away at most. As August 25 wore on, news arrived that the German Foreign Office had wired embassies and consulates in Poland, France, and Britain to order the evacuation of German citizens by the quickest route. In Moscow, Voroshilov terminated the Soviet-British talks on the grounds that they no longer served any useful purpose. British and French press correspondents in Berlin were leaving for the frontiers, while neutral observers there reported anti-aircraft guns being set up all over the city and bombers flying overhead continuously, toward the east.

Only the members of the Proteus mission and the few whom they had taken into their confidence knew that by then in the former world, Hitler had already ordered the attack on Poland to commence at four-thirty the following morning, Saturday, August 26. That was how it had happened even without Soviet collusion; who, then, could doubt that Hitler, with the only real risk to his first major gamble in overt hostilities eliminated, would do other than take full advantage of his diplomatic triumph by pressing forward as planned with all the speed and force at his disposal?

And yet, strangely, that was not how things turned out. The dawn hours of August 26 came and went without news of an onslaught upon Poland. Late in the morning, Eden brought reports of apparent last-minute doubts and hesitation among the Nazi high command. The evening before, a Swedish businessman called Dahlerus had arrived in London as a go-between sent by Goering to convey Germany's willingness to seek an "understanding" on the current situation. And then, early in the morning, the British ambassador in Berlin, Sir Nevile Henderson, had followed independently to present Foreign Secretary Halifax with preposterous proposals from Hitler guaranteeing the integrity of the British Empire and pledging Germany to defend it in the event of its being threatened. So, even with Russia neutralized, his military preparations complete, and Overlord behind him, a single gesture by the Allies of their determination to meet force with force had been sufficient to cause Hitler to falter at the last minute. It was a sobering indication of how differently the events of the past several years might have run had such a precedent been set from the beginning.

Dahlerus returned to Berlin that evening with a noncommital reply, and was back in London again the following morning, Sunday, August 27, with a memorized six-point offer put together overnight by Hitler and Goering. But the proposals he brought were not the same as those conveyed previously by Henderson and seemed to be the start of a refrain that sounded painfully familiar after Munich. Chamberlain expressed skepticism that any settlement could be considered on such terms and sent the indefatigable Swede back to Berlin with an unofficial response, to report back by phone on its reception before an official version was sent with Henderson. The British position remained essentially that they desired good relationships with Germany, but would stand by their obligation to Poland if she were attacked. Germany's offer to protect the British Empire was politely declined.

Hitler agreed to accept this standpoint provided that Britain undertook to persuade Poland to enter into immediate negotiations with Germany. Accordingly, Halifax wired the British ambassador in Warsaw to prevail upon the Poles for authorization to inform Hitler that Poland was agreeable. This they did, and Henderson was welcomed back to Berlin on the evening of August 28 by an honor guard of SS to deliver the official British note.

Some of the more credulous of those involved were jubilant that peace had been secured, but others more experienced in Hitler's ways retained a cooler, wait-and-see attitude. Their wisdom was borne out by the official German reply, which reached London early on August 29 and stated that friendship with Britain could not be bought at the price of renouncing Germany's vital interests. It then launched into a familiar tirade of alleged Polish misdeeds and provocations and insisted on the return of Danzig and the Baltic Corridor. Finally, it demanded as an indication of good faith the dispatch to Berlin of a Polish emissary with full negotiating powers not later than August 30.

The last part contained the trap. By its arrogant insinuation that Poland was expected to send its emissary scurrying at the snap of Hitler's fingers—clearly an intended prelude to more of the kind of treatment that had been handed out to the ministers of previous victim nations—the demand made Polish rejection all but certain. If the Poles declined to send a negotiator, or even if they did and Hitler's terms were rejected, then Poland would be to blame for turning down a "peaceful settlement," and Britain and France would have a justification for washing their hands of the business.

"It's a strange feeling now that this is really happening," Anna Kharkiovitch whispered in an awed voice when the team assembled in Winslade's hotel room at midday to hear the latest. "History is actually changing moment by moment from what we remember, and it's because of what we did. It's uncanny."

Duff Cooper looked thoughtful. "Right now, Hitler could well be more confused than we are," he mused. "He's been confident that we'd seize the first chance we got to wriggle out, just as in your world."

"That explains what's happening," Bannering said, nodding. "He's trying to give us an out. He doesn't know that anything's been changed, and neither does Overlord. They can't know. They don't possess a connection to our world of 1975 and its history. They've only got a link to Overlord's world of 2025, and in that world this situation never happened. There, the Nazis faded away years ago."

By this time, none of the British diplomats or ministers had any stomach for another Munich. The Poles had never for a moment considered one. The British ambassador in Warsaw wired Halifax that they would sooner fight and perish than send a representative of their nation to be bullied and humiliated. If Hitler really wanted to negotiate, the Poles said, they would negotiate as equals in some neutral country.

Accordingly, Henderson arrived at the German Foreign Office at midnight on August 30 to deliver a note stating that Britain could not advise Poland to comply with the German demands. Ribbentrop, the German Foreign Minister, began aping Hitler at his worst by launching into a hysterical denunciation, but for once the shock-tactic of insult and intimidation failed to work. In a heated exchange that the German interpreter would later describe as "the stormiest I have experienced in twenty-three years," the Englishman outshouted the German, and at one point both men leaped from their chairs and glared across the desk so angrily that they seemed about to come to blows. When Henderson asked for the promised German proposals, Ribbentrop read them aloud in German, speaking so quickly that Henderson could do no more than gather the gist of a few of them, after which Ribbentrop refused to supply a written copy of the text. It was out of date in any case, he maintained, since the Poles had not sent a plenipotentiary as stipulated.

Henderson did finally obtain a copy indirectly from Goering the next day. The terms contained in the document turned out to be generous—extraordinarily so—and would undoubtedly have formed a meaningful basis for negotiations had they been conveyed to the Polish government in time. But Hitler had never intended that they should be. They were a hoax, intended simply to fool the German people and foreign observers, as they succeeded in doing to a large degree when Hitler broadcast them at nine o'clock that night, August 31.

For by then, the decision had been made. All the frantic eleventh-hour diplomatic scrambling that would continue into the night throughout the capitals of Europe was already futile. At a half-hour after noon, Hitler had issued his final directive for the attack on Poland to commence at dawn the next day, September 1, 1939.

Churchill, who had gone to France in a last-minute effort to sow more of the defiance that was taking root in England, had returned a few days before the end of August; his wife, Clementine, followed via Dunkirk on the thirtieth. They decided to move into their Pimlico flat to be nearer the center of developments, and arrived to find the newspapers carrying banner headlines of German armies pouring into Poland under an umbrella of ceaseless air attack, with the British Army mobilizing and the evacuation of children from the cities already in progress. The only light relief was Mussolini's declaration that Italy was staying out. Evidently, Il Duce had thought twice about taking on the French Army and the British Mediterranean Fleet. So much for the Pact of Steel.

That same afternoon another event occurred that had not taken place in the previous history, which symbolized the mood of national determination that the Proteus team's efforts had brought about. Prime Minister Chamberlain invited Churchill to become a member of the War Cabinet he was forming to conduct the war that he now saw no hope of averting. Chamberlain's eyes at last were fully open, and there would be no question in this world of staging a mere sham war to satisfy world opinion. Whether he would prove forceful enough for the job, however, was another matter.

At nine o'clock that evening, Sir Nevile Henderson handed Ribbentrop a formal warning that Britain would, without hesitation, fulfil its obligations toward Poland if the German forces were not withdrawn. The French ambassador delivered an identically worded note one hour later. The French would have to bear the brunt if the Germans attacked in the west; to facilitate French mobilization, Chamberlain tried playing for time when he addressed the House of Commons late on September 2. But the members would have none of it. After thirty-nine hours of unprovoked war in Poland, they were angry, impatient, and more than suspicious of anything that hinted of a Munich smell wafting from the government benches. After a heated session, the government was in a precarious position and more than likely to topple if it failed to deliver the answer the nation wanted, and soon.

The pace of events that the Proteus team had set in motion had now gone far beyond their capacity to influence further. For the time being, they were reduced to passive observers, able to piece together only a fragmentary picture from accounts brought by others of pandemonium in the Foreign Office, ceaseless phone calls to and from Paris, and rumors of a final ultimatum being issued jointly with the French.

Then a news bulletin early the following morning, a Sunday, announced that the Prime Minister would address the nation that morning at eleven-fifteen. Winslade and the others breakfasted with the Churchills before listening to the broadcast.

It had been obvious for some time that the inevitable social contact would either compel the Proteus people to reveal their true identities to Clementine or lie to her. Since Churchill had refused to contemplate the latter, she now knew who they were; one of his reasons for taking her to France had been to broach the subject in suitably detached surroundings. After her initial shock, she had adjusted to the situation with an aplomb that befitted a lady of her character and background.

"I suppose that if you're from 1975, you could, if you wished, tell what is going to happen to all of us . . . or at least, what happened in your world," she had remarked to Winslade over dinner the evening she arrived in London. "It tempts one to be curious."

"I could," Winslade agreed. "But would you really like me to?"

After a long silence, she said, "No. . . . On reflection, I don't think it would be very wise, do you?"

"I think you are very wise."

"Do you ever discuss such matters?"

"No."

"A most commendable precedent, Mr. Winslade. Yes, I agree—let's stick to it."

But on the morning of September 3, everyone's thoughts were focused very much upon the present. Conversation across the breakfast table was sparse and the atmosphere solemn as the hour of eleven passed. Then the announcer introduced the Prime

Minister, and the clatter of cutlery ceased and teacups were set aside as Chamberlain's voice came from the radio, sounding strained, but resolute.

"I am speaking to you from the Cabinet Room at Ten Downing Street. This morning the British Ambassador in Berlin handed the German Government a final Note stating that unless we heard from them by eleven o'clock that they were prepared at once to withdraw their troops from Poland a state of war would exist between us. I have to tell you now that no such undertaking has been received, and that consequently this country is at war with Germany. . . ."

Silence reigned for a long time after the address was over. Eventually Churchill said, "I must confess that despite the gravity of this moment, I find myself unable to suppress a certain feeling of elation. Glorious old England, although peace-loving and ill-prepared as ever, is about to answer her call to duty once again. After my dejection at hearing how in your world we groveled and were destroyed, this brings relief and serenity of mind indeed." He paused for a second or two and then shook his head sadly. "But how much we have sacrificed. The Rhine frontier, Italy, Austria, Czechoslovakia's fortress line, now Poland . . . all gone. How different it would have been if we could only have mustered our courage and determination years ago."

"True," Anna Kharkiovitch replied. She toyed with her teaspoon for a second or two and then looked up again. "But it's possible that in the long run it could turn out to be for the best."

Churchill looked puzzled. "How so?"

"Because, morally, the West's credentials are now beyond question," she replied. "The world has witnessed that every attempt at appeasement, reason, compromise, and accommodation has failed, and the only resort left now is force. If anything stands a chance of bringing America in on our side ultimately, this does. And that would be worth far more than all the things you mentioned put together."

"Provided, of course, that we survive long enough for America to get in on the act," Winslade commented.

"Yes," Anna agreed dryly. "Of course, there is always that."

Then a low moaning began somewhere outside the building and rose rapidly to a sustained wail. The sound was already familiar from airraid practice drills—the warning of enemy bombers approaching. "Well, one has to give the Germans some credit for promptitude, I suppose," Clementine conceded.

The party went up to the roof to see what was happening. The rooftops and spires of London lay spread out all around them in the September sun, and above, even as they watched, scores of silvery, blimp-shaped balloons of the antiaircraft barrage were rising slowly on every side. In the streets below, steel-helmeted air raid wardens were directing scattered groups of people toward the shelters. Everyone carried a small, square box, slung from a shoulder-strap, containing a gas mask. The bright red Post Office mailboxes had been fitted with a yellow warning panel that was supposed to change color in the event of a gas attack. So, finally, it had come.

"Now we'll see," Churchill murmured to Winslade through his cigar. Winslade nodded distantly as he stared out over the city.

In the world that the team had come from, the outbreak of war had not brought the devastating air assault on the cities of England and France that most people believed would be inevitable; Hitler hadn't wanted to provoke action in the West while the German forces were engaged in Poland, and in any case expected the Allies to opt out after the Polish cause had gone away. There were no grounds for supposing anything had changed in that respect in this world.

But the analysts advising Chamberlain and his government knew nothing about that, of course, and had produced gruesome forecasts of the numbers of dead and maimed to be expected on the first day of hostilities and through the following six months. Haunted by visions of entire city populations driven to hysteria by bombs, gas, and a collapse of social and medical services, the government had laid secret plans for the mass disposal of bodies by dumping them in lime pits and from hoppers at sea.

Even Churchill had mollified his views about Chamberlain when Bannering pointed out these facts. "If that is what he believed would be the alternative, it makes it easier to be more charitable before glibly accusing him of moral cowardice at Munich," Churchill conceded. "I still believe we should have fought, but I can see why he would consider the year that he purchased to be worth its high price."

In the team's world the Luftwaffe hadn't been turned on England until the end of 1940. "If that pattern is adhered to in this world, and if by the grace of God I should come to have any influence over the course of events," Churchill promised grimly, "we will be ready. And this time, come what may, we will never surrender."

Winslade stared for a second. "Do you really believe there's a God?" he asked curiously.

"It doesn't matter," Churchill said. "One should behave as if there were, anyway."

They then went down to the shelter a hundred yards or so along the street, taking with them a bottle of brandy and some of

Churchill's other "medicinal comforts." The incident turned out to be a false alarm, and they returned after half an hour to the flat.

Later that afternoon, Chamberlain spoke to Churchill again to offer him, as well as a seat in the War Cabinet, the post of First Lord of the Admiralty—the position that Churchill had held at the outbreak of the Great War in 1914. Churchill accepted at once, and by six o'clock in the evening was back in his old office and chair, with the same wooden map-case beside him that he had had made during his previous tenure, and inside it the same charts of the North Sea on which Naval Intelligence had recorded the movement of the Kaiser's High Seas Fleet. The signal WINSTON IS BACK was sent out from the Admiralty to all ships and bases of the Royal Navy.

So as far as major historic events were concerned—what had happened and when—the net effect so far of the Proteus mission had been to delay Britain's entry into the war by three days. Chronologically speaking, it didn't amount to very much.

But in terms of the underlying "how" and "why," there was all the difference in the world—grounds for hope, possibly, that the changes the team had been anxiously awaiting for many months might suddenly start coming in a torrent.

CHAPTER
23

WITH FIVE OF THE team—Bannering, Anna, Selby, Winslade, and Warren—now in England, demand for the vehicles at Gatehouse had slackened. So Ferracini and Cassidy, along with Ed Payne, borrowed the sedan for a night out on the town—a black, 1936 four-door Packard, built as solid as a tank, with a split windshield, rounded fenders, a grilled front, and a luxurious leathery smell pervading its inside. After crossing the river to Manhattan, they stopped at Max's to collect Janet, Pearl, and Amy, and then drove north out of the city, heading for the shore of Long Island Sound beyond Eastchester Bay. Going to the Glen Island Casino had been Ferracini's idea. He had been curious to see the place ever since Winslade described it to him in a limousine en route from a submarine berth in Virginia, seemingly a thousand years ago. Ferracini had particularly wanted to make it that night because the Glenn Miller Band was playing.

The parking lot around the building was nearly full when they arrived, and more cars were coming in through the gates by the minute. They spilled out, already in high spirits, and joined the stream of people converging upon the doors. The evening was warm and calm, with barely a breeze stirring the surrounding trees. The Casino stood out in floodlights against the smooth waters of the Sound, rippling silvery in the light of a half-moon set in a jet-black, cloudless sky.

They reached the door behind a party of people blowing squeakers, wearing party hats, and making a lot of noise. One of the girls with the group had a bunch of balloons and held them out invitingly. "I just got married today. Have a balloon." Amy took two and tied them to the front of her dress, and Janet screamed with laughter. Cassidy was wearing a derby that he had acquired at Max's somehow. Pearl had been celebrating something or other since early evening and was already a little tipsy. It looked as if it would be a good night.

The hall was packed and boisterous. The musicians, on raised tiers under spotlights at the far end, were wearing maroon blazers with black ties. They were already in full swing with a thumping, exuberant rendition of "Little Brown Jug." The lighting was soft, the air smoky, and the floor a mass of bobbing, twirling bodies clad in everything from white-jacketed tuxedos and evening gowns to tartan shirts and dungarees. A long bar crowded with people ran halfway along one of the sides, and tables, mostly taken, filled the remainder of the area around the floor.

As they began threading their way through the room, Glenn Miller himself rose to take the trombone solo. Ferracini stopped moving and stared. The distinctive profile, familiar now from the many photographs that he had seen since that day in Norfolk, Virginia—clean-shaven, high-browed, receding hairline, gold-rimmed spectacles—was discernible even at that distance. Many times during the training period at Tularosa, Ferracini had lain on his bunk alone in one of the billets and listened to recordings like this, trying to picture what the mission would be like. Now, in that moment, it seemed that the past had finally come alive. Or had the "present" that was now gone finally died?

"Hey, Harry, come on—I see a table." Cassidy's voice jerked him back from his momentary reverie.

Janet grabbed Ferracini's hand and tugged him along after the others. "What's up, Harry? Anyone would think you'd never heard a band before."

They arranged the chairs as best they could in the cramped space left between the people at adjacent tables, and sat down. Amy sat on Cassidy's knee. Cassidy grinned and cupped her balloons suggestively. She had a pretty face and blonde hair that curled forward to form points in front of her ears, and she was wearing a straight, pale blue dress, reminiscent of the flapper style of the twenties. She and Cassidy had been getting along well, on and off, in a casual kind of way ever since the first night that she and Janet had met him and Ferracini and brought them to Max's. Ed Payne managed to catch a waitress and ordered drinks.

Pearl reached into her purse, lit a cigarette, and tossed the pack and lighter down on the table. "So where did Gordon go?" she asked. "I haven't seen him for weeks."

"He had to go away," Amy replied. "Where did you say he went?" she asked Cassidy.

"Europe."

"Don't tell me—to look at pictures," Pearl guessed. "Is Gordon a collector or something? Always going somewhere to look at pictures."

"Just business this time," Ferracini said.

Pearl shook her head and sighed. "Do you know, I still don't know what kind of business you guys are in. Is it some kinda secret, am I just slow, or what? Everything I hear gets confusing."

"Why worry about it now?" Janet said. "I thought this was a night out. What happened to the party?"

"Yeah, what about the party?" Cassidy agreed. "Nobody's dancing yet, and we've been here at least five minutes. Well, I reckon there's—"

"Hey, cut that out!" Amy shrieked.

"The balloon burst."

"I heard a joke about balloons," Pearl said. "A balloon dancer, see . . . all she's wearing is these balloons, and a guy says . . ." She stopped and frowned. "No, wait a minute. . . . Oh, heck, I've forgotten how it goes. I'm always doing this."

"A girl shows up at a costume party, and all she's wearing is a black bra and a pair of black shoes," Payne said. He looked around the table expectantly.

Pearl shrugged; Amy frowned.

"Okay, I'll buy it," Janet said. "What is she?"

"The Five of Spades! Ha-ha!" Payne thumped the table gleefully, Cassidy roared, and the others joined in.

Ferracini grinned. "What's black and crispy, and hangs on the ceiling?" he asked. Nobody knew. Being an Italian American, he usually told it as a Polish joke. But suddenly he remembered that the day before, with Hitler's armies storming onward into Poland from the west, the Russians had attacked without warning from the east to complete the destruction of that hapless country. It wasn't a time for jokes like that. "A lousy electrician," he said instead. It was good enough, and the others laughed. Then the drinks arrived and jokes were forgotten for the time being.

Pearl took a long sip from her glass, then sat back and closed her eyes. She shook her head disbelievingly. "Oh, jeez . . .

shouldn't have started so early. I need to work some of this stuff off." She looked at Payne. "How come you haven't asked me to dance yet, Ed?"

"How about a dance?" Payne obliged cheerfully.

"That's what I like in a guy—decisiveness. I thought you'd never ask. Let's go." They stood up, and Payne took her elbow and steered her away in the direction of the throng on the dance floor, now jumping and gyrating to "I've Got a Gal in Kalamazoo-zoo-zoo-zoo-zoo."

Amy was now wearing Cassidy's derby. "Why did you tell that girl at the club you were a gunrunner in South America?" she asked, turning to accuse him.

Cassidy made a face of protesting innocence. "Me? When?"

"Yes, you—last Friday."

"What girl?"

"The dumb-looking one in the slinky dress. You know who I'm talking about."

Cassidy turned his palms upward. "Okay, you've got me. In my blameless innocence of youth, I'm unable to tell a lie. I did it to make you jealous. I figured it might improve my chances of getting laid—you might be easier if you feel you have to compete."

"Cassidy, you're impossible! I don't believe this."

Ferracini had gone quiet. In his mind's eye, he was picturing waves of Stukas peeling and diving over defenseless towns, and refugees with their children trudging along endless, weary miles of road, pushing the remains of their belongings in handcarts while behind them their homes burned. It was happening now, at this moment, while people drank and laughed and danced. Somehow, there was an air of unreality about it all.

He felt Janet's hand close around his arm. "Come on, Harry," she said in his ear. "This is no time to get melancholy."

She was right. There was nothing he could do. He nodded and summoned a grin. "Then do a better job of making sure I don't."

"Like to dance? I don't have to wait for you to ask."

"I don't feel athletic right now. How about waiting for something slower?"

"Sure."

Later, when the mood had mellowed, they danced for a long time. Janet didn't speak much but clung very close, as if she were trying to say something with her body that she didn't want to put into words. Ferracini was content to enjoy her closeness and softness while inwardly savoring the strange feeling of a woman giving herself, symbolically at least, to be his for the moment. This, too, was new to him. In his world, people had rarely given themselves to anybody. The prospective future had been too short and demanding for things like that.

Afterward, they went out onto the terrace, where people were taking a few minutes of fresh air and looking at the necklace of lights along the Long Island shoreline and the colored lamps of the boats on the Sound. Janet pressed close and snuggled in his arms for a while. At last, she loosened herself to study his face curiously for a few seconds. "I don't want to make you mad or anything, Harry, but . . . well, you haven't had a lot to do with girls, have you?"

There was nothing that he knew of to feel offended about. He grinned faintly and shrugged. "Not really." That was the easiest thing to say. His had been a world of constant threat and danger, where everyone lived each day with the feeling that time was limited. Under such conditions, sex was a stress reliever and available fairly freely; but deep commitment, involving as it did too much risk of pain and loss, was more often avoided. In this world, it was the other way around. People dug emotional hooks into each other and got possessive even before there was anything to get possessive about. There seemed to be a whole minefield of unwritten rules and conventions, and he had decided that he had better things to do than get mixed up in them. Or was that a rationalization? Was he unwilling to risk being rejected for doing the wrong thing?

Janet misread his frankness as a signal for help. She moved closer again, kissed his mouth, and whispered against his shoulder, "Don't get any wrong ideas and think I do this all the time, Harry, but we could make it so it's just us . . . alone, I mean. Jeff's working late and will be staying with a couple of the guys at the university tonight. The flat'll be empty."

Ferracini looked out at the water. "I don't know if I want you to get that involved."

Janet giggled softly. "Harry, you really do say the strangest things at times. Sometimes I think you're from some other planet."

"What I mean is, before long I'll be going away," he told her. "I don't know exactly when, and there's no telling how long. I just don't want . . ."

Janet didn't show any great surprise. "Overseas?" she asked.

"Yes."

"But you will be coming back again, won't you?"

"Sure."

Janet didn't seem reassured. "Is it . . . well, dangerous?"

"Look, I really can't go into it. . . . We've talked about this before."

Janet moved back to see his face. "I guess I've been half-expecting it for a while," she said. "Jeff worked out his own theory. Want to hear it?"

"Tell me," Ferracini said.

"He figures the government is worried about Hitler and the Nazis getting the bomb that he's always talking about, and that you're with a secret part of the Army that's been trained to go into Europe and sabotage their program."

"Even though we're not at war?"

"Jeff thinks it's important enough for that not to matter. Anyhow, there's a good chance we will be, the way things are going. And even if we don't, it could still be done undercover, through a deal with the British, maybe. Jeff figures that perhaps that was why the King of England came over to see the President a couple of months back."

"Ingenious," Ferracini granted. He hoped he was managing to remain poker-faced enough to conceal just how ingenious. "Am I supposed to comment?"

Janet sighed. "No, I guess not. It's just that, well, when you do go away, wherever, I want you to know that I'll be thinking about you. You know what I mean. Don't think nobody cares what happens."

Ferracini drew her closer and looked at her face for a long time. She met his eyes unblinkingly. "Really?" he asked at last.

"Really." She nodded.

He hesitated for a second. "What you were saying about Jeff a few minutes back . . ."

"If you go away, I'd like to think you'll remember me, too."

"We could slip away and get a cab, I guess . . ."

"I did just happen to bring my coat out with me."

"Well, yes, I had kinda noticed."

"You never miss anything, do you?"

"Only lots of opportunities, maybe."

Janet laughed and took his hand. "Then don't make this another one. Come on, let's go."

CHAPTER
24

ON SEPTEMBER 11, FRANKLIN Delano Roosevelt, President of the United States, sent a curious letter to Churchill, congratulating him on becoming First Lord of the British Admiralty again and welcoming further communication on a personal basis.

For a head of state to initiate such contact with a subordinate minister—and one not responsible for foreign dealings, at that—of another state was unorthodox, to say the least; and what made the incident more remarkable was that they were not even casually acquainted. They had met once, briefly, at a luncheon in London in 1918 that Roosevelt had attended as Assistant Secretary of the Navy, in the course of which neither had made much impression upon the other. In the years since then, apart from a common appraisal of the dangers of Nazism, their positions on most issues had been diametrically opposed. Churchill's rigidly conservative, traditionalist ideology had nothing in common with the pragmatic experimentalism of Roosevelt, who was idolized by the American unions and the acknowledged leader of American liberalism. With views on the New Deal indistinguishable from those of ex-President Hoover, who had remained aloof after the capsizing of laissez-faire capitalism and insisted that the wreck would right itself in time, Churchill had called for an end to Roosevelt's "ruthless war on wealth and business," while Roosevelt in turn had dismissed Churchill as a backward-looking, has-been politician. How, then, to explain this sudden gesture of sympathy and solidarity?

The answer lay in the grasp that both men shared of twentieth-century strategic realities, which transcended domestic issues: they both understood the role of sea power as the vital instrument of world power, and the dependence of both nations—indeed, of the entire Western democratic world—on joint Anglo-American naval supremacy.

Roosevelt, following the doctrines of the American strategist and naval historian Admiral Mahan, whose writings he had devoured in his youth, recognized naval power as the key to America's future defense, and more importantly, recognized the need to develop a policy of cooperation, not competition, with the Royal Navy in order to counterbalance the rise of Germany and Japan. Steam and electricity had shrunk America's oceanic moat and made her part of a single cultural and ideological heritage that stretched from the Hawaiian Islands to the Rhine. American interests and security counted as much on the British Fleet as Britain's maneuverings for a power-balance in Europe did on American reinsurance in the western hemisphere. They faced common adversaries back-to-back, and shared naval strength was essential to protect both their rears.

The British had recognized this convergence of interests, too, which was the main reason for their benevolent neutrality during the Spanish-American War, and their quiet encouragement of the U.S. annexations of Hawaii and the Philippines before Germany could annex them. It also explained Britain's concessions in the Alaskan boundary dispute and to the American insistence on control of Panama. America, for her part, had reciprocated massively with her entry into the Great War in 1917.

America couldn't afford to let Britain and France go down. Despite lofty phrases about keeping the world safe for democracy, the simple fact was that to save her own hide, America would have to halt the have-not nations in their drive to loot the haves, and the Maginot Line was her first line of defense. It had been true in 1917, and it was true now.

Roosevelt, in his letter, had referred to the coincidence of his and Churchill's having occupied similar positions during the Great War. Then he had gone on to use the telling phrase that the current situation was "essentially similar." The letter, in language that another global strategist would understand, had signaled their unity of viewpoint and purpose.

How he wished there were more people in Congress with

similarly broad conceptual horizons, Roosevelt thought as he sat back from his desk in the room he had made his "oval study." He watched Secretary of State Cordell Hull and adviser Harold Ickes depart with the three senators they had been talking with about the 1935 Neutrality Act that he wished he'd never signed; a vote on easing the restrictions against shipping arms to belligerents would take place at the end of the month—October.

He preferred working here to his official office in the Executive Wing. It was a comfortable room, with dark green curtains, white walls, chintz covered furniture, and he had given it a personal touch with dozens of personal knickknacks, family mementos, stacks of books and stamp albums, numerous model ships, and selected treasures from his collecton of naval charts and pictures. The desk had been a present from Queen Victoria. It was made from the timbers of a British ship abandoned after becoming trapped on northern ice; the ship had subsequently been saved by American whalers, and restored and returned to Britain by the U.S. government.

Roosevelt, in his fifty-seventh year, President since 1932, had thinning hair starting to turn gray, a broad smile that came readily and showed his teeth, and wore gold-rimmed pince-nez on a large, straight nose that suited his rugged, square-jawed head. He was naturally big in stature and had developed massive arms and shoulders after a polio attack eighteen years previously, which had left him with both legs paralyzed and would have ended the careers of many lesser men. He, however, had bounced back into the political arena to become Governor of New York State, and then President at a time when the nation's distressed condition had presented government with perhaps its greatest challenge. He had responded spectacularly, and whatever some financial and economic experts might have had to say from the comparative shelter of later years about the real efficacy of his measures, the sheer dynamism of his "First Hundred Days" had been enough to inspire the people that the strength of Uncle Sam was committed on their side. The plunging indicators of prosperity and confidence had leveled out and then begun rising again in the succeeding years, and his reelection in 1936 had been a landslide of popular endorsement.

His second term, however, perhaps predictably, was proving to be a rougher ride. In his own words, he and his New Dealers had "earned the hatred of entrenched greed." With the worst of the Depression behind them, the forces of the far right were now pouring out of their trenches to attack those who had dented their self-esteem by exposing their pretensions to knowledge that the public had once taken for wisdom. On another flank, his move to alter the structure of the judicial branch—in effect, to liberalize it after a number of Supreme Court rulings that parts of the New Deal were unconstitutional—had proved to be miscalculated and had failed. The experience had demonstrated that, irrespective of his continued personal popularity, there were certain principles and institutions that the American people cherished above individuals, and which they were innately suspicious of any attempts to meddle with.

In this category was their determination, having disentangled themselves from the Old World and its problems, to stay disentangled, and not to involve their sons in the very squabbles that they themselves had come halfway around the world to escape. The solid isolationist phalanxes of Congress reflected this mood, and if Roosevelt believed privately that America would have to enter the war sooner or later, clearly he would have to tread carefully in any attempt to reshape the nation's perceptions.

Until quite recently, he hadn't been at all sure that he wanted to make any such effort. Munich and the events after it had filled him with a sense of hopelessness and despair, and by the summer of 1939 he had practically resigned himself to the thought of retiring from public life to enjoy his family and his personal interests for whatever time might be left. But Chamberlain's eleventh-hour firmness over Poland, which Roosevelt hadn't expected, had given him new heart; and then the appointment of Churchill first to the War Cabinet and then to the Admiralty had rekindled all his old hopes. His letter to Churchill had also been partly an expression of the jubilation he had been unable to contain.

In fact, the sudden turn of events had been so invigorating that he was even entertaining thoughts of flouting convention and running for a third presidential term. It was only a thought. He hadn't mentioned it to anyone yet, not even Eleanor.

In the meantime, however, there was the next meeting to think about. While Pa Watson, his appointments secretary, was marshaling the next group of visitors in the corridor outside, Roosevelt drew the top folder of his stack across the desk and opened it to quickly refresh his memory.

Oh, yes, it was a follow-up to the meeting that Alexander Sachs had finally obtained on October 11, after a two-month wait, to hand-deliver the letter from Einstein. A little tough on Alex, but how much free time could anyone expect a President to have when the fuse to the global powder keg had just burned down? Roosevelt turned over the sheets in the dossier and scanned the underlined sections and the marginal notes he had made. Uranium research at Columbia . . . possible source of enormous energy . . . single bomb might destroy a city . . . Nazi program? Also present besides himself, Sachs, and Watson had been two ordnance specialists, Colonel Adamson from the Army and Commander Hoover from the Navy. "Not a relative!" Watson had penned jokingly by the latter name in his briefing notes. Roosevelt smiled. The transcript of the October 11 minutes showed the meeting ending with Roosevelt's words, "Pa, this requires action."

The action had taken the form of appointing an Advisory Committee on Uranium, to be chaired by the Director of the National Bureau of Standards, Lyman J. Briggs. The committee had scheduled its first meeting to take place at the Bureau on October 21 and sent out invitations to the scientists whose names Sachs had given as being involved in the work.

But then something unusual had occurred. Leo Szilard had contacted Watson to insist that a group representing the scientists be granted access to the President before that date. *Demanded as absolutely imperative. Fixed for Oct. 16.* Roosevelt's eyebrows rose as he read Watson's note of the conversation. "Demanded, huh?" he murmured to himself. "Boy, this had better be good." Then he set the file aside and looked up as the five visitors filed into the room.

Roosevelt already knew Einstein. The professor and his second wife, Elsa, deceased three years now, had stayed as overnight guests at the White House early in 1934 after moving from Europe; they had actually arrived in 1933, but there had been a mix-up with the first invitation. Roosevelt spoke German well, and he and Einstein had found much to talk about concerning the darkening European scene and their common love of sailing.

Szilard, the Hungarian scientist referred to in Einstein's letter, was with him, and Colonel Adamson was back again after being tracked down by Watson at short notice. The other two names, however, were unfamiliar: Professor Mortimer Greene, and a German, Dr. Kurt Scholder.

Roosevelt sat back and beamed when the introductory formalities had been completed. "Okay," he invited. "Shoot."

Szilard, uncharacteristically nervous from his sense of the gravity of the occasion, sat forward on the edge of his chair. "Mr. President, thank you for agreeing to my most irregular request," he began. "I'm sure that when you have listened to us, you will agree there was good reason for it. I'll come straight to the point . . ."

"Please do," Watson interjected. "We've had to make time by squeezing you in."

Szilard nodded. "The fact is," he continued, "that what we have to say has nothing to do with uranium research, although that, too, is an important subject. The real matter that brings us here is far too sensitive to have risked committing to paper in any form." Adamson and Watson frowned. Roosevelt's chin tilted upward a fraction, the movement alone doing all the asking that was necessary.

"If I may." Mortimer Greene reached inside his jacket and took out an envelope, from which he drew a photograph. He half-rose to give the picture to Watson, who passed it to the President. It was an enlargement of a photograph in a document from the microfilm library that the team had brought with them from 1975.

Roosevelt's brow creased as he stared at the picture. Then his expression changed from puzzlement to baffled incredulity as the impossible implication of what he was looking at sank in. He looked up, and his mouth started to open. "Oh yes, it's quite genuine, I assure you," Szilard said.

"Be thankful, perhaps, that happen every day, something like this does not," Einstein offered, trying to be helpful.

Roosevelt blinked and looked down at the photograph again. It showed a Christmas family gathering in front of a large, gaily decorated tree, with smiling people, children dressed in their Sunday best, and lots of packages and wrappings lying around. The family was his, and the place was clearly their mansion at Hyde Park, by the Hudson, halfway between Albany and New York. He himself was standing in the center with Eleanor; three of their sons—John, James, and Franklin D., Jr.—were there, with daughter Anna Eleanor; and there were in-laws, grandchildren, and other relatives that he could identify immediately.

The problem was that he couldn't remember a Christmas on which this particular picture could have been taken. For one thing, there was a female cousin sitting with a baby on her knee that seemed to be hers, yet she had never had one and had only recently announced her engagement. And even more perplexing was the note scribbled across the lower right-hand corner in what was unmistakably his own handwriting. It read:

> To Catherine & John
> with happy memories to relieve these trying times
> affectionately
> Franklin D. R.
> Christmas, 1941

Nineteen forty-one?

Roosevelt set the photograph carefully on the papers before him, stared at it for a few seconds longer, then took a cigarette from the box to one side and inserted it into his holder. "I think you people had better explain," he said at last, looking up.

The decision finally arrived at, as Winslade had hoped, was to try all-out for a working return-gate as first priority, which would automatically give them the bomb—from 1975—if they succeeded. A lower-priority program of ongoing atomic research would be maintained in the meantime as insurance in case they didn't succeed. This arrangement had the added attraction that the second area of activity could continue to provide a convenient cover for the first.

The other thing Roosevelt ordered was that the remainder of the Proteus team be brought to Washington. "I want to meet every one of this bunch," he told Watson. "And besides, every U.S. citizen ought to be able to talk to his President. What difference does it make which copy, or whatever, of the U.S. they're from?" He thought for a moment and then looked at Greene. "How long did you say they've been cooped up in that warehouse in Brooklyn?"

"Since February," Greene replied.

"Did the soldiers there bring uniforms back with them from 1975?"

"Yes, as a matter of fact they did."

"Well, you can tell them that I want them to wear their uniforms when they come here," Roosevelt said. "It'll be good for their pride and morale." He made an empty-handed gesture at Watson. "Things would have taken a pretty bad turn if soldiers of the United States Army had to creep around in disguise to meet their own Commander-in-Chief, wouldn't they, Pa . . . and at the White House of all places? If anyone gets inquisitive, they can just say that the subject's classified and they're not permitted to talk about it."

The meeting at the Bureau of Standards that had been fixed for October 21 did take place as scheduled. For the record, an appropriation of $6,000 was approved to commence the U.S. nuclear weapons program. The transcript of the proceedings depicted Adamson as a closed-minded officer of the old school, unwilling to consider new possibilities. At one point, he was recorded as asserting that moral superiority, not gimmicks in weaponry, brought victory. If that were so, Eugene Wigner retorted, the Army's budget could be cut by thirty percent. Edward Teller concluded that Hitler's "moral superiority" had just smashed the Poles.

But that was, after all, only for the official record.

CHAPTER
25

IN THE HISTORY OF the Proteus team's world, Hitler had delivered a major speech to the Reichstag on October 6, 1939, proclaiming his desire for peace. He had done no more than correct the injustices inflicted upon Germany at Versailles, he maintained, and he offered to settle the few remaining differences between Germany and the West at a conference. The West's leaders, however, unable to back down in the glare of world opinion, but at the same time unwilling to initiate serious hostilities, had remained inert. This had led Hitler to conclude that they needed a stronger justification if they were to disentangle themselves from the war.

The Russians, sensing what was coming and anxious to improve their security, had begun pressuring Finland for border readjustments after seizing eastern Poland, and eventually opened hostilities against Finland at the end of November. With Russia thus preoccupied for the time being, Hitler ordered preparations for an attack into France through Belgium and Holland. Bad weather caused several postponements, but the blitzkrieg finally rolled westward on January 30, 1940. The French, already demoralized internally and faced with three Fascist dictators—Hitler, Mussolini, and Franco—on their borders, sued for an armistice without any great show of resistance.

The screen before the gathering of people in a darkened room of Churchill's flat in Morpeth Mansions showed newsreel extracts of German tank columns passing through French villages, artillery batteries in action, and thousands of bedraggled Allied prisoners being marched along roads by grinning Wehrmacht guards. Arthur Bannering's voice continued its commentary above the whirring of the projector. "Hitler agreed to a cease-fire on condition that France be partitioned into a German-occupied sector and a sector under a pro-German regime that would also administer the French colonies. The French accepted, leaving the British Expeditionary Force across the Channel in an impossible situation. It, too, was forced to surrender in March."

"They couldn't have been evacuated?" Churchill queried from where he was sitting in the center at the front, facing the screen.

"Everything had been half-hearted," Bannering replied. "Nobody had expected an attack of such ferocity. The Army wasn't equipped to fight a real war, never mind to stage an evacuation."

"Hmph," Churchill grunted.

Churchill had moved into quarters above the War Room at Admiralty House, which besides keeping him close to his official duties, freed his own flat at Pimlico for use as an operations center for the Proteus team. Professor Lindemann, who was sitting by the fireplace, had also moved into Admiralty House, ostensibly to set up a statistics department for aiding the Navy with scientific analyses and advice. It was now November 1939, and the trusted inner circle that knew about Proteus had grown somewhat since the outbreak of war.

The film showed German soldiers demolishing the wall of a museum building and then moving a railroad coach outside. Bannering continued, "The French surrender was formally signed in April, in the same railway carriage that Marshal Foch used to dictate the surrender terms to Germany that ended the Great War. It was moved for the occasion to the same spot in the woods at Compiègne that it had occupied on November 11, 1918."

Scenes of the surrender formalities followed, and then the view changed to one of German troops embarking and their ships putting to sea. "In May, Hitler's forces invaded Denmark and Norway. The British position was hopeless—the Norwegian ports would enable the Germans to tighten the U-boat blockade; we had no allies; and all of our equipment, along with most of the Air Force, had been lost in France. With the end in sight, Mussolini entered the war by attacking Egypt and British East Africa. Despite the treaty terms forbidding it, Hitler seized the French Fleet at Oran, which in combination with the Italians gave the Axis the Mediterranean. We had no choice but to withdraw the Navy to Gibraltar, leaving Egypt exposed."

Bannering's voice took on a bleak note as he relived the anguish of years that were both long gone and imminent. "After that, the rest of Europe fell in with what was obviously the winning side, and we were soon overwhelmed. Spain opened its borders, enabling Hitler to take Gibraltar. Malta fell. The Balkan states aligned with the Axis to form a second strategic pincer closing on the Persian Gulf through Greece and Turkey, in addition to the Italian offensive across North Africa.

"In November, Halifax, who had replaced Chamberlain as Prime Minister, sought a truce by offering to give up Egypt. But Hitler was unimpressed, since the collapse of the whole Middle East was now unavoidable, anyway. Seeing a chance to eliminate a possible base for future American operations, Hitler demanded occupation of the British Isles."

The picture on the screen showed formations of massed Luftwaffe bombers, and then changed to more by-now-familiar shots of explosions, fires, and falling buildings. This time, however, the scenes were of London streets and landmarks. Gasps of protest came from some of the viewers. Bannering concluded somberly, "The remnants of the RAF were destroyed in the first three weeks. We were defenseless. Nothing was left to oppose the air bombardment or the invasion forces massing in the ports across the Channel. The Royal Family and other prominent figures were taken to Canada, and German troops began landing in England, unopposed, on the last day of the year. The British surrender was signed on January 1, 1941." The final sequence showed Hitler driving triumphantly through London at the head of a victory parade, along streets lined with panzer tanks and gray-coated German soldiers.

Winslade switched off the projector. Over by the door, Brendan Bracken, a close friend and aide of Churchill's, turned on the lights. Heavy silence lasted a few seconds while the mood dissipated, and then murmurings and muttered comments broke out all around the room. Admiral Pound, the First Sea Lord and a former naval colleague of Churchill's, looked across at Bannering. "So was that when you got out, Arthur—with those people right at the end?"

Bannering shook his head. "I went a couple of months earlier with one of the departments that had been relocated to Canada in October."

Desmond Morton, another of Churchill's close acquaintances since the Great War days, stroked his chin thoughtfully.

He was a former artillery officer who had added to his Military Cross the distinction of being shot through the heart and living normally ever since with a bullet in him. "Then that would mean there's a . . . copy, or whatever, of you, walking around somewhere in London at this very moment, wouldn't it?"

"Yes," Lindemann tossed in. "As a matter of fact, he's been hoping to catch a glimpse of himself ever since January."

"Extraordinary!"

At the front of the room, Churchill rose to his feet while the screen was being retracted out of the way of a large map of the world affixed to the wall. He turned to face the room and raised a hand. Silence fell quickly. Winslade came forward to sit down in the chair that he had occupied earlier. "Now you have seen the rocks of disaster to which our course of only a few months ago was leading," Churchill said. "But let no one suppose that we now know how to avoid the worst. On the contrary, the situation here seems to be, if anything, even worse than that which existed without our meddling. We are at war with greater determination, certainly, but against that our prospects for success have surely weakened since Russia has been converted from cynical neutrality to active alliance with Hitler."

Nobody could be sure how much of what had changed in this world was really a result of the team's actions, and how much of it would have happened, anyway. Sometimes the subtleties of the web of causes and effects that linked their actions to seemingly disconnected, faraway events were astonishing.

Churchill continued, "Corporal Hitler's October 6 Peace Speech to the Reichstag, we are told, took place in both worlds. The version we heard in this world, however, blamed me specifically for the war. Since my counterpart held no office in the Proteus world, it is clear that our actions are already altering the behavior of the Nazi leaders in Berlin.

"Furthermore, as we know, Chamberlain and Daladier are staunchly refusing even to consider a conference while German armies stand on ground that they have seized by force; in the previous world they were too paralyzed by the rush of events to reply. This difference, too, can be attributed to the Proteus operation."

Churchill spread his hands appealingly. "On the other hand we have the deplorable incident of the *Royal Oak*." In the middle of October, a German submarine had penetrated the defenses of the British Fleet's home base at Scapa Flow, off the north of Scotland, and sunk the battleship *Royal Oak* at anchor. "That did not happen in the previous world. As head of the Admiralty, I can assure you we would have been better prepared if it had. It's difficult to see how anything that we have done could possibly have brought about that change.

"But what are we to make of the recent vote by the U.S. Congress to repeal the arms embargo section of the Neutrality Act?" Churchill asked. This decision allowed American arms and munitions to be sold to belligerents as long as they were paid for in cash and transported in the buyer's own ships, which favored the Allies because of Britain's naval strength. "Was this no more than a whim of a different timeline? Or was President Roosevelt, who became disillusioned in the previous world, sufficiently inspired by our last-minute resoluteness to step up his pressure on Congress? If so, then again we can take credit for bringing about the difference.

"In short, how reliable a guide are the major events in that previous world to what is going to happen in this one? We are searching feverishly for a pattern."

He paused and surveyed the room for a moment before concluding. "If German planning has followed the same course as before, we know that the blitzkrieg in the West has already been ordered. Only the foibles of the weather are causing its postponement. Previously the attack came finally at the end of January, but with all the uncertainties, who can say if that will be the case again? It could come tomorrow."

Churchill raised an arm and extended his index finger for emphasis. "But nevertheless, we dare not risk making this knowledge generally available within the government. If word were to find its way back to Hitler and his masters that they no longer have a monopoly on this extraordinary time-technology, we have to assume they would try for an immediate victory by introducing atomic weapons now, instead of waiting until 1942. Thus, everything depends on the scientists in America. We over here can only hold firm and await results with hope."

It was an anticlimactic note to finish on, and the room remained quiet. Churchill nodded to Winslade to take it from there and sat down.

Winslade rose, rubbed his hands together for a few seconds while he stood looking at the map, and then turned to face the room. "But that isn't to say that we can't take advantage of our foreknowledge to reap some benefit," he said briskly. An immediate stir greeted the statement. This was what everyone had been waiting to hear. "Let's be honest with ourselves and admit that in view of the security precautions that we've all agreed are essential, we're not going to see any fundamental alteration in government policy in the next two months. We assume, therefore, that the blow upon Belgium will fall late in January, as before. We

hope, however, that because of what people like Winston have
been doing, the French will hold out better this time."

Winslade paused, but no one spoke. He turned to gaze at the
map again, and then ran a finger along the jagged coastline of
Norway. "Hence, this area, remote from all the action, should be
very quiet. Now, while we as a group may not control the country,
we do pretty much have the Navy—the First Lord and First Sea
Lord are sitting right here.

"The plan we have worked out is this—to take advantage of
the attention being focused on the Western Front during these
spring months by using the Navy to put ashore a landing force
here, in northern Norway. Publicly, the justification will be to aid
Finland through Sweden. In our world, the Finns surprised everybody by giving the Russians a bloody nose, and there was a lot of
popular support and sympathy for them. We see no reason to expect anything different in this world. The government, however,
will believe that the purpose of the operation will be to cut
Hitler's iron-ore supply line from the Swedish mines here at Gal-
livare, and down here through the port of Narvik."

Winslade smiled crookedly for a second. "But the real reason
will be to forestall the Nazi invasion of Norway, which we know
will take place in May. Hence, we can deny Hitler not only his
iron ore, but also the additional U-boat bases that he's planning
to seize on the Atlantic seaboard."

There was a short silence while the listeners digested the
proposition. Then somebody asked, "How sure can we be that
the Germans will stick to May?"

"Nothing's certain," Winslade conceded. "But so far at least,
the timeline differences that we've observed seem to be in details
rather than in anything substantial. Events should tell us if that
principle is continuing to hold. According to our experience, for
example, the Russian attack on Finland should begin two days
from now. Whether or not that happens again will be a good test."

"How well-prepared are we to mount an expedition like
that—in training and equipment, I mean?" Desmond Morton
asked doubtfully. "Let's not forget how much of a start the Germans have got."

"Harvey?" Winslade invited, looking at Major Warren.

Warren answered from a chair by the door, near Eden and
Duff Cooper. "Not so well-prepared as we'd like," he admitted
candidly. "The biggest thing that the people I've talked to don't
comprehend yet is the power of planes against ships. If the Luftwaffe manages to get bases within effective range of the operation, we're in trouble. Carriers can't compete with land-based

aircraft, and the British Navy doesn't have enough carriers, anyway. Forget battleships. They've had their day."

"But the Luftwaffe won't be anywhere near because they'll be preoccupied in France," Churchill said. "And if the German Navy tries to intervene, well, we know how to take care of them." Laughter came from one or two places, somebody raised a query, and the discussion turned into a technical debate on the relative merits of land- and carrier-based aircraft and battleships. Warren caught Winslade's eye and held it for a moment. Winslade shrugged.

There was another part to the plan, too, which only the original, inner core of people knew about.

Hitler's return-gate to 2025 was located near Leipzig, in the eastern part of Germany, just under a hundred miles south of Berlin. It was contained in a rock-hewn cavern deep beneath a chemicals and munitions manufacturing complex at a place called Weissenberg. There could be no hope of defending the West effectively while it continued to exist. And since there was still no news of a connection back to 1975, Winslade had decided on his own initiative to do something about getting rid of it.

"We were supposed to be just sappers sent ahead to build the bridge for getting the tanks across," he had told Churchill. "But it doesn't look as if the tanks will be coming. Therefore, I propose that we attack the target ourselves, without any further waiting. Eliminating that machine must be our overriding priority."

Eliminating it would be the goal of operation "Ampersand," tiny in scale but immeasurably great in importance, that would be timed to take place while the other events in Europe were drawing attention elsewhere.

Having provisionally agreed on the outline of a plan, the group waited to see if Russia would confirm Winslade's prediction by attacking Finland, as she had in the previous world. She did, right on schedule, on November 30. Encouraged that their information was continuing to prove reliable in its essentials, Winslade sent a message to New York, readying the rest of the mission's military contingent for an immediate move to England.

CHAPTER
26

COLONEL HANS PIEKENBROCK, CHIEF of the Abwehr's secret intelligence and espionage section, stared dubiously at the file lying open on his desk. He reached across the desk and took the glossy pages from an American illustrated news magazine that Lt. Col. Boeckel was proffering from the other side.

"And this is the picture?" he murmured as he examined the color photograph on the top sheet. It showed two men shaking hands in a spacious, elegantly furnished setting, while several others looked on from behind. The scene was of representatives from a couple of South American states saying farewell to U.S. officials in the entrance hall of the White House after talks following the October conference of American nations. Piekenbrock was interested not in the foreground figures, however, but in the small group of uniformed soldiers behind them that the cameraman had inadvertently captured, just inside the edge of the frame. They were standing in a loose huddle, possibly waiting their turn for an appointment. A couple of men in civilian clothes were with them, also.

Boeckel passed across an enlargement of part of the picture, which the Photographic Department had produced at his request. "If I may, sir . . ." He indicated two of the soldiers, who were standing together on one side—one tall, with a yellow mustache, caught in the act of waving a hand as he said something; and the other, darker. "Fritsch sent us the article because he says he's certain that those two were among the gang he described in his earlier report." Boeckel picked up a further enlargement, showing very grainily, but discernibly, the shoulder patches and collar insignia on the tunics. "I did a routine check to identify the unit they're from, but the result was puzzling. There's no record of those designations in any of the U.S. Army manuals. And if you look carefully at the uniforms themselves, you'll notice that they differ from the standard American pattern in a number of subtle ways. Again, we have no record of anything quite like them."

Piekenbrock sat back in his chair, his fingers steepled below his chin. Then he got up and walked over to the window to stare down at the traffic on Bendlerstrasse. "Let's run through this very quickly once again," Piekenbrock said at last. "First of all, this man Fritsch gets himself mixed up with American gangsters somehow and ends up at this house outside New York. But these mysterious men in masks, who walk up walls and put hoodlums in the hospital with their bare hands, appear from nowhere, seize the whole place, and hand it over to a rival gang."

"What appears to be a rival gang, anyway."

"Whatever. And Fritsch sends you a report of this affair, including an account from the New York newspapers."

"At the time, it seemed to have nothing to do with anything except American criminals," Boeckel said. "But we kept the matter under review, nevertheless."

Piekenbrock held up a hand. "You did the right thing. Anyway, it now turns out that these men are not criminals, but American soldiers. Also, they belong to a hitherto unknown unit, which might conceivably just have been formed. They appear to have undergone some extraordinary training. And now they show up at the White House . . . to meet whom? Could it be the President himself, perhaps? If so, why? Who are they?"

"I have been giving the matter some thought," Boeckel said.

"And have you come up with any ideas?"

"Well, it's merely a speculation, you understand, sir, but it seems to me that the U.S. military has been developing a secret unit to specialize in undercover urban activities—sabotage, assassination, or other such missons. The raid on the gangster's house could have been a practice exercise with the added benefit of having some redeeming social value—perhaps by eliminating some criminal elements that the authorities couldn't touch legally."

Piekenbrock raised his eyebrows. "You mean the police didn't know? Wouldn't that be a bit risky?"

"Not as risky as the real thing and someone else's police," Boeckel pointed out. "It would be the ultimate in training realism."

"Hm, yes—ingenious, I'll grant you that. Go on."

Boeckel tapped the file lying on the desk. "The warehouse that Fritsch identified in Brooklyn could be their camouflaged operations base. What I suspect is that they've been running an elaborate exercise to see if they can remain invisible for a protracted period in a major city while merging with the criminal fraternity and carrying out active operations, all without any cooperation from the authorities, or even any official knowledge that they exist. Having tested their methods, a visit to Washington could represent their 'graduation,' as it were, before becoming operational elsewhere."

"Such as?"

Boeckel shrugged. "Well, we all know that Roosevelt would like to get into the war, but Congress and the people won't let him, openly. A good guess might be that they're being sent over here—maybe even to Berlin."

"And assassination, you said, might be among their specialties?"

Boeckel drew a long breath. "With some obvious names as targets."

Piekenbrock nodded. Clearly, his own thinking had already led him to the same conclusion. "That could also explain why Roosevelt should be involved personally," he mused.

"Exactly, sir."

"Hmm . . . I think we should find out more about this warehouse if we can," Piekenbrock said. "Not Fritsch—he's just an amateur. Reads too many boys' books and takes risks. Get one of the professionals onto it—someone like Musketeer. But I don't want anyone breaking in or doing anything reckless if they're likely to bump into the kind of people that Fritsch described. That will be all."

"Yes, sir." Boeckel stood up and gathered the file and papers together.

"I just want to know a bit more about the place, some idea of what goes in and out," Piekenbrock said. "Low-key—know what I mean?"

"I'll start on it right away."

"Very good. Oh, and Boeckel—about that secretary of yours. She's an attractive woman. It's not a good idea to flaunt it so much when Lady Luck smiles your way, you know. I'm hearing jealous noises from several directions. I know the Führer wants us to make more Germans, but he never said anything about making a public spectacle of doing so. I trust I make myself clear?"

"Oh, yes, sir. I'm sorry. I'll be more discreet."

"Very good. I'll say no more. Good day. Heil Hitler."

"Heil Hitler."

CHAPTER
27

FERRACINI'S UNCLE FRANK HAD brought him here once as a young boy to see the place where he had been born. And from time to time as he grew older, when Ferracini felt sad or lonely, he had come back to this part of Queens to walk the streets that had made up the world of the parents he had never known, as if sharing the memories of the sights and scenes they had lived among somehow brought him closer to them.

The building that he remembered as derelict and boarded-up on the corner of a dingy street now had bright red curtains and flowerpots in the upper windows, and a bicycle shop was open for business on the ground floor. What he had known as an auto-parts dealer's next door, with a sparse assortment of gaskets, fan belts, cans, and tools clipped to a pegboard behind its dusty window, was a busy delicatessen. The liquor store beyond that was still a liquor store; the hardware store was still a hardware store, although it looked more old-fashioned, with tin bathtubs hanging over the doorway, drums of kerosene and turpentine inside, and a bench out on the sidewalk stacked with bundles of firewood, candles, balls of twine, and all kinds of brushes. What had been a TV store was now selling vegetables, and the gap where a burned-out shell had stood was a house with green painted woodwork and children's drawings chalked on the wall by the door.

The street as a whole, though recognizable and not without its scars, had a different feeling from the tired drabness of the scene he remembered from long ago and yet to come, in another world. It felt alive and colorful, as he had pictured it in his daydreams; the way he would have liked it to be.

Ferracini thrust his hands deep into his overcoat pockets and walked slowly past the houses and shops; the church standing behind trees inside walled grounds; the school at the bottom of the hill and the hospital beyond, halfway up—the world that his older brothers and sister had grown up in before he was born. He wasn't exactly sure why he had come back again now; he had never thought of himself as sentimental.

Orders had come through from Winslade for the Special Operations force to be ready to move to England. A detachment of plainclothes U.S. Military Police would be taking over security at Gatehouse. This was just something that Ferracini had felt he had to do before they left.

Just curiosity, he'd told himself, not nostalgia. It was Janet's day off; she'd wanted to come with him, but he had said no. It was something he'd wanted to do alone. He would go back to the flat afterward and say good-by to her and Jeff.

He stood for a long time on a corner, staring at his parents' house from a short distance along the opposite side of the street. It had become run-down by the time Frank had first pointed it out, and Ferracini remembered feeling disappointed. Now, however, it looked cheerful and clean, with freshly painted woodwork, bright curtains, and its small front yard neat and trim. A light drizzle began falling. Ferracini turned up his collar, but remained standing on the corner, his mind filled with memories of the stories his aunt and uncle had told him of times gone by, and of the photographs in the albums that he had pored over as a boy.

As soon as he saw the woman in the dark coat appear around the corner at the end of the street, he knew why he had been waiting. It was his mother. The dark-haired girl walking beside her and gripping her sleeve would be his sister, Angela, who had been four in 1939. He watched as they came nearer on the far side of the street, his mother small, frail, and hunched slightly with the weight of the shopping bag that she was carrying, and Angela chattering and skipping a step or two in every few. They arrived at the house, entered the front yard, and as she turned to close the gate, his mother paused for a moment to glance curiously at the bareheaded, tousle-haired young man in the overcoat, watching from the corner. For a fraction of a second, the distance seemed to telescope, as had the time, and he felt as if he were looking deep into the face that he had seen only in pictures—a brave and determined face, yet at the same time gentle as only a mother's can be, lined by a lifetime of struggle and sacrifices that had deserved better reward. Then she turned away and disappeared into the house.

After a while, Ferracini began walking slowly back the way he had come. It wasn't a tear on his face, he told himself. The rain was getting heavier. He had only come out of curiosity, after all.

Early the next day, in a chemistry laboratory at Columbia, Jeff was crouched down before one of the cupboards beneath the workbench, holding a list of apparatus required for the morning's experiment in one hand, and lifting out tripod, beakers, Leipzig Condenser, test-tube rack, and burner with the other. As he was finishing, a foot planted itself in his field of vision, and a tall, thinnish figure with glasses materialized above. "Did you bring it?" Asimov asked.

Jeff closed the cupboard door and stood up. "Bring what?" he asked, at the same time feeling a pang of guilt as he remembered. Harry had showed up at the apartment the evening before to announce that he was leaving for an indefinite period; after his earlier admission to Janet that he would be going overseas, the mystery and excitement had driven all thought of Asimov's story from Jeff's mind.

"The draft you said you'd read over," Asimov replied. "The story about the spaceship trapped in the gravity field that can't communicate out because its frequencies are shifted. You promised you'd let me have it back today."

"Oh . . . oh, yes." Jeff reached for his bag on the stool behind him and pulled out folders and papers. But even as he started making a show of rummaging through them, he had already remembered with a sinking feeling that the manuscript had been lying near some things of Harry's that Harry had scooped together and taken with him the night before. He was pretty sure, too, that it had no longer been there after Harry had gone. "I . . . I must have left it at home," he mumbled. There was always a chance that Janet might have set it aside somewhere.

Asimov's face dropped. "Hell and dammit, Jeff! I wanted it tonight to work in a couple of new changes I've thought of," he grumbled irritably.

"Sorry, Isaac, it slipped my mind. I'll look for it tonight."

"Look for it?" Asimov blanched. "My God! You don't mean you've lost it?"

"No, of course not."

"Okay, well, try and let me have it tomorrow, will you, Jeff?"

"Tomorrow," Jeff repeated, managing a sick smile.

* * *

Meanwhile the five outgoing members of the Proteus military contingent—Ferracini, Cassidy, Payne, Ryan, and Lamson—were assembling with their personal kit in the mess area at Gatehouse. The other baggage and equipment for England had already been sent ahead by ship to Liverpool, in two duplicate shipments because of the U-boat hazard. They themselves, following confidential arrangements made between Roosevelt's and Churchill's staffs, would be flown to England in a converted U.S. Army bomber; for official records, the bomber would be making a test flight to evaluate transatlantic delivery routes for long-range military aircraft. As to what was supposed to happen after that, all they knew was that they would undergo some kind of training and then proceed to active operations "somewhere overseas."

"We'll go in by sub," Cassidy told the others as they collected their things in final preparation to move out. "Wait and see—straight into the Baltic. Five dollars says it's by sub."

"They wouldn't risk it," Ryan said. "Too many British subs operating around the Baltic. The German defenses would be on alert all the time."

"Where else, then?"

"Up from the south—Mediterranean, through Italy," Ryan said. "Why else d'ya think they brought Harry along? He looks the part, see."

Cassidy looked at Lamson. "Any guesses, Floyd?"

Lamson shrugged and heaved a backpack onto his shoulder. "Who cares? Guessing isn't gonna change anything. It could be an air drop."

Mortimer Greene and Kurt Scholder were waiting to escort them to the front of the building. The two FBI agents who would be accompanying the party to Mitchell Field on Long Island came forward to help with the bags. After a last look around at what had become, since January, a home in many ways, they filed through the doorway in the partition that separated off the machine area.

Some of the scientists were working as usual. Einstein was puffing his pipe and listening to Fermi, a small but vigorous man with lively brown eyes and an immense brow formed by his receding hairline, who was gesticulating excitedly as he talked. Szilard was busy at one of the consoles, and Teller had been around fifteen minutes or so earlier. In addition, partly to make up for the loss in technical assistance that the departure of the troops would entail, more technicians and scientists had been recruited to the group.

Einstein and Fermi stopped talking and came to say their farewells. Szilard got up from his console and joined them.

"So the time has come, yes?" Einstein said. "What should one say on an occasion such as this? To each of you, may your own kind of God, whatever that might be, go with you. And to anyone that doesn't have one, well, you might find one that suits you. But whatever, good luck, my boys."

"Good luck," Szilard repeated as lots of hands were being shaken in turn. "Let's hope that we manage something useful over on this side to back you up."

"Not good-by, but *arrivederci*," Fermi said. "I'm sure you will all be back again sometime, when the Fascists are no more. Before then, too, all of America will be fighting with you. You will see."

Teller reappeared just in time to add his own good wishes, and then the group walked through the front area of the warehouse to the loading bay where another guard was waiting in the bus.

As the bus passed the Brooklyn Bridge, Ferracini stared across the river at the familiar skyline and thought of all the things he had found that he had never imagined existed, and which would now have to be left behind. Always in his life it had been the same. Perhaps, he brooded inwardly, some things were better left undiscovered.

Back at Gatehouse, Einstein came through from the machine into the mess area and ambled over to the side-table where the coffeepot and tea urn stood. "Enough work for one morning. Now I will relax a little," he murmured. Scholder and Greene, who had returned from the front of the building and were talking over cups of coffee at the large table, nodded to acknowledge his presence. The place seemed strangely quiet and empty with none of the troops around. Einstein poured himself a cup of tea from the urn, stirred in a spoonful of sugar, and sat down in an armchair nearby to refill his pipe. More voices sounded from the other side of the partition. A moment later the door opened again, and Szilard came through with Fermi and Teller. Szilard, as usual, was doing the talking.

"In each element of the superposition, the object-system assumes a particular eigenstate of the observer. What's more, every observer-system state describes the observer as perceiving that particular system state. . . ."

Einstein sighed and looked around while he sipped his tea. His eyes roamed over the mess of oddments and litter that the troops had discarded in the last stages of packing and eventually came to rest on an overflowing trash bin standing near his chair. On top was a thin wad of typed sheets of paper. Einstein lifted it from the bin and set it down on his knee to scan casually while he lit his pipe. "Ach so, der spaceship that goes to the stars, ja?" he murmured to himself. He turned the page and settled himself back more comfortably, moving his feet to make room as Fermi came over to pour some coffee.

"In each element, the system is left in an eigenstate of the measurement," Fermi said over his shoulder. "If a redetermination of the earlier observation is made at that stage, then every element of the resulting superposition will describe the observer with a memory configuration in which earlier impressions are consistent with later ones. That makes it inevitable that any observer will perceive the system as 'jumping' into an eigenstate randomly, and then remaining there for subsequent measurements on the system."

"Yes, I agree," Teller said. "The main point, though, is that . . ."

In the chair, Einstein smiled delightedly and nodded his approval. "Ah, so here we have General Relativity. . . . Yes, very good, very good. . . . Trapped in the intense gravity field, eh? . . . Oh, is not so good. . . ."

"Each memory sequence yields a distribution of possible values," Szilard was saying. "And each of the distributions may be subjected to statistical analysis."

"Yes, exactly!" Fermi answered, waving his hands. "That's my point. The conventional statistical interpretation *must* emerge from the formalism itself. Every observer must deduce that his universe obeys the familiar statistical quantum laws. The universal state vector becomes a tree, and every branch corresponds to a possible universe-as-we-see-it."

"*Mein Gott!*"

The exclamation from Einstein stopped the conversation dead. The others looked at him as he rose slowly to his feet with a strange look on his face, while the papers which he had been reading fluttered to the floor. "Are you all right?" Szilard asked cautiously.

Einstein didn't seem to hear. "The communications link didn't work . . . because time at the two ends didn't run at the same speed. . . ." he murmured distantly.

Szilard looked at Teller, then at Fermi. They all shrugged. Scholder and Greene watched with puzzled expressions. "If you will excuse me, I must go back to my calculations and think some more," Einstein said, still sounding faraway. He began moving toward the door, at the same time nodding rapidly to himself. "Yes, suddenly a chink of light . . . possibly, possibly," they heard him mutter as he hurried out of view.

CHAPTER
28

THE FLIGHT TO BRITAIN was uneventful. A chilly, misty December dawn was breaking when the plane finally landed at Prestwick, on the west coast of Scotland, where the five Americans were met by a Captain Portel and a Lieutenant Cox of the Royal Navy. The arrivals were tired and bleary-eyed, and after brief introductions everyone climbed into a wagon to drive ten miles to Kilmarnock, where they would catch the London train coming from Glasgow. The conversation was forgettable and fully in keeping with the bleak scenery of wet, gray stone houses, the soggy-looking hills in the background, and the cold, ungodly hour of the morning.

The station cafeteria was just opening when they arrived, and they had time for a ham and cheese sandwich and a pint mug of strong, sweet, steaming tea, which quickly put life back into their cramped limbs and restored some color to their faces. A Christmas tree was standing in one corner near the stove. Opened on display in front of it was one of the hamper boxes, containing various items of food and candies, jars of chutney, pickles, and preserves, and knitted articles such as socks, mittens, and ear muffs, that the local branch of the Women's Voluntary Service was sending to "The Boys at the Front."

As they stood around the stove warming themselves, Payne

commented on the frivolities being reported in the American press. "All that the troops in France seem to be doing is digging holes and playing soccer for newsreel cameramen," he said. "Is that really all there is going on over there to write about?"

"I suppose everyone's relieved that all the things the experts were promising for years didn't happen," Portel replied. "They told everyone the sky would be black with Heinkels and Dorniers, wingtip to wingtip, within hours. There were thousands of papier-mâché coffins piled up ready, all the hospitals were standing by with acres of empty beds . . . and nothing happened. Now, of course, it's all the government's fault for not knowing anything about anything. But you can't blame poor old Neville for everything. He's not a bad bloke really—does his best, you know."

With evacuations, the military call-up, and relocations of key personnel and government departments, about half the families in England had at least one member on the move somewhere, and the train down to London filled quickly until even the corridor was packed with baggage and people, with many khaki, navy, and RAF uniforms. A lot of troops got on at Carlisle, but by that time Portel and his party had found themselves a compartment.

"They won't tell us how many lives the bloody blackout has cost," Lieutenant Cox said. "But it's cost a lot more than anything the Germans have done. Personally, I wouldn't be surprised if we end up patching things up with Hitler and calling the whole thing quits. I mean, if either side were serious, they'd have done something about it by now, wouldn't they?"

Even the sinking of the *Royal Oak* had been "a pretty good show by Raeder's chaps," in Portel's opinion. Ferracini was incredulous as he listened. It was all still a game of king-size cricket. A sporting, "Well hit, sir!" had been earned by the other side. It didn't seem to have registered that what had been knocked for six was over eight hundred British sailors.

But at least the British were doing something, he reflected. "What do people in America think?" Cox asked him.

Ferracini had to answer, "To be honest, most of them have forgotten there's a war on over here at all."

There were innumerable stops and delays, and it was dark when the train arrived at King's Cross Station. They emerged, stumbling over curbstones and sandbags, into an eerie, black, treacherous world of unseen steps, corners, and lampposts, vaguely outlined buildings, and shuffling bodies. Pedestrians materialized suddenly in the gloom, most of them carrying flashlights and wearing at least one piece of white clothing, usually an armband, coat, hat, or scarf. In the roadway itself, drivers cautiously inched their way forward, guided only by thin pencils of light coming through slits cut in their headlight masks.

Portel vanished into the murk to find a cab. How, Ferracini couldn't imagine. "Man, oh man, I never realized Broadway was so beautiful," Cassidy's voice muttered from somewhere behind as they stood waiting.

Portel evidently knew the ropes and reappeared after what seemed a miraculously short time with a taxicab, into which Cox squeezed with half the group. Then, to prove it hadn't been a fluke, Portel repeated the performance by finding another cab for the rest. Twenty minutes later, they were all reunited at the Kensington Garden Hotel near the Albert Hall. Rooms had already been booked, and Major Warren and Gordon Selby were waiting to welcome them. While the arrivals from New York went upstairs to clean up and change into fresh clothes, Portel and Cox went for a quick "noggin" in the bar with Warren and Selby; then, their charges safely delivered, the two British officers departed. The others reassembled for a late dinner, which Warren had arranged to be served in a private room.

"It's a lot different here from Manhattan," Gordon Selby said as they sat down. "I still haven't figured out how the cabbies find their way around at all."

"Doesn't anyone talk about anything else but the blackout?" Ryan asked.

Selby grinned apologetically. "I must be picking up English habits already," he admitted. "The big scare's over, so now they grumble—about the food rationing, about the Civil Defense people sitting at their posts and drinking tea with nothing to do all day, about the lousy benefits that the wives of the guys who are drafted get paid. . . ." He nodded. "But sure, mostly about the blackout."

"How about the trains—have you tried them yet?" Cassidy said. "They're really something."

"But in this England, we just walked on," Lamson reminded him. "We didn't need any travel permits stamped by the local Polizeiführer. The Gestapo weren't on the train checking papers. That's something, too."

"That's a point," Cassidy agreed.

"The saddest part's the big toy stores," Selby said. "They're all trying to keep up a business-as-usual face with lonely Santas sitting around among mountains of train sets and dolls, but there aren't any kids. They were all evacuated out of the cities at the beginning."

"But they are starting to trickle back in again, especially with the time of year," Warren added.

One lump of sugar for the coffee was allowed per cup. Each person received one pat of butter and one of margarine for the rolls, and the waiter pointed out which was which.

Ferracini turned his head to scan the room after the waiter had left. "Is this place safe to talk?" he asked.

Warren nodded. "It's okay. We checked it before you guys arrived."

"Then about the mission—what happens next?" Ferracini asked. At last—this, of course, was what had been burning in all their minds.

"We're gonna go in and take out Ay-dolf's return-gate," Cassidy said before Warren or Selby could reply. "Why act like you don't know, Harry? None of us thinks we came along just for the ride."

Nevertheless, all eyes remained fixed on Major Warren. He seemed unsurprised. Nobody had expected him to be. He nodded.

"Where is it?" Payne asked.

Warren frowned in the act of raising his fork to his mouth, and hesitated. "You've all come a long way, and the subject isn't really appropriate to this evening," he said. "Leave it until tomorrow, okay? It's going to be a busy day. First thing in the morning, we'll be coming back here to pick you up for breakfast with Claud, Anna, and Arthur. After that, you're all going to meet Churchill and Professor Lindemann for a preliminary briefing."

"Is that when we get to meet the British half of the act?" Ryan inquired.

Warren shook his head. "Forget it." The others exchanged puzzled glances.

"There isn't going to be any British half," Selby explained.

"Just us—everyone here except Gordon," Warren said. "He has to stick around to help get a bomb program moving if we don't make it."

Ryan frowned. "So what happened to this idea of getting British replacements for the backups we were supposed to have gotten from JFK back in July?"

"That's out," Warren said. "The politics between the British and the French stinks. The generals are all playing ostrich with their heads stuck in the last war. The staff in London doesn't get along with their commander in France. He doesn't get along with the French, and none of them gets along with the war minister. Some of them have even started bitching behind each other's backs direct to the King." Warren shook his head. "It's all a mess.

I've talked about it with Claud, and we've agreed we'd be better off staying out and running our own firm in our own way."

Six men were going to pit themselves against what was probably the most heavily protected place in Europe—or, very likely, anywhere. Ferracini slumped back as the enormity of what Warren was saying hit him. He caught Cassidy's eye for a second, and for once even Cassidy seemed dazed. Selby, watching, attributed their expressions to fatigue. "Anyhow, you guys have come a long way. Let's save it all for tomorrow and try to get some sleep tonight, eh?" It was all right for Selby. Selby wouldn't be going.

Cassidy leaned back in his chair. "Just us, period, or will we be using local contacts?" he asked.

Warren waved his hand decisively in front of his face. "Not another word about it until tomorrow morning," he ordered. "Gordon, tell us again what you were saying earlier about that crazy horse and cart."

"There's a famous old firm of hatters in London, called Scott's," Selby told the table. "They've always used a horse-drawn delivery van—a kind of tradition now. It's very distinguished, with nice woodwork all painted and varnished, and liveried coachman and footman in cockaded top hats.

"Well, I saw it this morning trotting down Bond Street with everything just the same as usual, except that the guys have traded their hats for steel helmets—I guess until the war's over." He shook his head. "These people . . . I don't know . . . I'm not sure it's so inevitable that Hitler will walk all over them. Sometimes I still think it could go either way."

"We all know what happened last time," Lamson drawled laconically.

"True, but they were under the wrong management," Selby said. Then he added, "If only something could be done about that. . . ."

Payne caught the curious note in his voice. "What are you trying to say?" he asked.

Selby glanced uncertainly at Warren. Warren gave an almost imperceptible shake of his head, and Selby steered the conversation to other things.

Later in the evening, after the dinner party had broken up and the others had turned in for the night, Ferracini, Cassidy, and Ed Payne caught Selby on his own in a quiet corner of the lobby. "What did you mean earlier, Gordon, when you said something about changing the management?" Payne asked as they sat down around him at a table.

"Oh, nothing really . . ."

"Who do you think you're kidding?" Cassidy said. "Come on, give. We're curious."

Selby hesitated, then emitted a long sigh and nodded. "Anna's convinced that Claud and Arthur are up to something that they're not letting on about," he said, lowering his voice. "Claud has taken more key people into his confidence over the gate and what's going on in the U.S. He says it's to stiffen the country's morale, but Anna doesn't think that's the main reason."

"What does she think, then?" Ferracini asked.

"That Claud's meddling again," Selby said. "It gives him direct access to more of the nation's policy shapers. He's having dinner tonight with Lord Salisbury and Leopold Amery, which is why he wasn't here. They're both among the people who have been saying some pretty tough things about the way the government's been handling the war so far. You see, it broadens Claud's base for pulling political strings. Chamberlain might be a sincere guy and all that, but he's just not a war leader. Churchill's the only one with any fighting spirit in the whole War Cabinet. Anna called him 'a cuckoo put in a nest of baby hedge-sparrows.' Now she thinks Claud is carrying out preparatory maneuvers to capitalize on having gotten Churchill in there."

"You mean some of the sparrows might be kicked out before much longer?" Payne said.

"That," Selby agreed. He paused for a moment. "Unless the idea is to bring down the entire British government, which might explain why Claud and Arthur are being so secretive."

The others stared at him incredulously. "Surely not?" Payne protested. "Not even Claud would try to pull off anything as audacious as that."

Selby smiled in a strange, humorless kind of way. "That's exactly what I told Anna," he said.

"And what did she say?" Payne asked.

"She agreed," Selby replied. "She said her imagination must have been running away with her. Why, it would be almost as audacious as trying to go back in time to change history!"

CHAPTER
29

LONDON IN DAYLIGHT STRUCK Ferracini as a caricature of a city at war. The superficial trappings of wartime were in evidence everywhere, to be sure: shop windows boarded up or crisscrossed with adhesive tape; balloons overhead; signs over sandbagged entrances indicating public airraid shelters; lots of uniforms on the sidewalks; but the people seemed like the mildly embarrassed hosts of a lavish masquerade party trying to act as if nothing had happened when none of the guests had shown up. Many of them were no longer bothering to carry their gas masks, he noticed, which the American newspapers had made a big thing of back in September.

All the superficiality reinforced the impression he had formed before leaving the U.S. that England still didn't fully realize it was at war, or if it did, nobody comprehended what war with modern totalitarianism meant. In September, the country had been grimly resigned to a mood of "let's get it over with." But since then the officially promulgated horror stories had been proven wrong, and the people had concluded that they'd have been better off trusting in their own instincts all along. Now all authority was suspect, if not openly ridiculed. Foreigners—Germans, Italians, French, Russians; they were all pretty much the same—were too excitable and not very bright. They just needed to be left alone for a while to sort out their squabbles and calm down. Then everyone would be able to forget the fancy dress and other nonsense, and get back to being decent and civilized.

Yet at the same time it was a pleasantly different England from the one Ferracini had known previously. The grimness and the crushing despair that had come after years of universal impoverishment, material and spiritual, were absent. And there wasn't a swastika to be seen anywhere. In the tradition that had remained unbroken through centuries, it was free.

That was the whole problem with the English, Ferracini was beginning to see: They were simply incapable of conceiving how things could be otherwise.

The preliminary briefing for Ampersand took place in a vault beneath the Admiralty buildings on Whitehall, which on Churchill's instructions had been permanently reserved for undisclosed, highly classified naval business. All ten of the Proteus team now in England, i.e., everyone except Mortimer Greene and Kurt Scholder, were present, along with Churchill, Lindemann, and a confidential secretary to record the proceedings.

Ferracini had learned something about Churchill during Proteus training, as had all the team, and had gleaned more from further reading during the months at Gatehouse. He knew that Churchill had fallen from favor in the Great War, made enemies among British socialists and conservatives alike, and was alleged to be erratic and impetuous. But against that, Churchill had been one of the few who had consistently foreseen and warned of the dangers that others were only now beginning to wake up to, and he had died gun in hand behind a barricade, defending what he believed in. In Ferracini's book that said he couldn't be all bad.

Besides that, Ferracini had never found reason to doubt Claud's judgment. As he stood in a corner sipping tea—he was learning already that the English couldn't do anything without having a cup of tea first—and watching the stocky, red-haired, bulldog-jawed figure standing by the shrouded table in the center of the room and grumbling to Winslade about bureaucratic pigheadedness and red tape, Ferracini could sense already that Churchill was an exception to the general picture he had begun to form of the British. Back in 1975, Claud had fought hard to get the mission planners to accept Churchill as the first contact. Ferracini was already responding to Churchill's personality, even though Churchill hadn't as yet really said anything. Whatever else might be going on between other English and French generals, politicians, or whomever, Claud had found the team a good general manager. It was a shame, Ferracini thought, that he couldn't do the same for the whole country.

The session began with a few introductory words from Churchill, in which he welcomed the newly-arrived Americans to Britain and expressed the hope that many more would be following before it was too late. Then Winslade picked up a pointer and took the floor, while Major Warren let down a set of successively larger-scale wall-maps showing Europe and parts of Germany.

"I'm sure there's no need to tell you what the objective is," Winslade began breezily. He glanced around to confirm his guess, then raised the pointer to indicate a region just over a hundred miles southwest of Berlin. "From this moment on, the Nazi return-gate will be referred to as 'Hammerhead,'" he said. "It's located here, in the Leipzig area, deep underground at the chemicals and munitions plant near Weissenberg." He paused and looked around expectantly.

"Leipzig?" Cassidy repeated. He looked at Ferracini. "That was where we went on that other assignment back in '71 or '72 . . . to bring back those papers and stuff that somebody had copied from some local archives."

"Purely a coincidence," Winslade said with obvious insincerity. He turned and unveiled the table in the center to reveal a detailed model of the Weissenberg plant. "The target, gentlemen," he said.

The site was roughly square, and from familiar kinds of structures and the vehicles that had been included to indicate scale, looked about a mile or so along a side. The back lay along the bank of a river, probably the Elster, and consisted mostly of loading docks and moorings for barges. One side of the plant was flanked by trees cut back to leave a clear strip outside the boundary fence; on the other side, the land rose toward a bluff of open, rugged high-ground overlooking a bend in the river. The front faced an expanse of open ground that ended at a workers' residential suburb of Weissenberg, consisting mainly of brick rowhouses.

A road and rail spur led in via a freight entrance, and a branch of the roadway ran outside the fence for some distance to the large main gate. The fence itself was unremarkable for an industrial installation, a high wire construction with floodlights at intervals and a number of small side gates.

A cluster of what looked like office and laboratory buildings stood inside the main gate, and behind them stretched a confusion of factory buildings, processing towers, storage tanks, reaction vessels, smokestacks, and vats, all tied together in tangles of pipework, roadways, rail sidings, and canals, along with all the other paraphernalia of a large chemicals manufacturing complex. Whoever built the model had even added a few puffs of cotton-wool smoke to some of the smokestacks for realism.

But there was also something odd, Ferracini realized as he looked more closely. And now that he had noticed it, it continued getting odder. In a remote corner of the site, on the uphill side toward the bluff, a much smaller zone projected out from the main site area like a later addition, but was fenced off from it. A separate road and rail link branched off the spur outside the main plant and followed the perimeter to enter the fenced-off zone through its own, formidable-looking gate.

Everything about this appendage seemed out of place. The constructions inside it were squat, windowless, and solid-looking, with sloping walls, suggesting more a fortress or a system of blockhouses than anything connected with the rest of the plant. The surrounding enclosure consisted of three well-spaced fences with the strips between filled by tangles of barbed wire. And the watchtowers at the corners and halfway between looked as if they contained more than just floodlights.

"Quite an asset to the German war economy," Winslade commented after a suitable pause. He moved forward and pointed out various details. "For the most part it conforms to standard layout. The area over here is devoted to bulk chemical processing. This inner fence—here, along here, and around to here—encloses the munitions manufacturing compound, which produces heavy artillery shells and Luftwaffe bombs. Filling and assembly of the shells takes place in this group of buildings . . . of bombs in this group . . . and the finished products move through to final storage here, by the railhead, before shipment out. There's also a 'specials' section, here, which handles things like on-off experimental devices and low-volume test batches. Casings aren't manufactured on site, but come in by rail."

Winslade moved around a corner to reach the rear of the model. "The power plant is at the back by the coal-yard and unloading wharves, and the place next to it is a central boilerhouse for raising process steam. The buildings inside the front gate are administrative offices, and the ones behind, quality assurance and research labs. Here, outside the front gate, is the works' cafeteria and social club. This is the medical center, and that, a training school for apprentices."

There were no questions. By the time they left, everyone going on the mission would know the place as well as the streets they had grown up in. Winslade quickly scanned their faces and then went on, "But there is something unusual, as I suspect some of you have noticed already." His manner became less casual as he tapped the pointer on the casemate-like buildings of the fenced-off corner annex. "Here, in 1935, the Ordnance Department of the German Army began constructing a research and testing facility for secret work on explosives and rocket propellants. Because of the nature of the work, and because those who mattered knew that war would be only a matter of time, it was built underground, and its surface buildings made bomb-proof. However, when the basic construction work was completed two years later, the Nazi high command ordered the site to be handed over to the Todt construction organization of the SS. Hammerhead was dismantled, moved there, and reassembled from a place it had occupied in the Bavarian Alps—not far from Berchtesgaden, as a matter of fact, which was why Hitler's mountain retreat was built there."

Churchill interjected, "My first reaction was that only a lunatic would put a vital installation that close to a munitions plant. However, I am assured it would be unaffected even if everything on the surface blew up at once."

"It's more than strong enough and deep enough," Lindemann confirmed.

Winslade put the pointer down, slipped one hand into his jacket pocket—he was outfitted as a British naval officer that morning—and made a sweeping gesture over the model with the other. "On the other hand, this location offers many advantages. No one will question the need for security. Strange-looking objects going in and out will attract no undue attention. It has good road, rail, and water freight-handling facilities. And it lies within easy traveling distance of Berlin."

He turned and gazed back at the model. "The surface portion of the installation that houses Hammerhead is referred to by the people at the plant as the 'Citadel.' All that the average worker knows is that it's a place the SS owns—you stay away from it and don't ask what goes on inside. Hammerhead itself is situated several hundred feet below in an artificial rock cavern, behind concrete roof, walls, and floor all tens of feet thick.

"There are two elevator shafts giving access, one at each end. The main one is under the large hexagonal blockhouse that the rails disappear into, there, and there's a smaller emergency shaft at the rear. Each shaft is protected by its own system of alarms, armored doors, and guard posts. A permanent garrison of three hundred fully equipped SS infantry is housed inside. Both shafts connect to the facility on two levels. The connecting corridors are covered by observation and gun ports and can be sealed off from the inside. As an additional precaution, the approach passageways are also protected by gas-injection and flame-throwing devices." As he finished, Winslade wheeled to face the Special Operations squad and beamed at them challengingly.

A tomblike silence descended. Churchill allowed his gaze to flicker curiously over the faces of the Americans who were hearing all this for the first time. At last Ferracini said dryly, "I, er . . . I assume you're not expecting the six of us to take it by a frontal assault."

Winslade smiled as if he had been enjoying a small private joke. "There are limits, Harry, even to the things that I consider reasonable."

He turned back toward the table and slid away a movable section of the model to reveal a cutaway view of the underground installation and the two shafts leading down to it. The model showed other things down below ground, too, such as rock strata, piping ducts, and drainage channels. Also, there was something that looked like another vertical shaft of some kind. It lay under the general plant area, outside the Citadel and its defenses.

"The first industry on this site was a soap and dye works that grew around a potash and rock-salt mine dating from the late Middle Ages," Winslade went on. "Although no mining has been done for over a century, some of the old shafts were found to be still in existence when the later plant was contructed, and subsequently when parts were extended. They were usually sealed or filled in, but some that proved useful were cleaned out and retained." He indicated the shaft that the partitioning of the model had revealed. "This one, for example, still exists underneath one of the waste collection and disposal plants—that's the building and the tanks behind it at the top, there. To avoid dangerous reactions between inappropriate substances—acids and organics, for example—a number of separate waste-handling systems are used. In general, solid wastes are taken off down the river in barges, and liquids are simply dumped down old mine shafts such as this one and get lost in the collapsed workings and galleries below—very simple, and very cheap."

But there was a further channel, running from the lowest level of the underground Hammerhead installation, diagonally downward and in under the main plant area to meet the old mineshaft deep down. Winslade traced it with his pointer. "I said earlier that the excavation housing Hammerhead was originally intended for secret chemical work. That, too, required a waste-disposal system. It was provided by this sloping conduit, which as you can see discharges into one of the main plant's disposal shafts." Winslade smirked apologetically through his spectacles, unable to resist it. "The armadillo's anal orifice, as it were," he told the listeners.

"And that's our way in?" Ryan said. Just at that moment he wasn't in the mood for bad jokes.

"Quite."

There was a short silence. At last, Payne said, "With all that protection up top, well . . . it seems kind of strange that something like this was overlooked."

"The place isn't serving the purpose it was built for," Winslade reminded everyone. "That conduit has never been used. There was a lot of confusion and mislaid blueprints when the SS took over from the Ordnance Department. It's almost certain that nobody there today even knows it exists. It took us an enormous amount of detective work to find out about it ourselves, which involved tracking down one of the original construction engineers from 1935 . . . all kinds of things."

"So all we have to do," Cassidy summarized, "is get across to the other side of Germany with a war on, get inside the plant and into that shaft, go down it a few hundred feet and follow the conduit up into Hammerhead, blow the target, and then get out again after we've stirred up a hornets' nest of three hundred SS."

"Yes," Winslade agreed pleasantly. "Except for one other thing. The conduit joins the main disposal shaft quite deep down. We ought to assume that it lies below the surface of the liquid that's been poured down there, perhaps some considerable depth below. That, ah, would be another reason, of course, why somebody responsible for security wouldn't consider it very seriously as a possible means of entry."

"Exactly what kind of liquid are we talking about, Claud?" Ferracini asked suspiciously.

"Impossible to say," Winslade replied. "It varies with the different processes being scheduled around the plant, and that kind of thing. But you can generally count on a mixture of acid solutions, cyanides, nitrides, arsenic compounds, organics . . . in other words, it'll be highly toxic and probably corrosive. Also, the gases trapped above the liquid surface are most likely lethal."

This time everyone in the group was too stunned to say anything.

Winslade let the mood linger for a few seconds. Then he informed them, "But the sealed canisters being shipped from New York were brought with the mission as insurance against precisely this kind of eventuality. They contain kits of specially developed protective clothing, complete with breathing apparatus, and other equipment. We've already made arrangements for practice and familiarization sessions for you all, first at the Royal

Navy's submarine and escape school at Portsmouth, and then in a more realistic environment at a flooded tin mine in Cornwall."

Winslade, true to form, had delivered the worst up front and was saving no nasty surprises. As the initial shock started to wear off, the others found their voices, and then the questions began coming thick and fast.

If this stuff did turn out to be corrosive, how long could these suits be expected to give protection? Cassidy wanted to know. It depended, Winslade told him. It was no accident that one of the party, Captain Payne, was a chemist. The equipment included an analysis kit, and the answer to the question would depend on his findings at the time.

How would they descend the shaft and get up the sloping conduit? They would be spending some time at the limestone caverns in Derbyshire for a course on caving techniques and equipment. What did the shaft walls consist of? What was their probable condition? How big was the conduit, what was its gradient, and how slippery was it likely to be?

What was at the top of the conduit? A steel coverplate resting on a steel-rimmed concrete seating, secured by eight one-inch-diameter bolts. Thermite charges would be used to melt the fixed nuts holding the bolts.

And when the seal was broken, then what? The conduit opened into a basement level of Hammerhead, containing pumps, air circulation equipment, and other machinery, with the return-gate itself on the level above. Since the precautions against intruders were directed upward, not down, an experienced team proficient in stealth should have a reasonable chance of placing demolition charges and effecting a safe exit. "And if not . . . well, that's why we attach so much importance to initiative training," Winslade completed.

A silence followed, punctuated by shuffling feet and long intakes of breath. Then Ferracini said, "That's all very fine as far as the assault goes, Claud, but how are we supposed to carry suits, weapons, caving and other gear, plus enough explosives to do the job, halfway across Germany?"

"You're not," Winslade replied. "That side of the operation depends on factors that couldn't be anticipated, and therefore, hasn't been finalized yet. You'll be traveling in pairs, but the details will be the subject of another briefing at a date yet to be fixed."

"Couldn't we just fly into Berlin from Sweden or somewhere as American neutrals—journalists or something?" Ryan asked.

"Too many problems with being kept under surveillance by

the police all the time," Winslade answered. "Best not to risk it. As for getting the equipment there, we're looking into several alternatives. Air-dropping it is one possibility. Another is smuggling it in independently. Again, this will be covered in detail later."

"How about contacts in the area?" Cassidy asked finally. "Can we expect local help?"

In reply Winslade looked inquiringly at Churchill, who looked at Lindemann. Lindemann cleared his throat. "Oh, my department, I think." He stood up and moved a couple of paces forward. "As some of you may know, I spent some years in Germany after the Great War. When the Nazis came to power, I made several return visits to help endangered European scientists, especially those of Jewish descent, to escape and find suitable employment in the West. Leo Szilard was also involved in that, as a matter of fact. Anyhow, to answer the question, yes, I have been making discreet inquiries through channels I prefer not to disclose, and it should be possible to arrange some help for you from people who are opposed to the Nazi regime enough to want to help, and whom I consider sufficiently reliable."

Winslade added, "But we won't say more about them for now. Naturally, each pair of you will be given the name of your own contact only."

There remained only one further question. Payne asked it. "When?"

Major Warren answered. "At present, we're aiming for the end of February." He looked at the squad and treated them to an imitation of a sadistic leer. "But don't get carried away with visions of a nice, cozy Christmas. We've got one or two other things lined up in addition to what Claud talked about. You've all been having it too easy for too long back at Gatehouse. For the next month, we'll all be getting back into shape. I've booked us all a vacation on assault course training—as guests of the British Army."

Anna Kharkiovitch was sitting at the back of the room with Gordon Selby, reflecting on what had been said. It was obvious that long before the mission's departure from 1975, Winslade had seen fit to take elaborate precautions against a possible failure to reestablish contact. How much had Claud known all along, and how much more might he know now that he wasn't telling? Was there no chance of any of them ever returning? Had there never been any chance?

Or was the explanation nothing more sinister than Claud's habit, inculcated by a lifetime of working amid secrecy and intrigue, of never telling anybody more than they needed to know to do what needed doing at the time?

As always, everything connected with Claud was murky, enigmatic, and uncertain. And that, to a woman of Anna's disposition and temperament, added up to: infuriating.

CHAPTER 30

CHRISTMAS WEEK, 1939, BROUGHT great excitement to the scientists working at Gatehouse. For the first time, the monitoring instruments connected to the return-gate indicated that it was picking up pulsed energy. The only evidence was a flickering trace on the screen of a primitive oscilloscope hooked up to a typically outlandish Fermi improvisation of coils, vacuum tubes, and bits of wire, but the characteristics of the pulses confirmed that the long-awaited contact between different universes had at last been initiated. Much had yet to be done before meaningful information could be exchanged, let alone physical objects, but it was a start. A fine seasonal present for all involved.

In one of those inexplicable flashes of sudden insight that illuminate the lives of the truly great, Einstein had realized that a crucial but unquestioned assumption—that time at the two ends of a connection between future and past would run at the same speed—was without any proven foundation. In day after day of debating and theorizing that usually went on all through the night over take-out snacks and endless coffee, the red-eyed but excited scientists reexamined and reformulated their basic premises and eventually produced a revised mathematical model. The equations deduced from the model revealed that, indeed, as Einstein had suggested, the rates of time-flow at the two ends of a link would not be the same. They would differ, in fact, according to the fourth power of the time interval between the ends, with time at the future end running slower; thus, if time ran twice as slowly a certain distance into the future, it would run sixteen times as slowly twice as far into the future, and so on. The exact relationship depended on certain constants that could only be found by experiment, and which were not yet known.

This explained why the 1975 machine had failed to contact them. Before a projector could link with and power a return-gate, it first coarse-scanned the designated zone of spacetime with a probe "beam," closing the connection only when it detected the formation of a multidimensional field resonance across the dividing interval. For the probe to lock on, a precise synchronization had to be achieved with certain wave functions generated at the return-gate end—analogous to a radio receiver's having to be tuned to the same frequency as the transmitter to pick up a station. Synchronization depended on timekeeping, and if no allowance were made for the difference in time-rates at the two ends, the link-up wouldn't work. It really was—well, almost—as simple as that.

With the key fallacy exposed, the rest was expected to follow fairly rapidly, and the scientists set up preliminary experiments to determine the unknown constants. This required little more than modifying the operating ranges of some of the electronics, which was a straightforward task, and the first tests produced an incoming signal that was identified as a component of the probe beam. Measurements of the pulse rate and other parameters, and comparison with the known design data for the machine transmitting from 1975, showed that, from the 1939 reference frame, time would be flowing slower in 1975 by a factor of 5.7.

Getting the link to work wouldn't be as easy as twiddling the tuning knob of a radio to the correct position, however. Because the people, including Kurt Scholder, who, in 1975, had rushed through the construction of the system from purloined German records hadn't fully understood the fundamentals, the return-gate wasn't designed to be "tunable"; and the fixed mode that it worked in was wrong. Putting it right would require the reengineering of some components and the complete redesign of others. By mid-December, a stream of requisitions and specifications for the required parts was going out to suitable laboratories and workshops. Thanks to Roosevelt's involvement, there was no problem in obtaining whatever level of authorization was needed to ensure top-priority response.

Once that work was under way, the scientists followed up

some rough calculations they had poduced which suggested that, even though all modifications had not been completed, a partial interaction between the machine and the probe beam scanning from 1975 ought to be possible. When the first of the re-engineered components came in and were fitted, the scientists set about putting their hunch to the test.

"It's right on the threshold," Scholder announced, peering at a sensitive light-spot galvanometer wired into the jumble of apparatus that was strung together on a portable bench placed near one of the control panels. "It's rising again. . . . Close—nineteen point two. Very close . . . fading slightly now, eighteen-nine . . . eight."

The green trace flickering on the tiny screen that Fermi was watching swelled for a second or two, then shrank again. "Q must have been above ninety-eight percent of critical that time," he said. He adjusted a control on the panel and checked a reading. "I've reduced beta to five. Recharge the bank and let's try that again with everything else the same."

Einstein, Teller, and two of the assistants looked on, Einstein puffing his pipe and watching with amused interest like an amiable science teacher; Teller more intent, serious, and a shade edgy after almost forty-eight hours without sleep. It was Christmas Eve, and they had just finished installing the first of a set of resonant cavity devices delivered to Columbia University that morning from a precision engineering firm in New Jersey. Although the device wouldn't be enough to support the communications channel, the hope was that it might just give the system enough responsiveness for the probe beam to find it. That would be an important milestone reached.

"Up to charge," Scholder said. His voice was calm and matter-of-fact. "Loop energized. Okay . . . the ramp's climbing now."

Fermi took up the commentary. "Nineteen . . . nineteen-point two . . . point three . . ." He tensed visibly with excitement. "Three-five . . . point four . . . my God, it's going to make it!"

Teller stepped forward and peered over Fermi's shoulder. "Q is critical now," he said.

"Nineteen point five!" Fermi exclaimed. At the same instant, an orange lamp glowed on one side of a panel crudely hacked out of sheet aluminum, and a pointer on a dial next to it swung up from zero on the scale and steadied.

Scholder smiled tiredly as Fermi whooped and slapped him on the back. "We've got contact!" Teller shouted behind them. "The probe beam's reacting!" The assistants standing with Einstein cheered, and other figures began appearing from places around the rig to see what all the fuss was about.

The readings confirmed that although the return-gate system was responding, the partial resonance that it was setting up was too feeble for the probe to lock on and open the auxiliary channel. The interaction itself, however, should have induced a disturbance in the physical dynamics of the beam sufficient to alert the operators at the far end to the fact that the probe was encountering something. If that condition could be maintained, it offered an opportunity, perhaps, for conveying a crude form of message by making and breaking the energizing circuit in a coded pattern.

They had already agreed to try it if the test succeeded, so no time was lost on deliberations. As soon as the pointer registering contact had stabilized, Scholder commenced flipping the energizer supply switch up and down, using it as a Morse key: P-R-O-T-E-U-S . . . P-R-O-T-E-U-S . . . P-R-O-T-E-U-S . . .

He continued until Fermi announced that the fleeting contact had been lost. It reappeared a few minutes later and then died completely. "We were lucky to get that," Teller commented. "It was right on the threshold all the time. We're not going to achieve much more until the phase modulator amplifiers arrive."

"Edward's right," Fermi said, sitting back in his chair. "And we won't see them until after the holiday. I vote we all take a break. Hitler or no Hitler, tomorrow is reserved for my wife . . . assuming I still have one. What's the point of preserving freedom if you're never free for a moment to benefit from it?"

The others agreed. They shut down the system and collected coats, hats, and papers to take home. After a final round of salutes, best wishes, and arrangements made by some to get together later in the evening or sometime for dinner the next day, they broke up to go their various ways.

Teller agreed to take Fermi in his car and drive Einstein to Princeton before returning to his own apartment in Morningside Heights. "You know, it's a strange thought," Fermi remarked as the three of them walked through the machine area toward the front of the building, where the vehicles were parked. "If they do spot the perturbations in 1975, then with a dilation factor of almost six, only two months or so will have gone by in their world since the Proteus people left."

"If it's the same 1975," Teller said. "We don't know how many universes might be aiming probe beams back at the zone we're in. How do we know we've hit the right one? What's the probability of another 'crossed wire'? In fact, just how does the whole mess manage to keep itself untangled at all?" He sighed heavily as they descended the steps of the loading dock. "There's so much that we don't know."

Fermi was equally baffled. Instinctively, the two of them looked at Einstein. "I haven't the faintest intention of spoiling my Christmas by even thinking about it," he informed them as they climbed into Teller's car.

A plainclothes military policeman opened one of the large doors to let the car back out. Evening was closing fast. Flurries of snow filled the air, and slush from an earlier fall still covered the ground. Just as Teller was about to engage first and move away, a shout came from across the road—a woman's shout. The three in the car looked around.

A week or so previously, someone had rented the small store-house with adjoining office shack across the road. It had been standing empty since the summer. One day, a truck had appeared to unload a few crates, but the only signs of life observed since then by the Gatehouse security guards had been a woman going in and out once or twice, her car parked outside for most of the day, and a light inside the window. The officer in charge of security had requested a routine check, but nothing amiss was found. Now the woman was running toward them and waving.

"Don't go—wait a minute!" She arrived, puffing, at the car, a woman in her mid-forties, perhaps, a little on the plump side, wearing a fur hat with earpieces and a heavy tweed coat. Teller wound down the window. "Thanks," the woman said. She rested her purse on the window ledge and got her breath back. "Sorry to trouble you, but I've been an idiot. I left my headlights on, and now the battery's dead. Could I get a start off yours? I can't use those hand-cranks, and I do have some cables."

Teller glanced at the others, nodded, and was about to reply when the security guard who had opened the door came over and intervened. "That's okay, sir, you carry on," he told Teller. Then, to the woman, "I'll come over in just a second and crank it for you, ma'am."

"Thank you. You're so kind."

"All part of the service." The guard waved Teller on his way, and the car moved off along the street. Then the guard turned and began walking back to close the warehouse door. The woman followed him, but he stopped and raised a warning hand. "Ah, wait out here, ma'am, if you don't mind," he told her. "I'll just be a few seconds."

The woman, who was known as "Musketeer," stopped obediently. She could see from where she was standing that there was nothing remarkable inside the doors. But she had managed to get a good view of the three men in the car. Albert Einstein she had recognized immediately. She hadn't known the other two, but she'd got a good shot of their faces from the car's window ledge with the camera built into her purse. And there had been plenty of time to memorize the license-plate number.

CHAPTER
31

THE WINTER OF 1939–1940 was the coldest that Europe had experienced in forty-five years. Around Britain the Channel froze off Folkestone and Dungeness; the Thames was solid ice for eight miles from Teddington to Sunbury; and in parts of Derbyshire the snow drifted up to the roofs of farmhouses and cottages.

On the fifth day of the New Year, Minister of War Leslie Hore-Belisha resigned, the first of Anna Kharkiovitch's "baby hedge-sparrows" to be pushed from the nest, and there was a reshuffling of ministers; the machinations that Winslade and Bannering were orchestrating from behind the scenes were producing tangible results. Whether these would add up to enough and in time, however, was another matter.

Ferracini and the rest of Ampersand knew no more about the incident than appeared in the papers; they didn't have too much time to care what might be behind it. They spent the Christmas and New Year period with one of the British regiments training on Dartmoor, a bleak expanse of wild and windswept heath, scrub, hills, and bogs on the Devon-Cornwall peninsula. Officially, they were listed as American volunteers temporarily assigned to the unit pending further posting elsewhere.

Although the course was tame in comparison to the brutal

physical and psychological demands of the three-month screening process that would-be Special Operations volunteers endured, everyone in the Ampersand group was grateful for the program of calisthenics, combat sports, and swimming that Major Warren had imposed during the months at Gatehouse. For a month, they raced with full battle-packs over treacherous, ice-bound assault courses; hauled themselves, cursing and perspiring, up climbing nets; scaled walls and ramparts; and negotiated swaying plank and rope bridges over deep ravines. They trudged for days on cross-country marches until blisters appeared and hardened on all the old, familiar spots on their feet; and they went through open-air physical drill, jumping, climbing, vaulting, and performing team sit-ups, squats, and presses with telephone poles, ten men to a pole.

During the course, they saw why Warren had abandoned his idea of replacing their missing reinforcements with British volunteers. Perhaps letting them see the reasons for themselves had been part of his purpose in arranging the program.

It wasn't that the British troops lacked guts or spirit. Far from it. The Tommies for the most part were enthusiastic and hard-working, didn't complain too much, and accepted the inevitable screw-ups and lousy breaks that were the soldier's lot with cheerful resignation. Lean and hardy like their American counterparts after the years of the economic slump, they were keen to get over to the other side, get the job done, and come home again. They knew that was how it would happen because that was how it had always happened.

That was the problem: They had no idea what they were up against.

They were inexperienced, naive, and totally trusting in officers who belonged to a world that had ceased to exist. The Germans were "all wind and trousers," a lance corporal from Wigan told the Americans over a supper of bullied beef, beans, and gravy. "They like marchin' oop an' down wit' flags an' bands, an' pushin' poor little booggers like Poland around, but when somebody who means business finally puts 'is foot down, they soon go scurryin' for their 'oles." The same mistakes hadn't been made this time as in 1914. The Maginot Line was there now, and the blokes behind it were ready.

Ready for what? Ferracini wondered.

Their combat training consisted almost entirely of a few sessions on a rifle range and in grenade pits—with limited ammunition—and formalized, old-school bayonet drill. They learned how to dig trenches, shore them up with timber, and fit duckboards;

how to blanco webbing; and how to shine boots. It was ironic: yes, all the things were being done right that should have been done in 1914. But this was 1940.

What of antitank weapons? What of tactics for dealing with massed, air-supported armor smashing through on narrow fronts and racing along main roads at speeds that would have left the Great War commanders paralyzed? The German field tractors could haul rubber-tired, six-inch guns up rough hillsides at forty miles per hour to bring close artillery support right up behind the tanks. How could fixed batteries, dug in miles behind a front that would supposedly remain static, be expected to counter them? What of cooperation with friendly tanks and aircraft? The German commanders used radio to keep track of movements in the highly mobile, fast-changing situations that they anticipated. How could generals who still depended on dispatch riders and runners hope even to know what was happening, let alone do anything to affect it?

At one training session just after New Year's Day, Ferracini, Cassidy, and Lamson looked on in disbelief while a British brigadier, complete with knee-high cavalry boots, white walrus mustache, and port-wine complexion, gave instruction on tackling the Junkers 87 dive bomber—the infamous Stuka—with a rifle. "You'll find it quite straightforward if you keep your heads," the brigadier assured his attentive flock. "Stand up to them and take them high on the climb, like a pheasant. A brace a day per man would add up to a jolly good bag—what?" Confident laughter greeted the remark. The Americans didn't laugh.

The next day, the hand-to-hand combat instructor, a big, sadistic sergeant from Glasgow who liked knocking the new recruits about, picked on Floyd Lamson as a stooge and came out of it lightly with a cracked collarbone, torn cartilage in the neck, and a raw shin. Cassidy explained hastily to the shocked C.O. that Lamson had ancestral blood from an Indian tribe notorious for its instability.

"They were the ones who wiped out General Custer," Cassidy told the officer, while Lamson winced inwardly. "His grandfather was a cannibal. It's not really his fault. . . . And they do make good scouts." The C.O. gave Lamson the benefit of the doubt and dismissed the affair with a plea for him to at least try to behave like a civilized Christian. The number of beers subsequently bought for Lamson at the pub not far from the camp by grinning young Britishers more than compensated.

The British weren't the only ones gearing up to fight the last war all over again. The French, if anything, were worse; and from what Ferracini and the others had heard and read in the course of almost a year in America, the majority of U.S. generals still seemed to be having trouble grasping that the planet continued beyond Maine. It wasn't so much that they were slow in responding to change. Leaders and rulers always had much to lose and little to gain from the disruptions brought by change; therefore, invariably, they constituted the conservative elements of society. That much had been true throughout history. The difference this time was that the thinking of one side was being shaped by minds whose experience came from eighty-five years in the future.

Even so, the Ampersand troops agreed privately, in the four months that had gone by since the beginning of September, the West's leaders should have learned more from Poland than they had.

The New Year was colder and icier than usual, even in Berlin. Despite years of incessant, vitriolic Nazi propaganda, the majority of the population hadn't wanted war. In contrast to the scenes of frenzied jubilation amid which the German armies of 1914 had marched off to the fronts, the streets had remained quiet and empty at the news of Poland's invasion. Now with things like the blackout, a war surtax of fifty percent on top of income tax, the virtual disappearance of gasoline, the introduction of ration cards for food, soap, shoes, and clothing, and coffee's replacement by a coarse substitute made from roasted barley seeds, the average Berliner felt the cold of 1940 psychologically as well as physically.

The scene in the Tiergarten presented a curious contrast, with children skating on frozen ponds, and sandbagged anti-aircraft batteries brooding menacingly beneath snow-laden camouflage nets. Colonel Piekenbrock and Lieutenant Colonel Boeckel were taking a lunchtime stroll from the Bendlerstrasse. They walked slowly side by side, caps pulled low, faces tucked down behind the upturned collars of their greatcoats, snow crunching beneath their jackboots.

"There's no chance of mistaken identity?" Piekenbrock said. His breath turned to white vapor in the cold air as he spoke.

Boeckel shook his head. "The faces were identified independently by three experts. Also, the car was registered in Teller's name. We're quite certain."

They walked on in silence for a while. "So what do you make of it?" Piekenbrock asked. Boeckel knew by now that this tendency of Piekenbrock's didn't mean he was perpetually devoid of ideas. It was simply his way to ask a subordinate's opinions before voicing his own. It helped him recognize talent, and it disarmed yes-men.

"Well, we seem to have uncovered a small, but highly professional, unpublicized unit of the American Army, specially trained in guerilla methods and undercover operations. They've even staged practice missions from a disguised base in New York."

"Agreed," Piekenbrock said, nodding.

"And now we find Einstein visiting this same base. Not only that, but he's with Teller and Fermi, both of them specialists in the same field." Boeckel glanced at his superior uncertainly.

"Oh, yes, yes," Piekenbrock said, waving a leather-gloved hand impatiently and thrusting it back in his pocket. "You can say it. Einstein is a great scientist. Never mind the nonsense that Goebbels churns out for the masses. And you say that this Hungarian and the Italian specialize in the same field. What field is that?"

"I made inquiries at the Kaiser Wilhelm Institute," Boeckel replied. "About a year ago, an important experiment was conducted here in Berlin which caused an international stir among physicists investigating the inner structure of atoms. Apparently, there are good reasons to suppose that atomic processes involving the element uranium might release quite large quantities of energy—enormous quantities, in fact. Some of the scientists at the KWI say it could lead to a revolution one day in powering industry, ships, and so forth. And in weapons."

Piekenbrock frowned. "Atoms? But they're just tiny things, aren't they?"

"Extremely so, sir."

"Amazing. Anyhow . . ."

"It seems that both Teller and Fermi are noted for their work in that field. In fact, Fermi was awarded a Nobel Prize for his contribution. He ran away to America when he went to Sweden to collect it."

"A Jew?"

"His wife—partly."

"I wonder if we can really afford to lose too many people like that in the long run. Anyhow, that's not our department."

They came to a small hump-backed bridge over a frozen stream and stopped for two Wehrmacht generals going the other way. The generals returned their salutes as they passed. They carried on walking again, and Boeckel continued, "In the last year, official interest in uranium has been expressed in England, France, and America. Also, in America especially, there has been a marked decline in the amount of information being published on research connected with the subject. In other words, it seems that the West might be taking this notion of extra-powerful weapons seriously."

"Do you think this could have something to do with the super-bombs that the Führer has been telling us we'll have in two years?" Piekenbrock asked.

"Yes, I think it could," Boeckel replied. "It seems that both sides are onto the same thing."

Piekenbrock nodded. "And the Americans have trained a special unit to infiltrate Germany and conduct espionage or sabotage operations on what our people are doing," he completed. "These scientists were probably going to the training base in New York to give technical briefings on what to look for and things like that, eh? It makes sense. I think we can forget this idea of an assassination squad being sent after the Führer."

"My conclusion also," Boeckel agreed. He waited for a moment; then, seeing that Piekenbrock wasn't about to reply at that point, he went on, "I've been doing some further checking that suggests there might be still more to the story."

"Oh?"

"There seems to be some kind of a network of people involved on both sides of the Atlantic. For instance, Fermi and Teller are both at Columbia University in New York. Another Hungarian, called Szilard, is also involved there. He isn't on the official staff, but lives in a hotel along the street. Now, he was previously engaged in similar work in England. One of the people whom he worked with was a Professor Lindemann, who is a personal friend of Churchill's and also his most trusted scientific advisor."

"Ah, so *Der Lügenlord* appears in the picture, does he?" Piekenbrock murmured. "Lying Lord" was the German newspapers' latest term to describe Churchill. He was also referred to widely by his initials, WC, which were written on the door of every German toilet.

"Lindemann spent some years here in Germany, and he and Szilard were mixed up in getting Jewish scientists out of the country," Boeckel went on. "Now Lindemann has moved into Churchill's Admiralty headquarters in London. Einstein stayed at Churchill's Chartwell mansion when he was in England in 1933. Einstein and Szilard were colleagues in Germany. Teller was there, too, at the time. He met Fermi in Italy before Fermi went to America. You see, the same names keep appearing. They're linked in some kind of pattern, but I haven't managed to interpret it yet."

Piekenbrock halted at a junction in the path. Boeckel waited. A short distance away, an old woman was struggling to haul a wooden sled carrying a sack of coal, while a small boy pushed in the snow behind. Coal was the worst of the shortages that winter. Reportedly tens of thousands of homes in Berlin were without heating at all.

"If they are all part of such a network, then our American friends would no doubt stop off at England on the way, wouldn't they—to coordinate with the Churchill end of the operation?" Piekenbrock said at last.

"Very probably," Boeckel agreed.

Piekenbrock nodded slowly. "I'd like a special watch kept for them at the places they might be expected to appear—Churchill's naval headquarters in London, for example," he said at last. "It would be a useful confirmation of our guesses, and we might get a better idea of what they're up to." He paused. "How much of our work on uranium is going on at the KWI? Is it concentrated there, or are things going on at other places, too?"

"It's a confused situation," Boeckel said. "The KWI people are working under a Professor von Weizsäcker, with support from the War Office. But there's another professor, called Esau, who's running a setup for the Education Ministry over on Linden, and the Ordnance Department has something going at Gottow. It's not clear how all the pieces fit together. Sometimes, I think it's easier to find out what the enemy's doing than these infernal bureaucracies of ours."

"Well, get a picture together of what's happening, and especially where," Piekenbrock said briskly. "I'd like a list drawn up of the major centers where work is in progress on this uranium business. If we do get wind that those Americans are on their way over here, it might be as well to know what their potential targets might be."

"I'll begin at once, sir."

"You've done some good work, Boeckel," Piekenbrock complimented. "Keep it up. You should go a long way. . . . Oh, and I trust that things are under control concerning that matter to do with your secretary?"

A puzzled frown crossed Boeckel's face. "She's gone, sir. She was transferred to Hamburg."

"She was?" Piekenbrock managed to look genuinely surprised. "Oh, yes, I'd forgotten. Well, behave yourself with her replacement."

"That won't be difficult," Boeckel said glumly. "They've given me a hag who's at least fifty. She's as fat as a carthorse and has bad breath."

Piekenbrock strolled on, admiring the patterns of snow on the trees and avoiding his subordinate's suspicious glances. "Did they really? Oh well, these things happen, I suppose. Isn't that just too bad."

On January 10, an incident occurred that had not taken place in the Proteus team's universe: Two German officers made a forced landing at Menchelen, in Belgium, after their plane strayed off course. They were carrying copies of the German plan of attack in the West, which took the form of a thrust through the Low Countries as the Allied commanders had anticipated, and which the Proteus team's history confirmed.

The German planning staff had been urging Hitler to delay the attack because of the continuing atrocious weather—again, a departure from events in the Proteus universe, where conditions had been less severe. With the loss of the plans, Hitler conceded and ordered the campaign in the West to be postponed until spring.

Hitler also decided that adhering to the captured plan would be too risky and called for a new one to be drawn up. He began paying close attention to a scheme that General von Manstein, the new commander of the XXXIII Army Corps, had been urging for a fast-moving armored thrust through the Ardennes, far south of the originally proposed points of attack. The French considered the area impassable to tanks and hadn't committed much of their strength to its defense. Even if the Germans did attack in that region, the French reasoned, they would need six or seven days to bring up their heavy artillery—ample time for the French reserves to move into covering positions.

Von Manstein agreed with these calculations. Therefore, he wasn't proposing to use heavy artillery; he would use ground-attack bombers, instead.

CHAPTER
32

DIVING AND THE USE of scuba equipment were part of the basic training of all Special Operations troops; so were parachuting, skiing, mountaineering, and travel across all types of terrain from arctic icefields to tropical jungles—in short, just about every means available for carrying warfare to an enemy. Furthermore, Paddy Ryan, in an another coincidence that Winslade refused to comment on, had previously been an instructor at the Navy's Underwater Reconnaissance & Demolition training base in Florida. Hence, none of the Ampersand group who arrived at the submarine school in the second week of January needed any introduction to flippers, masks, wet suits, dry suits, or underwater breathing apparatus. After a day's practice to refresh basic skills, therefore, they were able to devote the rest of the time to the main object of their stay at Portsmouth: learning to use the the special equipment, both consignments of which had arrived safely from New York via Liverpool.

Each suit consisted of an inner and an outer garment. The body-hugging inner was made of soft sponge rubber to trap bubbles of insulating air close to the skin, covered by a layer of treated flannel. The outer was a hooded, tight-fitting suit made from double-thickness oilskin impregnated with paraffin wax.

The design was based on underwater dress as it had developed by the 1970s, but with the added features of gloves and over-gauntlets attaching at watertight wrist seals, tighter-sealing face masks, and hard outer helmets, colored for ease of identification.

The aims were not only to prevent all contact with the surrounding medium and to afford good heat insulation, but also to minimize the spread of liquid inside the suit if a leak did develop—the rate at which fluid under pressure could penetrate even a pinhole was surprising. And if the contents of the mineshaft were corrosive and somebody suffered a major gash? Well, that was one of the reasons why the person picked as medical officer, Ed Payne, just happened to have specialized in chemical burns.

Unlike regular scuba gear, which supplied compressed air from backpack tanks, respiration was effected by means of an oxygen rebreathing system worn on the chest, far less bulky and unlikely to prove a hindrance in confined spaces. In addition, the suits were equipped with saturated magnetic-reactor telephones, which required no cords and functioned like radios up to distances of a few hundred feet; they were compact and required no electronics or heavy batteries.

Some of the concepts employed were novel by the standards of 1940; for example, one-piece face masks instead of goggles that squeezed eyes uncomfortably at depth, and on-demand regulator valves delivering air at the pressure of the working depth to inflate the lungs against the weight of the overlying water. Care had been taken, however, to exclude any totally implausible innovations. Thus, any equipment falling into German hands might cause a few raised eyebrows, but it would be unlikely to arouse further suspicions.

"Well, the way I figure it has to be is like this," Cassidy said, sitting forward and lifting his leg onto one of the cross-girders to adjust part of his harness. "You know what Kurt said about all these universes branching off from each other every time an atom flips its lid, or whatever he said they do?"

"Uh-huh." Ferracini, clad in his own suit except for its face mask, leaned out from their perch on the steel-lattice gantry spanning the top of the fifty-foot-deep escape tank, and looked down at the muddy brown surface of the water six feet below. Major Warren and Captain Payne were on a wider platform in the middle of the gantry, from which a set of lines disappeared down to where Lamson and Ryan were demolishing obstructions at the bottom. The water in the tank had been dyed opaque brown to simulate the liquids at the bottom of the shaft at Weissenberg, and the team was having to learn to work by feel and communicate via a system of touch signals instead of the diver's usual hand signs. Payne had commented that the color was appropriate to Claud's quip about armadillos.

"And every universe is a possible version of what might have happened, somehow different from all the others," Cassidy went on.

Ferracini nodded. "That's the way it sounded to me, anyhow."

"Okay, so once two branches divide and go separate ways, they can never merge again, right? In other words, once two versions of a past exist that are different in some way, they can't lead you to the same future, okay?"

"I dunno. . . . Well, maybe. . . . What is this, Cassidy? Since when have you—"

"Shuddup a minute, Harry, this makes sense. Now—"

"Well, excuse me."

"Sure, but now think about this. If you build a machine that sends people or a message—anything—back into the past, it has to create a new branch—in fact, a whole new tree of branches that begins right at the instant that the whatever-it-is appears. Now, all of those new branches have to be different from the line that was already there and led to the future that the whatever-it-is came from. They have to be different because they've got a whatever-it-is on them—like a machine in Germany back in 1925, for instance—that the line that was already there doesn't have. Therefore, anyone who comes back through that machine can't do anything to change what's on the line that was already there because the line he's on now—the new line—leads someplace else up the new tree."

"Wait a minute . . ." Ferracini held up a hand while he thought over what Cassidy said. "Okay, so . . ." He stopped, and his eyes widened.

Cassidy nodded vigorously before Ferracini could say any more. "That's right. Overlord must have known at least that much, seeing as how they figured out the original system and all that. So, any idea of them thinking they could change their own situation by setting up Hitler to take out the Soviets is baloney. They'd have known that nothing they did could change anything to do with where they were at."

"So what did Overlord think they were achieving?" Ferracini asked, puzzled.

Cassidy shrugged. "All I can think of is that they didn't figure they'd change their own universe, but set up a new one that suited them better. Then they'd pack their bags, move in, and take it over."

"You mean after Hitler had gotten rid of the Soviets and set it up for them?"

"Exactly—except that he had other ideas and shut down his end of the connection before they made their move."

And that was where the world he had grown up in had come from. Ferracini couldn't fault the reasoning. Slowly, a frown crept over his face as he thought about what it meant. "Are you saying that Claud must have known about it, too—that he's been holding out?"

"Either that or he got it wrong," Cassidy said.

"Claud doesn't usually get too much wrong."

"That's what I figured."

"But if Claud knew, then . . ."

"If he knew, then he'd have known also that the same applied to our universe," Cassidy completed. "Nothing we do here can change the situation that JFK and the rest of them are in back there. All we can affect is the future of the branch we're on now."

On the platform behind them, Payne said something into his telephone and looked over his shoulder at Warren. "Ryan says they're done. They're coming back up now."

Ferracini and Cassidy collected tools and other items in preparation for going down next. "So what are you saying?" Ferracini asked. "That Claud had the same idea—our world had no future worth talking about, so he decided to transfer to another one that had more going for it?"

"If you were him, which one would you rather retire in?" Cassidy asked.

"I'll tell you when I've got a better idea where this one's leading."

"But at least it's got chances. See my point?"

Ferracini stood up and thought about it while he fastened lines, knife, and tool belt, making sure that everything was tied and buckled such that it could be released instantly if it got caught in something. "So how come he never told anybody?" he said at last.

Cassidy spread his hands in a what-else-do-you-expect? gesture. "If we're stuck here, we're stuck, but if it does turn out to be true, how many of us honestly feel now that it would be such a lousy deal? We've had a year to get used to this place, and it could be a lot worse. Now that we're all adjusting, Claud doesn't talk too much about Gatehouse, anymore—hadn't you noticed? He talks about Hammerhead. See what I mean? It's what happens to this world that he's interested in, not the one we came from."

"Einstein and all those scientists back there with Mortimer

and Kurt—are you saying it was all a waste of time from the start? Claud knew it was?"

"I'm not sure," Cassidy admitted. "But let me ask you this: Would you have had anything to do with this mission if you'd known for a fact before we left that it was gonna be a one-way ticket?"

At the end of the week, Winslade came down from London to see how things were going. He showed up looking like a nine-teenth-century English squire, in checked tweed suit, complete with topcoat, shoulder-length cape, deerstalker hat, and smoking a curved briar pipe. He announced that from the latest intelligence reports the German attack might not materialize at the end of January, after all. The improvement in Allied resolve might be part of the reason; the weather could have something to do with it. Nobody was sure. But in any case, the Allied plan was to meet a German thrust as far forward as possible by advancing into Belgium at the first sign of a German move westward.

There was a lot of popular support for Finland, still putting up a good fight against the Russians. The Norwegian and Swedish governments, however, were balking at the thought of granting the Allies passage to render any aid. The British, for their part, now that war had come, had no qualms at the implied prospect of fighting the Soviet Union in addition to the Nazis.

"They've taken the view that Stalin is as bad as Hitler, and if they're going to get rid of one, they might as well get rid of the other while they're at it," Winslade said. That the opposition the British were talking about taking on was more than ten times the population of their tiny island didn't seem to bother them at all.

CHAPTER
33

ON THE LAST DAY of January, the scientists at Gatehouse again made a crude contact with the 1975 system by establishing what Scholder described as a "partial resonance." This happened five weeks after the first occurrence, which had taken place on Christmas Eve. There had been delays in getting some of the redesigned components delivered; others had had to be scrapped and reordered, and progress in general had not been spectacular. Scholder repeated his attempt to attract attention at the far end by morse transmission, but nothing new was accomplished. Greene telephoned the news to Winslade as a matter of course, and Winslade asked to be informed immediately of any further developments.

In Europe, the German assault in the West that had overwhelmed France and led to Britain's defeat in the previous universe failed to materialize. By the end of the first few days of February, those with inside knowledge who had been anxiously following the situation concluded that the invasion wasn't coming. At last, the strengthened Allied determination seemed to have shown results and altered the course of history for the better.

Reassured and emboldened, Churchill and his followers stepped up their pressure for action to forestall the Nazi move into Scandinavia, which in the Proteus world had taken place in May. Accordingly, on February 5, the Allied Supreme War Council decided upon intervention in Norway. The plan adopted followed closely the lines that Winslade had outlined at Churchill's flat in November, namely that the public justification would be to aid Finland, while the government would believe that the real objective was to cut off Germany's iron-ore supply from Sweden.

On February 16, the British destroyer *Cossack*, acting on direct orders from Churchill, sailed into a Norwegian fjord to apprehend the German ship *Altmark*. Although the Norwegians were supposed to have searched the *Altmark* and had reported negatively, Admiralty intelligence held that the ship carried British seamen taken prisoner by the German pocket battleship *Graf Spee*, which had later scuttled itself after being cornered by British and New Zealand warships in the South Atlantic in December. A boarding party from the *Cossack* found 299 British prisoners aboard the *Altmark* and forced their release, causing immense satisfaction and jubilation among the British public— and to hell with whatever international law had to say about it.

The incident also provoked concern among the German high command, who were under no delusions about the pretext of Allied aid to Finland. If the British hadn't hesitated to violate Norwegian territorial waters for something as inconsequential as freeing a few prisoners, the Germans reasoned, surely they would be at least as likely to shrug off Norwegian neutrality for the far greater prize of denying Germany its ore supplies. Accordingly, the Chief of the German Navy, Admiral Raeder, began pressing Hitler to move the date for the Norway invasion forward.

Meanwhile in England, after three more weeks of wriggling and squeezing through Derbyshire caverns, rappelling down slippery ropes into flooded mines in Cornwall, and working blind in watery, slime-filled blackness, the Ampersand team was recalled to London for a further briefing session in the vaults below Admiralty House.

"Your Spanish visas have been fixed by nameless people at the U.S. State Department working through a CBS front," Winslade said as he handed two American passports across the desk for Ferracini and Cassidy to inspect. Winslade had acquired himself a permanent office at the Admiralty and was back in his British Navy uniform. "They'll get you from Paris to Madrid. From there, you fly to Rome as Joe Hennessey and Pat Brewster— a news reporter and sound engineer both with CBS, traveling together for a planned broadcast from the Vatican reviewing the first year of the new papacy. Italy is on good terms with the

Franco regime after the aid that Mussolini sent in the Civil War, and travel on that route isn't too restricted."

Cassidy studied his passport carefully. "And if anybody checks, the CBS office in Rome will confirm they're expecting these guys to show up?" he queried.

"Of course."

In a chair beside Cassidy, Ferracini examined the ID card, travel permit bearing official French and Spanish stamps, and other documents that Winslade had produced, all conjured up by a clandestine section of the MI6 department of British military intelligence. They were good; where appropriate, they had been given a worn and aged look. "It says here that we sail to France direct from New York this week," he remarked.

Winslade opened a folder and began laying a series of items out on the desk. "Copy of a New York *Herald Tribune* from last Monday to put in your briefcase . . . two theater ticket stubs from Saturday—Broadway . . . dated receipt for shirts and pants from menswear store on Third Avenue . . . letter from wife to hotel address in Paris, postmarked Bensonhurst, Long Island, with snapshots of children—congratulations." Ferracini studied them briefly one at a time and nodded. It went without saying that all their clothes, shoes, pocket contents, and personal belongings would include nothing of British origin.

Lindemann, sitting on a couch by the wall, was the only other person present this time. Each of the three pairs making up the Ampersand operation would be told only their own cover identities and route into Germany. Ferracini and Cassidy knew nothing of how, or under what guises, Warren, Payne, Lamson, and Ryan would be traveling. They didn't even know for sure who would be partnering whom, and therefore, if worse did come to worse, they would be unable even to describe the other pairs involved in the mission. Pairs whose descriptions were known were easier to spot than individuals.

"In Rome, you change identities," Winslade went on. He handed across two files in red binders. "When you arrive, contact the American Consulate. Somebody there will give you instructions for exchanging your documents and belongings for two new sets. The details are given in these files. Memorize them. They're to be returned before you leave. Basically, you become Niels Jorgensen from Denmark, and Benito Cassalla, an Italian. One of you is a schoolteacher, the other an artist, and you share a common interest in classical archaeology. You've been spending the winter in Italy looking at Roman architecture and ruins—you'll be given plenty of sketches and photographs in Rome to substantiate that, and there'll be notes for you to copy in your own handwriting. You're returning to Denmark by train via Bologna, Verona, and Munich, with a change to make at Berlin for Hamburg and the Danish frontier."

Winslade spread his hands. "But you never make your connection in Berlin. You get off the train early, at Leipzig. It will be nighttime, and if you're stopped at Leipzig station you can say that as foreigners you were confused by the blackout and thought the train had reached Berlin. Wait until the train is just about to leave to make sure you'll be left stranded, which will be your reason for checking into a hotel for the night." Winslade looked at Lindemann and raised his eyebrows in an invitation for him to continue.

Lindemann cleared his throat. "I will introduce you to someone who'll be able to fill you in on current details regarding hotel registration, police checks, and so on," he began. "Now, for the next morning. Near the center of town is a square known as the Rathausplatz. One of the streets leading into it is called Kanzlerstrasse, a narrow, cobbled affair with a bierhaus on the corner, under a clock. A short distance along Kanzlerstrasse, you'll find a shoemender's with the name Hoffenzollen outside. You're to go in there and say that you've come for the shoes that were being heeled for Fräulein Schultz. You should be asked if she has recovered from her cold yet. You are to reply, 'Yes, she's much better now. It's been such a dreadful winter.' "

"And follow instructions from there on," Winslade said. "You both know the drill."

Ferracini and Cassidy glanced at each other, but neither of them had any immediate questions. "What about the gear?" Cassidy asked, looking back at Winslade.

"We've decided against air-dropping it," Winslade replied. "Instead, it's being independently routed, in two containers again, each going a different way. Each consignment will be enough to do the job."

"Independently routed" was a trade euphemism. It meant that the equipment would be transported separately by people who were considered more expendable than the six Ampersand specialists. If a container fell into the wrong hands and the people handling it were caught, they would know neither what its contents were nor its ultimate destination; nor would they know that a second container even existed. If both containers went astray, at least the team would be preserved, with the option to try again later by some other means.

Assuming all went well, however, the Ampersand personnel would be able to retrieve the containers once they had been brought to safe drop points by the anonymous "other parties," as

Lindemann called them, and after at least one of the Ampersand pairs had found its contact. But as a further precaution, until both conditions were satisfied the containers would not be retrievable.

The whereabouts of a container would be represented by a standard six-figure map reference, of the kind that Ferracini and Cassidy were already familiar with, Lindemann explained. After safely depositing their container, the other parties involved would place different small ads in two of the local papers. To anybody who knew how to decipher them, each ad would provide one half of the map reference. The Ampersand people would know which ad to look for in one paper; their local contact would know which ad to look for in the other paper. Thus, only when the two had met would reconstruction of the complete map reference become possible. The second container would be obtained in the same way, but of course the two ads relating to it, and the group of other parties responsible for placing them, would be different.

After completion of the mission, escape would be effected via a submarine rendezvous off the Baltic coast. A method of coded telephone calls to the American Consulate in Berlin had been worked out, whereby dates and timings for the rendezvous could be fixed with the British Admiralty via Washington.

Departure date would be the end of February. The remaining time until then would be devoted to becoming familiar with details of life in contemporary Europe, memorizing cover stories, and all the usual precautionary chores.

A knock sounded on the door just as they were finishing up. The naval sentry outside opened the door, and Churchill came in to inquire on progress. The papers that day had applauded his decision to send in the *Cossack* and said it exemplified the kind of spirit that the government should be showing more of; he was in a jaunty mood. "They'd have all ended up in a prison camp if we'd waited for our illustrious friend to move at his usual funereal pace," he told them. Churchill's latest choice epithet for Chamberlain was "The Undertaker from Birmingham." He waved Ferracini and Cassidy back into their chairs as they started to rise and rubbed his palms together as he stood looking at them. "Well, and how does the plan strike you? You'll be the ones more affected by it than anybody."

"It seems . . . very thoroughly worked out, sir," Ferracini said.

"As fail-safe as you could hope to get," Cassidy agreed.

Churchill nodded, satisfied. "As the man in Brazil said when asked how his mother-in-law's remains should be disposed of,

'Embalm, cremate, and bury. Take no chances.' With an enterprise of this importance, a comparable measure of prudence seemed in order."

Winslade smiled. "Why Brazil?" he asked.

"I have absolutely no idea. That was how I heard it."

"We'll be talking to the last two of you tomorrow, and then it'll be hard swotting and memorizing for the rest of the month," Lindemann said.

"And you feel confident that you can do it?" Churchill asked, looking at the two young Americans.

"Sure," Cassidy replied, shrugging nonchalantly. If the mission screwed up, he told himself, whatever he said would have ceased to matter, anyway.

Ferracini answered more circumspectly. "The chances look good. Having the unexpected on your side always helps."

"Splendid." Churchill beamed from one to the other. "I know there's no necessity for me to spell out how much depends on the success of this undertaking. Therefore, I'll spare you any speeches. But you know, I have a feeling that this venture in co-operation across the seas will turn out to herald a grand alliance between our countries before this is over. That may sound strange in view of the current climate of isolationism on your side, but things like that can soon change. Did you two know that my mother was an American, by the way?"

They talked until lunchtime, at which point Churchill and Lindemann left to keep an appointment with some admirals to discuss U-boat matters. Winslade had arranged for the rest of them to meet Arthur Bannering and some of the others for lunch. They locked the room, ascended two levels, and went out by the front entrance. "You should be getting used to this London by now," Winslade said as he trotted briskly down the main steps with Ferracini on one side of him and Cassidy on the other. "Quite a change from what you'd seen where we came from, eh?"

"It looks nicer without any of the wrong uniforms around," Cassidy said. "Say, Harry, do you remember what this building we were just in used to be?"

"Southeast Region Gestapo Headquarters," Ferracini said.

"And making sure it doesn't become that again is what the mission is all about," Winslade said as they began walking in the direction of Trafalgar Square.

In the single room that he had rented in a dingy office building almost across the street, the man with the telescopic camera removed the plate on which he had snapped the trio coming down the Admiralty House steps and added it to the pile he had been accumulating all morning. He sighed with boredom and glanced at his watch as he inserted another slide into the camera. Five more hours, and then a crowded bus home, a supper of pie and chips in the transport café down the street, maybe a pint at the corner pub, and then back to his seedy bed-sitter in Willesden. To think he'd believed all those stories about a spy's life of wine, women, fast living, and excitement. He hadn't even received the money for the rent and the film yet!

At the end of the month, Ferracini and Cassidy departed by air from Croydon for Paris as scheduled, the other four having already disappeared during the preceding few days for destinations unknown. A day later, Winslade received an urgent call from New York: Something was happening at Gatehouse again—another partial contact with the 1975 machine. It was faltering and intermittent, but this time the scientists were managing to sustain it. Mortimer Greene felt there was a good chance of connecting fully at any time.

If a contact with 1975 seemed imminent, everyone agreed that Winslade as head of the Proteus group should be present, all the more so since his task in England was finished for the time being. If need arose, the Ampersand operation could be halted anytime within the next week—Ferracini and Cassidy at Rome by a message to the American Consulate there, and by similar means in the cases of the others. But the first thing was to get Winslade back to the States as quickly as possible. President Roosevelt had been interested to learn that Anna Kharkiovitch was a historian who had specialized in the politics of the times, and he sent a request via Churchill for her to come over with Winslade. Once more, he arranged for an American military aircraft to be made available for the journey.

"Just imagine, dinner with the First Lord of the British Admiralty last night, and now a personal invitation from the U.S. President," Anna said to Winslade as a Royal Navy car drove them toward the airport at Hendon, in the northern outskirts of London. "My word, I am becoming popular in this world! Do you know, I don't think I'd mind all that much if we never went back to ours at all."

Winslade smiled and pretended not to notice the pointed look that she flashed at him beneath the joking words. "It's election year over there," he reminded her. "Roosevelt's just hoping for some campaign tips, I bet."

Anna sighed. "You know, Claud, you have this rare gift for really boosting a woman's ego."

"Oh, it's no gift, I assure you. It requires lots of practice."

Anna's face became serious and distant all of a sudden. "It

could mean good news," she murmured thoughtfully. "Very good news, in fact."

"How come?" Winslade asked her.

"It could mean that, privately, Roosevelt has already decided to run for a third term," she replied. "Now that, Claud, would really be a change from what we remember, wouldn't it?"

CHAPTER
34

WINSLADE'S FACE WAS SERIOUS as he and Mortimer Greene followed Anna up the steps of the loading dock in the front area of Gatehouse and walked toward the façade of boxes and crates screening the rear of the building. The two plainclothes military policemen who had driven with Greene to meet the plane disappeared into the front office to report back to the guard commander.

"I don't like it," Winslade said. "The bumbling amateur business could be a clever second cover. You say that documents from Abwehr headquarters were found in his apartment? That's enough in itself to make me worry. Canaris is no fool, and he's got some sharp people working for him."

"Yes, but those documents only dealt with routine matters," Greene said. "There wasn't anything that specifically pointed either to us here or to the mission. And if Fritsch were any kind of a professional at all, he'd never have left even those lying around like that."

"I still don't like it," Winslade repeated as they threaded their way toward the hidden door that led into the machine area. "I'd like to talk to him myself, later."

On their way back from the airfield, Greene had told them of the man the guards had caught snooping around the building the day before: a German by the name of Walther Fritsch, who had immigrated several years previously. He was being interrogated elsewhere, but a preliminary check had revealed that he was known to the FBI, who had dismissed him as something of a comic figure working outside the regular German espionage services, and probably not worth the bother of apprehending. In fact, American counterintelligence had found him a useful aid to unraveling the labyrinthine tangle of the Nazi information-gathering organization by feeding him planted information and tracing its path through the system. Now it appeared that this assessment might have been dead wrong. If Berlin had gotten wind of what was going on at Gatehouse, the consequences could only be disastrous.

The machine area had a busy look; lights winked, machinery hummed and whirred overhead and all around; and technicians worked at readout screens and control panels. Kurt Scholder was standing with Szilard and a technician by a large table covered with charts and papers that had been set up in one of the spaces below the machine. Fermi was tinkering with something in the background, while Colonel Adamson, who had been present at the first meeting with Roosevelt at the White House, looked on, along with a lean, sallow-faced man whose face was unfamiliar. Teller was talking to somebody on the walkway above.

A round of handshakes welcomed Winslade and Anna back. Greene introduced the stranger as Harry Hopkins, a roving presidential aide who had come from Washington in order to make a report on progress. The feeling of expectancy that hung in the air made elaborate preliminaries seem inappropriate.

"A good flight?" Scholder inquired.

"As good as could be expected," Winslade said.

"The Ampersand operation?"

"They all left on schedule."

"Still no attack in the West?"

"Nothing."

Scholder nodded and changed to more immediate matters by moving back a pace and raising an arm to indicate the panel behind him. "Here we have a most peculiar situation, which has developed only in the space of the last few hours. We managed to stabilize the conjugate function this morning, and now we're reading probe resonance harmonics in the sigma-tau spectrum—and at full strength, not low level."

Winslade's brow creased. "You don't mean rho-sigma?"

"No, that's the point. The locking signature is clear and unambiguous."

The frown on Winslade's face deepened. He explained in answer to Anna's questioning look, "It means we're encountering a probe beam from the other end that's trying to lock on. But it's a full-power beam to activate the main transfer gate, not simply the auxiliary communications channel." He turned to Scholder. "And have you had any luck with the communications side?"

"No. There's nothing. That subsystem is completely dead."

"How about the beam that's seeking—did you try a lock-on initiation to see if it would work?"

"Not yet. Since you were on your way, we decided to wait until you got here," Greene said. He looked at Scholder. "Has there been any change in quality?"

Scholder shook his head. "Not really. It's still oscillating near threshold. We lost it for fifteen minutes about an hour ago, but it has restored itself since."

"But it could die on us at any moment," Greene said.

From what the instruments were saying, the chance was there now to connect the gate through to 1975. In just a few minutes' time, perhaps, they might be able to walk into the cylinder a few feet above their heads and be back in their home time.

Winslade clasped his hands behind his back and paced a short distance away across the floor. There was really little to think about, but checking one last time for anything he might have missed before committing himself to a decision had long ago become a habit.

"This intermittency worries me, Claud," Scholder called across, reading Winslade's action as hesitation. "If I could give details of the modifications here to the engineers at the other end, they would be able to make suitable compensations. It would give us a more stable link."

"We have to go for it now, Claud," Anna urged. "If there's a chance that the Germans might be onto us, we can't risk losing even a day."

Winslade turned and came back again, smiling faintly at their anxiety. "Then let's go for it," he said. His manner became more brisk. "Okay. Kurt, start priming for lock-on initiation right away."

"I can handle that," Szilard offered. Winslade raised an eyebrow. Scholder nodded.

"Fine," Winslade said. Szilard moved away to commence organizing the people around the machine. "You'd better collect your information, Kurt," Winslade said. He looked at Greene. "I'll go through with Kurt if we connect, and leave you to carry on in charge here, Mortimer. Anna, you'd better come with us to start filling in our political people on what's been happening here in the last year." His gaze fell on Harry Hopkins and Colonel Adamson. "And perhaps some kind of representation from this era wouldn't be out of place as a gesture."

Hopkins held up a hand protectively. "Now wait a minute, I'm just here as a passive observer, remember? President's orders. You're not getting me inside that thing."

Winslade looked at Adamson. "Keith, how would you like to be the U.S.A.'s first ambassador to another time?"

"Not thirteenth?" Anna queried. "What about us?"

"Depends how you look at it," Winslade said. "We're from 1975. This is 1940. Nineteen forty is earlier than 1975."

Adamson was taken aback. "I really don't know about that. . . . I don't have any orders that say anything about—"

"Fiddlesticks," Winslade said. "Your orders are to facilitate our mission by all the means at your disposal. Well, this facilitates it. Here . . ." Winslade tossed him the briefcase that Scholder had finished cramming with papers. Then he turned and led the way to the steel stairway behind. Adamson shook his head helplessly, then sighed and followed.

They climbed the steps and walked along the railed platform flanking the return-gate cylinder to the access port, an opening like a large doorway without a door, leading into the boxlike construction at the end of the cylinder. In front of the port, the walkway widened into a broad platform of steel-mesh flooring, above which a system of pulleys and hoisting tackle hung from overhead girders: There was no telling what might need to be brought through the gate—nuclear bombs, maybe. Winslade positioned himself in the center of the platform, facing the port, and Adamson drew up uncertainly a pace or two behind him.

A minute or so later, Anna and Scholder joined them; Scholder was clutching a second briefcase. Fermi appeared with one of the technicians and went over to a local monitor panel that communicated with the main control area below, where Greene had remained with Szilard. A group began forming at the back of the platform to watch, including Teller, Harry Hopkins, Einstein, and George Pegram from Columbia.

A hush descended as Fermi and his assistant donned telephone headsets and began making adjustments on their panel in response to instructions from the control area below. "Field coupling is established," Fermi announced. "They're getting a stronger reading of the section fundamental."

"It's connecting!" Scholder whispered, moving closer behind Winslade. "That's the probe beam centering." Winslade nodded.

Beside Scholder, Adamson stared into the blackness of the opening in front of them and licked his lips apprehensively.

"It's locking now," Fermi said. A sequence of lamps changed
color on the panel in front of him, and a display screen switched
to a different data format. "Yes, both . . . and positive," he said in
a lower voice, answering something coming over the telephone.
"Nine-eight, and eight-eight . . . yes. . . . No, I don't think so.
Very well." He turned and glanced at the group on the platform.
"Szilard's making them double-check something. We'll be a minute or two."

"Typical!" someone snorted.

"But probably best," Scholder said.

The silence was broken only by occasional snatches of
voices from below and Winslade whistling through his teeth.
Anna stood immobile, staring expressionlessly at the port.
Adamson began fiddling nervously with a button of his jacket.

The minute or two dragged on endlessly. Then Fermi turned
back toward the panel suddenly, nodded his head a couple of
times as he began talking into the telephone again, and then announced, "We're connected! The loop's closed. We're starting to
draw power now."

Even as he spoke, the others on the platform felt a mild
vibration surge through the structure. A dull red glow, like that
in a photographic darkroom, illuminated the inside of the port.
The chamber beyond it was long, rectangular in section, and
bare. "That's it," Scholder said.

Winslade set his jaw firmly and advanced toward the port.
The others followed. "Good luck," Teller called from behind, and
other voices joined in. The four entered the port and went
through to the inner chamber. Those left outside clustered together a short distance back, so they could see in.

The glow changed slowly to a uniform orange that filled the
chamber as if the air itself were incandescent. The four figures
stood motionless, bathed in light. The light became brighter, and
the figures seemed to become translucent, as if they were losing
substance. The orange became yellow, then a pale blue, and the
outlines of the figures disappeared. Violet followed, then black.
Finally the subdued red glow returned to reveal . . . nothing.

The chamber was once again empty.

Three thousand miles away in Italy, the train heading northward to Germany via the Brenner Pass was thirty minutes out of
Rome. "Tickets and papers, please," the inspector's voice called
along the corridor. "Have all tickets and papers ready."

"Papers, papers, always papers," the gray-bearded man with the woman in the green coat grumbled as he fumbled in the bag next to him. "Another ten years of the Fascists and we'll all be living in a desert. They'll have used up all the trees making their tons of wastepaper."

The woman smiled nervously at the others in the compartment. "Please excuse my husband. We've had a tiring trip. It makes him irritable. He doesn't mean everything he says."

"Better not to say it, then," the man in the center seat, wearing a business suit, snapped, while the young, sharp-faced woman sitting across from him sniffed disapprovingly and looked away. Ferracini gave the woman in the green coat a reassuring wink as he felt in his inside pocket for the folder containing his and Cassidy's documents. Beside him, Cassidy stared silently out the window.

The door from the corridor slid open, and the inspector, a big man with a thick black mustache, moved into the compartment. Two young, armed policemen in black uniforms waited outside in the corridor. The inspector took the papers of the couple and the man in the center seat in turn, examined them, and handed them back with a grunt. Next came Ferracini and Cassidy's turn.

"Signore Jorgensen from Denmark and Signore Cassalla," the inspector commented as Ferracini handed him the folder. He scanned the documents quickly. "Was winter in the north too harsh for your friend?"

Ferracini grinned. "If an excuse to go where it's warmer presents itself, then take it," he said in Italian, which he had spoken since childhood.

"And what excuse did he manage to dig up?"

"An excellent phrase to pick," Ferracini said. "We are both archaeologists, you see. We spent the winter in Italy, and now we are going to my friend's place in Denmark to write our paper. Caesars may turn to dust and the greatest empires end in ruins, but we will never be out of a job." The remark was intended as a sly dig at Mussolini. A touch of insolence tended to help in situations like this, Ferracini had learned. People who were too anxious not to offend often had something to hide.

"Do you speak Italian?" the inspector asked Cassidy.

"A little only."

"In order." The inspector handed the folder back. "Perhaps when Hitler has finished with the Maginot Line you will have more ruins to occupy yourselves with."

"Perhaps," Ferracini repeated neutrally.

The papers of the remaining occupants passed scrutiny without incident. When he had finished, the inspector backed out into the corridor and closed the compartment door. "Tickets and papers, please. Have your tickets and papers ready," he called out as he moved away.

The bearded man took out a cigarette case, and the sharp-faced young woman buried herself behind a newspaper. The man in the business suit looked at Ferracini and Cassidy. "I am also an expert in archaeology," he informed them pompously. "What period do you specialize in? Mine was the Mesolithic in Western Europe, particularly Ireland and Brittany. The evolving patterns of flint microliths from that region tell such an interesting story, don't you think?"

Ferracini groaned inwardly. This was exactly the kind of thing he had been dreading. But before he could say anything, Cassidy turned his head sharply from the window and glared across the compartment, his clear blue eyes blazing. "We would not waste our time on the subhuman cultures of barbarians and savages," he declared shrilly in German. "The sole origin of human progress lies in the racially pure Germanic ancestral warrior tribes uncontaminated by non-Aryan blood, as taught in the official science of the Reich. All else is lies fabricated by Jews and decadent academics to hide their racial degeneracy. They will be exterminated. Heil Hitler!"

The man sat back in his seat abruptly. Oh, they were *those* kinds of archaeologists, were they, his expression said. "Pardon me," he said, coldly. And with that he took a book from his pocket and immersed himself in it. Cassidy nodded curtly and turned his head away again. Beside him, Ferracini eased himself back in his seat, exhaled a long breath slowly and silently, and pulled his hat down over his eyes to feign sleep.

The white incandescent haze that had enveloped them faded slowly, and solid surroundings materialized. Different surroundings.

The inner chamber of the Gatehouse machine was gone, and instead they found themselves standing on a shiny metallic floor inside a much larger space formed by two sides curving together overhead to form a semicircular roof, like a short, high tunnel. The surface was of some milky white substance glowing with an inner light, and formed a ribbed pattern interrupted by metal ring structures at intervals.

On either side, gaps along the length of the floor separated it from the walls. The walls continued their curve downward and out of sight below, as if the tunnel were circular in section and the "floor" a platform supported halfway up inside it. Ahead of them, the platform led to a large set of double doors. Behind an observation window above the doors, faces were staring down at them.

Colonel Adamson could only stand bewildered. Winslade looked quickly from one side to the other. He seemed puzzled and uncertain. Anna Kharkiovitch frowned as she took in the surroundings, and shook her head uncomprehendingly. "Claud, what is this? I don't understand. This isn't the place that we came from in New Mexico. It's not the machine at Tularosa at all. I've never seen any of this before."

"But I have," Kurt Scholder said grimly. "It isn't even the U.S.A. This is Pipe Organ—Overlord's secret installation in Brazil. Somehow we've arrived in 2025!"

Ahead of them, the large doors were beginning to slide open.

CHAPTER
35

THE DOORS SLID ASIDE to reveal a brightly lit antechamber, with smaller doors leading out from either side and another set of larger doors facing from the far end. Higher up, a glass-enclosed gallery looked down from the corner formed by two of the walls, and from it a railed stairway descended to the floor. A tall, lean-faced man with a short beard and receding hair was already hurrying down the stairs, followed by another man and a woman. He was wearing a white topcoat over a jacket and light blue shirt, plain at the neck. He looked agitated. As the trio reached the floor, one of the side doors opened and more people spilled out, babbling and gesticulating excitedly.

Kurt Scholder's mind raced to take in the situation. This was the other end of Hitler's link to the world where the totalitarian state had been masterminded. It was from this place that Overlord's agents had departed to make contact with the leaders of the discredited Nazi party of 1925.

The timings of transfers in and out of Pipe Organ had always been crucial, Scholder remembered from his time here, thirty-four years ago now by the scale of his own bizarre life span. A departure of even a few seconds from the planned schedule had been enough to send the program directors into hysterics, which could explain the pandemonium among the people who were appearing in the antechamber ahead. Why this should be so important, Scholder had never been sure; but it might provide the best chance for saving the situation, or at least of preventing its rapid deterioration into a total disaster.

He murmured quickly to the others, "Try to split up if we can, temporarily. If we're all interned and immobilized together, we'll never get out. I'll need a diversion when we get among them. They're used to Nazis—confuse them. Bluster."

The tall, bearded man stepped inside the doors and gestured frantically. "Come on! Get out of the lock. Who are you people? Where—"

"We?" Scholder cut him short with an indignant screech as he and Winslade began marching toward the doors. Behind them, Colonel Adamson hesitated for a split second and then moved hastily to catch up as Anna Kharkiovitch jabbed him in the ribs. "Who are we? We should be asking who you are if you don't know us! What kind of reception is this?"

The lean man was taken aback. "I don't understand. . . . There must be—"

"Where is Herr Oberkeltner?" Winslade demanded, bellowing in German. "We were advised that he would be already waiting. He is not. And I don't see Freidergauss. This is intolerable! Someone will pay."

The four arrivals walked into the antechamber, and a general melee ensued as more figures appeared on the stairs and through the side door. The bearded man turned to another, who was looking baffled and turning through sheets of paper in a folder. "What has happened?" the lean man demanded. "Those names—where are they?"

"I'm sorry, Director Kahleb . . . I don't seem to see them," the other man faltered. "This doesn't make—"

"Get them out of the way," somebody else shouted. "TG297 is nine seconds late already. Mathers, call Control. Start bringing the beam up now."

"I'm trying. Channel's busy."

Voices were babbling on all sides.

"Dammit, use the emergency code!"

"But who are these people?"

"Oh, God, we're all in for it now."

"Well, they must have. They're here. The schedule must be in error."

"Impossible, I tell you!"

"What kind of organization is this?" Winslade screamed at the top of this voice. "Where is the nincompoop in charge?"

Another side door opened and more people appeared, but

they seemed uninterested in the tumult going on in the antechamber. Two men wearing side arms and dressed in white caps
and uniforms of dark gray, satiny material cleared a path to the
open doors through which Winslade's party had just come. Then
some more men, a couple in white coats and the rest in unfamiliar styles of clothing, ushered through a small group wearing the familiar attire of the 1930s; this group had evidently been
waiting to depart. At that point, the man called Kahleb succeeded in shepherding the others out of the antechamber and
through the other side door.

The near end of the space they were now in was predominantly white in color and suggested a reception area of some
kind, with soft carpeting, chairs and low tables scattered in clus-
ters, and a counter running along one wall. On the opposite side
were several seats facing video stations that resembled computer
work terminals. Farther back, an open partition of shelves and
colored designs screened the rear area, which looked more like
an instrumentation room. It had lots of wall panels and electronics cubicles, and the farthest part, occupying the lower section of a split-level floor, seemed to form a windowed bay looking
out over a vaster space of machinery and activity below.

Still waving his hands and protesting loudly, Winslade
marched to the center of the floor with Anna. Adamson moved
instinctively to follow, but Scholder caught his sleeve. Winslade
and Anna became the focal point of attention, drawing the tide of
people around them. Scholder nudged Adamson closer to a door
near one end of the counter.

"Will you kindly calm down and identify yourself," Kahleb
shouted above the din, at last losing patience with Winslade's
ongoing tirade. "Carrying on like this won't resolve anything."

"Who do you think you are to talk to me like that?"
Winslade shouted back.

"My name is Kahleb, and I am responsible for Section F-1,
Transfer Operations Control. I—"

"Well, you very soon won't be! I want to talk to the Control-
ler General."

"This is outrageous. I—"

"I insist!" Winslade walked over to one of the terminals and
stooped to hammer something into its touchboard. The screen
flickered for a moment, and every eye in the room was drawn
irresistibly to see what would appear on it.

"Now," Scholder hissed, and pushed Adamson through the
door next to them.

They were in a small room with a sink and faucets, re-
frigerator, coffee maker, several food closets, and a stack of boxes.

Another door opened out the far side. Scholder waved Adamson on through, and they came out at a junction of three short corridors of bare concrete walls. There were iron stairs going up and down, more doors in every direction, and an elevator just a few feet away. But they hadn't covered enough distance to be able to risk waiting. Instead, Scholder led the way downstairs for one level and pressed the call button there.

The elevator was of the kind that had doors on two sides—as Scholder had probably known already and Adamson was beginning to realize. They stepped in, but instead of selecting a floor, Scholder opened the opposite door and let them out the far side. Then, as the doors were starting to close again, he reached back in to send the elevator up. At that instant, the noise of a door bursting open came from upstairs, followed by excited voices. Scholder and Adamson walked quickly away, turning a couple of times into more passageways, and came to another elevator. At this one they went down.

"I'm the one who should be concerned, Keith," Scholder said, catching the look on Adamson's face as the car lurched into motion. "This is literally back where I came in."

Adamson pulled himself together with an effort. "I'll file a complaint when we get back."

"The advisability of that might depend on where we get back to."

"Assuming we ever get back anywhere." After a pause Adamson said, "That was pretty quick thinking, Kurt. I'm impressed. But where do we go from here?"

The elevator stopped, and the door opened. Scholder held up a restraining hand while he peered out. Then he motioned Adamson quickly across the landing and opened a door. The inside was pitch black and noisy, and a gust of warm air came out. Scholder switched on the light to reveal a room full of motors, compressors, air circulation equipment, and ducting. Some shelves stood near the door with buckets, brushes, and cleaning aids. There was a small handcart like those used by janitors, and next to it a steel closet. Scholder opened the closet and gave a satisfied grunt as he took out a grimy oversmock. "You'll be all right in here for a few minutes," he said as he pulled the smock on over his suit. "I'm going to try to get us some better clothes. Our own are too conspicuous."

"And then what?"

"Then we pay a visit to someone who might be willing to help us."

"Who?"

"Oh, in a way you already know him," Scholder replied. He

put a couple of bottles of cleanser and some rags on the handcart
and pushed it onto the landing. He smiled mysteriously, closed
the door on Adamson's puzzled frown, and walked away pushing
the cart.

Scholder reached the metalworking and machine shops on
the lower levels of the complex a few minutes later and entered
the changing room outside the washroom and showers. Two men
were talking by the staff lockers, and Scholder fussed around in
the background with a bottle and cleaning rag until they went
into the showers. Then he quickly checked the lockers and found
enough of them unlocked to provide a mix of garments that he
judged to be his and Adamson's sizes, choosing baggy and loose-
fitting items to allow a margin of error. He dropped the clothes
into his cart, bundled up a couple of white work coats and
stuffed them in on top, and a few seconds later was on his way to
rejoin Adamson.

They changed silently in the cramped space of the machinery room and emerged as passable imitations of bona fide Pipe-
Organ workers, provided no one looked too closely at the
photographs on the badges pinned to their work coats. After they
had reentered the elevator, Scholder pressed a button to take
them back up several levels. As the car commenced moving, a
grille overhead in the ceiling announced, "Attention. Attention.
Unauthorized persons are at large in the Security Area. All personnel are to return to their assigned work stations immediately
for security checking. All personnel to assigned stations. Repeat . . ."

"We were just in time," Scholder murmured. "That means
they'll be sealing off all movement between levels in a few minutes."

The car stopped, and they came out into a wide, carpeted
hall with potted plants and pastel walls. Figures were hurrying
this way and that between corridors leading away in different
directions, and to one side some people came out of an adjoining
elevator at almost the same time. "What's it all about, any idea?"
one of them asked.

"Haven't a clue," Scholder said, sounding irritable. "What's
it ever about? They're probably springing another drill on us."

"Typical! It's only Security that never has anything better to
do around this place."

More of the gray-uniformed guards appeared and fanned out
to position themselves by the elevators. "Hurry up," one of them
told Scholder and Adamson. "You heard the announcement."

Scholder nodded and walked briskly away, with Adamson
tagging along and doing his best to look as if he knew where he

was going. They went past a series of paneled doors and came out into a more open area of laboratory benches, experimental equipment with lots of gleaming metal and glass, desks, computer stations, and partitioned-off offices. Unhesitatingly, Scholder led the way through the maze of shoulder-high screens and glass-walled clean-rooms to the door of one of the corner offices. He crashed in without slackening pace and signaled in the same movement for Adamson to close the door behind them.

Two desks were inside, facing each other by the far wall. The man sitting at one of them looked up with a start. "What the hell? . . ."

Another man, who was standing and had been about to put something in the drawer of a table behind the other desk, wheeled around. "Who are you?" he demanded indignantly. "Didn't you hear the alert? You shouldn't be here. What section are you from?"

Scholder smiled reassuringly. "Not so tense, my friend," he said. "You should take things more easily, like Eddie here."

The man at the desk frowned. He was in his mid-forties, perhaps, and had a rounded, open face with wide, pale eyes and sandy hair. Beside him, a screen displayed rows of mathematical symbols. "How do you know who I am?" he asked suspiciously. "I don't know you."

"Don't you?" Scholder looked amused.

Eddie stared at him for a second or two, then shook his head. "No."

Scholder turned his head toward the younger of the pair, who was still standing. He was wearing a white sweater with dark pants and had sharp, intense features, straight, wiry black hair, and a thin, obstinate mouth—definitely German in appearance. "When you were seventeen, you had a skiing accident on the Dente Blanche, which left a distinctive scar on your left forearm and upper arm." Scholder glanced at Eddie. "Did you know about that?"

"No, I didn't," Eddie sounded mystified. "Why? What does that have to do with anything?"

Scholder looked back at the younger man. "Your sleeve—show us that scar."

"Why should I? First I want to know who the hell—"

"Please."

The word was a command, not a request. The man hesitated, then nodded and pulled back the sleeve of his sweater to reveal an L-shaped pattern of scar tissue. "Satisfied? Now would you mind explaining?"

In reply Scholder pulled back the sleeve of his own coat, unbuttoned the cuff of his shirt, and turned it back. The same scar was there, faded somewhat by thirty-four more years of wear, tear, and living, but unmistakable.

"You see, I, too, am Kurt Scholder," he said. "This used to be my office when I worked for you, Eddie—or at least, another version of you. And yes, I have to admit that we are the ones responsible for the excitement. We need your help to conceal ourselves until after the security check, and then we can talk." He looked back at the gaping copy of the person he had once been. "I'm sure you'll cooperate, Kurt. I am you, after all. And you wouldn't want to get yourself into trouble, now, would you?"

CHAPTER
36

LEIPZIG HAD NOT YET become the city that Harry Ferracini remembered from the early 1970s of his own world. In that world, the promises of glory, affluence, and power that had intoxicated the German people and dulled their senses while the Nazis were taking over the nation had long been forgotten. Instead of fulfilling their destiny as the proud and noble Master Race, they had awakened from their stupor to find themselves slaves to a ruthless, self-proclaimed elite wielding a total monopoly of authority and power. Subscribing to no code of ethics, the members of that elite had been subject to no restraint except loyalty to their kind. Free to command the labor of defenseless peoples and to plunder the resources of entire nations through the unchecked use of terror, they had lived with their courts of followers amid luxury and splendor undreamed of by the Caesars, while the children of the craftsmen who built their palaces starved in rags. Thus, the Nazi leaders had inherited the utopia that Overlord sought to recreate.

But the beginnings of it all were there already Ferracini could see as he and Cassidy walked slowly, hands in pockets, through the streets in the full light of morning. He could see it in the Nazi flags hanging from the windows; in the youths in brownshirt uniforms with swastika armbands, swaggering through the crowd, their jackboots crunching on the cobbles, their thumbs hooked jauntily in belts with silver-eagle buckles; and in the boarded-up shops with Jewish names overhead. And the fear—fear of ever-watchful police; fear of never knowing which relative, neighbor, or workmate might be an informer; fear of arbitrary search and arrest, interrogation on a whim, internment without trial—that was there already, too, in the faces of the people.

Cassidy stretched as they walked. "You know, Benito, I'll never complain about the seats on a coast-to-coast flight again," he muttered. "A day and a half in that goddam train! What were they doing at all those stops, changing the boiler? Anyone would think there's a war on."

"It's not the seats. You're too long and lanky. I've always said you're too long."

"It is the seats. Everything's designed for mutants and amputees. . . . And anyhow, supposing you're right, exactly what am I supposed to do about it?"

"It's too late now, Niels. You ended up in the wrong job. You should have gone in for basketball or something."

"Oh, is that so? And who'd have saved your neck like I did the last time we were in this city?"

They split up as they came to the Rathausplatz. It was a market day, and the square was filled with stalls and people. Ferracini stopped to buy a paper at a curbside kiosk, while Cassidy crossed the street and wandered around the square, stopping finally in a doorway at the corner opposite the bierhaus with the clock over its entrance as Lindemann had described. From there he could observe the whole square and see along the winding, cobbled lane that a sign confirmed was Kanzlerstrasse.

Ferracini came into the square on the far side a minute or so later and walked slowly along the shopfronts to the bierhaus. He turned the corner into Kanzlerstrasse and had followed its single narrow sidewalk for only a short distance when he saw the shoemender's with the sign "Hoffenzollen" ahead of him on the opposite side. It was a small place with a protruding gable, whirly leaded windowpanes, and paint flaking from its green door. Ferracini could see nothing unusual or suspicious. Even so, he kept walking to the next corner and stopped there to stamp his feet in the slush, beat his arms across his chest, and take a quick look around. Then he turned and retraced his steps.

He could see nobody loitering without obvious reason; there was no sign of anyone watching the shop from across the street; nobody was sitting in parked vehicles. He looked back along the street. In his doorway across the marketplace, Cassidy raised a hand to his mouth and yawned. It meant that no one had followed Ferracini up the street. Satisfied, Ferracini crossed and entered the shoemender's. The door creaked, and a bell tinkled overhead.

It was dark inside after the daylight, and the smell was a mixture of mustiness and leather. Ferracini's eyes adjusted after a few seconds, and he made out a battered wooden counter with shelves behind it stacked with used shoes, a rack carrying polishes and laces, and an empty display case—under war regulations, real leather had disappeared for the duration. He registered a hammer, a knife, and some shears lying together on one of the shelves, and a faded picture of horses in a frame with cracked glass hung on the wall opposite the counter, behind the door. A corner bureau was stuffed untidily with envelopes and papers. The calendar above it still showed January.

The sound of a tool being tossed down onto a bench came from a door leading to the rear, followed by somebody belching and a heavy shuffling of feet. Then a giant of a man appeared, with black, unkempt hair and a thick ragged beard that gave him a wild look. He was wearing a leather apron, and his rolled-up shirtsleeves revealed massive forearms ending in two hams of fists that looked as if they could have crushed house bricks. His lips were drawn back, uncovering strong, even teeth that seemed to shine in the gloom. He dragged a leg as he moved.

"Good morning," Ferracini greeted. The giant placed two palms on the counter, raised his chin in a silent query, and waited. "I, ah . . . I believe you have some shoes being heeled for Fräulein Schultz," Ferracini said. "I was told they should be ready about now."

"Fräulein Schultz, eh?"

"Yes."

"You are a friend of hers? I don't know you."

"I'm a friend of a friend, as it were. Just visiting, you understand."

The giant stared at Ferracini expressionlessly for a few seconds. "One moment." He turned and shuffled back into the workshop. More sounds followed. Then Ferracini caught the faint click that only a trained ear would have recognized as a revolver being cocked. Ferracini moved instantly and flattened himself against the wall out of a direct line from the doorway. He felt along the shelf behind him, and his fingers closed around the hammer and the knife.

"And how is the Fräulein?" the giant's voice inquired from beyond the doorway. "Has she recovered from her cold yet?"

"Yes, she's much better now," Ferracini called back. "It's been such a dreadful winter."

Ferracini's ears followed the hammer being released, the safety catch reengaging, and the gun being returned to its hiding place. By the time the giant reappeared, Ferracini was standing nonchalantly behind the counter again. The giant put down a pair of lady's boots, tied together by the laces and strung with a label. "Go to the address on the ticket tonight, after eight," he said, keeping his voice low. "You will be collected there. You didn't leave your bags at the hotel, I hope?"

"No—a luggage locker at the station."

"Good. Leave me the tags." The luggage had served its purpose. Ferracini and Cassidy would have no use from now on for clothes purchased in Italy.

"Thank you."

"And good luck."

Ferracini rejoined Cassidy a few minutes later a block away on the far side of the square. "It looks okay," Ferracini said. "I've got a pickup address for tonight. Until then we've got the rest of the day to kill."

"A movie?" Cassidy sighed.

"I guess so. Any idea what's on?"

"You wouldn't believe it."

"What?"

Cassidy gestured, and Ferracini turned to find a billboard behind him. The big attraction showing at the Marmorhaus that week was *Adventure in China* with Clark Gable. "Now all they need is yellow cabs and Max's place just along the street."

Ferracini's mind flashed back across a million light-years of trains, planes, English winters with submarine schools and army assault courses, London buses, and U.S. Army Air Corps bombers over the Atlantic, to the lights and sounds of Broadway and Seventh Avenue. All of a sudden, somehow, he wished Cassidy hadn't said that.

Meanwhile, over a hundred miles to the north, near the town of Kyritz, Inspector Helmut Stolpe of the local Gestapo was standing in the charge room of the area Security Police Headquarters. A half-dozen or so uniformed SS men and a couple of SD (the intelligence branch of the SS) were standing around smoking and talking, while in the back of the room behind the desk the *Polizeiführer* shouted into a telephone. The sounds of vehicles stopping, feet clattering, and a voice barking orders came from outside.

The young man standing next to Stolpe in an *Unterschar-führer*'s uniform of the Waffen SS was probably in his mid-twenties. He looked haggard after the activity of the previous night, with tangled hair, a stubbly face, and the front of his tunic unbuttoned. He drew nervously on a cigarette as he talked. "But I've been there, and you haven't. You don't know what Heydrich's *Einsatzgruppen* are doing in Poland. The people don't know. Even the Army doesn't know. Nobody tells them. They all think we were sent there to stop saboteurs and partisans in the rear. But it's not true. They're killing anyone they think might be capable of organizing—teachers, doctors, unionists—thousands of them. And the Jews . . ."

Stolpe was unimpressed. "You should know better than to talk like that," he growled. This kind of softness had lost the last war. He was offended at finding traces of its contamination among the SS of all groups—the elite whom Himmler had selected to become the new order of Germanic knights. "Were you cracking up? Is that why they sent you back?"

The sergeant took no notice. "Old people, cripples, women with babies . . . We made them strip there in the snow, and we shot them down into the pits with machine guns. Thousands of them . . . day after day . . ."

"That's enough," Stolpe snapped. "Weren't you taught that the State embodies the will of the People, and therefore whatever the State does is legal? Go away and think about how many Germans died because of traitors and scum in the Great War. This time it will be different." He caught sight of one of the security officers beckoning him from the door that led through to the rear of the building. "I have things to do. If you take my advice, Sergeant, you'll learn to control that tongue of yours. Schooldays are over now."

Making a mental note to recommend that somebody talk to the sergeant's commanding officer, Stolpe walked across to the security officer and was ushered into a passage. It had rooms opening off it at the near end and farther back led to cells. The security officer indicated the medical room, and Stolpe entered to find an SS major and second lieutenant watching while a police doctor and an assistant stood by the table in the middle of the room, examining the first of the four bodies that had been brought in a half-hour earlier.

"What happened?" he asked in a neutral voice. From the part of the face that hadn't been shot away, he judged the man on the slab to have been middle-aged. One shoulder of his jacket was covered in a mess of congealed blood and tissue mixed with splintered jawbone. The doctor was cutting away the clothing while the assistant went methodically through the pockets and laid the contents out on a side-table.

"Three of them were spotted receiving something from a small boat at night a couple of days ago near Rostock," the major said. "The other one joined them later, and they began traveling south with a truck full of turnips."

The other corpses were still on the floor, lying covered on the litters they had been carried in on. Stolpe stooped to turn back the first cover to reveal a teen-aged youth in a blood-soaked overcoat riddled with holes. "Any idea where this boat was from?" He dropped the cover back.

The major shook his head. "It slipped away before anyone could get close. The coast guard was alerted but failed to intercept it. That was why we decided to let the reception party go and keep them under observation—to see what they were up to." He shrugged. "The boat? From Denmark or Sweden, possibly . . . or maybe even from a British submarine."

The third body was of a man with a mustache; there was a single neat hole in the side of his head. "And?" Stolpe prompted.

"The instructions were bungled, and some oafs at a road checkpoint about ten miles from here tried to detain them. They turned out to be armed, and they resisted. Two of the guards were killed, but the others managed to keep them pinned down while we were called out. The rest you can see."

Stolpe turned back the fourth cover to find himself looking at the almost serene features of a woman who looked as if she had been quite attractive. Her face, however, seemed unnaturally low down as she lay facing upward; Stolpe realized it was because her head had no back to it. "She was the last," the major explained. "Suicide—through the mouth."

"A shame." Stolpe replaced the cover and straightened up. "And what were they concealing beneath the turnips that was worth so much sacrifice?" he asked.

"Nothing. But the truck had a false bottom. What was inside was interesting. Come and see—it's next door." The major nodded to the lieutenant to carry on and led Stolpe back into the passage and along to one of the cells. Inside, an SD security officer and Erwin Poehner, Stolpe's colleague from the Gestapo office, were unpacking several large bundles that had been sealed in rubberized canvas. The items they had already taken out were arranged on the cell's two bunks.

Stolpe picked up a strange, black, one-piece, hooded garment made from a greasy, rubbery material. He examined it curiously for a while, and then tossed it back down to look briefly at, in turn, some kind of transparent face cover, with valves and tubes fitted to it; a body-harness with peculiar metal cylinders and slings for attaching tools or weapons; and a kit of heavy underwear. On the other bunk lay a pile of ropes, snaplinks, pitons, and other unidentifiable metal devices in assorted shapes and sizes. "Make anything of it?" he asked, looking back at Poehner.

Poehner shook his head. "I've never seen anything like some of this stuff. I don't know if they were planning to join the fire brigade or climb the Eiger. And do you want to know something else, Helmut? There's enough explosive in those sacks over there to sink the *Bismarck*. This is going to have to go a lot higher up."

And that, Stolpe told himself, groaning beneath his breath, would mean spending the rest of the day writing up a report and filling in forms about it.

CHAPTER
37

THE ADDRESS TURNED OUT to be a rowhouse in a shabby working-class district east of the city center. It was sparsely furnished, and the sole occupant a thin, bespectacled, baldheaded man, who said his name was Dr. Mueller. He effused a dismal cheerlessness that reminded Ferracini of the farmer depicted in *American Gothic*. He spoke little, and when he did speak, he sounded tense and nervous. Before they started asking questions, no, he didn't know who they were or where they were from, and neither did he want to; all he knew was that they would be picked up the next morning. What happened afterward was none of his business, and why he was doing what he was doing was none of theirs.

Along with, inevitably, new sets of papers, Mueller provided some clothes appropriate to their new roles—a crumpled suit with vest, necktie, felt hat, and overcoat for Ferracini, and for Cassidy a workman's leather jacket, shirt, sweater, and corduroy pants. Together they ate a funereal supper of black bread, sauerkraut, and a morsel of sausage and dry cheese apiece. Then, tired from their journey, Ferracini and Cassidy retired to spend the night sharing a straw mattress on the floor in a damp and drafty upstairs room. The place was clearly a "human drop-box," a transitory link in the chain. "Mueller" would evaporate as soon as they had left, and whatever attempts might be made to trace them to their origins, the trail would end right there.

The next day had dragged through to lunchtime before a man in a belted raincoat at last appeared at the front door to collect them, introducing himself as Gustav Knacke. He was short and stocky, with a brisk, chirpy attitude that inspired confidence; he had black curly hair, a tight mouth upturned at the corners, and dark eyes that seemed to be darting constantly everywhere and missing nothing. His breezy, uninhibited chattiness came as a welcome relief after the austere, silent presence of Dr. Mueller.

Knacke worked at the Weissenberg plant, he told them as they drove out of Leipzig in a noisy, smoky Fiat that had seen better days. He was a chemist involved in the development of firefighting and safety equipment. His wife worked as a clerk at the same plant. They would be putting up "Ferdinand" and "Juggler"—Knacke knew Ferracini and Cassidy only by their Ampersand code-names—until the time was ready. There would be more clothes at the house to replace the things they had left in their bags.

"Gasoline is practically impossible to obtain as a private citizen, but I use the car on company business," he told them as he drove. "Take these in case we're stopped. They're worker's passes for Weissenberg. You're a plant maintenance supervisor and an electrician. If anyone asks, we've been to Leipzig this morning to get parts for a critical repair job. Yes, the parts are in the trunk. Here are the receipts. Read them so you'll know what we've bought."

"Is that how you're planning to get us into the plant later?" Ferracini asked.

"Yes."

"So you must be where the six of us come together," Cassidy said.

"That's right."

Each of the pairs coming into Germany would have its own contact like the shoemender, who would know nothing of where they were bound. Also, no doubt, Knacke didn't know where the bodies that he retrieved from the "drop boxes" had come from.

"How about the others?" Cassidy asked. "Have any of them shown up yet?"

Knacke shook his head. "Not yet. It's still early, though. But we shouldn't be talking about that until . . . oh-oh."

Two armed policemen were standing in the road ahead, and another was walking forward with one hand raised and the other pointing straight at them. Knacke stopped the car a few feet away and his two passengers tensed, but the policeman turned away and walked back to rejoin the others. Then they saw they were at a railroad crossing, and vehicles from the other direction had been stopped, too. A minute later, two locomotives in tandem rumbled through, pulling a train of freight cars, followed by flat-cars loaded with shrouded field guns and gray-painted tanks emblazoned with the black cross of the Wehrmacht.

"You see, that's what we get," Knacke exclaimed, tossing up his hands. "Swindles, always swindles. Our illustrious Dr. Ley will produce a 'People's Car' for under a thousand marks that everyone can afford, the Führer promised. And so they invented a pay-before-you-get-it plan—neat, eh?—in which every worker pays five marks a week, or more if they can squeeze it out of you. When you have paid seven hundred fifty marks, then you get your order number that entitles you to a car as soon as they start coming off the line. But the number is all you get. Nobody has seen a car yet. And the factory that they built with our money at Fallersleben—more cars per year than Ford turns out in America, they said—is making tanks." He threw up his hands again. "What good is that to me? Am I supposed to take my wife shopping in a tank?"

Ferracini and Cassidy grinned at each other as the car began moving again. Ferracini settled back in the front seat to see where they were. Yes, he knew this area. Some things were as he remembered; others had changed. Or rather, they hadn't changed yet. It was a strange kind of reverse déjà vu.

Director Kahleb frowned. He was seated at one end of the table in the room upstairs from the reception area, where Winslade and Anna had been taken after Scholder and Adamson's disappearance a half-hour previously. Nothing was making sense. "If your intentions are as innocent as you make out, why did your two companions run away like that?" he asked. "I still haven't heard a good answer."

"How should I know without asking them?" Winslade retorted. "Perhaps they think everyone is insane here. I can see why they might."

The silver-haired man whom Kahleb had summoned held up a hand. "We can go into that when Shelmer arrives," he said. He looked at Winslade. "Now, getting back to the subject, you say you've never heard of the Nazis. You're not with Hitler at all?"

"Hitler?" Winslade blinked at him with a mystified expression. "You mean Adolf Hitler?"

"Well, of course. Who else?"

"The madman? But he was assassinated, oh . . . I don't know how many years ago. What does he have to do with anything?"

"How could we be connected with him?" Anna Kharkiovitch chipped in.

"You are from 1940," Kahleb said, just to be doubly sure.

"Yes."

"And there wasn't a Reich Führer back there, where you came from?"

"Führer?" Winslade looked blankly at Anna.

"They must mean the Central European Commissar," she said, doing a good job of sounding as if she were trying to be helpful.

"Oh, yes, of course." Winslade looked back. "That would be Comrade Georgi Yussenklovov."

"So you're with him, then," the silver-haired man concluded, nodding in a way that said they had gotten somewhere at last.

"No," Winslade said.

There were groans followed by a baffled pause. "Look," Kahleb said wearily, "let's start all over again. . . ."

One of the scientists listening from the side of the room turned his head and leaned toward another standing next to him. "This is completely unprecedented," he whispered. "It shouldn't have been possible, but it sounds as if we cross-hooked into a wrong universe entirely. It must have something to do with that interference we've been getting."

The Knackes' home was a solid, respectable, brick house with a tiled roof and ivy-covered walls, comfortably secluded behind hedges and shrubbery in a quiet area of woods and houses about five miles from Weissenberg. Gustav Knacke said that it had been built by his father, who had been a teacher of theology and philosophy at the University of Leipzig. It seemed the family had a long history in the area.

Knacke took them in the back door of the house and started a fire in the living room. They would have to make themselves at home for the rest of the afternoon, he said, since he was expected back at the plant. He would be back later in the evening with Marga, his wife. He cautioned them to stay inside the house, to keep the fire low to avoid advertising that the house wasn't empty, and not to answer the door or the telephone.

"Neighbors!" he exclaimed despairingly as he left. "Because their own tiny-minded lives are so dull, they poke their noses into other people's. Fortunately, the houses are far apart around here, and we have lots of trees. But it's better to be safe." He shook his head. "They send you cards at Christmas and wish you good morning with a smile on their way home from church, but give them half a chance and they're rushing to get themselves in the good books down at the police station. They bully their servants and grovel to their bosses. I fear it's part of the mentality of too many Germans."

Cassidy found a spare blanket in one of the closets, and after taking off his boots, stretched out on the couch in front of the fire and went to sleep. Ferracini had never known anybody with the stamina to go for such lengths of time without rest when the situation demanded, or the capacity for so much sleep when it didn't. He himself felt moody and restless.

He prowled about the house, getting his bearings. It was a sober, but at the same time tastefully decorated and dignified place, with paneled entrance hall and stairs, solid furnishings of walnut and oak, and china and glassware in cabinets in the dining room. The library had floor-to-ceiling bookshelves and a grand piano. There was a music stand near the piano with the score of a Mozart sonata lying open on top, and a violin case was propped against a nearby chair.

Ferracini took down some of the books at random and turned idly the pages. Plays and poems—Goethe, Schiller, Shakespeare . . . *Lives of the Great Composers* . . . art, history, and gardening. . . . He moved along to another section. *Analytic Functions of the Complex Variable; An Introduction to Differential Geometry and the Theory of Curvature; Physics since 1900.* . . . And farther on, *Eastern Mythology; A History of Thought.*

He found himself growing depressed. So much had been created; so much had been discovered; but apart from what he'd learned at school, he had been taught only how to kill and destroy. A craftsman might work for months, applying the knowledge gained in a lifetime in order to create something that any fool with a hammer could smash in a second. On the face of it, nothing worthwhile should have lasted. Yet the strange thing was that over the ages cities and nations had grown; works of art and science had accumulated; civilization had spread. Didn't that say that mankind's creative and constructive instincts far outweighed its destructive element? Man's overriding compulsion was to build and preserve. The interludes of destructiveness constituted the aberrations.

If that was so, then the whole world that Ferracini was from represented the supreme aberration, and he himself was just as much an aberration along with it. The resentment that had never been far below the surface welled up anew as the realization came home to him of just how much he had forfeited to that world and those responsible for shaping it. Now, finding himself face to face with a remnant of the world that had died, the full comprehension at last dawned on him of the true nature of the hideous force that he had been fighting all through his professional life.

His sense of purpose became suddenly clearer than it had ever been. It was as if his life until now had been a preparation for this moment. He found a grimly satisfying irony in the thought that all the knowledge and skill he commanded in the arts of destruction would now be concentrated on the task of destroying, in a sense, the world that had made him a destroyer. And he knew that if he succeeded, he would remain a part of the new world that would come into being, to share whatever new future lay ahead. He would have earned his place in it.

Frau Knacke was a proud and handsome woman, the kind whose looks sharpen and take on character with years, rather than fade. She had a full figure, which she carried well, raven black hair just starting to show gray streaks, a firm mouth, and deep, intelligent eyes. "You can stay here for as long as you need to," she told Ferracini and Cassidy as she showed them into one of the bedrooms upstairs. "The beds have been aired, and you will find more clothes, shaving gear, and so on in that closet."

The room was furnished with two beds, a long couch in a bay window, two small armchairs facing a low table, a wardrobe, and a chest of drawers. Sporting trophies stood on a shelf with some books and some models of Great War biplanes. A picture on the wall showed several rows of laughing youths wearing short pants, ties, and school blazers.

"We have two sons," Frau Knacke explained. "Wolfgang is in Berlin, studying to be a chemist like Gustav." She smiled sadly and shook her head at the insanity of it all. "The other one, Ulrich, was conscripted and is now with an artillery battery somewhere."

"He's supposed to be in Poland," Gustav said, sucking an empty pipe in the doorway. "But we know he isn't." He gave a sly wink. "We got a letter from him last week. He said he would send Marga some shoes like Aunt Hilda's. But our Aunt Hilda, you see, brought back a souvenir pair of wooden clogs from her honeymoon in Holland. So we deduce that Ulrich's unit has been secretly transferred to the West. There'll be something big happening in that direction before very much longer, you mark my word."

How had it happened that these people were providing hospitality to two men who were enemies of the very regime that their son had been called away to risk his life defending? Cassidy brought the subject up later when they were having dinner. "Why are you doing it?" he asked. "I mean, we're in a strange situation here. We can't help being curious."

Gustav mopped up the last drops of his soup with a piece of bread. "I suppose you could say we both believe that certain things in the world run deeper than the colors printed on maps and count for more than flags and anthems, or fanatical ideologies. Those are transient, trivial things, things invented by men, which relate only to the petty day-to-day affairs of men. They pass and are forgotten. The universe won't remember or care."

He glanced at Marga. She smiled faintly and gave his hand a reassuring squeeze. Gustav looked at his guests. "But there are other, more permanent things—things that don't change with a whim."

"How do you mean?" Ferracini asked.

"We are both scientists, you see," Gustav said. "I'm a chemist. Marga used to teach anthropology at Leipzig."

"I resigned because of the lunatic racial doctrines we were expected to teach because they suited current political needs," she said. " 'Nazi Science'! It's the poison they are pouring into the minds of young people that we are prepared to fight against."

"Truth, of course, pays no attention to political needs," Gustav went on, "or to the needs of any other kind of ideology for that matter. What is true will remain true regardless of all the wishful thinking in the world that would have it otherwise. And the purpose of science is to discover what is absolute and unchangeable, inherent in the fabric of the universe and completely uninfluenced by man's passions or by whether or not we even exist at all."

"You make it sound almost like a religion," Cassidy commented.

Gustav nodded. "Albert Einstein—you've heard of him, no doubt. I saw him once from a distance, you know. Einstein said that scientific research is the only thing that qualifies as a religion. If religion claims to deal with the absolute and the universal, then what could be more absolute and universal than the things revealed through mathematics and physics? But the systems that are called religions, what do they concern themselves with? Words that a person utters—which god he thinks he talks to. Whom somebody might choose to make love with. What books he reads. Trivial things, things that concern the behavior of people. There's nothing absolute or universal about that! Who do people think they are to imagine that the universe cares about their antics on this little speck of mud? Only people care about such things. But they persuade themselves that their little problems have cosmic importance." Gustav threw up his hands in a gesture of exasperation. "And these are the people who in the same breath accuse scientists of being arrogant! I ask you! Did you ever hear such an absurdity?"

"There are concepts of human progress and the advancement of freedom that we value above politics or national loyalty," Marga said. "Few people realize where this monstrous regime of Hitler's is leading. Have you any idea of the kind of world that would result if it isn't stopped?" Ferracini and Cassidy carried on eating and said nothing.

"It has to be stopped," Gustav said. "And we will help stop it in any way that is within our power. All other considerations must take second place. Your purpose in coming here is to hasten that result. That puts us on the same side in the only respect that matters."

Ferracini asked, "Out of curiosity, how much have you been told about our purpose? What do you know about why we're here?"

"Not very much," Gustav said. "Our place is simply to get the six of you into the plant."

"Our?" Cassidy queried. "You mean you and Marga?"

"There is another also, called Erich." Gustav said. "He is reliable. But anyway . . . after that? Well, since I have received no further instructions, I assume that you know what your mission is once you're inside. If you need further help, then presumably you'll ask for it."

Ferracini nodded. "That sounds good. Let's leave it like that for now."

Gustav's eyes twinkled, and he toyed with his fork for a moment. "But since an old friend of mine, Professor Lindemann, is involved, I suppose it would be no great feat of deduction to presume that you have come from England. But I wouldn't place your accents as English—more American if anything, I'd guess." He held up a hand hastily before either of them could reply. "No, please, don't say anything. It's better if I don't know. None of us can resist the temptation to let people know when we think we've been a little clever, eh?"

He folded his napkin and placed it on the table, then glanced at the clock on the mantelpiece. "Nearly time for the BBC news broadcast from London," he said. "Highly illegal, naturally, but by averaging out their propaganda and our propaganda, we generally manage to get a fair idea of what's going on . . . we think. It seems that there will be an armistice between the Finns and the Russians any day now. The Finns put up a good fight; but with the discrepancy in numbers there was never really any doubt of the outcome."

He got up from the table. "And after that, well, we don't have any jazz or swing, I'm afraid, but there is a collection of classical records in the library. Or perhaps you might like to listen to something live? Marga and I play quite a good piano-violin duet, you know, even if I do say so myself. Did you know that Reinhard Heydrich is supposed to be an expert violinist? He's very popular among the wives of the Nazi leaders because he can entertain at their dinner parties. I've heard he's been known to weep with emotion at the beauty of the music. Would you believe that—a man like him? What a curious mixture of baffling personalities this whole phenomenon has brought together."

Two days of inactivity went by. Gustav reported that he had no news of the other four. And nothing appeared in the newspaper small ads concerning the two loads of equipment that were supposedly on the way.

CHAPTER
38

THE YOUNGER VERSION OF Kurt Scholder looked around to make sure nobody was nearby, and then quickly unlocked the door of the laser optics calibration room. It was dark inside. On top of the heavy steel optical table, the ghostly forms of mirrors, lenses, supporting stands, and other pieces of equipment were outlined in dim violet light. He produced a flashlight, directed it into the pitch black space underneath the table, and held it steady while Scholder and Colonel Adamson moved boxes and cartons to make room for themselves.

"I still don't know what's going on, but I have to give you the benefit of the doubt," the younger Scholder whispered as they squeezed in. He helped them build a screen in front of themselves. "You should be all right here. I'll be back as soon as the check is over. It shouldn't take more than an hour or so." His footsteps hurried back to the door. Then the light from outside vanished as the door closed, and they heard the key turn in the lock.

Scholder and Adamson shuffled around to make themselves more comfortable, and all was quiet for a while. Then Adamson murmured, "I don't understand why they're so mystified about where you've come from. I mean, the people here know how this thing works, don't they? They must know about all these crazy branching universes and what that machine we've just come out of does."

"Not really," Scholder whispered. "I was aware of the physics, yes—when I was him, I mean—but I didn't know what the system here was really being used for. We were told that it connected to a research base in an uninhabited realm, which was being used purely for cause-and-effect experiments. I didn't find out what was really going on until later, after I went through from this world to the Germany of 1941 and found myself working on Hitler's bomb program. But of course, it was too late by then. They didn't issue us with return tickets quite so easily. Then when Hitler had the Nazi return-gate destroyed later, I was really trapped."

"Then only a select few in this place know the real purpose of what's going on?"

"Exactly. And the rest of the scientists here believe that they're privileged with highly confidential information. You see, the public at large has been told only about a breakthrough in physics that enables instantaneous transportation of matter over large distances. The scientists observe the secrecy very strictly. None of them wants to risk getting kicked out of what's probably the most exciting project they're ever likely to work on."

"Didn't anyone wonder where the bombs were going? You said you worked on them yourself. Didn't you wonder?"

"Final assembly was done at the other end, in Nazi Germany. We knew that nuclear explosives were being sent through, but we thought they were for engineering works at the far end—excavations and so on. That wouldn't have been unusual."

A short silence followed while Adamson thought over what had been said. "So what about the elite group, the ones who knew?" he asked at last. "Why did they cooperate? What did they imagine was in it for them?"

"I'm not sure," Scholder replied. "How can you ever be sure of human motives? Power, maybe? Prestige? Perhaps they thought they were going to become technical high priests in the Nazi utopia."

"Do you have any kind of plan in mind yet?" Adamson asked after a pause.

"I don't know. . . . If we can get the right help, simply to hold the control-room crew at gunpoint if we have to, I suppose, and force them to send us back where we came from. After that, who knows?"

"Sounds easier said than done."

"Got a better idea?"

Silence.

"No . . . I guess not."

"The first thing will be to try and find Claud and Anna. I wonder what's happening to them."

"I've lost all track of time," Adamson said. "How long has it been since we came out of that machine?"

Scholder uncovered the luminous dial of his watch. "About three-quarters of an hour," he replied.

Almost a week of nerve-racking inactivity had gone by at the Knacke house, interrupted only by two days that Ferracini and Cassidy spent reconnoitering the layout of the plant, making sketches and notes to update their information. Then Gustav Knacke arrived home after being out late one night and announced that "Druid" and "Saxon" had arrived, which told them that Ed Payne and Floyd Lamson had made it safely. Knacke had collected the arrivals from one of his drop-boxes and installed them a mile or so away in the barn of a vacated farm. The Jewish family that previously owned the farm had been forcibly resettled farther east, and the farm was awaiting new owners of approved Aryan descent.

That night, Gustav produced a pair of heavy topcoats, scarfs, and hats, and took his two lodgers via a trail through the woods to welcome the new arrivals with a bottle of cognac and a bag of provisions from Marga. Payne and Lamson had made themselves warm and comfortable in the hayloft of the barn; they were weary and hungry, but in good shape. They had traveled to Sweden and from there entered the port of Danzig as crewmen on a Swedish coastal freighter. Then they were supposed to have assumed the identities of two Red Cross officials to cross into Germany. However, after an incident in Poznán in which a suspicious railway police inspector and an overzealous guard had ended up in a carriage toilet with broken necks, they had jumped train and relied on improvisation and expediency to cover the remaining distance.

A day later, an ad had appeared in the paper that Ferracini and Cassidy had been watching, stating that somebody had twenty-three meters of fabric for sale at seven marks. The numbers were the odd digits of a six-figure map reference. On the same day, a different ad that Gustav had been looking for in a different paper supplied the even digits. A map revealed that the spot indicated by the combined numbers lay in a wooded area about eight miles away, where the only notable landmark was a small bridge crossing a stream. Ferracini and Cassidy drove with Gustav to a point on the road nearby and hiked down to the bridge. Not far away was a pile of brushwood and branches that had been left after tree-felling. One of the loads of equipment from England was concealed beneath the brush.

They returned that night and took the car down to the bridge on the first of several trips to transfer the cache to the barn. Gustav was intrigued when he saw the special suits equipped with breathing apparatus. "We're working on something similar to this in the lab I'm with at the plant," he said. "A contract for the Navy, you know—an oxygen rebreathing system for underwater use. And we thought we were years ahead of you people!"

"It's strange," Cassidy said as they loaded the bundles into the trunk and on the back seat. "This stuff shows up, and we'll probably never know who got it here or how. There are still a lot of brave people around."

"Yes, there are." Ferracini worked in silence for a while. Then he mused, "I wonder what happened to the other load."

Back in the office that young Scholder shared with Eddie, Eddie sat back shaking his head bemusedly and looked across at his Section Head, Dr. T'ung-Sen. "Now you can see why I figured you and John should sit in on this," Eddie said. "It's crazy, I know, but you can't argue with it—this guy is Kurt. There's no getting away from it. And if we accept that, there's no reason not to accept this cuckoo story of theirs, too."

"It's true," young Kurt confirmed. "Some of the things he's said—answers to questions I asked him—nobody else could have known."

T'ung-Sen brought both hands up to massage his eyes with his fingers. "A conspiracy of terror and tyranny to take over the world of a hundred years ago as a haven for our dying elites? My God, I don't know . . ."

John Hallman, Sen's opposite number in Plasmonics, stared at Scholder with a mixture of wonder and doubt. "So, who's supposed to be in on this?" he asked. "How many of the people here know what Pipe Organ's for?"

"Kahleb and Justinaux," Scholder replied. "Miskoropittis, Craig, Quincy, Bonorinski . . . people like that—everyone at D6 level and above, certainly. At a guess, say, oh, five to ten percent."

"What about Juanseres and the Security people?"

Scholder shook his head. "They're just doing a job."

"But how could a secret of that magnitude have been kept for so long?" Hallman objected. "Are you saying that all the other people who work here—us, for instance—could have been duped for this long? It doesn't seem possible."

"Don't underestimate the people behind it," Scholder told him. "They may be few in number, but they still have a lot of influence. But the time to tell you the whole story isn't now."

Hallman looked at T'ung-Sen. Sen spread his hands helplessly, shook his head, and said nothing. In the end, Eddie said, "Whether it's true or not will sort itself out later. The question that matters is, what do we do now?"

Scholder took the initiative. "It has to be brought to the attention of the CN for a full investigation," he said. "And if the authorities here won't cooperate, then the CN will have to send in a CIAF force to make them."

"Now wait a minute—" Hallman began.

"It's the only way," Scholder insisted.

"What about the Brazilian government? Are they mixed up in it?" Eddie asked.

"They know that Pipe Organ exists, obviously, but they believe the time-travel, cause-and-effect, research-station story. So they keep the subject classified."

"Look, would somebody mind filling me in?" Colonel Adamson said, sounding bewildered. "CN? CIAF? What are you talking about?"

Scholder explained, "The world we're in here hasn't had a major conflict since the end of the Great War, over a century ago in 1918. The major powers abandoned large national armies years ago, and since then have practiced other forms of rivalry based on healthier ways of competing.

"But local squabbles do break out from time to time, and situations occur that require firm-handed action. There isn't a world government, but virtually all of its nations belong to a Council of Nations that acts as a kind of world court for settling differences—like the League that you're familiar with, except this one works. And between them the world's nations support a global organization known as the Combined International Armed Force, which gives the CN a set of quite effective teeth."

Adamson nodded. "Okay," he said to Hallman. "So you've got the means here to deal with the situation. I don't really want to get involved. All I did was leave home this morning to spend a normal day at work. This is your century, not mine. Why can't you organize some people to take over that machine for just long enough to send us back where we came from? Then you can spend as long as you want figuring out how to get this place closed down."

Hallman stared at him incredulously. "Send you back? You've got to be joking! You can't expect to just materialize out of nowhere with a story like this and then disappear as if nothing had happened. Who knows what you may have started?"

"What do you mean, we started?" Adamson protested, becoming genuinely alarmed. "Look, it was your goddam machine that got us here. We—"

"You tapped into our line," Hallman retorted.

Scholder held up a hand and nodded resignedly. "If we have to remain for a while until this is cleared up, then so be it," he conceded. "But that's all going to take time. Meanwhile, there are still two more of our people in this place somewhere. I want to find them and get them out of wherever they are before we try anything else."

Hallman drew a long breath as if struggling to contain his patience, then exhaled abruptly. "Oh, the thing to do is hand it over to Security," he said. "I don't see that this is any of our business at all."

"That might be a bit hasty, John," Sen cautioned. "If there is something in this story, relying on Security could be a mistake. Their responsibility is to the wrong management."

Hallman looked disgruntled, but wasn't inclined to argue the point. "Well, what else then?" he invited.

"I suggest we take it to Dr. Pfanzer," Sen said. He glanced at Scholder. "Is he safe?"

"As far as I know, yes," Scholder said.

Hallman hesitated. On the one hand, he was a scientist with an aversion to getting mixed up in politics; on the other, he was a scientist—curious. This was much too intriguing to just dump on someone else and forget.

Before Hallman could say anything, the younger Scholder, who had been sitting with his chair tilted back and a distant expression on his face, looked at his analog and asked, "Just out of curiosity, does the word 'Proteus' mean anything to either of you?"

"Yes," Scholder said. "It was the code name for the mission that was sent back from 1975 to 1939. Why?"

"Ah, then that solves it," young Scholder said. "Before the alert, I was talking to some of the guys on last night's duty crew from Transfer Control. It seems there was a strange interference on the beam sometime early this morning. Nobody had seen anything like it before. It happened again just before lunch. What was so puzzling about it was that when they put the recordings of the interference through the computers for pattern analysis, it turned out to be coded in standard Morse. The word it spelled was 'Proteus.'"

"That was us," Scholder confirmed.

"I'm not sure I follow," Sen said.

Scholder explained, "When we had a partial resonance, we tried to signal to what we thought was 1975. . . ." His voice trailed away, and he seemed confused suddenly. "When did you say this happened—this morning? I don't understand."

"The last time was about three hours ago, and the first time was, oh, about four hours before that, I think they said," young Scholder replied.

Scholder turned toward Adamson with a puzzled expression. "But we sent that signal back at the end of January, didn't we, Keith? And the time before that was in December, Christmas Eve, to be precise. . . . I don't—" Then his eyes widened as the realization of what had happened suddenly hit him. "Of course!" he whispered. With everything that had taken place since their coming out of the machine, there hadn't been time to think. It hadn't even crossed his mind. "Oh, my God!"

"What is it, Kurt?" Adamson asked.

Scholder moved over to the two desks. "Excuse me a second." Eddie leaned aside while Scholder activated one of the video terminals. "Einstein—he was working with us—deduced that time would run slower if you move forward into the future. He worked out a fourth-power law that depends on the amount that you go forward by." Scholder entered a calculation into the computer. "Keith, do you remember that we said time would be slowed down by a factor of five-point-seven when we arrived?"

"Yes," Adamson said.

Scholder stared numbly as the result appeared on the screen. At last he swallowed hard and said, "That assumed we would be reconnecting to 1975, only thirty-five years into the future. But we've actually arrived eighty-five years into the future. But fourth-power law, that gives a factor not of five-point-seven, but of two hundred!" Adamson failed to grasp the implication at once. "We've been in this world for something like two hours now," Scholder said. "That means that back in our own time, sixteen days will have gone by since we were in New York! Back there it's the middle of March already. I'm afraid that you probably have a very worried wife."

Scholder nodded slowly to himself as a number of other things suddenly became clearer. Now he could see why the time-tabling of transfers to and from Germany had been so critical: Every minute lost at the 2025 end would equate to more than three hours lost in 1940. No wonder all the planning, and most of the meetings and conferences had taken place in Germany, not Brazil. But there was more to it than just that.

He looked at Hallman, his eyes deadly serious now. "We can't afford to fool with the CN," he said. "There isn't time. Do you realize what this means? Time is running two hundred times faster in the world we've come here from. For every two days that we spend talking here, over a year will pass by there—in a world where civilization is being overwhelmed and nations crushed by a form of barbarism that you people in your comfortable world here are incapable of imagining. But it was your world here that unleashed it. The bombs for 1942 are being readied here right now! Can you imagine that, Dr. Hallman? Can you imagine turning madmen with nuclear weapons loose in the world of a hundred years ago? Well, that's exactly what you've done. Now tell us again that we should just hand it over to Security and wait for somebody to talk to the CN."

A strained silence followed Scholder's outburst. Then Hallman nodded curtly. "Let's go and talk to Pfanzer."

CHAPTER
39

THE NEWS THAT CONTACT had been lost after Winslade, Anna, and Scholder disappeared into the Gatehouse machine with an American colonel had naturally caused great concern among Churchill's group in England. When over two weeks went by with nothing further of them, the concern turned to consternation.

With the likely outcome of Ampersand far from certain, the development of a Western atomic bomb to counterbalance the Nazi threat immediately assumed crucial importance; since most of the experts in America were trying to find out what had gone wrong at Gatehouse, the focus of atomic research shifted for the time being to Britain. The main centers of the British program were the universities of London, where a Professor Thomson was experimenting with fast and slow neutrons at Imperial College, supported by the Air Ministry; Liverpool, under James Chadwick, the discoverer of the neutron; and Birmingham.

At Birmingham, Lindemann introduced Gordon Selby to the group working on uranium fission under a Professor Rudolf Peierls and Dr. Otto Frisch—the same Otto Frisch who had brought the news from Sweden to Copenhagen in December 1938, of the Hahn-Strassmann experiment performed in Berlin.

He had been visiting England at the outbreak of war and elected to stay. One quick result of this collaboration was a realization by the Birmingham group that the critical mass of uranium 235 (the minimum amount needed for a workable bomb) was measured not in tons, as they had previously imagined, but in pounds. This altered radically their whole outlook regarding atomic weapons' feasibility. In response to a paper by Peierls and Frisch, and under heavy prodding from Lindemann, the government established a group that came to be known as the Maud Committee to monitor and supervise further nuclear work. Lindemann explained to the surprised British researchers that he had obtained Selby temporarily on an exchange deal that he'd worked with the Americans. "You'd be surprised what they're doing over there," he told them. "Some of the people they've got are way ahead of their time!" At least it was being honest.

Meanwhile, the Russo-Finnish war, which in the Proteus world had gone on until June, ended "prematurely," taking the planners of the proposed Norwegian campaign by surprise. Apparently, the Stalin-Hitler pact that had been concluded in this world had freed the Russians to send more troops to Finland, which resulted in a speedier decision. Thus, the main pretext for intervening in Scandinavia had gone away. Undeterred, Churchill pressed for a decision to proceed with the Norwegian landings, anyway.

"To hell with the Finnish business!" he growled at the next meeting of the War Cabinet. "We'll put mines in the Leads and go in when the Germans react. And if the Germans fail to react, then to hell with them, too. We'll go in anyway!" His secret reason, of course, was to forestall the German invasion expected in May. The War Cabinet was persuaded, and plans went ahead for an Anglo-French expedition to sail in early April.

But what Churchill and his advisers didn't know about was Admiral Raeder's urging Hitler, following the *Cossack* incident, to move the German invasion date forward. And Hitler had accepted the proposal, for the pact with Stalin had also released extra German forces. So, finally, the German force, too, was scheduled to sail in April.

In his large office behind high double doors on the top floor of Abwehr headquarters, Admiral Wilhelm Canaris, head of German military intelligence, studied the documents that Colonel Piekenbrock had laid on his desk. Canaris's assistant, Colonel Oster, looked down from where he was standing to one side of his chief's chair, while Lt. Col. Boeckel watched respectfully from a few paces back.

"So there's nothing positive that says they're actually in Germany yet," Canaris concluded.

"No," Piekenbrock agreed. "The photograph of those three coming out of the British Admiralty on February 18 was the last definite lead. If that idiot in New York hadn't gone blundering in against orders and gotten himself arrested, we might know more."

Oster grunted. "They were training in New York last June. Then a farewell ceremony, or whatever, at the White House in October. Now, London in February. . . . They're certainly getting nearer."

"Exactly," Piekenbrock said. He gestured at some of the other papers and clippings. "Now I find myself wondering whether these other things are just coincidences. Sumner Welles, the U.S. Undersecretary of State, visits Berlin and Rome in early March; James Mooney, a vice president of General Motors, is in Germany at the same time, supposedly on a private peace-seeking mission. Just coincidences? Or were they perhaps performing some liaison function with this sabotage group, which had already entered the country?"

"I can see your reasons for wondering," Canaris murmured. "So, what about this theory that they might be going after something connected with atomic research? Have we got any further on that?"

Piekenbrock looked inquiringly at Boeckel. "I've been checking through the list of places we know about, sir, and if anything, that theory seems less probable now," Boeckel said. "Professor Esau's work under the Education Ministry is running on a shoestring. As for the KWI, the people I've talked to there don't believe that any worthwhile result can be expected for years yet, if ever. Heisenberg's laboratory in Leipzig is involved only with theoretical issues. Diebner's team under the Ordnance Department at Gottow is still arguing for funds. . . ." He spread his hands. "You see, none of it qualifies as even worth worrying about at this stage, never mind as a serious threat. It can't justify an operation as elaborate as the one we've been picturing. That simply wouldn't make sense."

"Gottow," Oster repeated. "There's a lot of secret work on rockets going on there. Could that be the target?"

"A possibility," Canaris agreed. "Well, we can get the security there tightened up—it's an Army establishment. So, is there anything else to be done for the time being?" Piekenbrock and Oster shook their heads. "Very well, then—" He broke off as he saw that Boeckel wanted to say something more. "Yes?"

"There is one more thing, sir, something that I wasn't able to follow through," Boeckel said. "The SS operates some kind of se-cret installation at a munitions plant at Weissenberg, near Leipzig, which is described as an atomic research facility. I did try making further inquiries, but I was met by an extremely hos-tile response. Whatever Himmler's people are doing there, it's something they don't want us poking our noses into."

Piekenbrock nodded and looked back at Canaris. "Lieuten-ant Colonel Boeckel and I were discussing that this morning. That description could be a cover for something else."

"But you think the Americans might believe it," Oster said.

"Or perhaps they know something we don't," Canaris mused, half to himself. He drummed his fingertips on the desk and sat back in his chair. The whole regime was such a rats' nest of intrigues and feuds that it was a wonder anything ever got done. His own situation was no better. A former U-boat com-mander from the Great War, he identified strongly with the tradi-tions of the professional officer corps. Although he maintained superficially cordial relations with the heads of the rival organi-zations who eyed his exclusive control of military intelligence enviously—he and Heydrich had even become neighbors in the Berlin suburbs—he had nothing but contempt for Himmler, the jumped-up chicken-farmer, with his rabid anti-Semitism and mystic visions of neo-Germanic feudalism. And Himmler for his part distrusted anyone connected with the regular armed forces, which constituted the main potential opposition to his dream of establishing an SS state under his own private army.

So, was Canaris now supposed to make a free gift of this information to protect what was probably another of Himmler's private power-grabbing operations? It went without saying that if the information proved valuable, Canaris would receive no thanks or recognition. And anything else that might have been uncovered by Himmler's own police and intelligence networks—the Gestapo and the SD—would remain jealously guarded. There would be nothing reciprocal about it.

"Prepare a full report for submission to OKW," he said, refer-ring to the supreme command of the German armed forces. That was what he was paid for, after all. "We'll forward it to Keitel, and he can initiate whatever action he sees fit."

"You don't intend bringing it to Himmler's attention di-rectly?" Piekenbrock checked.

"I'll be damned if I will," Canaris replied. "We're working for the Wehrmacht, not Himmler. He has enough minions already. And besides, hasn't one of our officers attempted an approach in that direction already and been rebuffed? No, Hans, we'll stick to official channels and let Keitel take it to the Führer if he chooses.

Then the Führer can bring it to Himmler's notice if he deems it appropriate to do so. That, gentlemen, is his prerogative, after all."

Three more days had gone by with no sign of Major Warren and Paddy Ryan. As tends to happen with men brought physically and mentally to a peak of readiness and then left to idle, the troops were getting restless.

"Right now we've got a clear run in," Cassidy fumed, stamping back and forth in the hayloft of the barn at the disused farm. With four of them needing to stay in touch to compare notes and finalize plans, he and Ferracini now spent most of their time there. They didn't want to expose the Knackes to the risks of too many strangers being seen around the house. "We've been in Germany almost three weeks, Harry. How much more time do you want? Every day we lose increases the odds that something somewhere will screw up. Sooner or later you reach a point where you have to assume they're written off. Well, I say we've reached it. I say we go now."

Ferracini, who was sitting behind hay bales in the shadows a few feet back from an opening, keeping an eye on the approaches, shook his head. Until Warren showed up, Ferracini's seniority put him in command of the mission. "When the objective's this crucial, it's worth waiting a little longer if it means a third of our force. We give them one more full week."

"A week! Oh, Christ."

"It could be worse," Ed Payne said, sitting cross-legged, buddha-like among kit and blankets as he watched a pot of water heating on a kerosene stove. "I thought you said that last time you and Harry were here in '71, you lived rough out in the woods for a month."

"It was two weeks," Ferracini said. "The plant was into testing nerve gases by then. We wanted a sample for some department back in the States that was interested in the stuff, but our contact hadn't shown up."

Payne raised his eyebrows. "What, the same plant, you mean—Weissenberg?"

"That's right. We found out later that one of his messengers had been a Gestapo plant and turned him in. They roasted his feet with a welding torch, but he didn't talk. The informer wound up in the river with his head blown off."

"Yes, but that time was different," Cassidy said. "There was that chick who lived in that place down by the river. Do you remember her, Harry—the number with the red hair and green cat's-eyes? Lived with her brother, the guy who'd quit the Army after what he saw in Africa and was living under a new name?"

"You mean the lockkeeper?"

"Right, that's him."

Ferracini shook his head despairingly. "You asshole, Cassidy. I knew you were fooling around with his sister. Jeez, some guys just never learn."

"Man's gotta pass the time somehow," Cassidy grumbled.

"Go on over there, why not?" Payne suggested. "Maybe she's still around."

"She wouldn't be much good to him in 1940," Ferracini said. He sniggered. "Unless there's something about you that you haven't told us, Cassidy."

Payne lowered a bag of ground coffee into his pot. "You know," he said, changing the subject, "I was thinking about the work Gustav does at the plant on those gas masks and things. I think I've figured out another way we could have done the job, even if the stuff from England hadn't shown up. With all the—"

"Shh!" Ferracini tensed and craned forward as a movement among the trees beyond the farm buildings caught his eye. Then he relaxed. "Okay. It's only Floyd."

"Ah, food," Payne said. He reached behind him for the condiments and other items to begin preparations, while Cassidy lowered the ladder from the loft. Lamson came up a minute or so later and put down the sack he had been carrying. Payne opened it and pulled out two rabbits, a pheasant, and some potatoes, onions, and carrots. "Tonight, stew à la rustic," he announced.

"So, what's the verdict?" Lamson inquired. "Did we decide anything?"

"We give them another week," Ferracini told him.

Lamson nodded phlegmatically and drew a long, double-edged knife from under his coat. "Well, I hope you guys like rabbit," he drawled as he squatted down to begin work on his bag.

CHAPTER
40

"SOMETIMES," WINSLADE SAID, "I think life is just a process of discovering as you get older that you're not as clever as you thought you were when you were younger." He leaned back in the swivel chair and contemplated the two gray-uniformed security guards standing impassively inside the doorway at the far end of the room. A copy of the February 1940 issue of *The Reader's Digest*, which he had read on the plane from England to New York, had been found in his jacket pocket. Several of the articles referred to Hitler, the Nazis, and the war in Europe, exploding the nonsense that he and Anna had been fabricating to make time for Scholder. Now Kahleb and the others had retired to confer among themselves and await the arrival of somebody of higher authority who was supposed to be on the way.

Anna Kharkiovitch smiled faintly from the far side of a low, circular table at which they were sitting. "Well, perhaps the encouraging thing is that we flourish in spite of all our mistakes and imperfections," she said. "What a fragile, hopeless species we'd be if everything depended on our never slipping up or doing a thing wrong. We'd have been extinct long ago."

"That's one way of looking at it, I suppose. My word, Anna, I never realized you were so much of a philosopher."

"Didn't you?" Anna gave him a pointed look. Her tone conveyed more than the words alone said.

"I gather I'm supposed to ask what that means," Winslade said.

"I don't think there's very much about any member of the team that you don't know, Claud," she told him. "Oh, I know that everyone had to be carefully selected for a mission like this, that the least hint of an incompatibility problem would have been an automatic disqualifier, and that kind of thing. . . . But I'm talking about something else."

Winslade nodded. He didn't seem oversurprised. "Go on."

"Oh, lot's of things, Claud . . ." Anna waved a hand vaguely in the air. "The composition of the team, for example, especially the inclusion of Harvey Warren's military group. It was just too well matched to the needs of the situation that developed—Ryan a diver, Payne a chemist, all of them with operational experience in that area . . . as if you knew beforehand that Gatehouse would hit problems and we wouldn't get any backup. Then there was the way you left Arthur in England, trying to get Eden sent to Moscow in place of Strang, as if you already knew JFK's people weren't going to intervene in time. See what I mean, Claud? It's all too much of a coincidence. And just now, when you distracted everyone away from Kurt and Keith Adamson with that video, you knew what you were doing. I know it was only a standard directory or something that came up on the screen, but the point is you knew how to call it. You see, Claud, I've been wondering for a long time just how you come to—" She stopped speaking as a commotion of voices sounded from the far side of the door and grew rapidly louder.

The door burst open, and a knot of people led by two determined-looking men in dark suits marched into the room, brushing aside the guards who had been posted outside.

One of the two guards inside the room moved as if to unsling his weapon, then wavered. "Sir, I'm sorry, but—"

"Get out of the way," the taller of the two men in suits ordered without slackening pace.

"But our instructions—"

"Have been countermanded." The guards were too confounded to react, and within seconds the room was filled with people.

Kurt Scholder emerged from the throng with Adamson close behind and made for Winslade and Anna, who were on their feet. "You're all right. Good."

"Of course," Winslade said.

"These are the two people?" one of the men asked, looking at Scholder.

"Yes."

"My name is Pfanzer," the man said. "I head one of the project groups. Jorgassen here is an assistant director. Look, I don't know what to make of this story we've heard, but in case it's correct, we're getting you out of here until someone arrives from the proper authorities to investigate. We'll have to go to the Message Center before we can get in touch with them. Communications out of this place are restricted because of the secrecy of the work here. When we get there I suggest that—"

The sound of more tumult came from beyond the open door. Raised voices sounded from just outside, and then Kahleb appeared with a half dozen of his people. He was tight-lipped and angry. "You were ordered to let no one in!" he told the guards. "Who overrode me? What's going on?"

"I did," Jorgassen said, barring the way. "And exactly what's going on is something that we would very much like to know, too."

Kahleb caught sight of Scholder and Adamson. "Those are the fugitives." He waved a hand at the guards. "Detain them."

The guards looked uncertain. Before they could respond, T'ung-Sen and another man moved in front of them. "You're not under his orders," T'ung-Sen told them.

"You obey me," Kahleb said to the guards. "These people have no authority in this area."

"We are taking charge until some questions have been answered," Pfanzer declared, closing up alongside Sen. "Something highly irregular has been going on, and we mean to find out what."

"Don't be preposterous. Now, would you mind getting out of here and back to your own work?"

"Not until somebody explains where he came from," Eddie said, indicating Scholder with a nod of his head. "A full analog of Kurt Scholder here, but over thirty years older."

"Pah, you can't seriously believe that story!" Kahleb exclaimed contemptuously. "It's an elaborate hoax, for God's sake. They're from some kind of espionage ring, and they got in here illegally. That's what we were trying to find out more about. Why else do you think we were holding them?"

He looked sure of himself and sounded convincing enough to sow doubt. And his story was certainly less fantastic than the previous one. The mood of the room cooled. Some of the group that had crashed in exchanged uneasy glances. "Can you substantiate that?" Pfanzer challenged. He sounded uneasy now. Behind him the chorus of vigilante indignation was subsiding.

Kahleb pressed his advantage. "Substantiate it? I have no obligation to justify myself to you people, any of you. And even if I had, what would be the point of attempting to explain anything in the face of this kind of witch-hunting hysteria? I've told you— these people were apprehended after entering the facility illegally, and they have failed to give a satisfactory account of themselves. They are being questioned before the matter is handed over to the appropriate department. Now, would you kindly leave this to the people whose responsibility it is, and return to your own work, please?"

A swarthy, stocky man who was with Kahleb raised both hands and swung from side to side to address the whole room. "Okay, everybody, it's over—that's it. We appreciate your bringing in the other two, but let's all get back to work now and leave it at that. Come on, people, the fun's over."

Winslade thought frantically as he watched the situation that had seemed so hopeful collapsing like a house of cards. He had been pondering the strange situation they had walked into, searching for possible ways to exploit it, but hadn't said anything to Anna because of the guards. There seemed something providential in their having arrived at this of all places.

Hammerhead had been made unassailable by any form of assault from the surface. And Pipe Organ, likewise, was also impregnable from the outside.

From the outside.

That was the fatal oversight with both facilities. The designers had thought only of protecting against threats from the outside. But both Hammerhead and Pipe Organ possessed an additional way in that bypassed all the defenses: Although the two machines were separated by a gulf of time, they nevertheless stood back-to-back, each at the end of a connecting highway that led directly into the other—like a tunnel between the keeps of two castles. Guarding the tunnel would only make sense if it were possible for somebody to materialize inside it out of nowhere.

But that was exactly what Winslade and his companions had done. And the "tunnel" that they were at one end of led straight to the target of the entire Proteus mission. At the Ampersand briefing in London, he had described the mineshaft and waste conduit as a "back door" into Hammerhead, provided fortuitously by a twist of fate. But it was nothing compared to the wide-open door that was staring them in the face right now.

"Maybe you're right," somebody was saying grudgingly. "As long as no one's in any immediate danger . . . But you must understand our concern."

"Of course," Kahleb replied, sounding conciliatory. "I'd have thought the same thing. Now, will you please leave this to us?"

One of the guards was standing a few feet ahead of Winslade and to one side, but facing away to follow what was being said. He was at ease now, his manner relaxed and careless as the tension subsided. These were internal security police, little more than ceremonial guards, not battle-trained veterans or a rigorously selected elite like the Special Operations troops. Winslade thought of the risks that Warren and his men had accepted at his bidding. He could hardly refuse taking a risk himself to achieve the same objective, now that the chance was there.

"Isn't it about time somebody listened to us for a change?" he said in a loud voice, moving forward to command attention. All heads turned toward him. He raised an arm with his finger extended as if in emphasis, his movement so natural that the guard didn't even tense as Winslade brushed past him. Then Winslade whipped back in a sudden blur of movement, ducking into a crouch as he turned and driving his elbow back into the guard's solar plexus. He sidestepped as the guard buckled, and in the same movement straightened up to deliver an edge-handed blow to the back of the neck, taking the gun neatly from the guard's hands as the guard crumpled to the floor. He had leveled it at the second guard before the latter had his own weapon half unslung. The second guard froze. Anna Kharkiovitch gaped in surprise at Winslade for just a split second, then moved quickly to take the second guard's gun before most of the people in the room had registered what was happening.

Winslade backed into a corner from where he could cover the whole room and motioned Kahleb and his people to the far wall with a wave of the gun. The others who had confronted Kahleb were too shocked to react. "The side-catch is the safety," Winslade muttered to Anna, keeping his eyes on the others. "The lever behind the magazine selects solid rounds, left, or cannon, right. There's a three-position fire-selector in front of the foregrip—single-shot, burst of five, or automatic, sliding forward to back."

Anna inspected the weapon and checked it with sure fingers. "Okay."

The two guards from outside came in to investigate and stopped abruptly when they found themselves staring into two muzzles. "Not a move," Winslade warned, his voice sharp. "Now the guns, slowly, on the floor." The guards hesitated. One of them looked apprehensively at the figure sitting up and groaning on the floor, and complied. The other guard followed suit. "Kick them clear, over this way," Winslade ordered. "Now both hands high." He nodded to Scholder and Adamson to pick up a gun each. "Take their sidearms," Winslade said. Scholder and Adamson took the pistols from the guards' belts while Winslade and Anna covered them. "And now the ammunition clips. . . . Good."

Winslade surveyed the situation and gave a satisfied nod. His face split into a smile as he moved forward out of the corner. "No, ladies and gentlemen," he announced genially to the room, "I'm afraid the fun isn't over just yet."

CHAPTER
41

THE COLD LIGHT OF predawn was just touching the eastern sky above the Berlin rooftops as an SS staff car screeched around a corner into the Prinz Albrecht Strasse and stopped outside the main doors of Gestapo headquarters. The hunched street sweeper across the road and the two policemen clutching their capes around them against the cold as they stood talking on a corner opposite took little notice as a guard got out from beside the driver and hurried to open one of the rear doors. The stiff, primly upright, and sparsely built figure of Heinrich Himmler, probably the second most powerful man in the Third Reich, emerged, wearing an officer's greatcoat and black peaked cap with the badge of SS Reichsführer. He had a tight, downturned mouth, clipped mustache, and a receding chin, and blinked sleepily behind rimless pince-nez as the guard escorted him up the steps. The sentries heel-clicked to attention and opened the doors, and the two figures marched quickly through and crossed the deserted vestibule to the elevators.

Reinhard Heydrich, Himmler's deputy and head of the Reich Main Security Office, which incorporated both the Gestapo and the SD, was pacing impatiently to and fro when Himmler came into his office minutes later. At thirty-six, tall, blond, fair-skinned, with a firm-set mouth, straight nose, and clear-cut

features, Heydrich typified the Nordic ideal of Nazism's racial
fantasies. An incarnation of the technology of government by
brute force, he stood out from the majority of the Third Reich's
leadership by virtue of his supreme self-confidence and ability.
With a capacity to divorce completely all forms of emotion from
his work, including any personal spite, Heydrich combined the
technician's dispassionate pursuit of efficiency with the cynic's
readiness to exploit whatever was expedient. The result was a
calculated ruthlessness utterly devoid of any human considerations that frightened all who came in contact with him, including, at times, even Himmler.

"Good morning," Himmler greeted. "Well, what do you
have?" He had been awakened by a phone call a half-hour earlier,
in which Heydrich had said simply that there were urgent matters to discuss concerning "Valhalla," code name for the installation at Weissenberg that housed the connection to Overlord in
2025. A day previously, Hitler had expressed concern to Himmler
over the security precautions. Field Marshal Keitel, head of the
unified defense staff established in 1938, had shown the Führer a
report from Canaris indicating that the British and American intelligence services were coaching a picked espionage group to
specialize in matters connected with atomic research. Canaris
had mentioned Weissenberg specifically, and the skeptical tone
of some of his remarks had hinted strongly that he for one was far
from convinced by the SS's cover story. Hitler was worried and
had told Himmler to investigate.

"It's worse than we thought," Heydrich said. "A lot worse."
He gestured at the papers strewn across his desk and picked up
the file that he had procured from the Abwehr. "We're talking
about an elite military sabotage unit that goes all the way up to
Churchill and Roosevelt, personally."

Himmler puckered his mouth grimly. "Military? You mean
the American military is involved actively—a neutral country?"

"Exactly," Heydrich replied. "As I said, Roosevelt's involved
personally. What's the only thing that could be important enough
to justify that?"

"My God! Are you saying they know what's at Weissenberg?"
Himmler took the file and began scanning the pages rapidly.

"We have no firm indication of that, but Canaris's people believe it's the target. They've eliminated possible alternatives."

"Does Canaris know what it is?"

"No, I don't think so. But he suspects it's not what we say it
is."

Himmler looked horrified as he turned over the earlier documents in the file. "July, last year! Washington in October?

London? Surely this can't be possible! You mean they've known about it all this time?"

"And more," Heydrich said. "You remember that incident near Kyritz over three weeks ago—where four terrorists were killed when one of our units was called out to some shooting at a checkpoint? Well, the bodies have all been identified. They were all on record, which means they were just baggage porters. None were members of this Anglo-American sabotage squad. Therefore, the squad is still at large."

Heydrich held up another sheaf of papers. "And this is a laboratory report on the things found with the explosives they were carrying. It all came from England. And this is what part of the conclusion section says." Heydrich read, " 'The most likely conjecture is that this clothing was specifically developed to afford protection in hazardous gaseous and liquid chemical environments. A specific purpose, however, cannot be deduced.' "

"Chemicals!" Himmler gasped. "It has to be Weissenberg. Somehow they're going to try to get in through the main plant!" He paled visibly as the full implication sank in. "And if those materials were captured almost a month ago . . . oh, shit . . ."

"The saboteurs are already in the country," Heydrich completed. "And for a job as important as this, there won't have been just one shipment of materials."

Himmler turned away and stared at the map on the wall of Heydrich's office. Overlord would have to be advised via Hitler, but the immediate decisions would have to be taken locally, as was normal. The time dilation factor of 200—it had been 360 back in 1926, when the whole thing began, and was reducing constantly as the past "caught up"—meant that even if Overlord took an hour to respond, over eight days would have passed by in Germany. Strategy and long-term goals could be passed down, but not something like this.

"Contact the SS Oberstgruppenführer at Leipzig and have a detachment sent out immediately to take over gate security at that plant," Himmler instructed. "Also, have them secure the place and stand by in case of emergencies. Then get onto the Führer's headquarters and advise the commander that I wish to be notified at once when the Führer rises."

Heydrich looked uneasy. "Wouldn't it be advisable to secure the plant now, using the defense force that's garrisoned inside Valhalla, until the reinforcements from Leipzig arrive?" he said.

Himmler shook his head. "I'd rather keep them where they are in case we're wrong about these saboteurs entering through the plant. We would look very foolish if they got in while our crack guards were elsewhere checking workmen's passes. But make sure that they tighten up the entry procedures at Valhalla."

Heydrich hesitated for a second and then nodded. "It will be as the Reichsführer orders," he said.

"Also, get somebody to contact the Todt Organization and have them locate the engineers who were responsible for the structural changes. Bring them here, with complete plans of what was done. I want details of every conceivable means of entry."

Himmler glared at the Abwehr papers on Heydrich's desk. "It's inexcusable that this information has been withheld from us for so long," he seethed. "I suspect that our friend Admiral Canaris has been scheming to aggrandize his department at our expense. But this time he has meddled in more than he thinks." His eyes gleamed malevolently behind his pince-nez. "He is becoming dangerous. We'll take care of him later, after this other business has been resolved."

So this was it, Ferracini thought as he sat hunched in the back seat of Gustav Knacke's Fiat, moving with the early morning stream of vehicles, bicycles, and workers trudging on foot toward the Weissenberg plant. The culmination of years of intelligence gathering and planning back in his own world before 1975; the construction of the system at Tularosa; the recruitment and training of the Proteus team and its projection back in time; the setting up of Gatehouse; the move to England and the preparations since then: all to bring four men—Warren and Ryan had not made the one-week deadline—to this place on a clear, chilly morning on the first day of April. By the end of the day, it would all have been decided; either the incredible gamble would have paid a dividend worth years of effort, immeasurable human dedication, and the risk of many lives; or it would have failed.

The car passed the last of the workers' rowhouses on the outskirts of Weissenberg and rounded a bend from where the plant was visible, its main entrance only a half-mile or so away across flat, open ground dotted with clumps of gorse. Apart from the Citadel, which was operated and guarded by the SS, the chemicals plant was subject to no more than the normal level of industrial security, and Gustav anticipated little trouble getting the team in. The fenced-off compound enclosing the munitions-making area inside was tougher, but that was of no consequence since the plan didn't require access to it. Nevertheless, to be on the safe side, the Ampersand group had decided to infiltrate separately.

"Your friend isn't very talkative, Gustav," Julius said from the front passenger seat. He was a colleague who always rode to work with Knacke. "Or is it the early hour, do you think?"

"Oh, I don't really know him," Knacke replied. "He's just started—over in PM-4, I think he said. Somebody suggested I had a spare seat and would be able to give him a ride. Well, you know how it is with this war economy—can't really refuse." He glanced over his shoulder. "Is that right—you're in PM-4?"

"That's right," Ferracini answered. He had been speaking in deliberately broken German. "I start five days back on clean-the-pipes."

"What accent is that?" Julius asked.

"Is Spanish. Weather here is not so Spanish—all rain and fog."

"How come you're here?"

"I fight with Franco in war and then join Italians—go back work for Mussolini. But money better in Germany, they say, yes? So I go, but is lies. Give money, yes, then take away again."

"Oh, you'll get used to that," Julius said with a bitter laugh. "What do we call you?"

"Sorry, please?"

"Name—what's your name?"

"Oh. Is Roberto."

"So they've started cheating you already, eh?"

Ferracini thought for a moment. "Money, yes," he agreed. "But so what with money, anyhow? German girls okay-deal instead. Spanish girls all with very Catholic mamas—everything no-no until get married, then only if Pope say so. What Pope know about girls? So maybe Hitler, he do something good for Germans after all."

Julius laughed. "Hear that, Gustav? Roberto, you're okay."

The car slowed down as it approached the gate, and Ferracini reached into his pocket for the pass they had faked using blanks obtained by Marga. As Gustav had predicted, the security procedure at the gate was casual, and the car was waved on by a bored factory guard in response to three passes being pressed against the window. At that moment, Ferracini caught sight of Cassidy just outside the car, struggling to control a wobbly bicycle and holding his pass between his teeth. The guard waved him on without looking at it. In the back seat, Ferracini closed his eyes and breathed a long, silent sigh of relief. Payne and Lamson, who were coming in on a workmen's bus, would have no problem.

That left only the consignment of suits, weapons, and equipment. But that should already have been taken care of. The third accomplice, whom Gustav and Marga had referred to as "Erich," was bringing it in the scrap-metal truck that came early every other morning to collect swarf and turnings from the machining shops. Occasionally, it was searched on the way out, but never once had it been stopped going in.

Ten miles away on the far side of Weissenberg, outside a blacksmith's forge and mechanic's workshop with faded signs advertising oil and tires and an antiquated gasoline pump in front, the driver of the battered truck that had just had been towed in was arguing with a man in a leather cap and grease-stained boiler suit.

"Tomorrow? But that's out of the question! I've got to have it done right away, I tell you!"

"Oh, really? And who do you think you are? You're lucky enough as it is that I was passing by on my way here, otherwise you'd still be out on the road. I've got two other jobs promised this morning. You'll have to wait your turn."

Erich gritted his teeth in exasperation. "Look, I've got to get to the plant this morning. Just fill it up with cold water and I'll take it as it is."

"What, with a hole like that in your radiator? Impossible! You'll never make the first mile."

"All right, then—fifty marks extra on the price if you fix it right away."

"Well, I really don't know. . . ."

"Sixty! I must have this truck on the road."

"Seventy."

The wail of sirens interrupted, and both men turned to look as the traffic began pulling over to the side of the road. Moments later, two motorcyclists in steel helmets and SS uniforms came into view, followed a short distance behind by a convoy comprising a staff car and three trucks loaded with troops, racing from the direction of Leipzig. Erich's face fell as he took in the scene.

"Very well, seventy," he said tightly. "Provided you begin at once. And now, where can I find a telephone? It's most urgent."

A hundred yards away along the road, a black Mercedes carrying a swastika emblem on its door and flying an SS pennant nosed out of a side-turning onto the main road and roared off after the convoy.

CHAPTER

42

THE YOUNGER KURT SCHOLDER took a cautious step forward, then stopped and shook his head. Winslade kept the gun leveled and raised his chin questioningly. "Look, I still don't know what's going on, but I do know he's genuine," young Scholder said, inclining his head in the direction of Scholder. "This may cost me my job, but I'd like to help. If the true story is as you say, I don't want to just stand here doing nothing."

Winslade nodded. "Commendable," he acknowledged. "Any more?" The others who had arrived with Pfanzer and Jorgassen looked at each other and shuffled uncomfortably. "Specifically, I need somebody who knows the control-room operating procedures," Winslade said. "Or at least, somebody who is sufficiently familiar with them to make sure that the people in there do the right things."

"First, suppose you try telling us what it is you intend doing," Pfanzer suggested.

Winslade glanced across at the elder Scholder. "Kurt, the time dilation factor here will be much greater than for 1975, yes?"

"Yes," Scholder replied. "I wondered if you'd think of that."

"How much will it be? Any guesses?"

"About two hundred. I've calculated it."

Winslade nodded as if he had been half expecting something like that. "Then the parts for the A-bombs scheduled to go through for Hitler's 1942 offensive against Russia would need to be ready pretty soon."

Scholder's eyes widened as he began to see what Winslade was driving at. He performed a quick conversion in his head. For the bombs to be available by summer 1942, the components would need to be delivered, say, two years after the present time there—spring 1940. Twenty-four months at thirty days, divide by two hundred . . . He nodded. "It works out at about three and a half days from now. You're right. The components must be here now."

"They'll be through the big doors across the antechamber from the transfer lock," Winslade said. "That's the Dispatch Preparation Area, isn't it?"

"Listen to them!" Kahleb protested from where he and his group were glowering by the far wall. The guard that Winslade had floored was sitting up, clutching his stomach, and looking groggy. "They're insane. Are you going to allow yourselves to be parties to mass murder?" Anna Kharkiovitch silenced him with a menacing wave of the gun she was holding.

"I don't think we should continue this discussion in the present company," Winslade said. He began moving across the room. "Let's go next door." Anna and Scholder kept Kahleb's group covered while Adamson ushered the rest out behind Pfanzer and Jorgassen. "Make sure they don't have any personal communicators on them, Kurt," Winslade said. Scholder quickly frisked those who were left and came away holding several pocket sets and a wrist unit as well as the belt packs worn by the guards. Winslade indicated the room's permanent video unit to Anna with a nod of his head, and she obligingly shot it to pieces. "Sorry about that," Winslade told the indignant occupants as he backed out. "Don't try anything heroic. The door will be covered, and the same thing will happen to the first person who comes through." He posted Adamson outside with instructions to fire at anyone who tried leaving, and then went to rejoin the rest in the conference room that he and Anna had been taken to initially.

Inside, Anna and Scholder were still keeping the others at a distance, but their manner was less threatening now that Kahleb's people were out of the way.

"Now wait a minute," Pfanzer began in an alarmed voice as Winslade came in. "If you imagine for one moment that anyone here is going to help you send a live nuclear device through the link, then you are insane. We've only got your word about what's allegedly happening at the far end. But there are people there—

human beings. I'm certainly not going to lend my authority to getting anyone killed. I'll agree to, or condone, none of it, do you understand? None of it."

"Nobody's talking about sending through a bomb," Winslade said. "But the parts you've got downstairs are for devices that detonate by imploding a critical fission mass with shaped charges of conventional explosives." He looked back at Scholder. "That's what you worked on here, right?"

"That's you," Scholder said to his younger analog. "We make two experts."

Winslade looked at Pfanzer. "This is my proposition," he said. "You don't want to be responsible for anyone's getting killed. Well, neither do I. Now, whether you believe it or not right now, at the other end of that link is a world that your operation here has created, in which a war has already begun that will lead eventually to the destruction of Western civilization unless something's done to change it. I'm talking about deaths counted in tens of millions, not just a few who might be around when a bomb goes off."

"Very well, suppose we accept that for the sake of argument," Pfanzer conceded guardedly. "You still haven't told us your proposal."

"Simply that we disable the return-gate at the far end until the situation here is resolved by the appropriate authorities," Winslade said. "We go for the machine only, with a couple of strategically placed charges, without harming anybody. Then we call in the CN and have the whole place here put under CIAF control until everything's been investigated."

"Sounds reasonable," someone commented.

"Why disable the gate?" Hallman objected. "Why not simply call in the CN?"

"Because of the time factor," Winslade said. "Time is running two hundred times faster there. Delay could be fatal. A few days wasted here means years lost at the other end."

Hallman shrugged. "So? We just suspend operations at this end until further notice. I still don't see the necessity of disabling the gate."

"We can't risk leaving it intact," Winslade insisted. "We have the upper hand here for now, but that could change for any one of a number of reasons. The only way to be certain that the link won't be used for a while is to make sure that it can't be."

"And look at it this way," Scholder suggested. "Even if the gate is damaged to the extent that it will take years to repair, that's still only a matter of a few days here. You're not losing very much. But the result at the far end if the link became active again in the wrong hands could be catastrophic."

Eddie moved out to join young Scholder in the middle of the room. "Hell, someone's gonna have to start making decisions around here," he said. "Okay, I'll buy it. I'm with you, too."

"And me," another declared, following suit.

Dr. Pfanzer vacillated. "Again, exactly what are you proposing?" he asked Winslade.

"One group goes to take charge in the control room," Winslade said, speaking quickly in an urgent voice. "They have the duty crew bring up the beam and stand by to initiate a transfer. The two Kurts take another group through into the Dispatch Preparation Area to obtain explosives, detonators, and time fuses to make up several charges. Then we—just some of us; I don't want any of you people risking yourselves on this—make a transfer through to the other end, place the charges on short settings, and are brought back, hopefully before the 1940 end wakes up to what's happening."

"Is that likely?" Sen asked dubiously.

"I don't know," Winslade admitted. "But I'm willing to try. We're prepared to take the risks. All we're asking for from you is help."

"Ten seconds," Scholder said. "If it takes ten seconds to place the charges at the other end and get back into the machine, what will that translate into here? Nothing! It will be no time at all."

Pfanzer nodded. "And then?"

"Then we go to the Message Center and put a call through to CN Headquarters in Zurich," Winslade said.

"That'll really stir things up," Eddie said. "Security hasn't caught on to what's happening yet, but they will if you go holding up the Message Center at gunpoint. They'll all be heading this way. What happens then?"

"As long as that gate's out of action, I don't really care what happens," Winslade said. "Perhaps we'll hand over the guns and take our chances. You could tell them you didn't have a choice— we made you cooperate. That's all we're asking—a few minutes of cooperation. What's that to give if it saves millions of lives?"

"And what if we don't want to cooperate?" Pfanzer asked.

Winslade smiled apologetically and motioned with the gun he was brandishing. "Then, I'm afraid, we really would have to insist that you do so, anyway," he replied.

CHAPTER
43

FERRACINI FOLLOWED A CONCRETE path running between some oil-cooled transformers standing behind a wire fence on one side and a bank of pipes running down from a processing vat on the other, and came to the conveyor feeding the nitrate hoppers. He turned right, came to the roadway over a rail crossing, and began walking beside a long, black-painted, tin shed. It was all just as in the model he had studied in London.

A squeaking sound came from behind him, and a moment later Cassidy caught up and swung himself off his bicycle to walk alongside. "No problem," Cassidy said.

"I know. We came in just ahead of you. See anything of Floyd and Ed?"

"A bus passed me on the road, but I don't know if it was the right one."

"I guess we'll soon find out."

"Where's Gustav?"

"Parking the car. He'll be along in a minute."

They rounded one end of a building containing noisy rock-salt crushing machinery and walked along a narrow roadway with railroad tracks embedded in the cobbles. To their left lay part of the waste-processing plant that they were heading for: a jumble of steel supports and piping beneath several domed steel tanks; two larger, taller tanks stood behind. A short alley, in front of a single-story pumphouse just ahead, led left from the road-way.

They turned into the alley; here Erich was supposed to have left the truck. There was no sign of it.

Cassidy propped the bicycle against a wall, and they carried on past the pumphouse at a quickening pace to where the alley ended at a supporting wall beneath two more, horizontal storage tanks. To their left again, a short set of railed steps descended between the concrete-block foundations of the girders overhead and banked retaining walls. At the bottom of the steps stood a squat, brick-built, hexagonal building, which enclosed the top of the disposal shaft itself. Above it, behind a clutter of tanks, piping, and steelwork, was the rear of the waste-processing build-ing, from which several massive pipes ran down at a steep angle to disappear into the top of the brick hexagon.

The hexagon was a half-sunken construction, eight feet high and perhaps twenty across, with a narrow trench running around it, shored by a concrete retaining wall. Lamson and Payne were waiting crouched in the trench at the bottom of the steps, op-posite a three-foot-square steel hatch in the wall of the hexagon. "We've already checked," Lamson said before Ferracini could ask. "The truck's not around here anywhere."

For just a few moments, Ferracini's mind seized up. He closed his eyes and exhaled a long, despairing breath. Not now, he pleaded inwardly. Don't let it screw up now—not after all this. He shook his head a couple of times to clear it and looked about to check the surroundings.

The hexagonal building was low-lying, with a canopy of gird-ers, pipeworks, and tanks overhead. The retaining wall of the trench and the concrete formations above provided good cover, and this wasn't a busy part of the plant in any case. There was no great immediate danger of detection. On the other hand, the alley they had come down was a dead end; if they were challenged, there was no other obvious way out.

"We could get trapped here pretty good," Cassidy said, as if reading his mind. "Especially since we don't have any weapons." They were in the truck, too.

Lamson, however, had a toolbox with him. "Have you checked out the cover?" Ferracini asked him, indicating the steel hatch.

Lamson nodded. "I can get it off, no problem."

"Let's do that and check out the situation inside," Ferracini said. "That'll give the truck a few more minutes. Cassidy, keep a watch on the alley from the top of the steps." Lamson nodded and turned toward the hatch, while Cassidy went back up the stairs. Ferracini stared at the tanks and steel structures overhead. A continuous roaring of exhausts came from the pumphouse across the alley, and steam hissed from an outlet high on the back of the waste-processing building above. A locomotive whistle sounded from somewhere farther away in the plant. What he really wanted was time to think.

The disposal shaft, ten feet square as was usual for mines, was capped by a cylindrical steel shaft-head chamber, into which the discharge pipes from above connected. It was fitted with gas-tight inspection covers in its side, which were the team's intended means of entry. The brick hexagon formed an outer chamber enclosing the steel inner one. Thus, a double barrier prevented noxious gases' reaching the outside, enabling maintenance or inspection work to be performed with only one of the two covers being open at any time.

"There might be a way of getting down without suits," Ed Payne said as he passed tools to Lamson.

"How?" Ferracini asked.

"It's something I was thinking about to pass the time in the barn, just in case the worst happened," Payne said, straightening up. "The shaft-head chamber inside here should have sampling valves through the walls as well as manhole covers, for testing the gas mixture in the shaft. Now, this place makes ammunition, okay? Well, to make bombs and shells you use big pneumatic presses to mold the charges into shape. In other words, something you'll find available all over a place like this is a high-pressure air supply."

Ferracini nodded, all the time scanning the vicinity instinctively with his eyes. "Okay."

"If we could couple a high-pressure line to one of those valves on the inner chamber, it would raise the pressure of the gas trapped above the liquid in the shaft, and force the level down. We might be able to force it low enough to uncover the opening into the conduit that goes up into Hammerhead. If so, we could maybe rope down the shaft and get into the conduit without having to swim through any liquid at all."

"That would take time, wouldn't it?" Ferracini said.

Payne shrugged. "Yes. But that's about all we've got left."

Ferracini considered the proposition. At least it was something positive to be working on in case the truck didn't show. And as Ed said, they didn't have much else to do for the time being. "How long, do you think?" he asked.

"I don't know. It depends on how far above the conduit the liquid level is, what pressure we've got, things like that. If we could find a way of opening the inner chamber to drop a sounding line down without asphyxiating ourselves, I could figure out a rough estimate."

"Cover's off," Lamson announced. He lifted the steel plate, uncovering the opening into the outer chamber, and propped it against the wall.

"See how it looks inside," Ferracini said. Lamson nodded, took the flashlight from his toolbox, and climbed in through the hatchway. Ferracini looked back at Payne. "Gustav's mixed up with safety and firefighting gear. He might be able to get us respirators or something." He checked his watch. "Where the hell is Gustav? He should be here by now."

Payne became more enthusiastic. "We'd also need ropes, weapons, explosives, thermite to blow the cover at the top of the conduit—"

"One thing at a time, Ed." Ferracini went over what they had said so far. "Would it work? If we pressurize the shaft and force the liquid down, wouldn't that force a column of liquid up into the conduit, too? Wouldn't it get trapped up there and seal it off?"

"Yes, but only until the level of the shaft drops below the conduit outlet," Payne said. "Then the stuff in the conduit will drain back out and go down the shaft, like a bottle emptying when you tilt it. Bubbles will go up to the top and balance out the pressure."

"You're sure?"

"That's my department, Harry."

Ferracini nodded and was about to say something further when Cassidy came halfway down the steps. "Gustav's coming— in a hurry. It looks as if something's up."

Moments later, the sound of descending footsteps came from above, and Knacke appeared behind Cassidy. "What is it?" Ferracini snapped, reading the expression on Knacke's face.

Knacke shook his head miserably. "The truck's not here. Erich called Marga—she's been trying to get hold of me. He had a breakdown over on the other side of Weissenberg." He raised a hand before anyone could say anything. "That's not all. There's more—worse. A column of SS troop-trucks passed him coming in this direction, fast. It sounds bad. I mean, with two of your people and one shipment of gear lost, well, anything could have happened. I'm not even sure if there's time to get you back out of the plant."

"Hey, not so fast," Ferracini said. "Maybe we're not through yet. So what's Erich doing? Is he getting the truck fixed?"

"Yes, but Marga told him to call her again in her office before he tries entering the plant. If the SS take over at the gates or something, we couldn't ask him to try it. He'd have no chance."

"Can't argue with that," Ferracini said. He tried to estimate how much time they might have, but there were too many imponderables.

Lamson reappeared inside the access hatch. "Everything's fine in here, pretty much as we expected," he reported. "No surprises." He saw that Knacke had arrived, and nodded. "Hi."

"We've got all the surprises out here, Floyd," Ferracini said. "The truck's broken down on the other side of Weissenberg, and a column of SS is on its way here. It sounds like trouble."

Lamson's only reaction was to raise his eyebrows. "Better get this show on the road, then," he concluded laconically.

The wail of emergency sirens rose above the din of the surroundings. "That's gotta be them," Cassidy said, looking up and turning his head. "They must be at the gate."

"Get back up top," Ferracini told Cassidy. He drew Knacke closer and spoke rapidly and urgently. "Look, we have to get into a conduit that opens off the waste shaft that goes down underneath here. Very probably, the opening is below the liquid surface—that's what those suits you saw were for. The conduit leads up under what's inside the Citadel. Okay, Gustav?" Knacke nodded, listening intently. Ferracini went on, "Now, Ed's got this idea of running an air line in to uncover the conduit by pressurizing the shaft. We'll need coupling adaptors to connect into the sampling valves inside, breathing gear or something to get through the gas and garbage, lights, ropes, and explosives to blow our way out at the far end of the conduit, then take out the target. Also, we'll want guns."

"And how about some heavy clothing and lots of grease for skin protection?" Payne threw in.

Ferracini nodded. "What can you do?"

Knacke shook his head helplessly, boggling at the impossibility of it.

"Come on, Gustav, come on!" Ferracini urged, grabbing him. "Let's start with the air line. Can we hook into one anywhere near here? Where can we get union joints and couplings?"

Knacke found his voice. "There isn't time. It would take forever to raise that kind of volume to the pressure you'd need."

"You don't know that," Ferracini shot back. "You don't know for sure that it's even us they're after. And even if it is, they might not know where to look. A search could take hours to get here in a place like this."

Knacke licked his lips and went quickly in his mind over what Ferracini had said. "When you blow off the cover at the other end, the pressure would be released. Then the liquid in the shaft would rise back up again and seal off the conduit. How would you get back out?"

Ferracini looked at Payne. "Did you figure that out when you were thinking this up, Ed?" he asked.

"We force the level down far enough to set charges below the conduit to cave in the shaft and plug it," Payne replied. "That way, nothing can come back up after the pressure's released." That meant they would have to be inside the shaft when the charge was detonated. They'd all had enough experience with explosives to know that provided they were some distance back from the blast, the pressure wave would dissipate without causing undue discomfort. Miners blasted in enclosed spaces all the time.

"That means more explosive," Knacke protested.

Ferracini waved a hand vaguely. "Well, if we can't find enough in a place like this . . ."

Knacke shook his head hopelessly. "You can't be sure that the shaft will cave in and seal itself. You're talking about a shaft full of explosive gases as well as what's down there already— poisonous oxides, partly reacted nitrotoluenes, unburned TNT— all of it lethal. How do you expect to get through that?"

"What about the stuff you said you worked on—gas masks or whatever?" Ferracini said. "Could we get some of those?"

Knacke shook his head again. "They wouldn't be any good— not for that kind of mixture under pressure. Besides, a mask only filters out the toxins. It can't add anything that's not there. There won't be any oxygen down in that shaft."

"I thought you said something about an oxygen rebreather unit—the one the Navy was interested in. Wouldn't that do?"

"But they're just prototypes, and we only have a couple."

"Would they work?" Ferracini demanded.

"They might . . . but there are only two."

Ferracini looked at Payne inquiringly. Payne went through the alternatives in his head. "These rebreathers must use some kind of supply bottle," he said at last, looking at Knacke.

Knacke nodded. "One or two, worn on the chest."

"Okay," Payne said. "There ought to be a way to punch an inlet into a mask to inject oxygen from one of those bottles. Nothing fancy—it'd only need to hold up for a few minutes. The two guys with the proper breathers are inside the shaft. The two with the modified masks wait in the outer chamber. After the pressure's been raised to uncover the conduit and the shaft's been plugged, the two guys who are inside go through and open the top-end seal under Hammerhead. That drops the pressure. Then the other two waiting at this end open up the inner chamber, do a free-fall rappel down the shaft, and have a clear run up the conduit. If they move fast, they should make it."

They all looked at Knacke. Knacke spread his hands. "Maybe. . . . It sounds impossible. . . . I don't know." The others stared at him and said nothing. He began to say something, then faltered; gradually, a feeling of shame at his own negativeness crept over him. These were the men who would be going down there. They were prepared to face the dangers; but it was he who was finding all the objections. He rubbed his eyes, drew a long breath, and pulled himself together. "You're right," he said. "We have to try it. If we fail, let it not be because we were afraid to try."

Ferracini punched him lightly on the shoulder. "That's more like it, Gustav. Now you're talking like an American."

"I knew it!" Knacke exclaimed.

"So you're with us all the way, right?" Ferracini said.

"On one condition," Knacke said.

"Name it."

"One day, when this is all over and if we get out of it okay, you tell me what's inside Citadel."

Ferracini grinned wearily. "Okay, Gustav, you've got a deal."

Knacke's whole attitude switched to positive. "Those gas masks," he said. "The more modern ones carry the filters in the facepiece itself. They would be difficult to modify. But the older models used a separate pack, which would make it easier. I think I know where there are some."

"Mind if I make a suggestion?" Lamson asked from the hatch, where he had been listening.

"Go ahead," Ferracini said.

"Bombs make lots of gas fast. If you're gonna set a charge off down the shaft anyhow to plug it, then why not let that raise the pressure for you? It'd be a hell of a lot quicker'n what you're talking about. Wouldn't have to go fooling around with air lines at all."

Payne thought for a second, then nodded. "Makes sense. Why not?" he said.

Ferracini looked at Knacke challengingly. "See, Gustav—one problem down already. Okay, now, where's the best place to get our hands on some explosives around here—plenty of explosives?"

But Knacke had stopped listening. Instead he was looking up past Ferracini's shoulder with a questioning expression. Ferracini turned to follow his gaze and saw Cassidy beckoning urgently while he kept his eyes fixed on something above. Motioning for the others to stay put, Ferracini moved stealthily up to look from where Cassidy was crouching. His stomach tightened.

An open Mercedes staff car with a swastika emblem on the door had stopped at the end of the alley, and a figure clad in an SS lieutenant's uniform and holding a submachine gun was climbing out from the front. From the rear seat, a second officer covered while the first approached cautiously.

Then Cassidy's jaw dropped. Ferracini blinked, stared again, and then straightened up slowly into full view.

"Jesus!" Cassidy breathed. "I don't believe this, Harry. Holy Jesus Henry Christ . . . it's Paddy Ryan and Harvey!"

CHAPTER
44

WARREN AND RYAN HAD entered Germany from Holland on Bulgarian papers, posing as a dealer in precious stones returning from Amsterdam, and a civil engineer. Unfortunately, Warren's description had matched that of a French agent whom the frontier police had been tipped would try to enter via that route at about the same time, and the pair were promptly arrested.

The Germans quickly realized their mistake, but upon further questioning became just as convinced that the "Bulgarians" weren't who they claimed to be, either. Soon thereafter, an SS staff car arrived to collect them for interrogation at the SD regional office at Osnabrück, and they departed under the escort of a colonel, a lieutenant driver, and two guards. But the party never reached Osnabrück, and the two Americans ended up minus their captors and in possession of the vehicle. In the process, however, Major Warren had collected a bullet wound in the knee. The SS uniforms had enabled them to obtain treatment from a doctor, but the leg had since stiffened. Nevertheless, they resolved to keep their rendezvous. Impersonating an SS colonel and his chauffeur, they had motored across Germany with a purloined set of license plates without being stopped once.

Their problems hadn't ended there, however. After they reached Leipzig, their contact failed to materialize. Why, they never found out, but it meant that their link to the local coordinator of the operation—Gustav Knacke—was broken. Since nobody was going to come looking for them, and knowing that the four others of the Ampersand party ought to have arrived in the vicinity, they had spent two weeks driving brazenly around Weissenberg and the surrounding area in the hope of spotting one of the group or of being recognized themselves. But to no avail.

Then today, an SS convoy in a hurry passed them, heading in the direction of the plant. Accustomed to all-or-nothing gambles by that time, they followed at a distance and drove around to a side gate while the main column was unloading at the front, and the confused factory guards admitted them in response to Warren's shouting.

At least it solved the weapons problem, Ferracini thought as he lifted a canvas bag holding more Erma MP38 submachine guns and a case of ammunition from the trunk of the car. They had moved it to a less conspicuous position farther along the cobbled roadway at the end of the alley. Paddy Ryan picked up another bag containing Mauser 9mm automatics and cartridges, along with a couple of boxes of model 39 "potato masher" grenades. "We figured that if we were asking for trouble, we'd better be ready to do it right," Ryan explained as they turned and began walking back with their loads. "You wouldn't believe the things people leave lying around."

They turned the corner at the end of the pumphouse to find a man in stained overalls standing in the doorway, smoking a cigarette while he surveyed the scenery. He saw Ryan's SS uniform and looked at them quizzically. "What are you staring at?" Ryan barked. "Have you no work to do? Don't you know there's a war on?" The man mumbled something and disappeared back inside the pumphouse.

Meanwhile, Gustav Knacke, carrying a folded sack under his arm, had appeared back at his office in the Safety Equipment Development Section near the front of the plant. "Where've you been?" Franz, one of his colleagues, asked from the next desk. "Have you heard the news?"

"What news?"

"There's some kind of security flap going on. The SS are here checking all the gates. Instructions are to stay put. That's what the sirens were about. Didn't you hear them?"

"Oh, I thought that was a drill. Any messages?"

"Your wife called."

"Okay." Knacke sat down at his desk and dialed an internal number.

A few seconds later a girl's voice answered, "Works personnel office."

"Is Marga Knacke there, please?"

"Just a moment."

Gustav drummed his fingers nervously on the desk. A few seconds went by that seemed like forever. Then Marga said, "Hello?"

"Gustav."

Marga's voice dropped. "What's happening? You've heard the news?"

"Yes. But they're having their picnic, anyway—a change of plan, I gather. If Erich calls again, tell him they're supplying their own things."

"Yes, all right. I hope the weather stays fine."

"So do I. Must go."

"Take care."

Knacke rose, picked up the sack again, and walked on through the office to the laboratory area beyond. One of the technicians was working at a bench in the room where the oxygen rebreather units were kept. Knacke fussed around with a test assembly across the room for a minute or two, and then sent the technician on an errand. With the room empty, Knacke stripped one of the units off the dummy head and torso on which it was assembled, took the other unit down from where it was hanging on the wall, and bundled them into his sack, along with some of the oxygen bottles from the shelf above.

Then he went out into the passageway again and reached the storage rooms at the rear, where he closed the door behind him and began checking the closets. As he recalled from some tests he'd been involved in once, there ought to be several of the older-style gas masks here somewhere—the type used in the Great War, with concertina tubing running down to a filtration pack worn above the hip. He needed only three in addition to the two oxygen units, since it had been decided in a hasty conference that "Cricketer" wouldn't be going down the shaft because of the condition of his leg; instead, he would remain at the shaft head as a rear guard to cover the way out. The Americans still thought they had a chance of getting out—or at least, that was what they had told Knacke. He was through arguing. He stuffed the three masks and a spare into the sack, added a box of clean filter inserts, and then moved around a rack of storage shelves to the back of the room and opened the window.

Cassidy was standing in a doorway on the opposite side of the yard below. A sentry had been posted a short distance away at the end of the building, but he was facing the other way and watching the roadway. Cassidy stepped quickly out, nodding up at the window. Knacke tossed down the sack. Cassidy caught it and walked away. After closing the window, Knacke went out of the room, walked downstairs, and left the building by a back door. On his return to the waste plant, he made a detour to borrow a dolly from one of the materials stores, and used it to pick up a couple of empty oil drums.

Ferracini and Payne were inside the brick hexagon, waiting to open the inner, steel shaft-head chamber, when Cassidy returned with the oxygen units and masks. They had changed their regular clothes for oiled boilersuits, balaclavas, and woolens put on over a thick layer of grease. A hose had been run outside from one of the valves on the chamber wall to bleed off the excess pressure before they removed the cover. Ferracini was making a sounding line from a copper float stolen from a men's room and some cord knotted at measured intervals with the aid of the tape from Lamson's toolbox.

The clothing and grease, along with several hand-lamps and seemingly miles of coiled rope and cord, came from a burglarizing expedition by Lamson and Ryan. Since then, following directions given by Knacke, they had gone off again on the trickier mission of penetrating the higher-security Munitions Compound to get explosives. Major Warren was outside, keeping watch and placing weapons and ammunition where they would be ready to hand if needed. The SS had concentrated so far on securing the gates and the more sensitive installations, and had posted guards within the general plant area, no doubt in preparation for combing the place section by section.

Ferracini shook his head as he helped Payne make the rough-and-ready adaptations to the gas mask filtration systems for injecting oxygen. "Why does it always have to be like this, Ed? We had it all planned to the last detail—fixed lines down the shaft, cozy suits, even the little chemistry set. . . . Plenty of time at every step. . . . And here we are again—the usual no-time-to-take-a-shit foul-up." Behind them, Cassidy began stripping to grease his body before putting on one of the improvised combat suits.

"Do you realize the impact this'll have inside Hammerhead when you two blow that cap off the top end of the conduit?" Payne asked as he checked the pressure gauge on one of the inner-chamber sampling valves.

"What?" Ferracini asked as he worked.

"What Gustav was talking about earlier—a mix of hydrogenated hydrocarbons, nitrotoluenes, vaporized TNT, possibly cyanides—all exploding out under pressure. The effect on whoever's in there at the other end should be devastating, without any protection or anything."

Ferracini looked curiously at him, then at Cassidy. "Hear that, Cass? We may have an even chance of holding out till the rest of the guys get through."

"That's what I'm saying," Payne told them.

"That's the kind of news we could use more of," Cassidy said.

A form darkened the hatchway, and Knacke ducked inside. "No sign of Saxon and Zulu?" he asked. He still knew the team only by their code names.

"They're still away getting the explosives and stuff," Ferracini said. "Should be the last item."

Knacke nodded. "Then let me give you two a quick rundown on how these rebreather units work," he said.

Behind him, Major Warren heaved the first of the oil drums through the hatch from outside. Payne took it and rolled it across to a couple of wide wooden planks lying on the floor.

In the plant security manager's office, which SS General Heinz Rassenau had taken over as his temporary headquarters, a major entered and saluted smartly. "Yes, Major?" Rassenau inquired, turning away from the large wall-plan of the complex, which he and his executive officer had been studying.

"The second contingent has arrived from Leipzig, sir, and is disembarking inside the main gates," the major reported. At that moment, a telephone rang in the outer office. "Also, sector two is now secured, and squads Yellow Two and Yellow Four are moving in to begin searching sector three."

"Good," Rassenau said. "Form up the new men and begin on sector four at once. Also, put a call through to the commander of the Citadel and find out—"

"Herr General!" The voice of the security manager, tense and alarmed, called from the far side of the open door.

"Excuse me." Rassenau strode out to the outer office. The security manager was on his feet, holding a phone off the hook and covering the mouthpiece with a hand. "Yes?" Rassenau inquired.

"It's the supervisor of the Line Stores in R38, inside the restricted compound. . . ."

"Well?"

The security manager swallowed hard. "A foreman and another man have just been found tied up and gagged in an office there. Two men armed with machine guns forced their way in and got away with at least a hundred pounds of high explosive, plus some thermite mix, fuses, and detonators."

Rassenau's mouth compressed itself into a grim line. "So, we were too late after all," he muttered grimly. "They're already inside."

The security manager nodded rapidly. "They're inside the Munitions Compound. My God, they could blow half this place off the map!"

"We'll discuss how they got in there later," Rassenau promised icily. "Major, disregard that last order. Move all of the newly arrived troops through to the Munitions Compound and take four squads from the general plant area to seal it off—watertight, you understand. Then I want that whole compound searched, inch by inch."

"Yes, sir," the major acknowledged, and hurried away.

Breathing not too uncomfortably inside the mask, Ferracini could feel grease oozing between his fingers inside his gloves as he gripped the rope sling in which he was hanging from supporting bars rigged across the top of the inner chamber. The cover had been closed, and his world was now reduced to Cassidy's sinister hooded form next to him, vaguely outlined in the eerie dampness revealed by their lamp, and the shaft plummeting away into blackness below. They had sounded the liquid surface as lying one hundred ninety-eight feet below, which put the top of the conduit opening only twenty-five feet farther down—it could have been a lot worse. Their main risk now was being caught in a discharge from above. The best way to reduce it was not to waste time.

He nodded and hooked an arm around the supporting rope to cover his ears through his balaclava. Cassidy ignited a fast fuse attached to one of the lines going down the shaft, and the pinpoint of flame raced away into the depths toward the string of small charges suspended fifty feet below. Ferracini felt, more than heard, the concussion, and his body swayed wildly in its rope restraints. He had a split-second glimpse of the smoke front boiling up the shaft toward him, and then everything was blotted out.

Cassidy's fingers tapped an "okay" signal on his shoulder, and he acknowledged. He found the sounding line by touch, and a minute or so went by while he lowered the float, all the time counting the knots slipping through his fingers. At last he felt the line go slack as the float settled. Not enough. The detonations had raised the pressure and forced the level down, but not far enough. The opening into the conduit was still submerged twelve feet. He found Cassidy's arm and touch-signaled him to be ready to fire a second string. Cassidy signaled back that he was going to fire several. Ferracini began hauling the float back up while Cassidy reported the situation to the others in the outer chamber by tapping on the wall in Morse with an iron spike.

In the outer chamber, Lamson and Payne were kitted out ready to go, except for the masks. Payne checked that the sampling valve gauge had registered the pressure rise, while Lamson followed the signal being tapped through the wall. "Another twelve feet," Lamson called across to Ryan, who was by the hatch. "They're gonna set off a bigger string. How are things out there?"

Ryan relayed the news to Warren and Knacke, who were outside. "Quiet so far," he said, turning his head back.

Some flickers of light had begun penetrating the swirling murk, when the second string of detonations wiped everything out again. Ferracini's ears strained, but swallowing eased them. He could feel fumes starting to irritate his eyes: There were chinks where the mask didn't hug his face tightly enough, and the rising pressure was forcing gases through. He tried moving the facepiece around to coax it into a better fit.

Again he paid out the line and counted the knots. Two hundred . . . two hundred twenty-five. The conduit was clear! . . . Two hundred thirty . . . The float bottomed at two hundred thirty-six feet. They had over ten feet of shaft clear below the conduit. But how gas-tight was the shaft? Were its walls absorbent? Would the level stay down?

He signaled his findings to Cassidy, and together they slowly lowered the makeshift raft of oildrums and planks, to which was lashed the load of TNT that they would use to collapse and plug the shaft. The limited size of the inspection cover had forced them to make the raft in two sections and pass them through to be joined together inside the chamber. After what seemed forever, they felt the raft come to rest on the surface. Ferracini kept hold of one end of a guideline attached to the raft and passed the sounding line to Cassidy. The time had come for Ferracini to go down the shaft.

Feeling blindly, Ferracini checked that his submachine gun was securely strapped to his back, and that his automatic, dagger, ammunition pouches, tools, and grenades, along with the bag containing the thermite and accessories for melting the top-cover bolts were all firmly attached. Then he located the coiled rappel line and cast it away down the shaft. Finally he stood up carefully and turned in the sling, wrapped a turn of the rappel line around his back and under one thigh, unfastened his safety loop, and stepped backward into nothingness to go plummeting downward.

The line hissed through his gloves and over his greased clothing as he fell in long, swinging, pendulum-like bounds, using his feet to push clear of the wall. He could feel rocks and debris coming away from the sticky, crumbling sides. The blackness was absolute, and touch his only means of preserving any sense of direction. The shaft's square cross-section enabled him to orient himself by staying on one of its four walls, without which he would have lost himself completely. When he felt the warning knots that he had made ninety feet down the rappel line, he tightened the turn around his body to check his descent and walked himself gingerly down the final stretch, feeling his way with his feet. He found the conduit opening and hauled himself into it.

The footing felt fairly secure. He tugged slowly and deliberately on the rappel line three times to let Cassidy know he had made it. After a couple of seconds, he felt the line tugged twice in response. Then another pause, followed by three tugs from above. That meant that Cassidy had checked the depth, and the level of the liquid below Ferracini was holding steady. Relieved, Ferracini hammered a couple of iron spikes into the wall to fix the bottom end of the rappel line; then he took in the slack of the guideline from the raft, which was floating invisibly below, and used it to draw the raft over until it was vertically below where he was standing. Then he signaled Cassidy to come down.

So, in the end they'd had to do it all without telephones, Ferracini thought to himself as he fixed more spikes to anchor the guideline from the raft. It was amazing how, with practice, it was possible to construct a mental model of the surroundings by touch alone. He felt grateful now for the endless drills of working blind in the British Navy's tank at Portsmouth. Sometimes Ferracini had thought of Warren as too much of a stickler for details, yet those details had an uncanny habit of transforming themselves into life-or-death essentials. As always, Claud had picked the right person for the job. Strangely, he found himself wondering what Claud was doing while he was feeling his way about in a pitch-black pit full of poison gas and explosives somewhere under Germany, with the surface above swarming with SS. Probably wining and dining with Churchill and Arthur Bannering somewhere in London, Ferracini guessed.

Cassidy arrived and lodged himself alongside Ferracini in the conduit opening, and Ferracini guided him to the line securing the raft below. Then Ferracini used the rappel line to lower himself down from the conduit until he was kneeling on top of the raft itself. He found the box of detonators and fuses fastened to one end, and for the next fifteen minutes moved the raft slowly around the shaft to place a configuration of charges in the walls, packing the explosive deep into cracks, faults, and pockets wherever possible with the aid of an iron tamping bar brought down on the raft for the purpose.

When this was done, Cassidy pulled the raft back to a position immediately below the conduit, and Ferracini climbed back up, bringing the main fuse cord with him. The gases were densest at the bottom of the shaft, and his cheeks were streaming inside his mask. The nervous tension and the effort of his labors below were causing him to breathe heavily, and he could taste acrid fumes in his throat. He was starting to feel dizzy.

Cassidy had more fuse ready to attach to the cord that Ferracini brought up. Paying it out behind them, they began climbing the conduit. The conduit was steep, but having been tunneled down from Hammerhead rather than drilled, it was roomy enough for them to proceed steadily; also, its floor was cut into a series of stepped working levels, which helped offset the grade.

Ferracini's eyes were stinging, and he was struggling against an urge to cough. He opened the oxygen valve of his rebreather wider, which gave some relief; but he knew at the same time that this would exhaust its supply sooner. He was too muzzy-headed to calculate how long he had, or to really care that much. Keep plodding on—one, two, three, up a step; one, two, three, up a step. It would be worse after the next charge went off—more pressure. . . . Hoped he'd be able to keep going till they got out. . . . Oh, Christ, have to fight the SS then. . . . Keep plodding on— one, two, three, up a step. . . .

After a hundred feet or so they crouched on the conduit floor. Cassidy lit the fuse, and they covered their heads and ears.

Back in the outer chamber, the needle of the sampling valve pressure gauge jumped in the light of Payne's flashlamp. "That's it!" Payne said. "They've blown the shaft."

"They seem okay so far," Lamson relayed across to Ryan, who was still at the hatch. "They've blown the shaft."

"They've blown the shaft," Ryan told Warren and Knacke outside.

By the cover into the inner chamber, Payne and Lamson tensed and rechecked their equipment. When the needle dropped again, it would mean that the coverplate of the conduit underneath Hammerhead had been opened. That would be their signal to open up the inner chamber and go through.

Deep below, Ferracini and Cassidy were following the long

grade of the conduit upward—under the perimeter fence of the main plant complex; under the high-security zone around the Citadel; under Hammerhead. Ferracini was drenched with perspiration mixed with the grease. His head reeled, and he stumbled. Cassidy gripped him firmly and steadied him on his feet again.

In Gestapo Headquarters, Berlin, Heinrich Himmler was screaming into a telephone at the SS general commanding the Citadel garrison. On the far side of a table littered with construction plans, the two engineers from the Todt Organization were staring with appalled faces at the drawing spread out on top.

"They're not coming through the plant, you imbecile. They're coming *under* the plant! Do you understand me? *Under* it! . . . Well, get the dolts down from the upper levels. . . . Rassenau is wasting his time in the Munitions Compound. They're not in the Munitions Compound. They're coming in through number three waste shaft. . . . Yes, we've got him on another line, and he's sending his troops there immediately. But they may already have gone down. You must secure Valhalla. . . . What? . . . No, you fool, I've already told you that those shafts don't matter. There's another one leading right up your asses! They're going to come up right underneath you!"

Even as Himmler was shouting, a steel plate blew off a sealed opening on the lowermost level of the Hammerhead complex, and red-brown gas exploded out in every direction. Two hooded, black-clad figures wearing masks and brandishing submachine guns emerged, and the personnel in the vicinity started collapsing and choking.

While back in the waste shaft, two more figures were already on their way, hurtling downward through the darkness.

CHAPTER
45

MAJOR WARREN CROUCHED BY the hatch outside the brick hexagon, the steel cover of which had been temporarily replaced to avoid releasing a tell-tale cloud of smoke now that the inner chamber was open. It was secured by two nuts only for quick removal. A rapidly tapped message from Ryan on the inside told Warren that Lamson and Payne had entered the shaft; Ryan was about to throw down the getaway ladder—a pair of lines joined by loops, intended for climbing back up the shaft afterward—and then follow. Warren signaled to wish them good luck, then straightened and turned to look up at Knacke, who was keeping watch at the top of the steps. "Ryan's going now," he called. Knacke nodded, but didn't turn his head. Warren pulled himself halfway up the steps, grunting with the effort of dragging his leg. "Look, there isn't anything more for you to do here now," he urged. "Go while the going's good. This isn't a time for speeches, but you've done a great job. It won't be forgotten."

"Why should Americans be doing this?" Knacke asked.

"Much too long a story. And I wouldn't be allowed to tell it to you, anyway."

"Does whatever's under Citadel affect America, then?"

"The whole world."

Knacke nodded distantly. "I suppose that should make a difference. It's not easy, doing this. I am a German, after all."

"Yes. I'm sorry it had to be this way. But if it helps, this operation is directed against the Nazis, against what will happen if they're not stopped."

"I can imagine. That was why we agreed to help."

"You can't imagine."

At that moment a woman's voice called from somewhere nearby, sounding shrill with alarm. "Gustav! Gustav, are you here?"

Knacke reached for the gun beside him and peered over the walls and concrete blocks around the top of the steps. Marga, wearing a raincoat, was at the end of the alley. She was clearly distraught and looking around in desperation. "Marga!" Knacke called to her. "Over here."

A moment later a harsh voice from somewhere around the corner shouted *"Halte!"* Marga whirled around to look, emitted a cry, and began running along the alley toward Gustav. The clatter of boots running on cobblestones sounded, and a group of a half-dozen SS troopers appeared behind her. *"Halte!"* the officer leading them shouted again. He raised a pistol. Knacke shot him down as Marga's running figure cleared the line of fire. The burst also hit one of the others. A moment later, a grenade landed in the middle of the group, while behind Knacke's shoulder Warren was already picking up a second. The SS troopers scattered for cover amid another burst of fire from Knacke, and a second later the grenade exploded.

Marga tumbled breathlessly down beside Knacke at the top of the steps. "They found out where you were. I wanted to warn you they were coming, but—"

"Later." Knacke sealed her lips with a finger and thrust a gun into her hand. They'd had the foresight to learn how to shoot when they first found themselves getting mixed up in this business.

Shouts came from around the corner at the end of the alley, and a whistle was blowing. Bullets from somewhere whined overhead and pinged off girders. The officer that Knacke had hit was lying face down, motionless, with blood spreading across the cobbles from beneath his chest. The other soldier was on his knees, clutching one arm with the other and trying to get up. Two of the others made a dash from behind the corner and dragged him clear while the rest fired a covering volley. Knacke returned the fire, bobbing up to shoot over the wall in front of him, then falling and moving to the side to shoot around without exposing himself in the same position twice.

Marga was lying behind the top few steps. A couple of steel-helmeted heads appeared on top of the pumphouse across the alley. She fired up at them and they ducked down out of sight. Warren threw his grenade over the parapet of the roof, and it exploded a second later, sending roofing and pieces of skylight showering upward and blowing out two of the windows below. Warren tossed another grenade at the far end of the alley. An incoming grenade from somewhere to the right exploded in the trench at the base of the hexagon. Marga shifted her aim to fire at shadows moving inside the pumphouse windows.

Knacke exchanged more fire with the soldiers at the end of the alley. "They're regrouping," he called back over his shoulder between bursts. "They're going to rush us."

Warren was back at the bottom of the steps, loosening the two coverplate nuts with a wrench. "Fire anywhere," he shouted up at the other two. "Make noise. Hit the tanks—try to burst them. Then do as I say." He fired a long burst at the horizontal storage tanks over the end of the alley and followed it with a grenade. Reacting to the authority in his voice, Gustav and Marga shot at the tanks and pipes overhead and on all sides, while Warren threw more grenades. One of the tanks exploded, spewing a dense cloud of white vapor down into the alley just as the soldiers came charging around the corner. Then something inside the pumphouse caught fire, adding oily black smoke. "Take deep breaths—fill your lungs," Warren yelled, pulling on his SS colonel's cap and straightening his uniform. "Now, ready!" He yanked off the coverplate, and a thick, brown cloud vomited out to mix with the vapor and smoke, blanketing the surroundings with a choking, blinding fog.

Warren left a couple of grenades on long-delay settings to explode in the trench, then fired more shots into the air and hauled himself back up the steps through the murk. "Stand up! Put up your hands!" he ordered the other two, snatching their guns. Knacke was too bewildered to react. Warren struck him hard across the face. "Hands up, I said! Get back—back!" Prodding them with his gun, he drove them out into the alley. Figures were milling and colliding all around them. Warren fired back at the hexagon just as the grenades he had left in the trench began detonating, and more shooting broke out in the confusion.

The fog thinned to a haze at the end of the alley, which was now cordoned off by troops. Limping determinedly, Warren marched his "prisoners" through, coughing and weeping with their hands raised high. A sergeant and two privates moved forward to assist. "There are more of them back there," Warren shouted at them. "Go and give a hand forward." The soldiers rushed away.

They turned into the cobbled roadway and headed for the car. Behind them a brownish-yellow cloud was rising over the roofs and covering the surrounding part of the plant, with the sounds of shouting, gunfire, and more grenades still coming from beneath it. Fire sirens had begun to shriek, adding to the commotion. Soldiers were running by in the opposite direction, while others held back workers who were appearing from the surrounding buildings to see what was happening. Warren lowered his gun. "Relax now. Walk naturally," he muttered, and they transformed into just an officer and two civilians who could have been Gestapo.

Nobody challenged them as they reached the Mercedes, which was still where Ryan and Ferracini had left it. "Look as if you belong here," Warren told Marga as he steered her into the front seat. "You're driving." Then he climbed in the back with Knacke and handed the others their weapons. They pulled away, and an SS sergeant obligingly waved his squad back out of the way to let the car turn into the road.

At the side gate, however, things had changed since Warren and Ryan entered. Warren took in the situation rapidly as the car approached. The barrier was down, and an SS captain, a corporal, and two privates were standing outside the gatehut; three more soldiers were standing on the other side of the gateway, in front of a Kuebelwagen (the German equivalent to the Jeep) which was mounting a machine gun and had a driver and gunner at the ready inside. Very likely, more soldiers were in the hut, too. The corporal moved forward in front of the car with an arm raised, and the car slowed. A couple of the others raised their weapons, then lowered them again when Warren stood up and they saw his uniform.

"What's going on back there?" the captain began. "It sounds like—" He froze as his gaze wandered down from Marga's pale, tense face to the muzzle of the automatic resting on the top of the door. She fired and gunned the car forward at the same time. The captain reeled back against the wall of the hut, and the corporal dived clear; in the same instant, Knacke opened fire with a submachine gun on the others who were by the hut, while Warren shot the gunner in the Kuebelwagen on the opposite side and then lobbed in a grenade. The soldiers in front of the Kuebelwagen were still scattering when the Mercedes crashed through the barrier, and a hail of fire from its back seat kept the heads of the rest down as it roared away.

*   *   *

The bottom level of Hammerhead contained mainly power-generating machinery, ventilating equipment, and stores; the few people there had been incapacitated by the gas and fumes. There was no likelihood of their recovering sufficiently to attempt any heroics from behind in the next few minutes, and Ferracini and Cassidy moved fast, leapfrogging to cover each other, heading for the steel stairs that gave the only access to the higher levels.

A guard in SS uniform and a man in a white coat were starting to push the heavy door at the top shut when Ferracini came up the steps. He fired from behind a motor housing, and the guard reeled back; the other man crumpled in a heap in the doorway. More were trying to push the door from behind, but the body was blocking it. Someone leaned around to pull the body away, but went down on top of it as Ferracini fired again. Cassidy ran forward under cover of the burst to hurl two grenades through the doorway, following them with a burst of fire from a different angle. Then Ferracini moved up and cleared aside the two men he had shot.

He was looking into the chamber that housed the return-gate itself—similar in form to the machine in Brooklyn, which had been modeled on the same design. The main cylinder was above and ahead of him, with a railed platform running around it at half-height. The sides of the chamber were lined with instrumentation and equipment bays, ladders, and raised catwalks. Figures were shouting and running everywhere, with the greatest confusion in the area immediately behind the doorway, where the grenades had exploded among the people who had managed to get out from the lower level just as they ran into others coming the other way to investigate the commotion. More were starting to cough and choke as the gas from below began pouring through, and the confusion became a panic.

It wasn't a time for niceties. Ferracini raked the mass of colliding, convulsing figures with a long burst of continuous fire from the doorway, and Cassidy leaped on through, firing at the galleries above and shooting out the lights in the vicinity. Ferracini slapped in another magazine and followed moments later.

Once through the doorway, they spread out to gain a wider field of fire for mutual support, all the time working closer to the machine and moving into positions covering from different angles the entrance into the machine chamber. A figure staggered into view on one of the walkways and aimed a handgun at Cassidy. Ferracini sent bullets spattering off the surrounding girders before he could fire, and the figure retreated out of sight.

The scene was beginning to resemble a Brueghelian depiction of Hades, with the near end of the chamber darkened, smoke thickening and swirling around the looming bulk of the machine, and terrified figures retreating across a bloodstained floor littered with writhing bodies. The suddenness and violence of the assault had caught the SS guards present in the machine chamber completely unprepared, and the gas had impeded any organized resistance. Cassidy reloaded behind an equipment cubicle, and Ferracini concentrated on the stairs and platform above to clear a way to the machine.

Then the first squad of SS reinforcements from the upper levels came in through the entrance at the end of the chamber. But too fast, too reckless: They came straight out into bright lights and a crossfire directed from shadows. And they hadn't been prepared for the gas. They fell back in disarray, leaving several of their number behind. A voice outside the entrance shouted orders. More guards rushed in, but ran into the people who were trying to get out, and a confused melee ensued. Cassidy threw a grenade into the middle of it. In the resulting chaos, Ferracini reached one of the flights of steps around the machine and got up onto the platform fronting the transfer chamber.

The platform looked down over the area inside the entranceway, where SS guards were fanning out among the machinery and equipment consoles. Bullets rattled off the steel framework around Ferracini, and he could hear Cassidy firing below. He aimed a couple of quick bursts down through the rails at where some of the guards were sheltering, then ducked back behind the edge of the platform to begin frantically unpacking the explosives he was carrying.

Then he realized that his lungs were heaving. His oxygen was exhausted. He had no choice. He loosened the straps at the back of his head and pulled the facepiece of his rebreather unit to one side. Involuntarily his lungs gasped for air, and in seconds he was doubled over on his knees, coughing and retching. He was unaware of the light that appeared suddenly at the darkened end of the chamber as a second door opened to admit more SS from the emergency shaft at the rear.

Below, a group of SS had managed to work around between Cassidy and the door where he and Ferracini had entered, and they had pinned Cassidy down between one of the supporting columns and an electrical cubicle. Cassidy was changing position and firing desperately to defend himself from three directions, but he was cornered. He threw his last grenade; his gun ran out of ammunition. . . . And then Lamson and Payne appeared in the doorway from the lower level and mowed his attackers down from behind.

*   *   *

Leaving Kurt Scholder with Pfanzer and a couple of others to watch the dumbfounded duty crew in the control room, Winslade hurried downstairs to rejoin the people waiting outside the lock doors. Young Scholder handed him a bundle of cylindrical objects, each with a plastic pencil protruding from one end, similar to the ones that Anna and Keith Adamson were holding. Adamson had insisted on coming, too, and some of the Pipe Organ people had taken over the job of guarding Kahleb and company.

"They're all preset for thirty seconds," young Scholder said. "Just snap the pencils and get out." Winslade slung his automatic cannon across his back and looked at Anna. "All set?" She nodded.

Somebody came out of the control room and called down from the gallery, "The beam's locking now." At the same moment the double doors leading into the transfer lock began sliding apart. Inside, the chamber had begun to glow red.

"Stop that!" a voice shouted. Two figures in the golden, loose-fitting tunics of the Senior Directorate were striding out of one of the side doors, followed by Kahleb and others from his group. Gray-uniformed security guards appeared on the gallery above, running toward the control-room door. Somebody inside slammed it shut, and through the window they could see Scholder brandishing his gun. Pfanzer was waving frantically down and pointing at the transfer lock, while outside on the gallery, the guards began breaking the door down.

The doors opposite the transfer lock were open, and more guards were coming across the floor of the Dispatch Preparation Area beyond. "Go!" young Scholder shouted, and closed ranks with Eddie, T'ung-Sen, and the others while Winslade, Anna, and Adamson sprinted into the lock. The guards plowed into the wall of people, pulling them aside, but they were too late. The doors of the transfer lock were already closing.

Ferracini's face was pressed against the steel mesh of the platform flooring, but he was breathing again. Powerful fans in the ceiling ducts overhead were drawing up the clean air being injected into the level below. A foot landed near his head. Ferracini rolled away instinctively and found himself looking up at a hooded, black-clad form with window-covered eyes and face hidden by a mask with a ribbed tube leading out. He thought it was Ryan, but couldn't be sure. Across the platform, another of the team was running fuse cord between charges placed along the outside of the machine and connecting it to another cord leading up from below, while two more were firing down at the floor and up at the galleries. One was Cassidy; the other, who looked like Payne, was covered in blood and had one arm hanging uselessly.

A hand lifted at his body harness, and he kneeled groggily. The figure over him was Ryan. Ryan fired at something below, then picked up the charges that Ferracini had begun to unwrap and moved across the platform to add them to the ones that Lamson was placing. Ferracini looked along the machine wall and saw SS uniforms already up on the walkway, working their way along toward the platform. He reached for the submachine gun still lying beside him, aimed, and squeezed the trigger as they came out to make a rush for the platform.

Nothing! Empty!

Ferracini started to get up as bullets flew around him. Something seared the side of his chest and upper arm, and an impact on his shoulder sent him spinning around and sprawling across the floor again, in front of the access port into the machine. A grenade landed on the flooring just feet away from his face. He stared at it numbly, unable to react. Then Cassidy materialized, firing from the hip over Ferracini's head, and kicked the grenade away into space. Ryan was behind Cassidy, firing along the walkway on the other side of the machine. SS were coming along both sides of the cylinder now; more were coming up from below, climbing over the rail at the end of the platform. They had to hold them off until the charges blew—that was all that mattered now.

Payne went down, hit again. Then Ryan staggered and fell back against the side of the port entrance. Only Cassidy and Lamson were left fighting. Ferracini strained to pull another magazine from his ammunition pouch, but he couldn't make his arm move. He looked up and saw SS coming toward him across the platform, a blond, blue-eyed giant in the lead. For a second the giant looked down triumphantly, his lips curled back in a contemptuous sneer, made grotesque by a strange light that had begun glowing from somewhere behind Ferracini. Ferracini groped with his good arm for the automatic at his hip, but the giant was already aiming. . . . And then his head exploded like an overripe peach hit with a hammer.

The black-uniformed figures that had been moving up behind him disintegrated into pieces of bodies coming apart as they were hurled back against the rail at the end of the platform. Ferracini turned his head dazedly and looked up. That was when he knew he'd been hit worse than he thought. Because that was when he realized he was dead.

It wasn't the way he had imagined it—not that he'd spent a

great deal of time brooding over such things. But he'd expected all kinds of mystical, multicolored visions and exhilarating sensations, strange music, maybe, like the things the drug freaks talked about. . . . He'd never had any curiosity about drugs. The last thing a Special Operations trooper needed was scrambled brains. But the actuality was really quite . . . ordinary. Disappointing, somehow. It was ordinary, but in a distant, unreal kind of way. . . .

He saw an apparition of Claud standing over him, blasting away hoards of SS with some kind of an elaborate hand-held machine gun that fired miniature bombs and sounded like a train. Probably a hallucination expressing a subconscious wish, Ferracini thought with detachment. Anna Kharkiovitch was in it, too, firing another one. And even Keith Adamson—how had he gotten into this?—was there, running out of the machine, stooping, and dragging Payne back inside. Cassidy was slipping one of Ryan's arms around his shoulder, and Lamson was pulling a knife out of a limp SS body as it crumpled to the floor.

Then Claud was looking down and smiling in the way that only Claud could. "Come on, Harry, get up," the phantasm said to Ferracini's ghost. "We haven't got all day. I rather suspect that you've overstayed your welcome."

Anna Kharkiovitch leaned down and helped Claud heave him to his feet. It wasn't respectful. He was dead. Why couldn't they leave him alone? Then she was pushing him into the red light of the gate, with Cassidy helping Ryan just ahead of them and the sound of Claud still firing coming from behind. "No, wrong way," Ferracini heard himself mumbling stupidly. "We have to go the other way. Harvey's waiting for us up top."

And then he blacked out.

CHAPTER
46

GASPS SOUNDED AMONG THE people in the antechamber as the transfer lock doors slid open again. Winslade and the other two who had vanished only moments before were back, but now there were five more figures with them. They were clad in black, greasy suits with hoods, and masks covered their faces. Three were injured and being helped, two apparently unconscious. Ignoring the guards who were trying to herd them back against the wall, some of the scientists rushed forward to assist as the group began moving toward the doors. Winslade had an ugly gash where a bullet had seared his cheek, and blood was running down over his shirtfront and jacket.

The commander of the security force, Major Felipe Juanseres, who had arrived with Jorgassen behind the two gold-clad directors, stared grimly when he saw the limp, bloodstained figures being passed out of the lock, and the condition of the others. A wisp of stinging vapor from inside touched his nostrils. "Those are the ones," Kahleb said, moving to the front and pointing. "Those two, and the woman. He's the one who attacked the guard."

"Arrest them!" one of the directors ordered. The guards closed in around the lock entrance.

"Look at them!" Jorgassen protested at Juanseres. "Now tell

me it's only a scientific project at the other end. Those men have come straight out of a battle."

"Arrest them, I said," the director ordered again. "We are in charge of this establishment. You report to us."

On the gallery above, guards were hustling Scholder and Pfanzer out of the control room. Another man came out behind them. "The link's disconnected," he called down. "All the coupling functions have zeroed."

"You owe no loyalty to criminals," T'ung-Sen told the guards who were holding him and his group against the wall at gunpoint. "They're mixed up in murder, all of them."

"Mass murder," Eddie said beside him. The guards looked questioningly toward Juanseres for instructions.

"I gave an order," the director snapped.

"Your job is security," T'ung-Sen said to Juanseres. "There have been gross irregularities here."

"They have no authority here!" Kahleb insisted.

Juanseres looked from one group to the other. "That's enough," he declared. Then, to the guards, "Lock all of them up. That lot, those, all of them. They can all cool off until the matter's out of our hands. I'm calling in CIAF."

"You can't—" one of the directors began, but one of the guards jabbed him in the ribs.

"I said that's enough," Juanseres repeated. "I'm assuming full responsibility. My first duty is to maintain order here." He turned to the guards again. "Take them away. Detain those people in the conference room on R7, those in the executive lounge, and that group in the reception area. Get a medical team here immediately for these injured men and have the emergency room standing by. Take the people who are with them over there, too, to be cleaned up and checked over. After that, put them under guard in the staff canteen at the back. They can wait there."

CHAPTER
47

IT WAS DUSK. ANNA Kharkiovitch was sitting with Adamson at one of several tables in an airy room with white and orange walls. Some dishes of beef in a spiced sauce with vegetables and fruit had been brought in, but with the strain of waiting no one had eaten much. Scholder was pacing restlessly by the long window on one side. In the floodlit compound below, the first wave of CIAF aircraft had landed, and efficient-looking military formations in sky-blue uniforms were deploying quickly toward the gates and among the surface buildings of the Pipe Organ installation.

"Back home, it ought to be about the eleventh of April by my reckoning," Scholder said. "That means we've been gone six weeks."

"Just over five hours here," Adamson murmured.

Anna looked up. "So they would have taken how long? About a month to reach the objective in Germany?"

"Evidently." Scholder nodded. "A little longer than planned, but all the more fortunately so, it seems."

"Except for Major Warren," Anna said. "I wonder what happened to him."

"Well, I suppose we'll find out eventually," Scholder said.

"My guess is that it might be a while before any of us goes home."

"They can get us back then?" Anna said.

Scholder nodded. "I think so. But how much time might have gone by there when they get around to it is anyone's guess."

From what he had been able to gather in the short time he'd had to talk about the subject, the "interference" from the Gatehouse machine had been carried on a hyper-dimensional wave function resonating at frequencies that were slightly offset from the spectral group of the Nazi return-gate that Pipe Organ normally connected to. Out of curiosity, one of the shift managers in the control room had ordered the beam parameters to be set to the offset values, and the connection to Gatehouse had been the result. Duplicating the settings should reestablish the connection—provided, of course, that the people at Gatehouse didn't give up hope and abandon the machine in the meantime.

"I'm still not sure I understand this time business," Adamson said. "Why does any time have to have gone by in our world at all? If the machine here has got a knob you twiddle to select the date you want to connect to, or whatever does the same job, why can't you simply set it to the date that we left on, no matter how much time goes by here? That way, my wife wouldn't even have to know there'd been anything unusual about the day at all." His face knotted into a mystified frown as he followed the thought through to its unavoidable conclusion. "But come to that, why couldn't you set it to an even earlier date? No, that wouldn't make sense, would it? Maybe I'd decide not to come here at all. But I am here. . . . And then there'd be two of me back there, like you here, Kurt. But there weren't. Oh, hell . . ."

"You see, it gets complicated," Scholder said, nodding. "To rejoin the universe you left, you have to preserve the synchronization relationship. Otherwise—if you tried entering its past, for example, which implies being able to alter it—you'd simply enter a new branch instead, as we did when we came back from '75. You could do that if you want, Keith, but you wouldn't be back in the world that you left."

Adamson thought about it, sighed, and finally shook his head. "It's bad enough already. I'll wait it out," he agreed.

More CIAF aircraft descended vertically outside. Then one of the security guards outside opened the door at the far end of the room, and Winslade came in with Jorgassen and a man wearing a doctor's smock. Scholder turned, and Adamson half rose from his chair. "How are they?" Anna asked tensely.

"The one called Payne is in the worst shape, with a pretty

badly mauled arm and a hole in his stomach that's causing some internal problems," the doctor said. "Ryan is having a metal hip joint fitted right now. Ferracini's are just flesh wounds, but he's also suffering from acute poisoning from nitro compounds and a trace of cyanides."

"Fortunately, this is the twenty-first century," Winslade interjected.

The doctor went on, "As for the other two, they're both under sedation with nothing worse than nervous exhaustion. All of them should be fine in good time." Cassidy and Lamson had agreed to try to rest, but prowled agitatedly about instead; finally, they had been put to sleep. The doctor looked curiously at Winslade, then around at the others. "It's true then, what people are saying? You people really have come from the past?"

"You'll find out everything in due course, after the CN has finished," Jorgassen said.

The doctor looked disappointed. "Very well." He looked inquiringly around the group. "If there are no further questions . . ."

"I think not for now, anyway," Winslade said.

"They're going to be all right. That's the main thing," Scholder said.

"If there is anything else, we know how to contact you," Winslade told the doctor. "And thank you again for all you've done."

At that moment, someone called from the doorway and beckoned. "The CIAF people are on their way up here," Jorgassen said to the doctor. "We may need you to talk to them." And to the others, "Excuse us, please. We must go."

The others added their thanks to Winslade's, and the doctor and Jorgassen hurried away. Anna emitted a long sigh of relief. "Well, it could have been a lot worse," she murmured in a thankful voice.

The atmosphere had lightened. Winslade pulled up an empty chair, sat down, and poured himself some coffee. He patted the thick dressing taped to the side of his face. "And I, too, you'll all be relieved to learn, am expected to live," he informed them.

Outside the window to the west, the sky was reddening and turning the mountains into black silhouettes.

"So, you did it," Scholder said.

Winslade shook his head. "We never had a chance. They did it." He sipped his coffee. "But Cassidy said it was close. The Germans were on to it—they knew the objective and almost got there first. That was why our boys had such a bad time. I'd like to know how that happened. And all the equipment was lost—both shipments. The troops must have more or less improvised the whole mission, practically under fire."

"Extraordinary!" Adamson muttered, shaking his head.

"The SO units are very selective," Winslade replied. "They pick some pretty extraordinary people."

"I've watched them train . . . back in '75, I mean," Scholder said.

Anna Kharkiovitch was staring at Winslade, as if weighing whether or not the time was right to broach what was on her mind. Then the conversation lulled, and Winslade looked up to find her watching him. He held her eye and leaned back in his chair, his eyes twinkling and a vaguely playful, somehow challenging look on his face—as if he were reading her mind and daring her to speak. "Okay," she said evenly. "That isn't all that needs explaining, is it, Claud?"

Winslade raised his eyebrows as he took another sip of coffee. "Really?"

"Come on, no more games," Anna said. "It's time to pick up the conversation that we never finished." Winslade waited. "You knew too much about how the mission would probably go. You'd had all the right equipment prepacked. But that's not all." Anna enumerated the further points on her fingers. "One, you knew where we were as soon as we rematerialized. I watched your face. You didn't know how we'd come here, but you knew where we were. You knew the layout of the installation down there, and you knew that the bombs were prepared behind the doors across from the ones we came out of. Two, you knew how to operate that video. Three, you knew how to use those guns.

"We've followed you into this mission, Claud. We've trusted your judgment and never questioned any of your decisions. Some of the team have been hurt pretty badly. But the objective has been achieved. Now you owe us. It's time for some explanations."

Winslade finished his coffee and set the cup down slowly and deliberately. Finally, he nodded.

But before he could reply, the door at the end of the room opened and Jorgassen came in, this time with some people they hadn't met before. Two of them were wearing sky-blue uniforms with peaked caps and plenty of braid—presumably senior CIAF officers. Between the officers was a youngish looking man with wavy hair, a ruddy face, roguish eyes, and a mirthful half-smile playing around his mouth. He walked with a jaunty self-assurance and was nattily dressed in a clean-lined navy blue suit with pale gray lapels and trim, a blue-and-white-striped shirt worn with the neck open, and a pair of narrow-toed boots. Jorgassen motioned with a sweep of his arm as the others parted to allow the younger man through.

"It appears that the CN and CIAF have in fact been secretly investigating this whole operation for some time now," Jorgassen said. "So this business hasn't come as such a surprise to them. This is the person who has been in charge of their investigation." He broke off as he saw Winslade looking up with a broad smile that said he didn't need any introduction.

Winslade nodded with evident deep satisfaction. "Yes," he said, looking at the younger man, "I thought it might be you."

The other stared for a few seconds with an expression that combined puzzlement with a hint of uncertain amusement and suspicion; and then it changed slowly to astonishment as the realization dawned. "No!" he exclaimed disbelievingly. "It can't be!"

"Oh, but it can," Winslade assured him. "You should know if anyone does."

Anna looked from one to the other in bewilderment. She shook her head and looked again. She stared at Winslade, then back at the other man, mentally trying to picture him with perhaps thirty-odd years added and a little more reddishness in the face . . . then a pair of spectacles, and maybe a floppy hat. . . .

It was!

Anna slumped back weakly in her chair, for once in her life genuinely stunned.

It was Winslade—a younger version of Winslade!

CHAPTER

48

FERRACINI WAS LYING IN bed in a clean, airy room with sun shining on green mountains outside the window. His right arm and shoulder were strapped up. A dark-haired, dusky-skinned girl in a nurse's tunic and cap was tidying bottles and silver dishes on a glass-topped cart standing by the bed. He considered the situation at some length. If this was heaven, he wouldn't be feeling so lousy; if it was hell, on the other hand, he'd no doubt be feeling a lot lousier. He concluded that in all probability he wasn't dead after all.

"Hi," the nurse said, seeing that his eyes were open. "You're back. If you're interested, I have it on good authority that you're going to be just fine."

"Oh." Ferracini hadn't really thought about that, but it was nice to know. "Where is this?" he asked, lifting his head to see more of the surroundings.

"Near Juruena, in Brazil," the nurse told him as she pulled a cover over the cart.

Ferracini's head slumped back onto the pillow. What the hell was he doing in Brazil? He stared blankly at the ceiling for a while. The sounds came of the cart being wheeled away across the room and the door opening with a faint hum. Brazil? Wasn't that where the original machine was supposed to have been that started this whole crazy business off? He raised his head again just as the nurse was about to leave the room. "What year is this?"

The nurse laughed. "Don't worry, you haven't been out for all that long. It's still 2025." She disappeared, and the door closed behind her.

Ferracini let his head drop back on the pillow. "Oh, shit," he groaned, and fell asleep again.

Then the nurse was waking him, and it was evening. Shortly afterward, a doctor came in to see how he was doing while his dressing was being changed. Ferracini had a couple of nicked ribs, some torn muscle on his chest and upper arm, and a hole through his shoulder; he'd been gassed, too, the doctor told him. A few weeks of rest and he'd be as good as new. "What about the others?" Ferracini wanted to know.

"Payne and Ryan are still unconscious after surgery, but they'll recover," the doctor said. "Cassidy and Lamson are fine."

"Can I see them?"

"You feel up to it?"

"Hell, yes."

"Very well, but I'd like you to eat a little first."

The door opened and Winslade came in, wearing some kind of light blue uniform that Ferracini hadn't seen before. "Ah, yes, he is . . . splendid!" Winslade looked at the doctor. "Is it all right?"

The doctor nodded and waved a hand. "Yes. Come in."

"I heard you'd come around, Harry, and I came straight up," Winslade said. "You're looking a lot better now—your lips are the right color again. How do you feel?"

"He's fine," the doctor said. "I'll be in my office if you need me." He left. The nurse raised the bed so that Ferracini could sit up and propped pillows behind his back. Then she, too, left the room.

Ferracini nodded, "I guess I'll be okay." He tried to remember, but his mind still wasn't functioning clearly. He had a vague recollection of this being Brazil. "What's happened, Claud? This is that place Kurt came from in South America, right?"

"Right," Winslade confirmed.

Ferracini shook his head. It ached. "So what the hell are you doing here?"

"We got a message in England that Gatehouse had made another connection," Winslade explained. "So we flew back—Anna and I."

"Okay."

"But it was another crossed line. When we went through the machine, we found it had somehow hooked up with the Pipe Organ system in 2025, not the Tularosa system that we expected."

Ferracini brought his good arm up and massaged his brow. "So . . . how did we get here?"

"Pipe Organ connected to Hammerhead," Winslade reminded him.

"Okay . . ."

Winslade shrugged. "So we took the chance while we had it to come in through the back door of Hitler's return-gate and try taking it out that way—an unexpected extra string to the bow, you might say. But it turned out that you had just come in through the front door at the same time. The timing was excellent all around. I think we can congratulate ourselves on it."

That was right. Ferracini was beginning to remember fragments of the scene up on the platform: Payne and Ryan getting hit; Claud and Anna blowing the SS away; Keith Adamson being there. "But aren't they supposed to be all Nazis here or something?" he said at last. "How did you get access to their machine?"

"It's a long story, Harry. Worry about it later."

Ferracini drew a long breath, which started him coughing. He nodded. "Yes, maybe I will. . . . Oh, and thanks."

Winslade shook his head and, for once, looked solemn. "No. Thank you, Harry—you and all the others. The mission was a success. I've heard some of what happened at Weissenberg from Cassidy and Floyd. You did an outstanding job against odds that came close to impossible. Rest assured it won't have been for nothing."

Winslade left shortly afterward, and the nurse came back with a light meal of poached eggs, toast, milk, a glass of orange juice, and a couple of pills. Eating with his wrong hand was a slow business, but the food did something to get the acrid taste out of his mouth.

Before Ferracini had finished, there was a commotion of voices outside, and seconds later Cassidy and Lamson came in, leaving the nurse still protesting outside. They were both wearing scarlet dressing gowns over maroon pajamas, and bedroom slippers. "What did I tell ya?" Cassidy said. "He's fine. Say, Harry, in case there's a relapse or something, about that ten bucks you owe me. . . ."

Ferracini managed a grin. "Hi, you asshole."

"How're you doing, Harry?" Lamson asked.

"Soon be as good as new, the doc just said. What about Ed and Paddy?"

"Them, too, but it'll take a little longer," Lamson answered. "Ed's got some new holes, but they'll mend. Paddy's got a tin joint in his hip. It could have been a lot worse."

Ferracini shook his head helplessly. He wanted to talk about too many things. Then his expression grew sober. "I guess nobody knows what happened to Harvey, huh?"

Cassidy shrugged. "He might have gotten out. There's always a chance. I mean, what chances would you have given for us getting out?"

"I reckon so." Ferracini brooded for a few seconds, then pulled himself out of it with a determined effort. "So, what happens next?" he asked. "How about getting back? Has anyone figured that out yet?"

"Claud's working on it," Cassidy said. "But there's the usual, you know—complications."

"What kind of complications this time?"

"Well, you remember that thing Claud told us about after we got to England—that message he got from Kurt about Einstein figuring time would run slower at the future end of the link?"

Ferracini nodded. "Kind of. I never really understood it. But anyhow, what about it?"

"It's real," Cassidy said. "And not only that, the farther into the future you go, the more slowed-down you get."

"Look, I'm still not thinking too good. What's that supposed to mean?"

"It means that everything back where we came from is running faster by a big number."

"Like what?"

"Like about two hundred," Cassidy said. "You have to talk to Kurt or somebody because they've got all the information. But what it adds up to is that it's December there already. They're all getting ready for Christmas again."

Ferracini stared at him incredulously. "How long have we been here, for chrissakes?"

"Take it easy, Harry," Cassidy said. "Only a day plus some—a day and a quarter, maybe. You're missing the point. That's how it works. A day here means over six months gone by at the other end. That's why Claud's in a hurry to get something moving. I know it's crazy, but you know the way scientists are. When did they ever discover anything that made sense?"

"And that's not all of it," Lamson said. "Now we've got two of them."

Ferracini shifted his head to look the other way from the bed. "Two what?"

"Clauds."

"Now you're being crazy."

Lamson shook his head. "There's a younger one here, in this century—about thirty years younger. See, this is where he came from originally."

"Claud? He came from here?"

"From another version of here, anyhow. He wound up in the Nazi Germany of the 1930s," Lamson said. "But he escaped and got over to the States."

Ferracini looked dazed. "You mean like Kurt?"

"Right," Cassidy told him. "In fact, there's another one of him here, too."

"Another who?"

"Kurt," Lamson answered.

"But don't let us confuse you or anything, Harry," Cassidy said. "You need to talk to Kurt and Anna. They were in the middle of having dinner downstairs when we heard you'd woken up. They'll be up as soon as they're through. Like I said, they've got the information."

Ferracini stared at the tray of dishes before him as he downed the last of his milk. "Cassidy, I'm confused," he said. "I want to talk to Kurt and Anna. Why can't we go downstairs to them? Can you guys find any more clothes around here?"

"Sure you're up to it?" Lamson asked.

"Sure." Ferracini swung the tray aside, pushed off the blanket, and tried to stand. The room spun, and he sat heavily back down on the edge of the bed again, blinking dizzily.

"It's all them dames I kept warning you about, Harry," Cassidy said. "It kinda catches up at your age. Hey, Floyd, there was a wheelchair just outside. Bring it in here. We can put him in that."

Five minutes later, with Ferracini wrapped in a blanket, they wheeled the chair through a barrage of more protests from the nurse and out into the corridor. Two guards in sky-blue uniforms were posted at the elevators but didn't interfere with them. "Who are those guys?" Ferracini asked as they entered the elevator. "And what was that crazy outfit Claud was wearing? It looked the same, but with more brass."

"Oh, that's his by right," Lamson said. "He's a full colonel."

"Colonel? In what?"

"Wait till we get downstairs, Harry," Cassidy sighed. "Let Kurt and Anna handle it."

Twenty minutes later, they were sitting with Scholder, Anna, and Adamson at a table on a glass-enclosed terrace overlooking the floodlit central compound. The dinner dishes had been pushed to one side, and Ferracini was sipping from a glass of orange juice.

"Yes, that's right," Scholder said. "Claud was originally from this world—or, more strictly speaking, a parallel version of it, if you're up to the physics of what's going on." Ferracini nodded from the far side, where Anna and Keith Adamson had moved their chairs to make room for him to be wheeled up to the table. Scholder went on, "He was born in 1997, in Washington, D.C., and took up a military career, eventually specializing in intelligence work. Apparently he did quite brilliantly, and by the time he was twenty-eight, had already made full colonel with CIAF."

Ferracini nodded again. Unlike Adamson, he'd had plenty of time during the period at Gatehouse to talk to Scholder about the twenty-first century. He knew what CIAF was. "Okay, so what are you saying?" He put down the glass and rubbed his chin. "Claud's outfit found out the real story of what Pipe Organ was all about?"

"Yes. It involved a double level of deception. Obviously, the fact that something existed in a remote part of Brazil couldn't be concealed from the world. Also, it couldn't really be kept a secret that some kind of major breakthrough had occurred in physics. Well, the public was told that the facility here was an experimental establishment involved in a revolutionary matter-transport technology."

"Matter transport?"

"Like in science fiction," Cassidy said. "Remember that nut at Columbia that Jeff was always talking about?"

"Oh, yeah."

"Maybe he wasn't such a nut," Lamson mused.

"But clearly, the scientists working on the project knew better," Scholder continued. "They knew they were working on a time-travel system, or more precisely an alternate-reality transfer system. But they were given to believe that the subject was being kept out of the public domain until the potential impact could be assessed. The explanation made sense, and the scientists—all but a privileged inside group—accepted it. I was one of the ones who never questioned it."

"But what was really going on, of course, was that a world was being shaped in which Nazi Germany was being built up specifically to destroy the Soviet Union," Anna said. "The situation that brought about the decline of the traditional oligarchies in this world—the one we're in right now—wouldn't be permitted to develop. Instead, a war would be fomented in which the Nazis and the Soviets would destroy each other, and a post-Hitler era would then evolve in which power and privilege would revert to those who considered it to be theirs by right."

Ferracini raised his hand to halt her. "That's the part that I'm not clear about," he said. "Cassidy was talking about it when we were training back in England at that Navy school. Where was it?"

"Portsmouth," Lamson supplied.

"That's it. Anyhow, the way Cass figured it had to be was that no matter what you do, you can't change your own present. And none of the rest of us could find a fault in it. So, isn't it right?"

"It's right," Scholder agreed.

"So, surely the top guys here—the inside group that you talked about—must have known it, too. I mean, hell, they designed the machine and everything. But it doesn't make sense. Why would Overlord bother at all if nothing's gonna change their situation here in this world?"

"It's very simple," Scholder replied. "They create another world in which Hitler gets rid of Russia and sets up a system that's more suited to their tastes. Then they pack their bags, move in, and take over."

Ferracini blinked. "Of course," he murmured. It really was as simple as that.

"That's what the Nazi regime is there for," Scholder said. "Its end product was the world you came from."

Ferracini nodded. "So what went wrong? Overlord never showed up with their suitcases."

"After Russia was destroyed, and with the U.S. lagging, the Nazi leaders decided not to play ball," Scholder said. "Why should they? Why be janitors in someone else's world when you can grab it for yourself? They destroyed the link."

And Ferracini's world had been the result. "Okay, I get that much," Ferracini said. "So where did Claud come into it?"

Anna answered. "Claud infiltrated Pipe Organ by taking the place of a European playboy aristocrat who'd disappeared and changed his identity to elope with an heiress. He was curious and impetuous enough to get himself transferred through the system to see firsthand what was going on at the other end."

"But getting back wasn't so easy," Ferracini guessed.

"Exactly. Claud only got out of Hammerhead by killing and impersonating an SS guard," Anna said. "But to cut a long story short, he escaped from Germany to England, and got from there to the States. He landed there—in our world—in 1938."

Scholder interjected, "He was from an alternate version of this world, you understand. And the world he went back to wasn't the same as the one we've just come from. Events were different in both. That's why he appeared in 1938, but this world links to our 1940."

Ferracini massaged his brow. He didn't want to go into all that right now. But it would explain how Claud had been in Europe at that time, and how come he'd danced to Glenn Miller. "And he stayed through until '75, by which time he'd put the Proteus mission together," he completed.

"With some help from Kurt, who was trapped in Germany when the Nazis destroyed the link," Anna said.

"Claud made contact with me in the course of one of his espionage missions to Europe in the earlier years," Scholder said. "In fact, it was he who got me out, in 1955."

"And you knew he was from the twenty-first century?"

"Oh, yes," Scholder said. "With a job like that on our hands we had no room for keeping secrets from each other."

"So, why didn't you tell the rest of us?" Ferracini asked.

Scholder shrugged. "Claud wanted it that way. Psychological, I suppose. People on a team like ours—yourself, for instance—they like to think that the person they're working for is one of their own kind, not some kind of alien. Also, Claud didn't want to be regarded as a twenty-first century superman. People who think they're working for supermen can rely on them too much, instead of pulling their weight. Personally, I think he did the right thing."

"I reckon so, too," Cassidy said. Lamson nodded.

"Okay," Ferracini said. "I'll go along with that. So, how much had you figured out by the time Proteus was organized? Did Claud know that nothing we did was going to make any difference to our world?"

"No, I'm fairly sure he didn't," Scholder said. "I know I didn't, and the physics was my side of it."

"But you had your suspicions," Ferracini pressed.

"Yes, and we took precautions accordingly. It wasn't until we talked to Einstein that we knew for sure. I wasn't lying when I said I was a relatively junior scientist on the project here. You'll see for yourself if you meet the younger version of me who's wandering around somewhere. There were a number of big gaps in our knowledge. The time dilation effect, for example, came as a complete surprise."

Ferracini shifted his weight to make his arm and shoulder more comfortable, wincing as he pulled it too sharply. "So we couldn't do anything for JFK and his people after all," he mused. "It seems a shame after everything they did."

"Nothing that *we* did could have changed things," Scholder

agreed. There was a curious note to his voice. Ferracini caught it
and looked at him questioningly. Scholder went on, "However,
we know that just before we left, they were in touch with *somebody.*"

Ferracini blinked. "Say, that's right. Who's to say what might
have happened there?"

"Very probably, we'll never know," Scholder said. "But maybe
we can still create something better out of *another* world, which
would have had no chance. And perhaps, in the process, we
might enjoy a better future ourselves. And what's wrong with
that?" He shrugged. "All we have to do now is get back to it without losing too much more time. It's the end of 1940 there already."

Ferracini stared out at the darkened hills beyond the compound and recalled how much he had once despised that world.
Now he thought of it as his, and he missed it already. Like Claud
and Scholder, he had lost the world that should have been his,
and he had helped forge a new world. His place was there, and its
future would be his future. He wondered what had happened
there in the nine months that had gone by since the day at
Weissenberg. Had anything that the mission had done led to any
useful result at all? Or was that world, like his, destined to be
overwhelmed anyway?

CHAPTER
49

AFTER EVERYTHING THE TEAM had been through, Winslade wasn't anxious to tell the rest of them that, despite the success of Ampersand, the link back to Hitler's Germany could be re-established at any time. Indeed, he was loath to accept it himself.

Just a day and a half after the assault at Weissenberg, the instruments at Pipe Organ were indicating that Hammerhead was up and running again, and signaling to be reconnected.

"It was so obvious, and yet both of us missed it," young Winslade said as they stood among shiny equipment consoles and banks of indicator screens in the control room, watching the skeleton crew of operators who were monitoring events. "The Nazis had a spare set of parts somewhere to rebuild the machine. In fact, when you think about it, it's surprising they've taken even this long." After a day and a half in 2025, it would be January 1941, in the world at the other end.

Winslade nodded, unable for once to conceal his feelings of bitterness and self-reproach. "There's no excuse. With something so vital, of course they would have insured themselves against any kind of an accident. Damn!"

"And that's not all," young Winslade said. He hesitated. "Let's talk about it somewhere else." He led the way to the main doors and out to the elevators. A car arrived, and he selected

ground, several levels up. "I've just been talking to General
Forbes and Derrieaux, the vice chairman's aide," he resumed
when the doors had closed. "It's by no means certain that we'll be
able to keep this place shut down for very much longer."

Winslade stared at him, horrified. "You can't be serious!"

"I'm afraid I am—very serious. There's a real, and growing,
possibility that the operation here could be started up again—
conceivably quite soon."

"But how?" Winslade shook his head, unable for the moment
to accept what he was hearing.

"We underestimated them," young Winslade told him simply. "The power elites that still exist around the world have
learned to keep a low profile, but they can still pull a lot of
strings."

They came out of the elevator and cleared the security area
surrounding the access points down to the lower levels. From
there, a wide corridor brought them to the lobby of the main
surface building. "So what's happened?" Winslade asked as they
came out into the night air and began walking slowly along a
concrete path crossing the compound.

"The real villains are coming out of the woodwork now,"
young Winslade replied. "You know the people I mean—quiet,
but effective. Basically, they're setting a lot of international
wheels in motion to protest what they claim is criminal interference in a state's internal affairs, illegal use of CIAF, bypassing
of the international judiciary—you name it. And of course,
they've got cronies in every office, lawyers slapping injunctions
right and left already—the works. It could be a big problem."

Winslade had recovered from his initial shock sufficiently to
begin thinking more clearly again. "So what would that mean?
They could delay everything indefinitely if they chose while
they, what?—maneuvered the CN into allowing operations here
to be resumed pending the outcome of an inquiry?" He nodded
slowly to himself as the implication became clear. "Yes, of
course. With a time dilation factor of two hundred, they'd only
have to stall things for a short time here for their plans at the
other end to mature. Then they transfer themselves through,
sever the link, and are gone from this world long before the inquiry has established anything."

"Precisely how I read it," young Winslade agreed. "In fact, a
motion has already been put before the CN Emergency Cabinet
calling for CIAF to be pulled out of here. That gives you an idea of
how quickly the opposition is reacting."

Winslade shook his head. "They can't get away with it," he

protested. "It can't end like this. You know what's gone into this. There must be something we can do."

"What would you do?" young Winslade asked.

Winslade thought it over. "If they want an investigation, then let's give them one," he said at last. "But a genuine one, aimed at establishing the facts. We've got one thing they never bargained on—eight of us here who can testify from firsthand experience. What answer could Overlord come up with to that? We can prove what they're up to and expose their lies. If that much was made public, the CN would have to agree to an inquiry before they pulled CIAF out. That would be enough to keep Overlord's hands off the machine. That's what I'd do if I were you."

Young Winslade smiled faintly at the choice of phrasing. "But remembering that you're you, is that really what you want?" he asked. "Do you really want to get dragged into the whole mess—international lawyers, committees, hearings, injunctions and counter-injunctions? Have you thought how long that could tie you up here? Even a few months would mean almost a lifetime in that other world. Everything you hoped to see there would be over, one way or another, long before you got back. All of the people you knew would be gone. And even if you agreed, would that be fair to the other people who came with you?"

They stopped at the end of a line of CIAF transport aircraft, standing sleek and gray in the light from the floodlights. Winslade stared at the blackness of the forest beyond the perimeter fence and drew a long breath. "Yes, I know, I know. . . ." He sighed heavily. "But good God, we can't just stand aside and let it happen. You, in this world, you can't imagine what's at the end of that road—the destruction of everything that stands for decency and civilization. Terror as official policy. The enslavement of whole peoples. Genocide." He shook his head. "If staying here is what we have to do to stop it, then so be it."

"But if what the scientists suspect is correct, then a virtual infinity of universes exists in which it happens anyway," young Winslade pointed out. "So, you manage to alter the outcome in one of them. What does it matter? A big number minus one is still a big number. What have you accomplished?"

Winslade nodded distantly. "Yes, I remember—I used to be very analytic and calculating about such things. But it is true that you change as you get older, you know. I don't know if it's for the wiser, but I like to think it is. You're saying that it's pointless to try and change one world for the better if you can't change all of them. But by the same logic, you could argue that it's pointless for people to change themselves for the better if it doesn't change the whole world. Is kindness pointless because it doesn't wipe out all the unkindness everywhere? Is it pointless to save a life because others die anyway? Or to educate one child because others remain ignorant? I think not." Winslade paused and listened for a moment to the chirping and clacking of the night insects in the forest. "I'd say it's more the other way around. It's the small things that matter. The personal things in life are what decide if it was worthwhile. Leave all the universal truths and cosmic principles to philosophers and mystics. Those are the things that don't matter."

"I was hoping you'd say something like that," young Winslade said. "You see, we came to very much the same kind of conclusion."

Winslade turned, uncertain of what that meant. "We?"

"Myself, some of the senior CIAF people here, and a number of the scientists who were unaware of Pipe Organ's true purpose. We believe that you and the people with you have done enough without getting mixed up in this world's problems. You've all carried your share. Now it's time for us to pick up ours."

"You sound as if you're offering something," Winslade said. "What?"

"We can send you back," young Winslade replied, his voice low and serious now as he came to the point that Winslade realized he had been building up to all along. "Now, unofficially, while CIAF still controls this place. You've done enough to give that world you've told us about its chance to save itself. And you, too, should be given your own chance along with it—all of you."

Winslade turned fully to regard his younger self in the light from the floodlights behind them. "You'd do that—on your own authority? You'd go that far?"

"Yes. It's no more than you people have risked already. We've discussed it at length, and we all feel the same."

It was too good an offer to refuse. Winslade wasn't about to make things tougher by going through the motions of having to be persuaded. He nodded. "I'm grateful, very grateful. When did you have in mind?"

"We estimate two days to finalize the preparations," young Winslade said. "The legal squabbling ought to give us that long."

"Another two days. That's going to mean quite a jump at the other end."

"I know. But also, Payne's still quite weak, don't forget. I checked with the doctors, and they're not very happy about moving him before then."

Winslade exhaled a long breath. "Very well. Then the only thing left to worry about is the possibility of Overlord regaining control of Pipe Organ."

A grim look came into young Winslade's eyes. "That will not be the case," he promised. "We—the group here that I mentioned—have agreed that, regardless of whatever legal machinations might be attempted, the Nazi connection will not be restored. We are resolved to make such an eventuality impossible—permanently. That is our pledge to you."

Winslade gave him a penetrating look. "And what of the consequences?"

"They're part of the share that it's our turn to pick up in this world," young Winslade told him.

CHAPTER
50

ALBERT EINSTEIN GOT UP from the desk in his cluttered office on the first floor of the Institute for Advanced Studies at Princeton and went to the window to rest his eyes. Three years had gone by since the Institute had moved, in 1939, from temporary premises on the university campus to the new building of Fuld Hall. He preferred it out here amid the peaceful New Jersey surroundings of woodlands, meadows, and farms—all so different from the dreadful things that were happening everywhere now, it seemed. In Russia, the Germans had reached the Caucasus; the Japanese had taken the East Indies, the Philippines, and Southeast Asia, and were poised on India's border; Rommel was driving the British back into Egypt again. He wondered if civilization could survive it all.

He filled his pipe and looked back at the blackboard on the wall behind his desk, covered with symbols and equations representing his latest attempt to make some impression on the problem that had defied all his efforts since those momentous months in late 1939. Somehow, he knew, there was a way of constructing a unified representation of the superficially independent concepts of space, time, force, particle, and field that the symbols represented; and in that representation would lie the key to understanding how transfers between the many worlds implied by quantum-mechanics were possible. He had tantalizing glimpses of parts of the picture—special relativity unified space with time, and mass with energy; general relativity revealed gravitation as a manifestation of the geometry of spacetime. But the grand unification that he sensed intuitively, and which the physicists of at least one twenty-first century world had succeeded in formulating, still eluded him. Sometimes he wondered if he would spend the remainder of his years grappling with it.

A tap sounded at the door. "Ja?" Einstein looked around and ambled back from the window.

His secretary poked her head inside. "Sorry to interrupt, Dr. Einstein, but Dr. Fermi is on the telephone from Chicago," she said. Einstein wouldn't have a phone in his own office. "He insists it can't wait, I'm afraid. He sounds awfully excited."

"Ah, so, it can't wait, eh? Well, we'd better see what it is."

Back in the spring of 1940, after months had gone by without word of either the soldiers who went into Germany or the people who disappeared into the Gatehouse machine, President Roosevelt had decided that the West would have to rely on its own resources to defend itself. Accordingly, he had ordered all work on trying to comprehend the physics abandoned, and for the scientists involved to focus on a concerted A-bomb program instead. To this end the National Defense Research Committee had been formed under Vannevar Bush, president of the Carnegie Institute, which took over coordinating responsibility for nuclear fission research.

In the year that followed, the situation had become steadily more worrisome as Gatehouse remained inactive and nothing was learned of whether or not the German machine had been destroyed. In June 1941, therefore, Roosevelt had intensified the program further by having the NDRC absorbed into the new Office of Scientific Research & Development, operating under direct presidential control. The groups working on chain-reaction physics in the new organization were headed by Arthur Compton, Dean of Physics at the University of Chicago, and Compton had moved all of them to Chicago to be under one roof—a preliminary step to placing the whole program under direct military control.

"Enrico, hello. This is Albert Einstein. What can I do for you? I was told you sound excited."

"It's Gatehouse!" Fermi's voice gabbled. "We've just got a call from the people at Gatehouse. Something's happening there!"

"Happening?"

Since the arrest of the amateur spy early in 1940, there had been no evidence of further German interest in Gatehouse. Only a reduced crew of technicians was left there now, keeping alive a fading hope that something might happen one day, and sharing the boredom with a resident contingent of military police guards and FBI.

"It's activating—a full connection!" That was as much detail as Fermi would go into over the phone. "They might be coming back. Some of us are flying to New York right away. Do you want to get over there?"

Einstein blinked and sucked his pipe. "Why, yes . . . Yes, indeed. I'd like to be there very much."

"That's what we thought," Fermi said. "Okay, put your secretary back on the line and I'll get her to arrange a car for you. We should be there in something like five hours from now."

Around three o'clock in the morning, a knock sounded on the door and two CIAF guards entered. Cassidy had arrived a short while earlier to help Ferracini dress, and they were both ready to go as Winslade had instructed.

The last couple of days had been strange, with VTOL craft of all shapes and sizes buzzing in and out to disgorge and pick up lots of self-important people who strutted about carrying briefcases, talking in loud voices, and continually badgering the CIAF officers to be let into places they had no business going. Ferracini and the others had only a vague idea of what it was all about, but that hadn't prevented some of the visitors from pestering them, too. In the end, young Winslade had ordered the Medical Block to be sealed off, and he had tripled the guards on the entrances.

So, the troops had spent the last day with Ryan and Payne, who were both improving rapidly, playing with the room's call-up-anything-you-want video system, which combined computer, library, newspaper, stereo system, and TV. They had watched live shots of a platform being constructed in orbit; a documentary about a manned mission that had landed on Mars; an industrial espionage thriller set in Russia, China, and Europe; and other snippets of the world of the twenty-first century. Because of the security that had been enforced at Pipe Organ, however, phone capability was not included—a Message Center screened all call-out requests. The few that Cassidy attempted out of curiosity to some numbers advertised openly in the directory under "Sex Partners, Groups & Clubs" had been denied.

"All set?" one of the guards inquired, keeping his voice low.

"We're ready," Cassidy said.

"Nothing to carry?" the other asked, looking around the room.

"I guess not," Ferracini said. "We didn't exactly come here prepared for a vacation." They walked into the darkened outer room, where a night nurse was sitting by the far door, bathed in a circle of light from the lamp on her desk. "Where's Floyd?" Ferracini asked.

"He went on ahead with Paddy and Ed," Cassidy replied. "We'll catch up with them over on the other side."

They stopped in front of the nurse's desk on their way out. "Thanks for putting him back together again," Cassidy said to her. "You people did a good job, really. That's how he looks. It's normal."

"Thanks for everything," Ferracini said. "Sorry we have to rush off like this."

"We're sorry it couldn't have been longer, too," the nurse replied. "Well, whatever this is all about, and wherever you're going—good luck."

They went out in the corridor and along to the elevators, where two more CIAF guards were waiting with Anna Kharkiovitch and Keith Adamson. One of them was holding a car ready, and with few words the party descended to one of the underground levels. They followed a long, brightly lighted tunnel that led underneath the central compound to a concourse below the lobby of the main building. A couple of senior CIAF officers were waiting to take them through into the security area, and minutes later they were on their way down to the transfer lock, in the heart of the Pipe Organ complex.

They came out into another concourse and went through some doors on the opposite side to find themselves in the lock antechamber. A small group was waiting around the two gurneys on which Ryan and Payne had been brought across. It included the scientists T'ung-Sen, Hallman, and Eddie, as well as Dr. Pfanzer, both Scholders, and both Winslades. Up in the control room another handful of scientists, backed by a squad of CIAF guards, had moved the bewildered duty crew over to one wall of the room and taken their places at the key operators' stations. There was an air of urgency about the place.

Young Winslade came over to shake everyone's hand in turn, followed by young Scholder. "Well, that's all of you," he said. "I'm sorry your visit to our world couldn't have been longer. There's so much we could have shown you."

"I'm not sure exactly what's going on, but I do know you people are sticking your necks out for us," Ferracini said. "We appreciate it." Cassidy and Lamson echoed the sentiment.

"We feel we owe you at least that much," young Scholder

said. Then somebody came out of the control room and signaled from the gallery.

"I hate to cut this short, but time is critical," young Winslade said. "The beam's up and centered."

"It's time," Winslade told his party.

Ferracini moved up beside the gurneys and looked down at Payne. "Feel up to traveling, Ed?"

"If we're going home, I'll damn well get off this thing and walk if I have to," Payne rasped. Ferracini grinned.

"You'll have to stay out of trouble with that hip after we get back, Paddy," Winslade said, patting Ryan on the shoulder. "You'd never be able to explain away the X-rays."

A couple of CIAF troopers took the gurneys and began wheeling them into the lock. The rest of the party followed. Scholder lingered for a moment to shake hands with his younger analog. As he did so, he caught sight of the doors of the Dispatch Preparation Area on the far side of the antechamber beginning to slide apart. Behind the doors, some technicians were standing around a low, wheeled cradle carrying a fat cylindrical object covered by a shroud. They looked as if they were waiting to move forward with it. Scholder's eyes widened as he realized what the object was. "Kurt, those people back there—that's an assembled—"

"Go," young Scholder told him. "There isn't much time, and we have more work to do."

"But that's an assembled A-bomb under there. You—"

Young Scholder took him firmly by the arm. "We promised you that the link would never be restored," he muttered as he steered the older man into the transfer lock. "But we're on borrowed time already. We've received a directive relieving Colonel Winslade of his command. A force is already on its way here to replace him. They could arrive at any moment."

The CIAF troopers who had taken in the gurneys were coming back out. Young Scholder stopped at the doors and motioned the other inside. The elder Scholder turned to protest, but the doors were already closing. There was nothing more he could say or do. He turned back again and hastened to where the others were waiting. A red glow grew and engulfed them, and moments later the lock was empty.

It was like old times at Gatehouse. Einstein was there with Fermi, Teller, and Szilard; the machine was humming, its indicator panels flickering and control stations manned; and the coffeepot was brewing in the mess area at the back. Mortimer Greene stood tensely among the figures on the platform outside the entry port, not daring to believe fully that the light coming from inside meant what he prayed it meant. Gordon Selby was with him, having moved back from England over a year previously, and Arthur Bannering had flown up from his State Department posting in Washington.

"Locking established and beam pumping down," Fermi announced from the monitor panel to one side. "The primary node is relaxing."

The blue light inside the gate chamber faded, and then changed through green and yellow to orange. Gasps went up on all sides from the people on the platform as the outlines of human shapes became discernible within the glow. The orange dulled to red, which grew dimmer. The shapes took on solid form, and as the glow died, they began moving slowly forward.

"It's them!" Fermi shouted ecstatically from his vantage point by the port. "There's Claud and Anna! . . . Keith Adamson. . . . But there are more, too—too many."

The others were already rushing forward excitedly around him. Teller's voice rose above the cries of disbelief and uncontrollable laughter. "What's this? The soldiers are here!"

"Make way, make way," someone else shouted. "Two of them are injured. Right, bring them through."

Mortimer Greene stared at the ghosts as they came forward into the light. "My God!" he choked, and tears began running down his cheeks.

Beside him Selby and Bannering were standing too stunned to move. "Harry, Cassidy, Floyd," Selby stammered. "They're all here . . . but they can't be. . . ."

Szilard shook his head dazedly. "Those men," he protested to Einstein. "They're the soldiers, the ones who were lost in Germany nearly three years ago. How can they be here?"

Winslade was gripping Greene's shoulders and smiling. "Yes, it really is all of us. You waited, Mortimer! I knew you wouldn't let us down."

Cassidy came out into the center of the platform and stopped to pull himself up to his full height and fill his lungs with air. "We're home, guys," he called back. "I can smell it. Man, who'd have ever believed the Brooklyn waterfront could smell so sweet!"

"When is this?" Scholder asked. "What's the date? What time have we come back to?"

"November," Fermi answered.

"Which year?"

"Nineteen forty-two."

Ferracini came out and looked about him with a feeling of

wonder. It was, as Cassidy had said, home. Just as he remembered it. All around him, people were shouting, laughing, and back-slapping. His eyes came to rest on one, a tall, solidly built, gray-haired figure in a navy-blue blazer and open-necked white shirt, who was standing a short distance back, too overcome with emotion to respond. Ferracini needed a second or two to register the face—it had filled out a little and acquired a beard since he had last seen it. Then he grinned, and the grin broadened slowly. "Hey, guys," he called to the others. "It's Harvey! He made it out after all! Harvey Warren's here!"

Warren moved forward as the rest of the team came up on either side of Ferracini. Ferracini saluted. "Mission accomplished, sir. All present."

"Request permission to be excused standing to attention," Payne mumbled from his gurney.

At last a smile spread across Warren's face. "Permission granted, soldier," he said.

"So you got out," Ryan said, dropping the pretense of formality. "You fixed a rendezvous with the British sub?" Warren nodded.

"How about Gustav and Marga?" Cassidy asked. "What happened to them?"

"I brought them out, too," Warren said. "They're in Canada now, under assumed names. Their son in the army was taken prisoner by the British in North Africa. He's in a POW camp and doing okay. The other one's in Sweden."

"So the war is still going on," Anna Kharkiovitch said. "North Africa hasn't fallen? The British are still fighting?"

"Churchill is the Prime Minister now," Warren told her. "They don't know how to quit over there. He's turned the whole country into a fighting machine."

Anna stared at him incredulously. "Churchill is Prime Minister? You mean it's happening? We actually managed to change some things after all?"

"Change some things? That's not half of it," Warren said. "America's fighting! Roosevelt ran for a third term and was re-elected. We're in it against Germany, Italy, and Japan—all of them."

Anna gaped for a few seconds. "What about Russia?" she asked disbelievingly.

"Still going strong."

"No Nazi A-bombs?"

"No bombs."

Still seething with excitement, the crowd moved down from the platform, and MP guards came forward to help with the gurneys. "Can someone get us an outside line on one of the phones?" Colonel Adamson asked as they came down to the floor level and began moving through to the mess area.

"We must inform the President," Winslade said, nodding approvingly as he walked alongside. "But we shouldn't have to place a regular call. Don't we still have that direct line to the White House?"

"That's not quite what I had in mind, Claud," Adamson said, sounding apologetic. "I just wanted to call my wife."

CHAPTER
51

PRECEDED BY MOTORCYCLISTS AND a truck carrying armed guards, two armored staff cars climbed a winding, four-mile mountain road of widening mountain panoramas from Obersalzburg to the foot of a rocky crag near the top of Kehlstein mountain, in the Bavarian Alps. The vehicles rolled to a stop where the road ended, and the cars disgorged a bevy of braided and bemedaled officers of the Nazi high command. They converged toward a large stone archway framing an entrance, and fell in around a lean, stern-faced figure with dark, tempestuous eyes, a clipped black mustache, and a straight-combed forelock of hair showing beneath his peaked cap. He strode purposefully into the four-hundred-forty-foot-long tunnel that led into the mountainside.

"So now, admit it." Adolf Hitler challenged the corpulent figure alongside him. "Was I not proved right again in the end?"

"I have to agree that it seems you were," Hermann Goering said, puffing from the pace.

"Perhaps we shouldn't jump to conclusions," Martin Bormann cautioned from Hitler's other side. "It has been a long time."

"Pah, caution, caution—all I hear is people urging caution," Hitler sneered. "Boldness and nerve build empires. When will I hear people giving me answers with the same energy that they expend looking for problems?"

They had been about to board the train for Berlin at Obersalzburg station when a messenger from Hitler's Eagle's Nest caught up, bearing an urgent message from the director at Valhalla: The return-gate, rebuilt since early 1941 after the still unexplained security failure and the subsequent British-American commando raid, had become active again. The news had put the Führer into one of his expansive moods.

"Was it caution and timidity that got us the Rhineland?" Hitler asked as they stepped into the elevator that would take them up the last four hundred feet. "Or Austria or Czechoslovakia, both without a fight?" He surveyed his henchmen unsmilingly for a few seconds and then jabbed at his own chest with a finger. "They say I am a genius," he reminded them. "But shall I tell you a secret? Do you want to know what the real secret of being a genius is? Is it intellect? Brains? Education? The number of facts that a man can cram into his skull? . . . Eh?" He wagged a finger at them. "Books can hold all the facts you need. Graybeards and creaking academics can be hired. The roots of genius lie in the ability to make decisions, the will to stand by them and act in the face of adversity, and the nerve to see the action through unswervingly to its completion. The British call it 'sticking to your guns.' It's a good phrase."

They came out of the elevator and crossed a vestibule into the entrance hall of Hitler's mountaintop sanctum. An orderly came forward to assist the Führer with his greatcoat and take his cap, and the party moved on into the situation room, with its large map table, mural charts, and view of the jagged Bavarian peaks. "That is why I command, and the duty of Paulus at Stalingrad is to obey," the Führer went on. "The lesser will must yield to the greater. That is Nature's law, is it not? Paulus fails to comprehend the real issues in the East. His soldier's mind can function only at the tactical level. But a leader's vision is necessary to grasp the wider strategy."

"Yes, you were right about France and about Norway," Goebbels told his idol. "This will show you were right about Russia, too."

"Herr Director Mauschellen is on the line from Valhalla now," an adjutant advised, presenting a telephone handset.

"Yes, but how many agreed back in the early days of 1941 that I was right about Russia?" Hitler asked, taking the instrument. "How many had the courage to back me over Barbarossa when the repairs were completed and the new machine remained silent? 'Führer, we can't risk attacking Russia until the connection is restored,' Halder told me," Hitler said, mimicking the tone of the Chief of the General Staff. "Brauchitsch advised caution. You see, gentlemen, always it has been the same. But what would that have cost us? Two years!" He gestured with the handset. "But I had the nerve to move against Russia, even without any guarantee that the atomic bombs would be delivered in 1942. You see, I stuck to my guns."

Goering nodded and appealed to the others. "And now we are at the Volga and the Caucasus. All that would have been lost if we had waited."

Hitler raised the telephone to his face. "And now we shall see whether or not my confidence and my vision were mistaken," he whispered. Then, in a louder voice, "Hello, Herr Director Mauschellen? . . . Yes, this is the Führer speaking. . . . Oh, really? And what is the news?" Hitler listened while the room waited on tenterhooks. A triumphant gleam came into the Führer's eyes, and the others began exchanging reassured looks.

"Yes, one moment." Hitler covered the mouthpiece with a hand and sat down, at the same time directing a satisfied smirk at his followers. "It is as I predicted," he informed them. "The Valhalla connection has been restored. They are initiating the first transfer now." He made a contemptuous tossing-away motion with his hand. "So, we lost six months from the time the bombs were supposed to have been shipped through. What does that equate to at the other end—a day? Less?" He shrugged. "You see, it was nothing. Some kind of technical hitch could easily hold them up for that long. Probably the commandos who disappeared through to Overlord's end caused a few problems. The secret is to allow for the time difference and not allow yourselves to panic. That was why it was imperative for Paulus to stick to his guns in Russia. Now we will get the bombs, and the problem of Stalingrad will be resolved. And so will the whole problem of Stalin."

Goering was chuckling, his fleshy baby-face wreathed in delight. "That is so right! Two years—it seemed so long. But what was that at the other end of the connection? It was nothing. We were worrying about nothing."

"With hindsight, you can say that," Goebbels told him. "But it required genius to retain that perspective at the time."

Even Bormann was nodding grudgingly. "Perhaps I was too pessimistic, but that can be a sign of prudence, too." He was about to say something more, but stopped when he saw that a puzzled expression had come over Hitler's face. The relieved banter that had broken out across the room ceased abruptly with the realization that everything was not quite right.

"What?" Hitler was saying into the telephone. "What do you mean, an object has appeared inside the gate? What kind of an object? . . . How big and round? . . . On wheels? . . . Hello. . . . Hello?" Hitler looked up with a perplexed scowl on his face and leaned across the table to jiggle the telephone rest. "Hello, hello . . . Herr Director, are you there?"

"Operator," another voice said on the line.

"What's happened?" Hitler demanded. "I was talking to the director at Valhalla. Some fool has cut me off."

"Allow me to check, please." A few moments of silence went by. Then the operator came back again. "I'm sorry, my Führer, but all the lines to Valhalla have gone dead," he advised.

In an RAF photographic reconnaissance Mosquito flying at thirty-five thousand feet over the Leipzig area, the copilot-navigator's eyes widened above the top of his oxygen mask. "Bloody hell, Skip—look at that!" his voice crackled over the intercom through the roar of twin Merlin engines.

"Where?"

"Bank starboard—down there, two o'clock."

"Christ! What's going on?"

"Dunno. Looks like something's brewed up."

"God, I've never seen anything like that!"

"Not a bad show, what?"

"Where is it?"

"Just a minute—I'll have a look."

The pilot put the plane into a slow, banking turn to watch the rising cloud of smoke while the copilot consulted his maps.

"Has to be the chemicals and ammo place at Weissenberg, Skip. Someone must have dropped a match."

"It looks as if one whole end of it's gone up. . . . Strewth!"

They circled for a while longer, taking pictures. "Maybe Bomber Harris can cross this place off his target list for a while," the pilot said. "Oh, well, time to take the old bus home, I suppose. Pint of bitter at the Bull's tonight, George?"

"Not a bad idea at all, Skip. I don't mind if I do."

CHAPTER
52

WAS IT POSSIBLE TO pinpoint precisely what the Proteus team had done to bring about such a staggering change in the world's fortunes? Many factors contributed, but from the analysis that Arthur Bannering presented at the Florida resort where the team was sent to recuperate after visiting the White House, it all seemed to have hinged around two crucial developments that had not taken place in the Proteus world: Churchill's appointment as Britain's Prime Minister, and the reelection of Roosevelt for a third term as President of the United States. These events were connected, and Anna Kharkiovitch was suspicious that far more than had been revealed lay behind the circumstances that had precipitated them.

In April 1940, after the happenings at Gatehouse and Weissenberg, the Anglo-French expedition to Norway had sailed as planned. But following the postponement of Hitler's attack in the West, the German expedition sailed at about the same time—not a month later in May, as had been expected. The two fleets blundered into each other, and a confused series of landings and engagements took place up and down the Norwegian coast, lasting into the following month.

The result was a fiasco for the Allies and bore out all of Major Warren's dire predictions about the amateurish state of Britain's military preparations. It was conceivable that the Allies had survived the early encounters only because the enemy's advisers had never fought a real, large-scale war.

The British troops sent to Norway had no skis, and hadn't been trained in their use, anyway; the crack French *Chasseurs Alpins* mountain brigade did have skis, but they were shipped without the straps to secure them. A field communications unit, sent with its personnel in one ship and its equipment in another, was rendered *hors de combat* without the Germans' firing a shot when one vessel was rerouted in mid-voyage to a new destination, and the other wasn't. Troops were continually being embarked, disembarked, and reembarked in Scottish ports, while across the sea their hitherto undefended objectives were being occupied by the Germans. And no antiaircraft guns were sent.

But the biggest error, despite all the warnings, was the British failure to appreciate the impact of air power on a world that had been ruled by navies for centuries. The Luftwaffe quickly gained the skies after occupying bases in Denmark and Norway, and the Allied position became untenable. Evacuation of the expedition had commenced by the end of the month, which made all the more unfortunate a confident assurance to the House by Prime Minister Chamberlain only weeks before that Hitler had "missed the bus."

"If this is an example of what foreknowledge of history can do for us," Churchill had grumbled to a distraught Arthur Bannering, left to take the brunt after Winslade and Anna's disappearance, "we'd be better off without it!"

But the outcome of all this confusion was not such a disaster, after all. After a passionate debate in the British Parliament early in May, in which the government was censured not only for the Norwegian debacle, but also for its entire conduct of the war, Chamberlain resigned. For a while, it seemed that Lord Halifax would succeed him—as indeed he had in the Proteus world; but in this world, Halifax's disposition wasn't in tune with the new mood of the nation: He was not a war leader, and he knew it. Accordingly, Halifax declined, and the King sent for Churchill to form a government instead.

"Claud and Arthur set it up!" Anna insisted as she sat debating the affair with the others on the white sands of a Florida beach. "They engineered the whole thing. They knew the Norwegian campaign would be a disaster and that the government would never survive it."

"But how could anyone have known that Churchill would take over?" Selby objected.

"Who else was there?" Scholder asked.

"It was obvious that Norway couldn't succeed," Warren said. "And it did result in a god-awful shakeup of the whole British high command. But I don't know—would Claud really have risked something like that?"

"What about the other Claud?" Cassidy said. "Look how much he risked. It's the same guy, isn't it?"

"They knew it would happen, I tell you," Anna insisted again. "They set it up. Claud and Arthur brought down the entire British government."

A few yards away, Arthur Bannering sat nonchalantly reading a newspaper at a table underneath a sunshade, while Winslade, sphinxlike, smiled to himself as he gazed out at the ocean. Neither of them would say anything.

Churchill took office officially as Prime Minister to the Crown on May 10, 1940. And that, as chance would have it, was the day that Hitler unleashed his blitzkrieg in the West.

"I have nothing to offer but blood, toil, tears and sweat," Churchill told the House in his inaugural address. There could be no thought of making terms with the enemy; he knew where the road of capitulation would lead. "You ask, what is our policy? I will say: It is to wage war, by sea, land and air, with all our might and with all the strength that God can give us: to wage war against a monstrous tyranny, never surpassed in the dark, lamentable catalogue of human crime. . . ."

By then the whole European situation had acquired a momentum that was causing it to diverge from the history of the Proteus world much faster than anybody realized. As agreed, the British force in northern France advanced into Belgium to meet the anticipated German thrust, but Hitler had changed his plans. The main weight of the German attack fell not upon the Lowlands but farther south, in the Ardennes, and in days the Panzers had broken through the lightly held French line and were racing for the coast at Abbeville. The northern armies were trapped, and by the end of the month more troops were being evacuated in addition to those still coming back from Norway—this time over 300,000 of them, from Dunkirk.

Hitler didn't yet understand the change that Churchill's appointment signified. Taking the rapid collapse as evidence of the Allies' desire for a speedy end to their involvement, he signaled his adherence to the "understanding" that he still thought he had by holding the Panzers back for three crucial days while the Dunkirk evacuations went ahead. He publicly expressed absolute confidence that the British and French would then sue for peace, posing as the magnanimous conquerors by offering them generous-sounding terms.

Britain's reply came over the airwaves in Churchill's defiant, rasping tones: *Even though large tracts of Europe and many old and famous States have fallen or may fall into the grip of the Gestapo and all the odious apparatus of Nazi rule, we shall not flag or fail. . . . We shall fight on the seas and oceans, we shall fight with growing confidence and growing strength in the air, we shall defend our Island, whatever the cost may be. We shall fight on the beaches, we shall fight on the landing-grounds, we shall fight in the fields and in the streets, we shall fight in the hills; we shall never surender. . . .*

But it was too late to save France. Paris fell on June 14, and an armistice was signed a week later. Britain was left alone to face a Nazi-dominated Europe, just twenty miles away across the Channel. Invasion, surely, would be the next step. To oppose it, the Royal Navy was left with sixty-eight serviceable destroyers; there were just three hundred fifty tanks in all of the British Isles.

If the invasion had come, it would have been everybody's war. While farmers and factory hands drilled with iron railings and shotguns, the King had a shooting range constructed in Buckingham Palace grounds, where he, other members of the Royal Family, and the palace staff practiced assiduously with Tommy guns and pistols. He professed a distinct feeling of relief to Churchill that England was now on its own and disencumbered of foreigners that it was necessary to be polite to. The young Princess Elizabeth, heir to the throne, trained as an Army truck driver.

In the Mediterranean theater, meanwhile, the French battleships at Oran hadn't fallen into Hitler's hands as they had in the Proteus world; Churchill sent the Royal Navy there and sank them. A more cautious Franco kept Spain out of the Axis this time, and Gibraltar and Malta didn't fall. Churchill quashed requests for the Mediterranean Fleet to withdraw when Mussolini joined in the war, and instead, the Navy's torpedo bombers crippled the Italian capital ships in an audacious attack at Taranto.

These were the events that inspired Roosevelt, across the Atlantic, to run for a third term, and he was nominated as his party's candidate without any real opposition. "If we do win this war," Winslade told Anna as they settled down after boarding the train that would take the team back north to Washington, "it will have been won in July 1940, at the Democratic Convention in Chicago."

Even before then, Roosevelt's policies had shown the effects of the Proteus mission's intervention. After Dunkirk, prevailing over the U.S. service chiefs who had written Britain off, he sent Churchill shiploads of arms and ammunition, subverting the

Neutrality Laws by selling the materiel to a steel company, which resold it to the British government. In July, he signed an act expanding the U.S. Navy to include thirty-five battleships, twenty carriers, and fifteen thousand Navy planes, and in September shepherded a bill through Congress to supply Britain with fifty vintage American destroyers in exchange for leasing rights to West Indian bases. In October, the military draft bill became law, and Roosevelt's successful reelection made inevitable the eventual mobilization of America's stupendous industrial might to the British cause.

In the end, Britain was not invaded. Instead, Hitler, vowing revenge for having been let down on the "deal," decided to demonstrate the might of his Luftwaffe. Through the scorching days of August and September 1940, Goering's air fleets came in waves over England—and were decimated by the Hurricanes and Spitfires that Churchill, mindful of Bannering's warnings of what had happened in the Proteus world, had kept back from the forlorn fight in France. At night, the RAF bombers smashed the invasion craft being assembled in the Channel ports.

By September, the Luftwaffe's daylight attacks had been defeated. Incensed by the experience of his first defeat, the Führer switched his air force to a night-bombing offensive against London that lasted into the following year. Over seventeen thousand Luftwaffe bombers attacked the city between the middle of August and the end of October. In September alone, London was raided 268 times; the blitzkrieg continued through almost ninety consecutive nights of the cold winter months. But history didn't repeat itself. This time, Britain held out.

A convoy carrying most of the precious tanks was forced through to reinforce General Wavell in Egypt, and by the end of the year, the Italians had been hurled back and were in full flight across Libya.

In the Proteus world, Halifax had signed the formal British surrender on January 1, 1941. It was a very different New Year that the British, battered and weary though they were, could look forward to this time.

Since Overlord's whole purpose had been to eliminate the Soviets, the Russo-German pact of 1939 was plainly nothing more than a temporary expedient to be observed until Hitler was ready to attack. In the Proteus world, he had attacked in May 1941. Through diplomatic and other channels, Churchill and Roosevelt attempted to warn Stalin of what their secret information led them to expect. But Stalin remained—outwardly, at least—unimpressed. In April and May, Hitler secured his southern flank by gobbling up Yugoslavia and the Balkans, evicting a hastily improvised British force sent to defend Greece, and taking Crete by airborne assault.

Then, on June 22, three German Army groups consisting of 3,000,000 men, 7,100 guns, and 3,300 tanks, stormed eastward in a gesture of totalitarian good-neighborliness, and were halted at the very edge of Moscow and in the Crimea only by the coming of winter. At last, the beleaguered British had acquired a fighting ally—a strange bedfellow for somebody of Churchill's breeding and disposition, to be sure, but an ally nevertheless. And after more than a year of facing Hitler alone, that wasn't something to be sneered at.

"But in another sense it was the worst news," Selby told Scholder as the train clattered northward. "We took it to mean that Hitler would be getting the A-bombs, and therefore Ampersand had failed. That was when the British decided to merge their fission work with the U.S. program, and I moved back over here. FDR told everyone to stop fooling with the gate at that point and get moving on the bomb."

The biggest surprise of all had been in the Pacific.

In the Proteus universe, Overlord's agents had established relationships with the militant elements in Japan, who succeeded in bringing to power the former War Minister, Tojo. The Japanese contributed to the common cause by attacking the Soviets in the east from Manchuria in September 1941, a few months after the opening of the German onslaught on the western side. At the same time, they commenced amphibious landings in Malaya and the East Indies to further their own designs upon the former British and Dutch eastern colonies.

Intelligence reports came in early December of the Japanese troop transports sailing from their bases in China and Indochina. By December 6, as the Russians were launching a major counteroffensive along a 500 mile front before Moscow with the forces they had risked transferring from Siberia, the inner staff groups around Churchill and Roosevelt were convinced that the Japanese attack from Manchuria would come at any moment.

Then, on December 7, American cryptanalysts in Washington intercepted a message to the Japanese embassy instructing that diplomatic relations were to be broken off. The embassy was told to deliver the message to the State Department at 1300 hours. The Americans were puzzled. Why did the message talk about breaking off relations with the U.S. when Japan was going to attack the U.S.S.R.? Roosevelt hadn't learned yet, as Churchill had when France fell, that foreknowledge of events from another universe could be a mixed blessing. The U.S. remained blissfully off guard.

The Japanese embassy hadn't been notified of the urgency of the message; decoding was leisurely, and the diplomats didn't learn of the deadline until after the American code-breakers had. It was Sunday, and a further delay ensued in obtaining an appointment to deliver the translation to Secretary of State Cordell Hull. This was eventually accomplished at 1430 hours, not 1300 hours as had been stipulated.

1300 hours in Washington would have corresponded to dawn in Hawaii. When the message was finally delivered, Hull had just received the first reports from Pearl Harbor.

By then it was too late. Japan had jumped the wrong way!

But that was a year in the past by the time the team returned from 2025; and 1942 had seen a turning of the tide. In the carrier battles of the Coral Sea and Midway, the Americans had stopped the Japanese in the Pacific, and the Marines had gone ashore at Guadalcanal. In North Africa, the British under Montgomery had stopped Rommel at El Alamein and then gone over to the offensive, while to the west, the Americans landed in Morocco and Algeria. The Russians had stopped von Paulus at Stalingrad. The RAF were flying a thousand bomber raids over Germany, and the first wings of Flying Fortresses and Liberators had begun operating from England.

And on December 2, Winslade, Gordon Selby, and Kurt Scholder were among the group of scientists and officials watching tensely in a squash court at the University of Chicago as Fermi and his associates slowly withdrew the neutron-absorption rods from a pile containing 350 tons of graphite, 5 tons of uranium, and 36 tons of uranium oxide, built in the form of a flattened sphere measuring 26 feet across. Construction of the building that was supposed to house the project twenty miles west of Chicago in the Argonne Forest was behind schedule, so they had set it up instead beneath the grandstand at the Stagg Field stadium. Nobody had informed the University president or trustees.

The counters recorded a neutron multiplication factor of 1.006: the world's first nuclear reactor had gone critical. The rods were reinserted, and the multiplication dropped. The reaction was controllable.

Dr. Compton placed a call to James B. Conant, the chairman of the NDRC at Harvard. "Jim, I think you'll be interested to know that the Italian navigator has landed in the new world. The natives are friendly."

The scales of war were tipping rapidly.

CHAPTER
53

IN JANUARY 1943, THE Proteus team boarded a converted B-24 Liberator at Bolling Field, Washington, D.C., and were flown south to Brazil, across the Atlantic to Lagos, Nigeria, from there to Dakar on the tip of West Africa, arriving finally at Casablanca, on the Atlantic coast of Morocco. There, just over two months after American forces under General Patton had landed to wrest the area from the Vichy French, Roosevelt and Churchill, accompanied by their Chiefs of Staff, were meeting to review the war effort and agree on future strategy.

After resting the night at a hotel in the Anfa suburb of the city, the team was driven through sunny, palm-lined streets guarded by American troops to an outlying villa, where Churchill and Roosevelt held their private conferences, away from the main staff sessions. Relatively few individuals had been admitted to the Proteus secret even now, and the only other persons present were George C. Marshall, Chief of Staff of the United States Army, and Sir Alan Brooke, the British Chief of the Imperial General Staff. The meeting took place in a large, airy room at the back of the villa. Orange and lemon trees surrounded a lawn and pool outside the open French windows, and armed sentries patrolled inconspicuously below a high wall at the rear.

Churchill, cigar in hand and wearing a khaki bush shirt with baggy casual slacks, came around the map-covered table in the center of the room with a show of almost fatherly affection as the arrivals were shown in. He pumped their hands warmly and put his arm around Anna's shoulders to give her a hug. "It's a miracle!" he declared. "Impossible, I tell you, and yet here they are, back from the dead. We'd long given up any hope, you know."

"Except Mortimer," Roosevelt said as he wheeled his chair across the room. "He was the one who talked us into keeping the machine running. I figured he should know you people better than we did."

Marshall and Brooke were introduced. "I'm still not sure I believe it, you understand," Marshall said frankly. "I've read the report, and I can see you all standing here in this room, but I'm still not sure I believe it."

Brooke could only shake his head. "I don't think it's possible to express anything adequately in words. I've been told about the way things were in the world you all came from, and I can see for myself the differences in this one of ours. . . . Really, what does one say?"

"How about, 'Welcome back'?" Winslade suggested.

Brooke smiled. "That's enough? Oh, very well, then, welcome back, all of you."

"I wouldn't say that the changes were entirely our doing," Anna said. "You seem to have been busy, too."

Roosevelt nodded. "Oh, sure, we haven't exactly been idle during your absence. I think we've managed things about as well as could reasonably be expected . . . a few regrets and miscalculations with hindsight, but I guess that's life."

"Compared to the world we came from, it's astounding," Winslade said.

"And your wounds, Ed—I've been worried about them," Churchill said. "Are they mending satisfactorily? And what about you, Paddy, and you, Harry? How are you feeling?"

"Much better, thank you, sir," Payne replied. "Major Warren says I'll be back up to Special Operations standards in no time." Ryan and Ferracini said they felt fine.

Churchill nodded happily. "Splendid, splendid." He smiled and rubbed his palms together for a moment. "And now, we have something to show you that you should find interesting. Brookie?"

Brooke switched on a slide projector already positioned before a screen and inserted a frame, while Marshall closed a blind to darken the room. The picture was an aerial photograph, taken from a considerable height, of a tremendous plume of smoke rising over a landscape of low, rounded hills with open and forested patches. The smoke emanated from one end of a large industrial complex situated by a river. "Recognize it?" Churchill asked lightly. "It's from a set brought back by one of our Photo Recce flights a few days after you got back."

"I guess we could have told you earlier, but it would have spoiled the surprise," Roosevelt said, grinning unashamedly.

The Ampersand troops, who had memorized every detail of that layout, stared in astonishment and elation. Cassidy caught Ferracini's eyes, shook his head as if trying to clear his head of a dream, and then looked back at the screen. The picture was still there.

Winslade was blinking behind his spectacles. "He did it!" he whispered. "He stood by what he said he was going to do. He did it!"

"Yes," Anna mused distantly. "And I wonder what it cost him."

Alan Brooke gave them a while to study the picture, then commented, "If this bomb is as powerful as people tell me, I'm surprised that the effects are so localized. The main plant there is hardly touched. All the smoke seems to be coming from that annex area at the top there, right on the edge."

"Hammerhead was deep underground and heavily reinforced," Gordon Selby reminded him. "That would blanket most of the blast. Underground nuclear explosions usually vaporize a cavern and push up a surface blister, which gets sucked back down again to form a crater when the vapor condenses. To have punched through the surface at all, that must have been a fair-size bomb."

In response to further questions, the Ampersand soldiers filled in details of the operation at Weissenberg, and Warren described briefly his return to England by submarine with the Knackes. Then an orderly brought in soft drinks and refreshments, and Marshall opened the blind again.

"That was what Hitler was relying on, and now it's no more," Churchill said. "He's shot his bolt. This will prove to be the turning point of the war." He studied the food that had been brought in and selected a shrimp cocktail. "In fact, we've already begun planning the invasion back across the Channel into France. The code name we've given it is 'Overlord.' What do you think—appropriate, eh?"

The others smiled. "So, Hammerhead is finally destroyed," Scholder said, picking up a thin-cut, salmon-and-cucumber sandwich. "Can we assume, then, that the threat of a Nazi atomic bomb has been eliminated completely?"

"I wouldn't assume anything until this whole business is over," Marshall said.

"How likely are they to develop a bomb, anyway, through their own efforts?" Anna asked. "Obviously, they know it's possible."

"That's what I meant," Scholder said.

Heads turned automatically toward Gordon Selby. "Their reliance on Overlord probably means that their own program has been allowed to lag," Selby said. "And from what I've gathered from the Europeans I worked with and our own intelligence sources, the German program seems to be focusing on an approach with heavy water as the moderator, rather than graphite, which Fermi is using. Heavy water isn't easy to come by."

"In fact, the only installation under Nazi control that's capable of producing it in any quantity is a hydroelectric plant in southern Norway," Churchill said. "We sent an airborne commando unit to attack it in November, but the mission failed. However, we're sending in another group any day now—Norwegians this time. Let's hope they have better luck."

"But the final insurance is our own program," Roosevelt said. "Now it's under the military, General Groves is moving the whole thing out to new laboratories at Los Alamos to be run by Oppenheimer. We're going flat out for it. We could be wrong about the German effort, and the only insurance is to make sure we get a bomb first."

"Imagine what the world would come to if only Hitler had one," Churchill said.

"I don't have to," Winslade replied. His face grew serious. "You know, you may find you need the bomb for more than just insurance before this is through."

Churchill and Roosevelt glanced at each other uncertainly. "What do you mean, Claud?" Roosevelt asked.

Winslade carried his drink slowly over to the French windows and stared out at the garden for a moment. Then he turned to face the room. "The generation that's growing up in Germany today has been systematically brutalized by the Nazi system," he said. "It's in their schools, their youth movement, their media, their political ideology—everywhere. It begins even in the nurseries. They're conditioned to the worship of violence and the military cult, to view power and strength as the only criteria for establishing right. Their teaching idealizes the right of the strong to subdue the weak and glorifies the triumph of brute force as the expression of natural law."

Winslade shrugged and showed his empty palm briefly. "How do you get rid of a regime like this once it's taken root? You can't reason with it, because all you'll earn is contempt for what it sees as weakness. You can't bargain with it—a trading relationship implies equality, but all it understands is dominating or being dominated. You can't hope to coexist peaceably because your very existence represents either a threat or an opportunity—its obsession with might and mastery compels it to test its strength continually.

"If the only thing that it respects is might, then perhaps the only way to earn its respect is to speak its own language and show it might, devastatingly, without half measures—to beat it squarely on its own terms and outplay it by its own rules. In short, gentlemen, you knock the stuffing out of them. That might be the only way of getting this fixation out of their system."

There was a heavy silence. Then Churchill said, "Yes, but at what price? Do we end up indistinguishable from the evil that we set out to destroy?"

Winslade sighed. "Yes, I see the risk," he admitted. "But what's the alternative? The whole monstrosity doesn't belong in this world. It was never a part of it. It's an aberration that was imposed from the outside, like an infection. Sometimes it's impossible to get rid of an infection without damaging some healthy tissue. But if you succeed, the organism will recover."

"Their cult of ingrained authoritarianism is what provides the breeding ground," Anna said, picking up the analogy. "Why else did Overlord choose the time and place that they did? It has to be eradicated, permanently. The West tried to be decent and civilized in 1918, and look what happened."

Churchill looked at his three colleagues. "They're right, you know, Winston," Alan Brooke said quietly. "I wish there was another way, too."

"I wish I could argue," Marshall said. He drew in a long breath. "But I can't."

Roosevelt nodded.

And so it came about that at Casablanca, the United States and Britain agreed on a major intensification of the strategic bomber offensive, and on giving top priority to the Manhattan Project, as the A-bomb program was now officially called. Their war aim, as was announced publicly at the end of the conference, would be nothing less than the unconditional surrender of the Axis powers.

The only major outstanding topic was the machine at Gatehouse. "My understanding is that even if the particular world that you've just returned from was to leave us alone, there still exists a chance that any of the others might, deliberately or otherwise, tune in to Gatehouse, or whatever the appropriate phrase is," Churchill said. "Is that not the case?"

"Yes, that's it exactly," Scholder confirmed. "Crossed lines are possible. We've experienced a couple of instances already."

"And from what I hear, no one really understands them," Roosevelt said. "Not even Einstein."

"That's so," Scholder confirmed again. He'd spent most of his time since returning from Florida at Princeton.

"Let's go through this again," Marshall said. "Now, this machine in Brooklyn is only the return connection, is that right? You people came here originally by means of a projector that could send you into this world without any machine needing to be here at all. The return-gate is only to connect you back again."

"Correct," Scholder said.

Marshall nodded. "Good. Then what I want to know is this. If we didn't have a return-gate, what would be the probability of a projector in one of these other universes just happening to project something here—without anything acting as some kind of 'beacon' to attract it?"

"Oh." Scholder shrugged. "For one of them to just happen to hit this universe out of all the ones that exist in the branching system? Well, let's just say that accidentally finding a needle in a haystack would be a dead certainty by comparison." He shook his head. "The chances are next to nothing. That's why it doesn't happen every week."

Churchill glanced at the other leaders and nodded decisively, as if that was what he had been waiting to hear. It was clear suddenly that they had discussed the subject thoroughly beforehand. "Get rid of it," he said.

The Proteus people looked at each other, but none of them could pretend to be surprised. They had been asking the same question, too. Nobody tried to argue. This was clearly one question that Churchill and Roosevelt had already made up their minds about.

Accordingly, instructions were drawn up for the Gatehouse machine to be quietly and secretly dismantled, and for the pieces to be destroyed and dropped in the ocean; the design information and assembly drawings would be burned, and all references to the Proteus mission expunged from the official and private records of everyone who had been involved. Gatehouse would become once again just another warehouse on the waterfront in Brooklyn.

For considering what had been inflicted on it, the world wasn't doing too bad a job at all of getting itself back into shape. Other universes had interfered enough.

CHAPTER 54

NOTHING SEEMED TO HAVE changed very much when Ferracini and Cassidy came in through the door and went downstairs to the corridor that led past Max's office. The double doors leading into the club had been revarnished; the glittery wallpaper on either side was the same, and should have been changed. There was a new hatcheck girl.

"Say, what's a girl like you doing in a nice place like this?" Cassidy asked cheerfully as he handed his coat across the counter.

The hatcheck girl began switching on an automatic bored look; then she stopped, puzzled, and frowned. "Did I hear that right?"

"Who cares? Hi, I'm Cassidy. Who are you?"

"Lisa. I—"

"It isn't!" a voice exclaimed from a short distance behind them. "It can't be. But, my God, it is—Cassidy!"

"Hey, Max, you old rascal!" Cassidy roared. Max came out of the office, beaming beneath his high, tanned forehead and crinkly hair, and they shook hands. "So, how've you been, Max? I just said to Harry here a second ago that . . . say, that's strange. Where the hell did he go?"

But Ferracini had heard the voice singing inside the club.

He stood watching her in the spotlight for a long time from

just inside the door. She was wearing her hair tied up and high
rather than the loose and wavy way he preferred it, but it looked
good for her job; the button chin, high cheeks, and turned-up
nose were just the way he remembered. She was wearing a se-
quined gold and tangerine dress.

George had gone. There was a different piano player now, an
older man with a benign-looking face and a ragged white mustache. He reminded Ferracini of Einstein in a vague kind of way.
The place was busy, but most of the faces were strange. It was full
of uniforms now. Lou, looking as inscrutable as ever, was still
tending the bar in a black vest and white shirt with the cuffs
turned back. Pearl was on a stool at one end, and Sid sat with
some people at one of the tables.

"How the hell are you ever gonna enjoy life, Harry, if you
keep falling in love all the time?" Cassidy said joining him.

Ferracini grinned. "Worth coming home to though, huh,
Cass?" He saw that Max was there, too. "Hey, Max! How are
things? Say, you're looking just great!"

"You, too, Harry. Things? Oh . . ." Max waved a hand. "The
war may be bad for some, but it's not so bad for business. It's good
to have you two back. What about the others, Floyd and the rest?
Do you still see them?"

"It's good to be back. Sure, they'll be along later." Ferracini
hesitated. "Is Janet, ah, is she still—"

Max tilted a hand from side to side in front of his face. "Oh,
never anything serious. You know these women, Harry—they
have an intuition. She knew you were coming back. So, anyway,
where in hell have you guys been?"

"Top-secret presidential assignment," Cassidy told him.

"Oh, yeah—for three years? Still the same old Cassidy, eh?"

"Seriously," Cassidy said.

"Wanna know something?" Max nudged him with an elbow
and winked. "I got the exclusive agency rights on the Brooklyn
Bridge. Go ahead, make me an offer."

"Come on, Cass, let's get a drink," Ferracini said.

Max walked them over to the bar. "Look who's back," he
announced to the company.

Pearl looked around from her stool at the end. "Jesus, I don't
believe it!" A couple of the others there were old-timers and
pleased to see them back. Sid excused himself from the people at
the table and came over.

"Say, what's this?" Cassidy lifted Pearl's hand and admired
the ring she was wearing. "You? Now, I don't believe that!"

"Well, life's full of these little surprises," Pearl said in her
husky voice.

"Anyone we know?" Cassidy asked.

"You remember Johnny Six Jays?" Max said.

"You're kidding!"

"Sense of public duty," Pearl said. "Someone had to try and straighten him out. The only trouble is, I'm getting crooked." She sighed. "Most brides get a veil. I get a hood. It's the story of my life."

Lou set down the drinks. "On the house." Then a flicker of uncertainty crossed his face as he stood looking at Ferracini. "Did I tell you there was a guy in here asking for you and Cass, Harry?"

Ferracini blinked at him. "It's been three years, Lou. You sure you're talking to the right person?"

"Oh, sure. Lemme see now . . . on the short side, about that high. Pale face, mustache, wearing a hat . . . had dark glasses and kept 'em on inside. Acted strange all the time—kinda furtive."

Ferracini thought back. "Yes, I remember that now . . . the guy who was talking to George, right?" He shook his head disbelievingly. "Yes, you did tell me, Lou. We never found out who he was."

Lou turned away and pulled an old cardboard shoe box from a ledge at the back of the bar, crammed with dog-eared scribblings and slips of paper. He rummaged through the collection for a few seconds, then pulled out one of the slips, crumpled it up, and tossed it into a trash bin. Ferracini shook his head and looked away.

Out in the center of the dance floor, Janet had just begun her final number, when her eyes strayed over in the direction of the bar and she noticed something familiar about the tall, yellow-haired figure with a mustache, talking to Pearl, Max, and a couple of the others. For just a fraction of a second, she couldn't place the face. Then she saw who was with him, and her voice faltered involuntarily. The piano continued for a bar longer and then stopped. Some of the people listening at the front tables looked at each other with puzzled expressions. Janet recovered herself quickly and smiled. "Oh, dear, I'm sorry, ladies and gentlemen—I must have kicked out of gear for a moment. Can we start that one again, Oscar?" From the bar, the figure with dark wavy hair raised his glass toward her and grinned. The piano played again, and she sang.

Ferracini eased himself onto one of the stools and leaned back to rest an elbow on the bar. Probably for the first time ever, he was at ease in himself and content with the world. He tuned out what Cassidy was saying to the others behind, and let his mind drift back over the things that had happened to him since the return from that mission in 1975: getting mixed up in the strange project at Tularosa that had sent him into another world; setting up the machine at Gatehouse, then moving over to England, and crossing Europe for the operation at Weissenberg, only to be snatched into a completely different world again, this time in the future. And finally, coming back again. He hoped life wouldn't seem too tame now after it all.

And the people: the team he had worked with and been part of; the scientists—Einstein, Szilard, Fermi, Teller, Wigner. The statesmen and their aides and service chiefs—Roosevelt and Churchill; Eden, Duff Cooper, Lindemann; Hopkins, Ickes, Hull; Brooke, Marshall. . . .

And, of course, Claud. That was the only sad part about it: He would miss Claud.

Ferracini had seen the look on Claud's face when they were shown the reconnaissance photograph at Casablanca, and he suspected that Claud had made his mind up there and then. Claud had returned to the twenty-first century to be the star witness in his younger self's defense. He had gone to repay the debt that he felt he owed for what his younger self had done for him.

In fact, young Winslade's defense would have two star witnesses—Anna Kharkiovitch had gone, too. "It was something that started a while ago," Kurt Scholder had explained to Ferracini. "But they were both professional enough to put the job first."

The scientists had used Scholder's Morse system to signal for a reconnection. Then, in the machine's last operation before it was demolished, everyone who had been involved with Gatehouse had assembled there one final time to see Claud and Anna on their way.

They had invited Scholder to go with them to rejoin the world he had left as a young man long ago. But after much contemplation, Scholder had declined. Ferracini believed it was because of young Scholder, with the family that Scholder himself had once had. "This world is mine now—I'm getting too old to be gallivanting around among universes," Scholder had said. "And besides, Einstein isn't as young as he used to be, either. He needs someone to help him sail his boat."

Ferracini realized that Janet had stopped singing, and that people were crowding onto the dance floor as the band came back on with "String of Pearls." He saw Janet coming toward him through the crowd around the bar. She put her arms around his neck as he stood up from the stool, and they held each other for a long time. Then she stood back and looked at him. They both laughed, unable to find words.

Cassidy came over and broke the spell. "I'd have thought you two would have more to talk about than that after all this time," he drawled.

Janet slipped an arm around Cassidy's waist and kissed him on the cheek. She looked from one to the other. "It's amazing, neither of you looks a day older."

"Clean living, healthy food, and meditation," Cassidy told her.

"And you look just great, too," Ferracini said. "Better, in fact. How's Jeff?"

"Fine, last I heard," Janet said. "He joined the Navy. Right now he's somewhere in the Pacific."

"See, I said she knew you'd be back," Max said as he joined them.

"It was destiny," Janet said. "You believe in destiny don't you, Harry?"

"Sure," Ferracini replied. "Destiny is what you make it."

Janet studied his face with her light, green-blue eyes. "So is it over now, whatever it was?" she asked him. "You went away like you said, and now you're back. Does that mean you're back for good?"

Harry Ferracini took in the scene around them and thought how different it all was from the last time he had been in the Rainbow's End. The Army was present in strength; there were a lot of Navy; some Air Corps; Marines. Three British sailors had just come in the door with a couple of Canadians; some Australians were sitting at the far end of the bar, and he could see Free French and Polish uniforms among the crowd on the dance floor.

As had been true before in England, it was everybody's war now. Even President Roosevelt, he'd heard, had one son flying in a reconnaissance squadron over Africa; another was an executive officer on one of the destroyers that had taken part in the North African landings; a third was serving with the Marines in the Solomons; and another was an ensign on the carrier *Hornet*. The world that he believed in was standing up and defending itself at last.

And he thought how different it all was from the future that he had once faced as he stared out at a bleak, rainswept dawn from the bridge of a submarine off Norfolk, Virginia.

He looked at Janet and grinned. "Oh, yes," he told her. "You don't have to worry about that any more. I'm home to stay now."

EPILOGUE

DRIVING A CURRENT-MODEL 1947 Ford Mercury V8, Ferracini eased off the new highway and turned the car onto old, familiar streets of the Queens that he remembered. A lot of new houses were going up around the old area now, mainly single-family units on patches of green grass—the kind that the politicians were saying every American couple would own, now that the postwar economic collapse predicted by the doomsayers hadn't happened. Instead of making tanks and B-17s, the factories had switched to cars and refrigerators. Nobody worried about what would happen when everybody had one of everything; they'd start selling them two of everything, Ferracini supposed.

The news on the radio was talking about the Soviets' refusal to accept the plan that Marshall—secretary of state now—had announced for aiding European recovery, including Germany's. Ferracini changed channels to Bing Crosby singing "Don't Fence Me In."

The flowerpots still sat in the windows over what was still a bicycle shop. The liquor store and the hardware store hadn't changed. The delicatessen seemed to have expanded its business and had taken over the premises next door to become a neighborhood grocery. Ferracini parked in an empty space in front, got out of the car, and stopped to look around. Farther along, he could see the wall with the trees and the church behind it, and the school at the bottom of the hill. The building that had been a laundry looked different, somehow. He crossed the sidewalk and enterd the store.

A few people and some children were browsing among the self-serve shelves on one side. Ferracini spent a minute selecting a couple of items that Janet had asked him to pick up and walked over to the counter, where papers, magazines, candy, and tobacco were displayed. "Evening," the man with a black mustache and wearing a white coat greeted as he rang up the charge. "Anything else you need?"

"Just some information, maybe." Ferracini paused.

The storekeeper waited a moment, then looked at him questioningly. "Okay?"

"Do you happen to know if some people called Ferracini still live around here—farther down the street, almost to the corner?"

"Ferracini—the Italian people? Oh, sure, I know them. She's in here all the time with the kids. Yeah, they're still there." The storekeeper squinted and leaned forward to look at Ferracini more closely. "You're part of the family, too, ain'tcha? I can see the resemblance."

"Kind of distant. But tell me, did they just have another baby there recently?"

"She should have—she's been carrying it for long enough." The storekeeper raised his voice to call through a door behind him. "Hey, Barb, did Mrs. Ferracini have her baby yet?"

A buxom woman appeared in the doorway. "Yes, a couple of days ago. It was a boy."

"How . . . how is she?" Ferracini asked.

"Who are you? Say, you have to be a relative. Haven't seen you around here before." The woman nodded. "She's okay—they both are. I hear she had a hard time, and the doctor was a bit worried there for a while, but she'll be fine now. Want me to say who was asking?"

Relieved, Ferracini smiled and shook his head. "It doesn't matter, thanks. I was just passing through."

On his way back to Manhattan, he stopped to get gas and phone Janet at their apartment on Riverside Drive. She was still singing, and Capitol Records was talking seriously about a contract. He and Cassidy had invested in some war-surplus planes and were running an air charter business.

"Queens!" Janet exclaimed. "I thought you were having a day off. What are you doing over in Queens?"

"My folks came from there, remember?"

"But you never talk about your family, Harry."

"Well, this was different. There was just something I had to do."

"Taking in a ball game with Cassidy and Russ, more likely."

"No, not this time. Like I said, it was something I had to do—somebody's birthday that I didn't want to forget just this one time. See you later, hon, okay? . . . Oh, and yes, I picked up those things you said you wanted."

TECHNICAL NOTE

The "Many-Worlds" Interpretation of Quantum Mechanics

DESPITE ITS ENORMOUS PRACTICAL value and the success of its predictions, quantum theory is so contrary to everyday intuition that even after more than half a century, the experts themselves still can't agree what to make of it. The disagreement centers around the problem of describing "observations," by which physicists mean interactions in general.

Formally, the result of an interaction is a superposition of mathematical functions, each of which represents one of the possible outcomes. The difficulty to be resolved is that of reconciling such a superposition with the fact that in practice we observe only one outcome. In other words, how does the system (interacting bodies; apparatus and object; observer and observed) "choose" which of the possible final states to assume?

The "conventional," or "Copenhagen" interpretation is that whenever a wave function attains the form of a superposition, it immediately collapses to become one of the elements. Which element of the superposition it will collapse to is impossible to say in advance; a weighted probability distribution can be assigned to the various possibilities, however, and the predictions of such distributions have been amply verified by experiment. This is the basis of the familiar statistical nature of quantum mechanics.

The collapse of the wave function and the assignment of statistical weights do not follow from anything in quantum theory itself, but are consequences of an imposed *a priori* convention. This approach promotes the conclusion that the formalism of physical theory no longer represents reality, but reduces to a ghost-realm of potentialities—i.e., its symbols constitute merely convenient algorithms for making statistical predictions. But if this is correct, the critics ask, then what becomes of the objective reality that surely exists all around us? Einstein opposed this metaphysical solution of the Copenhagen school to his death, and his sentiments underlie much of the dissatisfaction that persists today with the conventional interpretation.

In his Princeton doctoral dissertation in 1957, Hugh Everett III proposed a new interpretation that denies the existence of a separate classical realm and asserts the notion of a wave function for the whole universe. This universal wave function never collapses, and hence reality as a whole is rigorously deterministic. By virtue of its evolution in time according to its dynamic differential equations, the universal function decomposes naturally into elements, and it is postulated that this process reflects a continual splitting of the universe into a multitude of mutually unobservable, but equally real worlds. It follows from the minimum-assumption mathematical treatment of this model that in each of these worlds the familiar statistical quantum laws will be found to apply.

In a sense, Everett's interpretation calls for a return to naive realism and the old-fashioned idea that there exists a direct correspondence between theoretical formalism and reality, which would doubtless have pleased Einstein. But maybe because physicists these days are more sophisticated, and certainly because the implications appear so bizarre, this alternative has not been taken as seriously as perhaps it deserves.

Its major weakness is that it leads to experimental predictions identical to those of the Copenhagen view, and therefore, no laboratory test can be designed to distinguish between the two. Indeed, the mathematics of the many-worlds interpretation yields formal proof that no experiment can reveal the existence of the other worlds contained in the universal superposition.

(This, of course, is where I took the greatest license in *The Proteus Operation;* but that's one of the perks of being a science-fiction writer as opposed to a scientist.)

A decision between the two interpretations may, however, ultimately be possible on grounds other than direct laboratory experiment. For example, in the very early moments of the Big Bang, the universal wave function may have possessed an overall coherence unimpaired, as yet, by condensation into noninterfering branches. Such initial coherence may have testable implications for cosmology.

For further details, including a comprehensive mathematical treatment of the theory, see *The Many-Worlds Interpretation of Quantum Mechanics,* edited by Bryce S. DeWitt and Neill Graham, published by Princeton University Press.